They Labor In Vain

They Labor In Vain

Michael David Szillat

They Labor In Vain

© Michael David Szillat 2012

Published by
Lighthouse Christian Publishing
SAN 257-4330
5531 Dufferin Drive
Savage, Minnesota, 55378
United States of America

www.lighthousechristianpublishing.com

To my beloved grandmother, May Auel,
faithful to the end

Unless the LORD build the house, they labor in vain who build.

Unless the LORD guard the city, in vain does the guard keep watch.

Psalm 127:1 NAB

PROLOGUE

Perched on the edge, a man stood between the doorway back to safety and the jaws of death. Amidst the darkness of the roof, a neon-red glow illuminated the nighttime shadows from the sign behind him that proclaimed, "Providential Insurance Company." A frozen breath of wind pierced his black tuxedo and threatened to rip the bowtie from his neck. Tentatively, he peered over the ledge upon which he stood, trembling.

I bet no one can even see me. No one will notice until I hit the pavement.

Uncontrollable tears blurred his vision, turning the taillights in the city street below into the churning chaos of hellfire.

A demon prodded the man, clasping a clawed talon onto his head. *This is all I am worthy of. This is what I deserve.* He took another look over the edge. Bundled against the winter cold, a few pedestrians hurried by, unaware of the conflict above them. From this height they seemed insignificant, hardly even human. Despair surrounded him like a swarm of locusts about to feed upon his soul. As if ensnared in the shadows behind the sign, a saddened angel fruitlessly struggled to approach the man, his lifelong companion.

With two wretched scarlet eyes, the demon glared defiantly over the desperate human prey on the ledge. An intensely cold spot in the man's shirt pocket bothered him, and he reached inside to retrieve the culprit, a small metal token. He clutched it tightly in his white-knuckled hand as if for strength.

Far away, a woman fell to her knees and whispered a name. In heaven, a saint touched Jesus and communicated the same name. Jesus nodded knowingly, laying His hand upon His heart, which emanated a piercing light. The light kept flowing.

From above, an invisible ray of empowering grace illuminated the angel on the roof, who then broke forth into a harmony of brightness. He glided hurriedly over to the man precariously balanced on the narrow raised ledge that encircled the roof. Just under the man's left foot, a loose fragment of concrete broke off and headed into the oblivion below. "Oh God!" he cried. The angel stretched out a hand and tugged at an indelible mark on the man's soul. For an instant, he let go of both despair and the token in his hand, even as he started to lose his footing. For a timeless moment, he felt himself suspended in the cold air, unsure of which way he had fallen from the ledge. Scenes from the past flashed before his eyes: his first car, his college graduation, his engagement party, his sister. "Theresa!" he called out before colliding with the roof in a painful thud.

Waves of relief crashed over him, flooding him with gratitude. With great effort he lifted himself off the cold concrete to a seated position. The world slowly came back into focus as he blinked his eyes and shook his inebriated head. Picking himself up, he advanced towards the open emergency exit door, beckoning with its pale light. For the first time in months he was happy to be alive.

Chapter One

In the late afternoon, Gregory Wesko typed furiously on his keyboard with contented efficiency. His summer sports jacket lay unceremoniously draped over the high back of his cushioned office chair. Lost in his work, Greg failed to notice the figure standing in the doorway. Not even the soft clearing of a throat caught his attention. Soon followed a light tapping against the doorframe. After a moment, a purposeful cough meandered its way across his desk. Greg refused to break his concentration.

"Hey, Wesko!"

The loud interjection paused Greg's flying fingers, but his face remained firmly fixed towards the computer screen in front of him. He stole a furtive glance at the form in the doorway. Smiling inwardly, he hoped that the darting of his eyes had gone unnoticed. With a grunt of feigned irritation, Greg resumed typing.

"Some nerve!" The stern feminine voice belied the woman's amusement. "He can't even break away for a tiny minute to plan lunch with a former office mate! I guess he's left me behind in the dust along with all the others, little old Joanna. Just too busy for lunch with the groveling masses!"

"You're right," Greg frowned firmly, "I don't have time for lunch with the groveling masses." Keeping his head facing forward, he cast a sideward glance out of the corner of his eye at the red-headed, fair-skinned Joanna Pearson. "But I do have time for an old friend!" A smile broke across his face. The twinkle in his light brown eyes put butterflies in Joanna's stomach, a reaction she had not expected.

"Then come by my desk tomorrow at 11:30!" she turned abruptly to go. Inwardly she warned herself. *Watch yourself, girl! This isn't the right time for those emotions. You'd better be on your best behavior.* She returned to her desk and tried to concentrate on her work, but images of Greg's broodingly handsome face and chords of his gentle baritone voice kept breaking into her thoughts. The clock on the lower corner of her computer screen read 2:48, still over two hours from quitting time. She turned to the framed embroidery on the wall of her cubicle that read, "I can do all things through Christ who strengthens me." *I hope you mean it! Especially if you want me to go through with this tomorrow!*

A darkening evening sky looked in on Greg through his apartment window. The sound of his feet against the tiled foyer floor was beginning to call him back to reality as he paced back and forth with a pile of mail still in his hands. He shuffled letters back and forth absent-mindedly.

What is going on? Am I losing my mind or just losing my touch? He continued pacing.

Nothing like this has ever happened to me before. Careless! Stupid! He chided himself as he stood in his dark apartment. The light switch beckoned in vain.

You worthless fool! What are you going to do now? How are you going to get out of this mess? No one is going to help you. You can't even rely on yourself anymore. You're a failure!

Greg cringed as a demon whispered lies into his ear. His empty heart opened its mouth to accept the flood of deceit and despair. He could not perceive that these ideas were not his own. They had a strong ring of truth to them, as if he had been hearing them his whole life. In fact, he had.

The light hush of a letter hitting the floor snapped him back to the present moment. In the dark he bent down to pick it up but could not read the return address. He reached for the light and the words sprang to life. *Theresa McAllen, 401 Retten Ave., San Antonio, TX 78227.* His sister's handwriting was as flamboyant as ever.

He headed through the living room to the study where he turned on an antique lamp in the shape of a baseball bat. Reaching into his desk, he pulled out a brass letter opener. As he lay the other letters down on the desk, the words on the top envelope caught his eye: CREDIT PROBLEMS? The gravity of his situation returned. Forgetting the letter opener, he slumped down into his swivel chair and ran his fingers through his hair. *What are you going to do? How could you have screwed up that account? How could you be so careless!*

Sitting forward, he propped his head on his hands, his elbows resting on the desktop. As if carrying on a conversation with himself, he continued. *I've been working too much. I've been working too late! Lisa said so herself. I need a vacation. Maybe both of us! But first I've got to straighten out that account. I'll fix this. I have to.*

With a shaky sense of security, Greg rose to his feet and headed for his bedroom, turning on lights as he went. He had just removed his tie as the phone rang. He reached for the phone he always kept in its charger on his nightstand.

"Hello?"

"Hi Gregory, I'm glad you're home."

"Lisa, it's so good to hear your voice! I was just thinking about you."

"You were!" Lisa kept her blush on her side of the phone. She had assumed he had forgotten to call, so she was planning to scold him for it. Now the words she had prepared were gone.

"Yes, I was thinking how I've been spending too much time at work and too little time with you. I want to change that."

"Music to my ears!" Lisa exclaimed. "When can I see you?"

"How about now?"

Forty-five minutes later Lisa set a brown paper bag down on Greg's kitchen counter. "Hunan

Wu" was emblazoned in red letters on the side of the bag. Greg had already set two places at his small dining room table. He was freshly showered and sat in shorts and a tee shirt waiting by his plate as Lisa brought out chicken with broccoli and shrimp mai fun in two serving dishes. She knew her way around his kitchen as much as he did, although lately they had frequented a number of local restaurants. One of their favorites was a local pizza parlor called "That Pizza Place." The owner, Joe Tropetto, was a friend of Greg's from East Granby Junior High. They had drifted apart after graduation and were pleasantly surprised to cross paths again as adults.

Greg tried to keep up casual conversation as long as he could. Lisa reviewed her day with him, and he was happy to let her talk. By the end of the meal she had also set forth her detailed plans for the week. Lisa relished the ostensible undivided attention Greg was paying her. Living forty minutes apart limited their visits during the week, and heavy work schedules often limited the length of their phone calls.

"You've been very quiet," Lisa noted as he poked at the last few noodles on his plate. "You sounded so happy on the phone. Did something happen in the meantime?"

"No, nothing happened in the meantime. It's what happened earlier today. I've been trying not to think about it, but I knew I'd have to let it out sooner or later. I thought I invited you over to get my mind off it, but I think I really needed to get it off my mind." A worried look crossed Lisa's face as he continued.

"It's not that bad, really. I'm having a problem at work."

"Is it Tony Franco again? Did he do something to you?"

"No. Tony's as unstable as ever, but it's not him this time. It's me." He paused but not for effect. "I seem to have misplaced about $20,000." Lisa gasped but did not speak. "I don't know where it went," he continued. "I discovered the problem just as I was about to leave work. I spent a few hours trying to locate it, but I just couldn't find it. It's missing from the Lewis account, one of the company's oldest."

Lisa sat in stunned silence for a moment before responding. "Maybe someone else transferred it without you knowing," she suggested.

"No, I'm the only one with access to this account. It's one of my newest responsibilities. No one can change the account without my password. There's no evidence of any unauthorized entries to this account. Not even any attempts. The money just vanished into cyberspace."

"So some computer out there is going on a shopping spree?" Lisa always tried to throw in a little humor. It was her best way of handling stress. Sometimes it worked. "Are you going to be in trouble for this?"

Greg started to rub his temples. "The worst that could happen is that someone finds out before I can correct the situation. Certain other people like my boss, Chuck, can inspect the account to see what activity has occurred. It would be catastrophic for him to find out. Either it will look like I'm incompetent or it will look like I'm a thief."

"Oh Gregory, they couldn't think that you took the money, could they?"

"Embezzling money from the accounts I'm responsible for would be a pretty stupid and blatant thing to do. I'd get caught for sure. But this is an old account with virtually no activity, and very infrequently audited. If I were to steal from one of my own accounts, it would probably be this one."

Lisa reached across the table and touched his arm. "Could you have misdirected the money, or do you think someone really stole it?"

Greg sat back and put his hands behind his head. "Both are unlikely, but the first option would be the easiest to deal with. If I lost the money, I can find it again. If somebody stole it, then we have a serious situation on our hands."

Lisa liked Greg's use of the word "we." She longed to be included in Greg's every move, but so often they were both too busy for each other. "I'll support you in whatever you have to deal with, Gregory."

"Which brings me to something else," began Greg, sitting forward. "I would like you to support me in deciding upon a vacation spot."

"Vacation?"

"Yes, not now, but soon. After I sort out all this mess at work. I said I wanted to spend more time together, so I think we should go away for a week or two. Let's leave our problems far behind and just be with each other. Let's really get to know each other again. Without the stresses, without the hurry."

It sounded so appealing to Lisa, but something inside her was deeply uncomfortable. "It sounds wonderful." Her words betrayed her hesitation. She tried to cover it up quickly. "Really, what a great idea! We can get away, be alone, have some peace." But Lisa felt anything but peaceful. The urgings of her conscience were not letting her rest. Greg picked up on it.

"Who are you trying to convince, me or yourself?" asked Greg, slightly perturbed. "I'm offering to take you away from all this craziness we've both been complaining about. The rush that keeps us from seeing each other, the hustle that's drawn out our engagement so long." He knew he had hit upon a sore point with her, but for the moment he did not seem to care. She did not seem to hear.

"I'm sorry, Gregory. I should be honest with you. I just don't feel right about going away with you alone right now. It doesn't seem right. Why not wait for the honeymoon? That will come soon enough. Anyway, can we really afford to take two trips so close together?"

Greg had a hundred counterpoints, but something inside kept him at bay. He didn't know that hundreds of miles away a woman inspired by the Holy Spirit was praying that his resistance to God would diminish. "Lisa, I don't feel like arguing about this right now. I meant it as a nice gesture, something I thought we both could use. Think it over, and let me know how you feel." Then he added, "I'm sure you'll come to your senses soon."

Lisa stood up and brought her plate to the kitchen. "I'll think about it," she said over her shoulder. Safely out of his sight, she set down her plate in the sink. Her hands were shaking.

The next morning found Greg frowning in front of his computer screen. He had intended to arrive an hour early, but a power surge had reset his alarm. Instead his internal clock had awakened him at the usual time to find a flashing 12:00 scolding him in red digits. Now as he sat staring at the black numbers on his monitor he felt acid accumulating in his stomach. Joanna's approach startled him.

"Hi, stranger," she greeted him. "You should close the door if you want to keep the riffraff out," she added.

"Hi Joanna. How are you?" He ignored her comment with his obligatory salutation. She noticed his faint scowl.

"You look pretty involved. Maybe I should go. Do you need anything?"

Greg did not look up. "Would you mind getting me a cup of coffee and maybe scaring up a doughnut? I forgot to eat breakfast."

Joanna was not sure how to handle Greg's gruff comment. She decided to chalk it up to a bad night's sleep and Greg's occasionally subtle sense of humor. "Someone down the hall from me brought in muffins. I'll snag one for you. You still take your coffee black?"

Suddenly aware that he had barked at Joanna like a servant, he looked up somewhat sheepishly. "I'm sorry, Joanna. You don't have to get anything for me."

"I know. How about that coffee? Cream or not?"

"No cream, thanks." As Joanna turned to go, he called out, "I appreciate it, Jo!" He watched her walk down the hall and turn the corner. Once she was out of sight, he returned to the matter at hand. The monitor screamed with numbers that suddenly seemed to swim before his eyes. Embarrassed, he quickly wiped away a few tears. He mistakenly ascribed them to exhaustion. The previous night's disagreement with Lisa had condemned him to a fitful sleep. Shaking his head to clear his vision, he tried to make sense out of the figures. Joanna's return and departure hardly broke his concentration.

Joanna prayed as she walked back to her desk. *Lord, whatever this problem is, please use it to convert his heart! Please see him through it. Bless him with wisdom. Prepare him for our lunchtime conversation.*

A quarter to twelve found Greg and Joanna sitting across from each other at *Indy's*, a nearby cafe with a splash of green tables under a bright red awning. It was a local favorite. Greg and Joanna waved as a party of six co-workers arrived and headed inside where there were larger tables. A light summer breeze meandered past the outdoor diners.

"So how are things on the fifth floor?" Greg asked after taking a sip of his iced tea. "How's Marvin treating you?"

"Fine, just fine," she responded. "You know how Marvin can be. Still demanding more work and fewer complaints. Lucky for me he's on vacation this week. Otherwise I would never dare to take a long lunch like this. It must be nice for you, with your own office, your own hours, and practically your own floor! Ever since you moved up to the sixth floor, it's been pretty boring."

"I would say it's been boring for me too, but I haven't had time to notice," Greg laughed, trying to put the missing funds out of his mind. "You talk about setting my own hours, but lately that's been about seven in the morning until seven in the evening. But who's complaining? The paycheck still rolls in every month."

"The almighty paycheck! I guess it makes it all worth it." She hesitated briefly before continuing. "What does Lisa have to say about your long hours?" She looked down into her diet soda.

"I don't think she minds too much. We're pretty independent people. Working until seven makes for some late dinners, but she has plenty to do without me. She has her own friends and her own career to keep her occupied."

"Is that all it does, keep her occupied?" Joanna asked.

"Well, no! She enjoys what she does. Anyway, she's also spending more and more time planning the wedding. We've agreed to leave most of that to her. She enjoys that too, and after all, I don't really have the time. If we waited for me to do the planning, we'd be old and gray before we ever got married!" Greg stopped as the waitress approached, armed with pad and pen. She took their orders and reported back to the kitchen.

"I guess a lot of engaged couples move in together at this point, but I'm enjoying the final days of my bachelorhood. I'm not opposed to people moving in together, you know, for any moral reasons. It's enough that Lisa changed her mind and decided to get married in a church. I figure that's enough religion for me!"

Joanna felt heat rising into her cheeks. She prayed for the right words. "Greg, you know that religion is important to me..."

As she trailed off, Greg made an attempt to stave off an uncomfortable topic. "I think we've been down this road before. You know my feelings about religion."

"You're right, Greg, I do think I know your feelings about religion. But that's not what I'm interested in. What I really want to know is your feelings about God."

"What's the difference?" Greg retorted.

"For a lot of people there really isn't a difference. But for me there is. The purpose of religion is to bring people close to God. Religion isn't God. My Christian religion guides me in my worship of God as I cultivate a relationship with Him. There are some people who are religious but don't know a thing about God. They have an outward appearance of being religious, but inside they're seething with evil. This kind of Pharisaic people gives religion, and God, a bad name."

"Pharisaic?"

Joanna kicked herself inwardly for using jargon instead of stating things clearly. "It means to be hypocritical, to make a show of religion while trying to steal all the glory for yourself. Like the Pharisees in the Bible."

"I've heard of them." Greg's desire to change the subject was beginning to show.

"And so, I'd like to know your feelings about God, rather than your feelings about religion," Joanna prodded.

"For me there isn't much of a difference. I never gave it much thought. My parents took my sister and me to church when we were young, but they stopped going after awhile. They even sent us to CCD class until Confirmation. Then they let us stop that too. After that we only went to Mass on Christmas and Easter with my grandfather, until he died."

"So you were Catholic?"

"Yes, and I guess I still am. What are you?"

"Methodist," Joanna replied. "I thought you knew that."

"With all this talk about knowing God without religion, I'd think you ascribed to one of those Eastern philosophies."

Joanna blushed. "That's not what I meant at all! Religion is very important. I just meant that God is the focus, not the rules and regulations. They are a means to know God's will." Tears started to well up in Joanna's eyes, adding to her frustration. *This is not going well at all! Lord, why am I having so much trouble? I can't seem to say the right thing.*

You are saying good things! she heard God answer. *You are planting the seeds, Joanna. One sows, another reaps. Now is not the time to ask him your question.*

Joanna felt a rush of joy but could not think of anything else to say to this handsome, troubled man sitting across from her under the red glow from the sunlight through the awning. She observed him for a few moments, not knowing where their conversation would turn next. The waitress arriving with their sandwiches broke the awkwardness of the situation.

Greg started for his sandwich but placed it back onto his plate. "Aren't you forgetting something?" he smiled faintly. "Isn't there something you always ask to do when we eat together?"

Joanna appreciated Greg's attempt to meet her. She folded her hands on the table in front of her. Greg followed suit. "Dear Lord, we thank you for this time together and for our friendship. We thank you for the food you have given us. May it nourish us and give us strength for the day. And we pray especially, dear Lord, that you would reveal yourself to us in a special way, and that we would come to know the height and depth of your love. Amen."

Greg added his "Amen" and then paused. "Joanna, I don't want this religion thing to interfere with our friendship. I know it's important to you, and I accept that, and I ask you to accept that it's not important to me."

"Greg, I understand that it's not important to you, and I will respect your wishes. But I will continue to be who I am, with no apologies."

"No apologies necessary," Greg replied.

Four o'clock rolled around with Greg still sitting behind his desk. He had not left his seat since lunch, and his muscles were protesting. His eyes were also beginning to play tricks on him. As had become his custom that day, he tried to ignore the phone when it rang, but he happened to glance at the caller ID. In an instant the phone was in his hand.

"Hello, Chuck!" Chuck Hollis was Greg's newest and toughest boss.

"Greg, I want you to make some appointments over the next two weeks to meet the clients of some of the larger accounts that were recently put under your supervision. Let's meet tomorrow morning to discuss the details." Greg's other line rang and obscured Chuck's next sentence. He saw that it was Lisa calling from her office where she worked in market research. Suddenly he remembered his plan to leave work early for their appointment to pick out wedding bands.

"I'm sorry, Chuck. My other line rang and I couldn't hear you."

Chuck summarized abruptly. "Meeting at 9 AM tomorrow in my office. We'll review some of your new accounts. OK?"

Greg nodded in agreement but neglected to speak.

"OK?" the phone crackled.

"Oh yes, OK. Bye, Chuck." Greg quickly hung up the phone and switched to the other line. "Hi Lisa!"

"Hi, honey. I'm just about to leave work. Are you ready to meet me at the jeweler's?"

Greg glanced up at the clock. "Yes, I can leave in about five minutes. Just have to shut down my computer," he lied. *And save my job!*

"OK, so I'll expect you to leave in about twenty minutes," she chuckled with resignation. "See you there! I love you."

"I love you too!" Drops of sweat began to form on his brow. *What if he wants to review the Lewis account? Maybe he noticed the missing money, and that's the real reason he called this meeting. I have to get that twenty grand back by 9 AM tomorrow!* Only one solution came to mind. He quickly navigated to a website for a bank where he had a margin account. He logged in and selected the menu option for electronic funds transfer. With a shaking finger he commanded the bank to transfer $20,000 to his Providential Insurance Credit Union account. To his great frustration, an error message popped up to inform him that the maximum transfer by phone per calendar day was $10,000. He built up his courage and selected the option to transfer the daily limit to the Credit Union. He would have to wait until the next day to transfer the rest of the money and figure out a way to move the total into the Lewis account untraceably, all before 9 AM. He shut down the computer and raced to meet the woman whom he could no longer afford to marry.

Chapter Two

"I want a larger share," the sniveling but confident voice conveyed in hushed tones. "Now that I know you want to keep it a secret from our partner," he added.

"You know very well that it was meant to be a secret from the start," the shorter man replied, waving his stubby hand in anger. "That was all part of the deal!"

"Things are getting complicated. Before you know it, you'll have another employee hiring a private detective. Imagine them joining forces!"

"If I go down, you're going down with me!" threatened the shorter man.

"Don't be so cliché," chastised the sniveler in his high, nasal voice. "I'd be more afraid of your partner and his thug than the police. The police can only throw you in jail."

"Nothing like that is going to happen. Look, you're already getting more when you work with me alone than when you work with my partner and me together. If you ask too much, there's no incentive for me to continue doing this little business on the side. So back down."

"We'll see about that!" sniveled the taller man.

"Hey, we've got to let things lie low for a while anyway."

"I doubt that," retorted the taller man. "Your original source is dried up; too much suspicion is already aroused. Now you're down to two – one shared with your partner and one shared only with me."

"What makes you think you're the only one helping us?"

"Oh please!" scoffed the taller man nasally. "Everyone else around here is such a boy scout! You know that."

"You can believe that if you want to," smirked the shorter man. "As far as I'm concerned, this conversation is over. I'm going home to my battle-axe of a wife before she calls here looking for me."

Early in the morning, the small, stout figure of Tony Franco paced nervously back and forth outside Greg's office door. Intent on executing his plan, Greg tried his best to ignore the frantic scene in the hallway. Greg had accomplished as much preparatory work as possible, and now he was forced to wait for his personal bank to open at 9 AM. When the hour turned, he planned to make a second transfer of funds from his outside account to his Providential Insurance credit union account. Once inside the corporate loop, transferring money to the Lewis account would be more feasible, although requiring a complicated and questionable procedure.

If Chuck called for a reckoning of the Lewis account at the impending meeting, at least the total funds would be correct. In his desperation, Greg felt tempted to pray for help.

"Greg, I can't stand it anymore. Aren't you going to let me come in?" the man in the hall whimpered.

"You didn't ask," Greg retorted with annoyance. "Come in."

"Thanks, Greg. I didn't want to be a bother," the man apologized.

"What do you want, Tony?" Greg barked brusquely.

"You don't have to be nasty, Greg. You're not nasty to other people," Tony complained.

"Other people don't pace outside my door for ten minutes," Greg pointed out. "I don't mean to sound rude, Tony. I'm just very busy today."

"As usual. Anyway, I'm convinced that someone wants me dead."

The drastic nature of the words caught Greg off guard. Tony had a history of mental illness and had even been institutionalized in the past, although Greg was uncertain of the details. Conflicting accounts circulated through the rumor mill, but Greg did not attempt to confirm or deny anything by broaching the subject with Tony.

Recovering from Tony's allegation, Greg attempted to dismiss the matter. "Come on, Tony, you've got to be kidding."

"No, it's true," he maintained. "First, I've been getting some strange phone calls. People hang up on me when I say my name. And then someone followed me home yesterday. They kept going when I turned into my driveway, but now they know where I live."

"Is your address unlisted?"

"Well, no," admitted Tony with embarrassment.

"Then anyone could find out where you live simply by looking in the phone book or on the Internet. They don't have to follow you home."

"Oh great! That makes it much easier for someone to hunt me down."

"Did you get a description of the car? A license plate?"

"It was a red car, that's about all I know," stated Tony simply.

"That narrows it down considerably," Greg scoffed sarcastically. He looked nervously at the clock on the wall. "I really have to get back to work, Tony."

"Do you think I'm in danger?" Tony asked expectantly.

"Not at all. You have to stop worrying. It won't get you anywhere."

"Thanks, Greg. I'll try."

As Tony exited the office, Greg murmured softly to himself, "I should take my own advice."

The crystal blue water parted before Greg's extended arms as he dove through the air. The cool water refreshed him, urging him to traverse its breadth. With his goggles he could see the bottom almost twelve feet below. He remained submerged until he reached a wall where he surfaced and slicked back his wet, dark hair. The familiar smell of chlorine invigorated him.

Greg frequented the gym three times a week on the way home from the office. It was the perfect way to work off the stress of the day, and today's stress had been heavier than normal. He wanted to clear his mind of the missing money, the Lewis account, his boss, and the enormous hole in his savings. The therapy of swimming helped him to sort out the day's details with a healthy outlet for the stress. He reviewed his frantic but successful efforts to cover the missing money in the Lewis account with his own. He had arrived only ten minutes late for his meeting with Chuck Hollis. Ironically, Chuck had not wanted to review the Lewis account, and Greg's urgency had been unwarranted.

By the fifth lap Greg had formulated a plan for the next steps in his investigation of the missing money. In the worst case, he could chalk up his personal contribution to the Lewis account as a loss and cash in money from one of his retirement accounts to cover the wedding. For Greg, the stiff tax penalty was worth the price of keeping his false pride intact.

Forty minutes later Greg pulled himself up the ladder and headed for his towel. As he stood dripping by the pool, he felt a strong indescribable yearning. Not accustomed to examining his interior life, he mistook it for sadness over the loss of so much money. He even tried to ascribe it to hunger or exhaustion. The real reason for his emptiness remained hidden from him. Greg had always been a fast and formidable problem solver, but his ability to deal with problems of the soul had been slowly atrophying over the years.

Dry and dressed, Greg left the locker room and took the stairs to the level where he had left his car in the parking garage. As the echo of his steps broke the cavernous stillness of the underground sea of automobiles, he suddenly realized he was not alone. Ordinarily he met a few people coming or going, but tonight the sound of soft steps far behind him seemed menacing. Perhaps the day's stress had put him on edge or perhaps Tony Franco's paranoia was contagious, but he could not convince himself that the fear was irrational. *They're after you!* The thought plagued him even as he quickened his pace. Although the car was only a few more rows away, the distance seemed unconquerable. Fumbling with his keys, he produced the right one and slipped it into the lock. In a flash he was behind the wheel with the doors securely locked. The engine purred to life at his command and he backed up.

A sudden jolt stopped him dead in his tracks. The sound of metal crunching still rang in his ears as he looked to the left and the right. A threatening figure approached with a stern scowl on his face. Greg cast a look in his rear view mirror and realized the source of the problem. In his panicked haste, he had backed directly into a passing car. He pulled forward slightly and heard the sickening shriek of metal releasing metal.

"Why don't you watch where you're going, mister! Look what you've done to my car!" As Greg got out of the car, the man put his hand on Greg's shoulder and directed him to the damage. "You just backed right out into me!"

Greg surveyed the consequences of his carelessness. Paint missing from the right rear door of the victim's car straddled a sizable dent. "I'm really sorry. I wasn't thinking, and I just backed right up without looking."

"Yeah, and look what you did! I just got this car last week."

A second appraisal of the car exposed small nicks and signs of wear that convinced Greg it had experienced previous scuffles, perhaps in a prior owner's possession. "I'll pay for the damages. Let me give you my address and phone number."

"Your car doesn't even have a scratch! Just one broken taillight. That's not fair. You're the one at fault here!"

"All I can say is I'm sorry. Why don't we avoid the insurance companies and just settle this matter ourselves? Give me a call in a few days and let me know how much you had to pay to fix it."

The man rubbed his chin. "How do I know I can trust you? Let me have your insurance information anyway. I'll probably need a new door. Maybe a new paint job for the whole car. Who knows?"

Greg reached into his glove compartment and produced his insurance information. He also took out a card from his wallet. "I'm going to write my home address and phone number on the back of my business card. That way if I don't come through you can let my boss know."

The men exchanged information and shook hands warily. "Are you OK?" Greg added.

"I don't know. Too soon to tell. I have back and neck problems already, you see. I'm sure this didn't help. I'll let you know." With that, the man entered his car and drove away in a huff. Greg stood watching as the victim sped off. His bumper sticker proclaiming "I'm Saved, R U?" disappeared around the corner as Greg's guardian angel winced.

Greg stood up as Lisa entered the restaurant. Rain had been pouring on the city since Greg's incident in the parking garage the previous night. The weather had taken an unseasonable turn, reminding the city of the rapidly-approaching autumn. Greg helped Lisa off with her wrap and took her umbrella. "It's good to see you," he said, giving her a quick peck on the lips. "They have a table for us already."

The couple was escorted past the bar to a dimly lit table in the corner of a sunken dining room. The aged cherry motif added to the darkness, leaving barely enough light to read the menus. It was not too dark for Lisa to read Greg's face. "Something wrong, honey?"

Greg continued looking down into his menu. "I feel bad," he started. "I've been keeping something from you. I should have told you yesterday."

An expression of concern immediately registered on Lisa's face. "What is it?"

Greg cleared his throat. "At work I..." his voice trailed off as pride prevented him from admitting the loss of his personal money, what was to be *their* money. "After work I had an accident. Actually, it was after the gym." The words spilled clumsily out of his mouth.

"Are you all right? Oh honey, why didn't you tell me right away?"

"I don't know. I really don't know. I guess I didn't want to concern you." Greg felt himself slipping into one of his weak moods. Often he mistook humility for weakness, so he usually tried to exude an air of strong, confident masculinity, or at least what he believed it to be.

"What happened?"

Greg relayed the story, leaving out his false suspicion of someone following him. Instead he blamed it on a half-truth. "I guess I was a little shaky after the incident with the money at work. I'm so glad I was able to recover it all," he lied. *And if you ever find out what really happened to the money, smart guy, maybe you can put it back into your account!*

"I'm so grateful you were able to straighten all that out. I knew you could do it, but I have to admit I was a little worried anyway. That was a lot of money."

The waitress came and took their orders. Greg requested a bottle of white wine as an aperitif. Casual conversation ensued until the wine arrived. Greg toasted their engagement and downed his glass. Then he replenished his supply.

Lisa took another sip and prepared herself to broach a difficult topic. "Gregory, I need to talk to you about something."

The concern in her voice passed Greg by. "What is it, sweetheart?" he smiled.

"It's about the vacation," Lisa began hesitantly. "I've spent a good deal of time thinking about it, and I've decided against it. There are a number of reasons why."

"Like what?" Greg's displeasure was apparent.

Lisa rushed in with her litany of prepared explanations. "First, it's a really busy time at work for both of us. Second, I'd rather save the money and apply it toward the honeymoon. And plus we've got all the wedding plans to work on. There's still so much to do! I haven't spoken to the caterer for a whole month."

"So?" Greg quipped. "I thought we had everything settled with them already."

"Oh Gregory, you know I have to touch base with them periodically. Things keep coming up and I have to make small changes. But there's another reason too."

"Here we go." Greg rolled his eyes in his head.

Lisa cleared her throat, which had suddenly gone dry. "This is the most important reason, Gregory. I just don't think it's appropriate. I would love to spend the time with you alone, but I think we need to have some supervision."

Astonished, Greg took a moment to replay Lisa's words in his mind. "Look, Lisa, we're not in high school anymore. We don't need a chaperone. I've never had a chaperone, and I don't intend to start now. The whole idea is ludicrous!"

The appetizers arrived. Afraid to lose her momentum, Lisa kept talking. "Gregory, remember we decided to wait until we were married? I think going away together is too much of a temptation. Where are we going to sleep?"

Greg hoped that the waitress had not overheard their conversation. When he was certain that she was well out of earshot, he responded. "We don't have to share the same bed. But we've gone away before and nothing has happened. And we shared the same bed then."

Lisa blushed. "I wouldn't say *nothing* happened. And we both know that even more would have happened if we hadn't had that problem with the toilet."

"The self-flushing toilet?" The humor of the memory broke some of the tension. "The first time that happened we really flipped out."

"I know," Lisa laughed. "And it saved us from going too far." She was instantly serious again, but more peaceful. "Neither of us thought that was a good thing then, but I'm grateful for it now. I've been saving myself for you this long. I don't want to ruin it."

Although Greg did not realize it, he was being enveloped in a cloud of grace. There were few footholds left in his heart, but grace managed to find them. His love for Lisa welled up with a new intensity that took him by surprise. "How can I argue with that?" he heard himself saying. "I appreciate your view, although I don't know if I can share your idealism. But I'll try for your sake." He paused for a moment to gather his thoughts. *Go anyway!* At first he thought the sense was urging him to break the tentative agreement they had just reached. Suddenly he realized what it really meant. "Honey?"

Lisa was brushing a tear away from her eyes. "Yes?"

"I think it would be a good idea for me to go anyway. I mean alone."

Lisa looked into his eyes and then up as if to heaven. When her gaze returned to him she spoke. "I agree. You should take some time to rest and refresh yourself. A vacation is just what you need."

"You don't mind?"

"Not at all." She took his hand. "I'll take a small break while you're gone too and visit my parents. I haven't been back to New Jersey in a while." Lisa's parents lived in the Watchung Mountains in a house on top of a gentle cliff. "I could stand to be refreshed too. And I've got a lot of catching up to do with them. I feel like it's been ages since I last saw them."

Greg squeezed her hand. "That sounds wonderful. I think this will be good for both of us. Thanks for understanding, Lisa. I love you."

"I love you too, Gregory."

Chapter Three

The roar of the engines sounded sweetly in Greg's ears as he sat with eyes closed in the aisle seat. Greg preferred to sit by the window but no window seats were available when he made his last-minute arrangements at the airport. He had arrived at the ticket counter with two destinations in mind, Las Vegas and Phoenix. Either one would offer easy access to the deserted areas of the Southwest he felt a strong desire to lose himself in, for perhaps in losing himself he would really find himself.

Greg had purchased a one-way ticket and reserved a rental car in Las Vegas. His tentative plans were to wend his way slowly to Phoenix and fly home from there. During his early childhood, Greg's parents had taken the family on a sojourn through Arizona, and Greg had idolized his so-called "Desert Adventure" in his memories over the years. Now Greg felt called to return in order to test the accuracy of his recollections.

A few minutes after take-off a voice announced that complimentary beverages were on their way. Greg leaned out of his seat and saw the cart full of refreshments proceeding slowly down the aisle. He decided to close his eyes until he could quench his growing thirst.

When he opened his eyes, the beverage cart was nowhere to be seen. His eyes ran up and down the aisle in vain pursuit of something to drink. *You missed your chance, nitwit!* He thought about ringing for a stewardess to bring him some water.

"You're awake!" a friendly voice startled him from the window seat. "Hope you had a good nap."

Greg looked to his left across the empty center seat to find a middle-aged African-American gentleman sporting a UNLV shirt. "I missed the beverage cart," Greg complained.

"I noticed that, so I ordered you a bottled water. I didn't know whether you liked pop or not. I hope you don't mind." Wrinkles deepened around the man's eyes in a way that revealed his propensity to smile.

Greg was genuinely impressed and grateful. "Thank you, sir. I really appreciate it. If you only knew how thirsty I am!" The man handed over the still unopened bottle of water and a plastic cup with half-melted ice. Greg accepted it and in a flash the bottle was half empty.

The man chuckled softly. "You know, it's too bad about that water."

"What do you mean?" Greg eyed him curiously.

"Whoever drinks that water will be thirsty again."

"Then I'll have to have another when the stewardess comes by."

"Wouldn't it be great if there were water which you could drink and never be thirsty again?" A sparkle gleamed in the man's eye, unnoticed by Greg.

"I guess it would be. I don't suppose you have any of that kind of water," Greg teased him.

The man looked down for a moment as an uncontainable smile broke across his face. *Lord, if that's not a lead in, I don't know what is!* "As a matter of fact, I do. In a manner of speaking." Greg raised his eyebrows and the man continued. "And I know where you can get some."

"Man, what are you talking about?"

"I'm talking about refreshment. True refreshment. You know, for the soul!"

"Oh come on, you're not from some cult, are you?" Greg retorted.

"No, I'm not. I'm a Christian. And I'm talking about Jesus Christ. Did you know that the conversation we just had was very similar to one from the Bible?"

"No."

The man relayed the Scriptural account of the woman at the well, where Jesus revealed himself to a Samaritan woman as the source of life-giving water. He went on to claim that whoever drinks this water will never be thirsty again, but it will become a fountain within him welling up to eternal life. Then Jesus told her that he was the Messiah, and she believed him because he was able to recount everything she had ever done.

"So he told her fortune and she never had to come to the well to drink again?" Greg summarized the story awkwardly.

"That's not exactly how I would put it. But she did come to believe in him, and in fact the whole town was saved."

"Interesting. Are you a preacher or something?" Greg asked.

"Travis Grenley," the man extended his hand. Greg shook his hand and introduced himself as well. The man answered Greg's question. "I'm a campus minister at UNLV." He reached into his pocket and produced a business card. "Feel free to look me up whenever you're in town."

"Thanks," Greg smiled politely, taking the card. Emblazoned in red letters next to an icon of a rugged brown cross read the words, "Have you prayed today?"

Maybe, just maybe.

From his twelfth-story hotel room Greg looked out on the carnival of lights below. The glow of the street presented the illusion of broad daylight. Although he was anxious to get an early start on his trip the next morning, he sensed that it was going to be a late night. He had no interest in spending time placing bets and pouring money into one-armed bandits, but the city itself held a certain irresistible allure. What he felt was not so much a desire to partake but merely an urge to explore what the city had to offer. As if mindlessly following a dormant instinct, he found himself in the elevator descending to the world below.

After he crossed the lobby, two large ornate glass doors slid open before him. The residual heat from the day's desert sun met him and beckoned him onto the sidewalk. Crowds of people passed him by as they headed to their next destination. The flashing lights above his head cast a pattern of orange and green on the sidewalk. In the windows of passing cars he could see the name of his hotel reflected in neon glory. Everywhere there was movement. The sensory input made his head swim.

Flashing, glowing lights assaulted his eyes from every direction as his feet took him down the wide sidewalk. From his left, a casino door flew open and two teenagers clad in black leather jackets erupted from the dark noise inside. Greg took a quick step back to avoid colliding with them. A casino guard followed them a few yards into the street before stopping to swear and shake his fist at the prey that had escaped. Greg found the racing of his heart and the pervasive excitement exhilarating, disposing him to do things he would not ordinarily do. *Go in!* He did not even feel the desire to resist. The doors gave way in front of him.

As he entered the casino, an unseen war broke out above him, evidenced only by the conflicting thoughts that raced in the back of his mind. He tried to ignore a quiet sense to take flight back out to the street and toward his own hotel room. *You deserve to have some fun, buddy! You've been working so hard.* This voice appealed to him much more.

He passed by rows of nostalgic slot machines, the kind that still accepted coins.

Reaching into his pocket, he found two quarters. In a flash they were gone. He searched desperately for a change machine. Spotting one a short distance away, he made his way through the crowds and wisps of smoke with great effort. The machine would not cooperate and kept rejecting his twenty-dollar bill. Uttering a mild expletive, he turned around and flagged down an attendant who handed him two rolls of quarters. He took them thanklessly and found another machine. He frantically popped the quarters in like a drug addict popping pills. The result of each roll of the wheels registered in his mind only for a second before the next quarter was dispatched. When three double bars appeared in his win line, his heart almost stopped. Two hundred and fifty quarters spewed out to the tune of buzzers and flashing lights. A few people shot glances in his direction, some with envy, some with admiration. He took a cup bearing the casino's name from a stack near the slot machine and filled it with his treasure. The event left him slightly dazed and confused about what to do next. His hand reached automatically for another quarter even as he wondered. It disappeared down the slot. As the machine waited for him to pull its arm, his conscience spoke up. *This isn't you. Don't do this any more.* Even as he considered this proposition, more words followed. *Yeah, you're not a gambler. You're a winner! Take your winnings and go have a good time!*

With hardly another thought, he shut off his conscience and found the cashier's booth. Soon he had new, crisp bills in his hand, which he promptly took to the bar. *Go ahead, you deserve it!*

The room was still spinning as he opened his eyes in the blinding light. He had left the curtains open, and the late morning sunlight streamed in with its heat. Groaning, he forced himself out of bed and made his way across the blurry room to the mirror. *You look like hell! What did you do to yourself this time?* His memory offered no answer. Vaguely he recalled roaming around the streets with a bottle of something in his hand until someone laid a firm grip on his arm and pried the item out of his fingers. The identity of the person and the contents of the bottle escaped him now. The last thing he remembered clearly was casting a roving eye on a woman across the bar and taking a swig from his beer. She had not returned his ogling.

Lisa! The thought of her released a flood of guilt from the pit of his stomach. He chided himself as he stumbled about the room, picking up some clothes and other items he had evidently strewn about the night before. A knock on the door startled him as he searched for his watch. "Housekeeping!" a pleasant-sounding woman yelled through the door. Greg assessed his situation and, deciding he was suitably clad, he approached the door and opened it a few inches. "Can I have a few more minutes?" he pleaded.

"Sure," she accommodated him. "You're not checking out today, are you?"

Greg realized that he was unaware of the time. "Uh, yes, I am. What time is check out?"

"Twelve noon. You've got about ten minutes. But don't worry. They won't care if you're a few minutes late. I'll be back later."

Greg thanked her and shut the door. He ran both hands through his disheveled hair as he decided that a shower was out of the question. He resumed his search for the watch Lisa had given him the previous Christmas. The counters and the dresser drawers did not have any secrets to reveal. He knelt down next to his nightstand and checked under the bed to no avail. Reaching over, he opened the nightstand drawer to discover a Gideon's Bible. The pages were open to the Gospel of Luke, Chapter 4.

And Jesus being full of the Holy Ghost returned from Jordan, and was led by the Spirit into the wilderness, being forty days tempted of the devil. And in those days he did eat nothing: and when they were ended, he afterward hungered.

And the devil said unto him, If thou be the Son of God, command this stone that it be made bread.

And Jesus answered him, saying, It is written, That man shall not live by bread alone, but by every word of God.

And the devil, taking him up into an high mountain, shewed unto him all the kingdoms of the world in a moment of time. And the devil said unto him, All this power will I give thee, and the glory of them: for that is delivered unto me; and to whomsoever I will I give it. If thou therefore wilt worship me, all shall be thine.

And Jesus answered and said unto him, Get thee behind me, Satan: for it is written, Thou shalt worship the Lord thy God, and him only shalt thou serve.

And he brought him to Jerusalem, and set him on a pinnacle of the temple, and said unto him, If thou be the Son of God, cast thyself down from hence: For it is written, He shall give his angels charge over thee, to keep thee: And in their hands they shall bear thee up, lest at any time thou dash thy foot against a stone.

And Jesus answering said unto him, It is said, Thou shalt not tempt the Lord thy God.

And when the devil had ended all the temptation, he departed from him for a season.

Another knock on the door brought him back to his present situation. In a flash he threw wrinkled clothes and unused toiletries into his overnight bag. Yelling, "I'm coming!" toward the door, he donned his old shirt and gathered his wallet and keys, forgetting the missing watch. He brushed past the maid at the door with a mumbled apology and headed to the lobby to check out.

A few minutes later he was in his rented jeep speeding south out of town toward Arizona. Clumps of sagebrush covered the land for miles in all directions. The wind whipped his unkempt hair to and fro and howled in his ears, drowning out the radio he had turned on out of habit. He was heading for the desert with all the grime from the night before still covering his body and soul.

But God was in pursuit.

Chapter Four

Gazing out the van window at the dark city skyline, Greg marveled that the buildings looked the same, unchanged by the events of the previous week. Time alone in the desert had awakened a feeling of transformation in Greg, or at least a yearning for it. Being greeted by the mundane and familiar upon his return was somehow disappointing, but Greg resolved to cling to the new perspective the open spaces had provided him. A strong sense that big changes were on the horizon evoked both apprehension and excitement. Messages from his desert retreat still pervaded every waking thought, some of which he embraced and some of which were too disturbing to analyze, at least for the moment. He decided to let the coming weeks help sort out the lessons he had experienced.

As his neighborhood drew near, Greg allowed himself to succumb to his aching to talk to Lisa. Before his trip, they had agreed to give each other space, which included a moratorium on calling each other during Greg's time away. He hoped that the absence had added more kindling to the flame in Lisa's heart as it had in his. The urge to call Lisa had become unbearable, and he had called from his cell phone as soon as he had deplaned. As yet his longing was unrequited, with Lisa's voice on her answering machine providing only a drop of water to a dry and thirsty heart.

The shuttle from the airport dropped him off at a hotel several blocks from his apartment. The walk back gave him a few more minutes to prepare himself for his old routine. As he pulled his wheeled luggage behind him, he felt determined to take responsibility for his own destiny and overcome the burdens he had left at home. A feeling of invincibility gave a spark of energy to his exhausted feet.

The front door greeted him with a whoosh as he slid his pass into a card slot protruding from the brick wall of his building. As he approached the elevator, a white sign caught his attention by the call buttons. *Elevator access to floors 1 through 5 only.* Greg was not surprised to find the elevator in partial service. In the past few years he had experienced many elevator problems, which seriously inconvenienced those who lived on the higher floors such as Greg. He entered the elevator and defiantly pushed the button for floor seven. The strip of black tape over the buttons for floors six through ten were not much of a deterrent. After a long day of travel, he had no intention of disembarking on the fifth floor and walking two flights of stairs.

The elevator passed the fourth floor where it performed its usual minor shakes and creaks. Greg eyed the floor indicator as he approached level five.

The elevator kept climbing in its typical rough fashion. A bell indicated his arrival at floor seven.

When the doors opened, Greg fell back against the elevator wall in shock. Through the yellow tape covering the elevator exit he could see only a blackened wall in front of him, charred by some unexplained conflagration. Recovering, he ran towards the tape in an attempt to peer down the halls as the doors shut in front of him. He scrambled for the elevator button panel, and in his haste punched the buttons for floors four, five and six.

The elevator came to an abrupt halt on the sixth floor. The doors opened, and Greg threw himself against a line of tape, which gave way with little effort. He abandoned his bags in the hallway and peeled some tape off himself as he ran down the left corridor to the stairwell. Marks from smoke and water on the ceiling above revealed the extent of the fire. With his heart racing, he flew up the stairs two at a time and encountered more tape across the door to the seventh floor, his floor. He ripped off the tape and opened the door.

The smell of smoke and dampness filled his nostrils and stung his eyes as he ran toward his own apartment with increasing anxiety. The pounding of his heartbeat in his ears was deafening. A gaping black hole where his front door had been sent waves of heat and panic through his body. Inside his eyes detected nothing but darkness. He stood motionless and unthinking for a full minute as he took in the sight.

"Freeze!" The sudden, stern command cost him his balance and he tumbled to the floor. "Put your hands behind your back!" Greg had barely started to obey when he felt handcuffs slap tightly closed on his wrists. In the next few seconds, Greg could not make out which words were being directed at him and which were being communicated into a radio.

"Greg Wesko! I'm Greg Wesko!" he found himself shouting with winded breath from his position on the floor. He had answered without the police officer's question even registering in his mind. He felt his wallet leaving his pocket. The officer rummaged through its contents and removed his license. A few glances at Greg and back to the license convinced him. A look of astonishment crossed the policeman's face. "We've got Greg Wesko here!" he shouted into his radio. A mild oath issued from the other side. "I'd like to take you downtown for a few questions, Mr. Wesko."

The policeman freed Greg from his handcuffs and helped him pick up his baggage on the sixth floor as they headed down to the lobby. The officer led the way to a police car on a side street near the apartment building. Greg could not muster up the courage to speak until they pulled out into the light traffic. "What happened?"

The officer seemed hesitant. "Frankly, we're still not sure. It looks like a gas leak caused an explosion on the seventh floor. Your apartment, in fact. The odd thing is, we thought you were dead!"

"Dead?" Greg could hardly contain his astonishment. A dark sense of foreboding swept over his body. "What made you think I was dead?"

The officer frowned. "We found a body inside your apartment. It was so charred that we haven't been able to make an ID yet. The explosion happened just last night."

Dots of panic began to darken Greg's vision. A merciless dread tightened its grip on his stomach. "A body!" he whimpered, wringing his hands. He had a strong desire to escape, to be anywhere but inside the police car.

"Did you have a roommate? Were you living with anyone?" the officer asked. Greg shook his head violently. "Any idea who it could be?" Greg could not answer. "Who has keys to your apartment?"

"Lisa! Oh, Lisa!" He ran a frantic hand through his hair. "Lisa had a key. *Has* a key!"

"Lisa Grozny?"

"Yes, Lisa Grozny! She's my fiancée. Officer, have you talked to her?"

The officer shook his head. "She hasn't returned from a trip she took to New Jersey to visit her family. Your mother gave us their number."

"My mother!" Greg's mind was racing in five directions at once. "Do my parents think I'm dead?"

"We made a number of phone calls to try to locate you. We explained that we hadn't made a positive identification yet. When we get to the station you can let them know you're all right."

Greg's thoughts returned to Lisa. He did not want to face the terrifying possibility. He surmised that to the objective officer, it did not really matter who had died in his apartment. He had no personal stake in the outcome. But somewhere, a loved one was never going to return home. A family was missing a member forever. *Oh God, is it my family? Did I lose my only real shot at a family? Don't let it happen to me! No, not me!*

In the police station Greg was led to an available desk to make a phone call to his parents in East Granby. The phone rang twice before a weary voice answered. "Hello?"

"Mom!"

It was enough. Tears choked off the voice on the other end of the line. Relief, gratitude, and release poured through the phone. Greg held the phone a few inches away from this ear until the barrage passed. He heard his mother yell the news to his father in the background, who indicated that he had surmised what had happened. "Your father wants to talk to you. Oh Gregory, we're so glad you're OK. Oh, we were so worried! Here's your father."

"Son, you can't imagine how relieved your mother and I are. To get a phone call like that, that your son may be dead! I wouldn't wish it on my worst enemy. I just can't imagine it."

"No, it would be terrible."

"Whose body did they find? An intruder?"

"I don't know, Dad. They didn't identify the body yet." Greg started to become agitated. "Dad, I don't know where Lisa is."

"What do you mean? Didn't she go on vacation with you?"

"No, I went alone. Don't worry, everything is fine between us." He decided against an explanation of his solo trip. "She went to see her family and hasn't returned yet."

"Then I'm sure she'll be back soon. Everything will be fine."

"I guess so." Greg sounded less than convinced.

"Good, son. You let us know what happens. Take care."

"OK, Dad."

"Goodbye." Greg murmured a goodbye after his father hung up the phone. It had been a characteristically short conversation. Standing up, he headed for the desk of the police officer who had been watching him during his call. The officer indicated for him to sit down.

"The medical examiner just got here a little while ago. I think she's made a positive ID on the body." At Greg's silence, the officer added, "We should know for sure very soon." Although the officer was accustomed to seeing people at their worst, his heart still went out to this man sitting here under so much obvious anxiety. He searched for something to say but found himself at a loss for words. "Don't worry," fell far short of the compassion he wanted to express. "I'll go check on the progress. My partner will wait here with you." As the officer departed, he offered a silent prayer for Greg in his anguish. Greg tried unsuccessfully to acknowledge the partner with a smile, but anxiety prevented him. The partner perused a few papers in his hands and then shuffled them back and forth apathetically. The clock on the wall advanced at a sickeningly slow pace.

The creak of an opening door and the tap of footsteps across the tiled floor sent Greg's stomach into a state of chaos. As the tapping repeated monotonously, thoughts solidified in Greg's mind. *This is it. The sound of those footsteps is going to bring you the news. It's either going to be good or it's going to be bad. It's as simple as that.* The voice continued. *It's what you do about it that matters.* Greg didn't want to hear any more. He stood up to greet a policewoman approaching with an unreadable expression. *What is she going to say?*

"Mr. Wesko?" she addressed him. At his uneasy nod, she continued. "I'm so sorry. The body appears to be that of your fiancée, Ms. Lisa Grozny. We'd like to get some information from you, when you're ready."

Greg's hands shot up to his temples. He pressed hard as if to squeeze something out of his mind. "No!" he shouted. "NO!" Like a shot, he took to his heels and fled the building, knocking a pile of papers off a desk in his flight.

"I guess he wasn't ready," remarked the seated officer. "Pick those papers up, would you?"

Greg was free of the police headquarters but felt a burden almost too heavy to bear. It was something he knew he could not outrun, but running was all he could manage at the moment. It seemed that he had never run so fast in his life.

The scenery made no impression on him. He did not mark his direction, and he did not notice whether anyone was there to see him or not. Had anyone seen him, they would not have seen any tears. He was running too fast.

As he ran, a few thoughts managed to surface despite his efforts to the contrary. He saw Lisa sitting in his apartment. Lisa over dinner. Lisa accepting his proposal of marriage. Lisa telling him she would not go away with him. *If she had just gone away with me, she'd still be alive!* The thought jarred him to a halt. He found himself in an unfamiliar part of the city, right across the street from a church. Oblivious to any oncoming traffic, he sprinted toward the church and climbed the steps. *Locked!* He ran from door to door. Every door was locked. At the side door, he fell on his knees and began to weep. As the cold from the stone chilled his legs, he began to talk quietly.

"Why did you do this to me?" he managed with faltering voice. "Why did you take her away? Oh God, why?" Raising his head, he continued, "And now you won't even let me in to see you!"

I'm right here!

"No you're not! You're not here! You're not with me!" he shouted with frustration. "You came and messed up my life, and now I have to pick up the pieces alone! Alone! All by myself!" At that moment, Greg blinded his eyes so he could not see, deafened his ears so he could not hear, closed his heart so he could not understand, could not turn, could not be converted, and could not be healed.

An angel hung his head and cried.

Chapter Five

The grief-laden fog surrounding Greg's desk broke just enough to reveal a figure pacing outside his office door. Lifting his unfocused eyes from the computer screen, Greg stared in the general direction of the door. His peripheral vision recognized the profile of Tony Franco.

"Yes, Tony?" Greg managed in monotone. When the sound of Greg's voice reached Tony's ears, he fled without speaking. A few seconds later muffled words of surprise and apology floated in from down the hall. Greg was still in the process of deciding whether to care about what had just transpired when Joanna appeared and knocked lightly. Greg attempted a smile. "Come in, Joanna."

Approaching tentatively, Joanna smiled uncertainly in return. "Are you getting any work done?" she asked, knowing better than to ask how he was doing.

"I'm halfway through the string of e-mails that have accumulated in my extended absence," replied Greg stiltedly.

"I ran into Tony Franco in the hallway just now. Literally. Actually, I should say he ran into me."

"He was just here but didn't say anything. I don't know what he wanted. I imagine he had that crazed look of his. I didn't really get to see his face."

"I didn't either," admitted Joanna. "He mumbled something to me as he ran off." Discussion of the incident lightened the mood, but only for a brief moment. "Can I get you anything? Maybe a cup of coffee?" offered Joanna.

Greg motioned to the four empty styrofoam cups lined up on his desk. "I think I've had enough for one morning." After an awkward silence, he added an obligatory, "Thanks, anyway."

"Are you up for lunch? If you don't feel like going out, I could pick something up," suggested Joanna.

"I brought a cheese sandwich," Greg responded. "Thanks anyway, again."

The two friends drowned in discomfort, Joanna standing just inside the office and Greg sitting at his desk. The unspoken sentiment was thick enough to cut with a knife yet could not be adequately expressed in words. "Greg, I..." Joanna trailed off, biting her lip.

"It's OK, Joanna. I should get back to work. There's a lot of catching up to do. Why don't you come by later in the week?"

Joanna nodded agreement, almost unable to speak. She blinked back a few tears. "Just let me know if I can do anything for you," she tendered in a hoarse whisper before disappearing into the hallway.

Greg continued staring at the doorway long after Joanna had left. When he struggled to return his focus to the computer screen, the black and white symbols began to swim before his eyes. Closing them, his mind drifted back to a cold day several weeks earlier.

Overcast skies watched over Greg as he sat with his parents and Lisa's parents next to the open grave. A few bitter tears escaped as the words of the final eulogy from the nameless pastor bounced off without registering. Almost close enough to touch, the silver coffin lay in front of him enshrouded with a tasteful display of white lilies. At the end of the ceremony Greg stood with the intent of approaching the coffin. As the crowd began to disperse, a small cluster of people offered another round of condolences, which all blurred in his mind. Joe and Marina Tropetto extended a general invitation to dinner whenever he felt ready. Joanna said she would pray for him. An entourage from work attended but had kept their distance, which he appreciated. No one had said the words he had needed to hear, and Greg wished that he could pinpoint what those words even should have been.

Finally Greg found himself alone. The casket hovered on a metal frame over the deep hole in the earth, waiting for the cemetery workers to return for the final lowering into the ground. In order to touch the coffin, Greg had to step up tenuously onto one of the metal support bars. The act made his legs shake, already weakened by emotion. For a moment he stood trembling at the side of the coffin. Then he collapsed on top of Lisa's casket, sobbing uncontrollably. With effort he kept himself from wailing out loud. Emotion poured out of his mouth and nose until his face was entirely wet. Happy memories and painful regrets tugged his heart in every direction, but overwhelmingly Greg felt deep and inconsolable loss. Finally out of tears, he stepped down and turned away, leaving the gravediggers to bury his faith, hope and love deep in the dark earth.

Some time after the funeral he returned to his old apartment to collect what he could salvage. With the investigation over and the floor deemed safe, Greg had received clearance to enter his apartment again. Joanna and his parents accompanied him to help sort out the mess. The fire chief had concluded that a spark had ignited a gas leak in Greg's kitchen. The explosion had blown out almost the entire apartment, and the fire had consumed most of what was left. The only items of value he could find were in his study. The desk had protected a few items of jewelry, including an antique pocket watch that had belonged to his grandfather. The last article he was able to retrieve was an unopened letter from his sister that had fallen underneath the desk, which had saved it. This letter, still unread, now sat in a pile on the floor in his new, empty apartment across town.

In the ensuing days, Greg turned off his emotions and handled logistics as well as he could. His sister tried to reach him several times, as she had been unable to make the trip due to a severe illness. With no desire to talk to anyone, Greg let the answering machine pick up his calls. Only those he could not ignore did he return.

Greg's boss advised him to take as much personal time as he needed to sort out the details and the emotions, but soon Greg longed to return to work for the distraction. At home he lay in his bed every night under scratchy sheets, waiting in vain for the world to change.

In his office, Greg shook his head to clear his thoughts and return to the tasks at hand. *Have to go on with your life, buddy. Have to throw yourself into your work. Put it all behind you. There's nothing you can do about it now but forget.*

As the day continued, Greg forged ahead with his new attitude. Hard work was the only place he could find any comfort since the tragedy. A few people trickled in to offer awkward attempts at sympathy, but he was not ready to appreciate it. For the most part, he found that people treated him as if nothing had happened. As the week wore on, he adopted a pleasant façade, broken only by an occasional pensive darkness. The pile of backlogged work was dwindling with exhilarating speed. Productivity, he found, was an excellent, albeit temporary, salvation.

On Thursday morning the phone rang even as Greg reached to make a call. "Wesko."

"Greg? Chuck. I need to see you immediately in my office."

Greg quickly gathered a pad of paper and some important reports he had finished the day before as he scurried up to his boss's office. He grabbed a drink from the water cooler just outside the oak door with the name Chuck Hollis embossed in gold. A short, husky man in his forties opened the door and indicated a chair across from a large, wooden desk. The darkly stained wood was polished to perfection. "Have a seat. I just realized that I need to get something."

Greg took the opportunity to study the room. The cream-colored walls were decorated very plainly. An old poster entitled "Challenge" hung behind the black swivel chair on the other side of the desk. A brass lamp with a green shade cast light on a few closed folders on the desktop, but the room was too dimly lit for Greg to read the folder titles. Ceiling lights bordered the room but did little to improve the atmosphere. A painting of a duck hunter in camouflage faced the chair where Chuck made most of his important decisions. The entire room impressed Greg as a waste of space.

"Sorry for the delay," Chuck offered as he made his way around the desk to his chair. "I needed to get some information from Amos." Amos Stockley was Chuck's boss and reported directly to the CEO. Chuck seated himself, taking a quick glance into a thick folder he had brought back with him from Amos' office. He closed the folder with a barely perceptible uneasiness, something quite uncharacteristic for Chuck. Not escaping his attention, Greg felt the urge to take control of the situation but could not form a cohesive plan of action. He sat, waiting for the dreaded unknown.

"Greg, I called you here this morning to discuss the Crucis account. There are a few things we need to go over. Some things which are unclear, but maybe you can shed some light on them."

The Crucis account! I was going to review that this afternoon! Greg chided himself for taking so much time off, allowing his emotional needs to interfere with the only thing he had left, his work, the uncertain center of his life. The late Emil Crucis had been a wealthy Hartford philanthropist who had established several trust funds shortly before his death seven years earlier. It was a large account that nevertheless required only routine attention. Crucis had crafted his own life insurance policy, payable to his three children in quarterly installments. They would receive payments until the money was depleted in about twenty more years.

"Greg, I don't know how to say this in a way which will not sound, well, let's say, accusatory. It has come to my attention that a sizeable quantity of money is missing from the Crucis account. As you know, every quarter funds are electronically transferred to three separate accounts, one for each beneficiary. Just last month, a request to change recipient bank accounts was approved. On the usual date, the funds were transferred to three bank accounts in Vaduz, the capital of Liechtenstein. However, funds were also transferred to the three original accounts. Were you aware of this?"

"No, of course not!" Greg's response was much more forceful than either of them had anticipated. Suddenly his temples began to pound as he realized the potential gravity of the situation. "I haven't had a chance to review that account since my return. I'm the only one authorized to approve such a change, but I don't remember doing it. In fact, I don't believe it's even allowed under the terms of the policy. Not unless the original bank closes, which apparently it didn't."

"No, I checked into that during your absence. I also checked with the bank in Liechtenstein. There is no traceable record of the transaction."

Greg realized that Hollis had known for some time but had waited to tell him. He wondered at his motivation for doing so. "So there is almost $120,000 missing," he mused aloud with dismay.

"Greg, I hate to bring up the topic, but I'm afraid we may be looking at a full-scale audit. It wouldn't be my first choice but it's mandated by company policy." The reports in Greg's hand burned to preempt the conversation and change the focus. But there they remained, growing heavier by the minute with his perspiration. The remainder of the conversation blurred into chaos, a mixture of Hollis' apologetic admonitions and Greg's perfunctory replies. As the meeting ended and Greg rose to leave, Hollis remained seated, following Greg to the door with a stony eye.

"Don't worry, Chuck, I'll figure this out." His words did not convince either of them. As soon as the door shut behind him, the hallway began to sway before his eyes. On shaky legs he made his way back to his office. *I will get through this. Believe in myself, that's what I have to do. I can do anything through my own strength, if I believe it.*

He wasn't fooling anyone.

The day had been long, difficult and fraught with emotion, although Greg had tried his best to keep his feelings bottled up inside. Having returned to his office from a meeting at the end of the day, Greg had intended to pack up his laptop and depart forthwith. To his great dismay, however, he encountered the nervous figure of Tony Franco swiveling back and forth in the guest chair, anxiously awaiting Greg's return.

"What do you want, Tony?" snapped Greg as he stormed into his office. Tony rose upon Greg's arrival, but Greg pushed past him in order to reach his desk. He began packing his laptop case without even raising his eyes to meet Tony's contorted expression.

"I'm sorry to bother you, Greg," he stammered apologetically. "I know it's late in the day, and you probably want to get home."

"That's right," Greg quipped.

"So I won't take much of your time. I just need someone to talk to, and everyone else seems to have left for the day."

"I saw Marvin Goldberg heading to his office just a few minutes ago."

"You know I don't get along with Marvin," Tony replied.

Greg sighed and placed his laptop carrier on top of the desk. Resigned to enduring a conversation with Tony, he sat down and began fidgeting with his mouse. "Tell me what's on your mind."

Tony resumed his seat. "I don't have a reason to live anymore. My wife wants a divorce."

"I thought you already were divorced," Greg asserted, ignoring Tony's predictable exaggeration.

"We never finalized it. We drew up the papers and even set a court date, but the day before the hearing, we called off the divorce. For the last few months we've been living apart, more or less."

"More or less?" Greg raised an eyebrow.

"Sometimes we try getting back together, but it never lasts more than a few days. So she doesn't bother moving anything out of her apartment. When she's with me, I feel happy. When she's gone, I tell myself that she will come back, and it keeps me alive. If the divorce goes through, then I won't be able to tell myself that anymore. I'm afraid I will die."

Greg closed his eyes and rubbed his forehead as he attempted to assemble the correct words. "Tony, I know it's hard to lose someone you love. Maybe it is even harder when that person is someone you can still see, still touch. It must make you think about what you could still have, and you wonder what you can do to fix it and make it all better. But no matter what, no one is worth dying over. You have to think of yourself and do your best to get through." Greg wanted to offer consolation, but his words failed to express what he truly intended and what he truly believed. A tear escaped from his eye, which he promptly wiped away.

"I'm sorry, Greg," Tony said as he stood back up. "I didn't mean to dredge up your sorrow. I should remember how lucky I am, that I still have my wife, whether she's legally my wife or not. I can't imagine your pain. It's selfish of me to think I'd rather die that live without my wife. I'd rather live and still have the potential of having my wife back. Thanks, Greg. Thanks for listening. I'll go now."

Greg opened his mouth to utter a good-bye, but a hoarse whisper was all that he could manage.

Greg arrived at his old apartment late in the evening. Nostalgia had never been his strong suit, but the conversation with Tony had compelled him to return for one last opportunity to reminisce. It was the first place he had lived alone. For two years he had roomed with a college friend after graduation, but his desire for independence had overcome the economic benefit of sharing monthly rent. Living solo agreed with him well, and the thought of such intimate sharing with a wife had caused him considerable agony. *Don't have to worry about that now.*

Memories began to well up in his mind as he stepped through the doorway. The housewarming party thrown by his former roommate, hailed as the "Glad-you-got-the-hell-out party." The struggle trying to get his new desk through the doorway into the study. The week he stayed at home in bed with an aching back after a ski injury. The phone call from his sister after two years of silence, announcing he was going to be an uncle. Quiet evenings with Lisa on the couch watching old movies. Arguments with her over their wedding and their future.

A gentle knock against the wall broke his reverie. He turned with a twinge of anger at the intrusion to find a small, heavy-set woman bearing a faint smile. "I'm sorry for your great loss."

In response to her apologetic tone, Greg attempted to don a more friendly expression. "Thank you. I lost everything in that fire." His candid admission took him by surprise, but he continued. "Everything of value. Burned up and gone."

The woman cast a glance down to gather her strength and collect her thoughts, trying to hide the emotions yearning to betray themselves upon her face. "I truly am sorry. I know how you feel. I lost almost everything in that fire too."

Sudden recognition registered in Greg's mind as he realized he had met the woman before. She had lived two doors down the hall from him. Their conflicting schedules had kept them from running into each other except on an occasional Saturday afternoon trip to the mailbox. A vague recollection of a single mother raising a young son crossed his mind. His stomach twisted in knots as he studied her face. "Your son?"

Raising her eyes heavenward before answering, the woman fought back tears. "I left him at home while I went grocery shopping. He hated to go to the store, and I didn't want to do battle with him after the kind of day I'd had." Pausing, she cleared her throat. "I could see the smoke pouring out the windows as I walked down the street. I dropped all my grocery bags." Her voice trailed off.

For the first time since the fire, Greg found something in his heart besides bitterness. That day, in front of the church, he had cast just about everything else out of his heart. Confronted with someone who had seemingly lost even more than he had, he felt the awakening of a stronger compassion that had long lain dormant. "I'm terribly sorry. I don't know what to say."

"It's okay." The woman forced a smile. "At least I know my son's in the Kingdom. My faith is the only thing that has gotten me through this tragedy, this terrible trial in my life. It's the only thing that ever does."

Greg reflected on her words. "The only thing that is getting me through this time is my work. Myself. My self-discipline. When it gets too hard, I just discipline myself to work harder. I think in time it will get easier," he paused, revealing his uncertainty. "Don't you think so?"

The woman folded her hands humbly. She knew about hard work. She knew about discipline. "I can't rely on myself. I rely on my faith. My faith in Jesus."

Her words grated on his nerves. *I've tried that, lady. Whatever faith I had burned up in that fire. Just when I thought I had found my faith, God ripped it away in a blazing inferno. You're a fool to believe that He will help.* Yet his own thoughts cut him deeply, as something inside knew that it was he who was playing the fool. "I hope that works for you. Faith isn't my cup of tea. Lisa and I had each other, and that was enough for us."

A moment of silence elapsed as the Holy Spirit prompted the woman to speak. "Did you know that I met your Lisa?" Greg looked at her in amazement. He did not even know the woman's name. "I bumped into her a couple times when she was letting herself into your apartment. She was a beautiful person."

"You talked to her?"

The woman nodded. "I even saw her the day of the fire. She was glowing and I told her so. She was carrying a package wrapped in gold paper. She said she had a big surprise for you but she didn't tell me what it was. I didn't pry. But I had my suspicions. She was overflowing with the Holy Ghost."

Greg's ears started to grow deaf as he began to write the woman off as a little crazy. "What are you talking about?"

"Your fiancée was a faithful woman. She invited me in once or twice and we talked about it. She had recently started going back to church, and she said her life was getting back on track. She wanted to tell you but didn't know how you would take it."

"I would have taken it just fine. I don't have any problem with her going to church. I would have even been willing to go with her sometimes, if she had told me." He looked away, hurt by the implicit accusation. "What made her think I wouldn't take it well?"

The woman prayed for guidance in her speech. "You see, she wasn't going to church just on Sundays. She was going every morning. Every day of the week. Had been for several months, more or less. I don't know exactly what was going on in her life, but I do know that she had found her faith in Jesus. I'm sure she's rejoicing with Him now in Heaven. And I know it breaks her heart to see you in such deep mourning here below."

Fat lot of good that does me now. "I appreciate your sentiments. Thanks for letting me know. I should be going now."

"No, no you shouldn't. Why don't you stay awhile? I'll leave you to be alone. But remember, you're not really alone."

In the silence of solitude he stared at the floor as conflicting thoughts tore at his mind and his heart. As profound as his loneliness had been in the past, it had never been as impenetrably thick as it was now.

Suddenly his eyes focused on a dull shiny object that weakly caught the light. He stooped over to pick it up. His heart skipped a beat as he beheld a piece of gold wrapping paper that had miraculously survived the fire. He fell on his knees, clutching the paper in his hands. The tears kept flowing long after his bent knees began to ache.

Chapter Six

The morning sun rose over the city skyline in a brilliant display of orange and red, conquering the deep purple hue of the receding night. Soft rays filtered through the dark blue curtains of Greg's bedroom, soaking the unwrinkled comforter in a faint bath of glowing light. In the corner on a chair, Greg's neatly folded pajamas lay on top of the latest issue of National Geographic. Silence pervaded the entire apartment, which had slowly filled up with new items, mostly purchased over the Internet. In the kitchen, the last few drops of water dripped silently from his new coffee pot, which sat inverted on a gold-wire dish rack. Greg had left his apartment in the pitch black of pre-dawn with the mental security of a clean and orderly apartment. Recently, Greg found it increasingly difficult to concentrate on his work whenever order was lacking in his physical world. It compensated for the growing disorder in his spiritual world.

A barely perceptible scraping of metal against metal, a slight jostling of the doorknob, and the front door of his new apartment creaked open. The dim morning light outlined the silhouette of a large man with a metal file in one hand and a small bag in the other. The figure guided the door to a quiet close behind him and paused to adjust his eyes to the dark. A few stealthy steps through the living room brought him to the doorway of Greg's bedroom. A quick scan of the covers and the folded bedclothes assured the man that he was alone in the apartment. He found the light switch and with gloved hands began his search.

Across town Greg tasted his cup of coffee to find it already ice-cold. For more than two hours Greg's body had been nearly motionless, his eyes scanning page after page of dates and dollars on the computer screen. After he scrolled through his last worksheet, he allowed himself to sit up, stretching his arms above and behind his head. *Everything is checking out. Everything is going to be fine. You're a smart guy. This will all be behind you soon. It has to be.*

A knock at the door caught his attention and he smiled to see Joanna, whose expression changed from concern to tentative joy to see him wearing anything but his recent customary frown. She stood in the entrance, uncertain whether to cross the threshold. "Good morning, Greg. I see you already have your coffee."

"I got here a little early today," he admitted.

"Especially for a Monday. I must say, I am glad to see you smiling. That's unusual for a Monday too."

Greg rested his head back against his folded hands. "Sundays are your Sabbath, and Mondays are mine, it seems. I looked forward to coming to work all weekend with great anticipation." *No, with great anxiety.* "I need to roll up my sleeves and get to work. That's the reason I get up in the morning."

A trace of disappointment marred Joanna's smile. "I was hoping you were feeling better. It's good to see you smile. I've missed the old Greg Wesko, and I've really wanted to talk to him. But honestly, I didn't know how much space to give you."

Joanna's candidness caught him slightly off-guard. He turned his chair to face her directly and laced his hands together on his lap. "I appreciate that, Joanna. I really do. I know I've been behaving like a real bear lately, and I apologize. It's been hard, as you know, and I needed the time to get myself together. Time to get back to my old self."

"After something like this, you're never the same. You can never get back to your old self. But you don't have to apologize. Or maybe I should just say that I accept your apology." She paused. "And why don't we have lunch sometime this week?"

"I'd really love to, Jo, but this week is completely crazy for me. If my schedule frees up, I'll give you a call." Greg grimaced inwardly at the skepticism written across Joanna's face. Wanting to maintain as much secrecy as possible about the audit, he had decided not to confide in anyone, even Joanna. "I'm not trying to put you off, Joanna, believe me. If not this week, let's definitely do lunch next week. Even twice!"

"I'll give you a ring later in the week to see how you're doing. In the meantime, don't hesitate to call if you need anything." Joanna felt prompted to say something more, but the right words would not materialize.

"OK, Joanna. Hey, you have a good day now."

"You too," Joanna hesitated as she began to close the door. Greg shot her an inquisitive look, so she added, "Bye, Greg," and departed.

As her heels clicked against the tile corridor, she was overwhelmed with the sense that she had failed her mission.

Shortly before noon, Greg decided to review the Crucis account one last time in preparation for the meeting with the corporate auditors after lunch. He had spent the better part of the previous week trying to beat the auditors to the punch in finding out what had happened with that account. According to protocol, they had been summoned to inspect every aspect of Greg's work in the minutest detail. There were several levels of audits, but the large sum of money involved with the Crucis discrepancy demanded a rigorous review. Greg expected to spend most of the remaining week with them, with several follow-up meetings afterward. The auditors had spent the morning with his superiors for a briefing of the situation. Greg's early morning efforts had uncovered several minor procedural errors from his early days, but nothing that warranted a reprimand. The incident with the missing $20,000 earlier in the year had been covered up so well that he doubted anything would be noticed. His plan had originally been to find the missing money and recoup the personal funds he had used. That plan had never been realized.

He typed in his password for the Crucis account and waited for the computer to accept it. With recent software upgrades, it now required an extra five seconds for the computer to grant him the appropriate access. In his impatience, five seconds seemed like an eternity. The screen cleared and a heading labeled *Crucis* appeared at the top of the monitor. Greg usually glossed over the perfunctory messages that accompanied logging into an account, but today they caught his eye. In two short lines, the computer informed him that he had last logged in on Saturday morning at 6:46 AM and that there had been seventeen unsuccessful attempts to log in since that time.

An acute uneasiness broke out in Greg's chest, spreading into his temples, which began to pound, and into his stomach, which suddenly tightened. A wave of nausea overwhelmed him. He had not come into work over the weekend, and he did not have access to the company's computer network from home. *Someone has access to my accounts. It can't be just a computer glitch. But then why were there so many unsuccessful attempts to log in afterward?*

Myriad questions flooded his mind, with only one plausible answer: someone else was tampering with his accounts. Someone had figured out his password and logged in over the weekend, perhaps many other times as well. But the subsequent seventeen unsuccessful attempts left him baffled.

A fresh idea in his mind, Greg glanced at his watch. "Almost an hour until the audit," he murmured to himself. With furious fingers, he looked up the number for the IT department. After a few rings and three computer-operated menus, he had a live voice on the other end of the phone. Without revealing the true reason behind his call, he inquired about the possibility of someone else breaking into his account or accessing his password. Greg could hear suspicion arising in the specialist's soprano voice.

"Sir, this sounds like a case I should refer to ISD, the Information Security Department. Do you suspect unauthorized access to your accounts?"

Greg hesitated, debating whether or not honesty would be the best policy. He opted for the truth, at least the partial truth, and related the login incident. He decided to withhold the fact that he was on the verge of an audit.

The woman at the help desk indicated that she would pass along the information to security, and someone would contact him within the hour. Meanwhile he should avoid any other activity in his accounts until he heard back from ISD.

As soon as he hung up the phone, he found himself struggling with feelings of regret about involving ISD, even though it seemed to be his most logical recourse. *It has to help with the audit. If I can show that someone has accessed my accounts illegally, I'll be off the hook. Maybe I can even get my $20,000 back. I'd have to be crazy not to let people know what happened.*

Greg sat back in his chair and lifted his head slightly toward the ceiling, closing his eyes and letting out a deep sigh. *When is that phone going to ring?* Patience had never been one of Greg's stronger attributes. Waiting for the Information Security Department to call back was excruciating, and Greg found his fingers drawn toward his computer keyboard. His appetite was gone, and the urge to continue his own investigation was beginning to take control. *If I could just do something besides sit here.* In the chaos of his thoughts, images of Lisa began to flash in front of his mind's eye. He found himself longing to talk to Lisa, to let her know what was happening. But an accusatory voice responded instead.

You never let her know the whole truth about the missing money the first time. Remember, you weren't in the habit of pouring your heart out to her in the past. Why should you expect to do so now? It's too late, and you've lost her. You're on your own now. That's the way you've always wanted it, isn't it?

"I don't know, I don't know," Greg found himself uttering out loud. "I just don't know."

A sudden knock at the door, and Greg found his pounding heart had leapt into his throat. He swore under his breath to see that one o'clock had arrived without a return call from ISD. Even though he realized that his visitors probably could not have heard his self-directed comments, he felt a rush of color rising in his cheeks. He stood to greet the team of corporate auditors with a cotton-dry mouth. Chuck stood with them, but Chuck's superiors were noticeably absent.

With the chime of his wall clock indicating five o'clock, Greg sat in the wake of the afternoon's introductory audit. A good deal of time had been spent reviewing the audit process and getting acquainted with Greg's accounts firsthand. In the pressure of the moment, he had forgotten about the computer help desk's instructions not to log into any of his accounts. The first ringing of the telephone during the audit recalled him to his senses, and he launched into an explanation of the suspicious activity in his account. Through the auditors' polite expressions, Greg could read that they were not convinced. *There is no way to prove that it really wasn't me who logged in on Saturday morning. Except that I have no access from home. Maybe I could get the security guard to vouch for me that I didn't come in this weekend. If he would remember...*

Greg reached for the phone and grabbed an emerald green notebook out of the lower right drawer of his desk. He considered it his accounting diary where he kept personal notes that he wished to protect from unfriendly eyes. On the other end of the phone, a rough voice crackled. "Security, Al speaking."

"Hi Al, this is Greg Wesko on the sixth floor."

"Hello, Mr. Wesko. What can I do for you?" Al Finch usually worked the evening shift and knew Greg from his frequent late-night hours.

"Al, I was wondering if you worked this weekend. I wanted to find out about something that may have happened here on Saturday."

"No, I had this weekend off. I was supposed to work but I switched with the new guy. You met him yet? His name is Jodah Sherman."

Greg did not recall meeting any new security guards. Al was the only guard with whom he was friendly, mostly due to Al's gregarious personality. During the day, employees could enter through the main lobby or through the employee entrance in the back of the Providential Insurance building through the parking deck. After hours the rear entrance was closed, and the only remaining access was through the main lobby. Employees had to ring for the security guard to open the front door. Sometimes this entailed a five or ten minute wait when the security guard was on rounds in another part of the building. Otherwise he manned the receptionist's desk in the main lobby or the guard office nearby. Anyone accessing the building between 5:00 PM and 7:00 AM had to sign in on a log sheet. Employees staying after 7:00 PM were required to call the security desk to let them know they were still in the building in case of an emergency. Then they had to sign out upon leaving the building.

"I don't think I've met him," Greg responded. "I think I'd remember a name like Jodah."

"He's from California or something. A real surfer type, if you know what I mean. Bleached blond hair and everything. I think he rides a surfboard to work." Greg had no desire to acknowledge Al's sense of humor at the moment. "Anyway, what do you think happened on Saturday?"

Greg thought quickly. "Nothing, really. I just think someone came in and played a joke on me. I wanted to know who was here on Saturday."

"Well, I can check the log book for you. A practical jokester on the loose, you say. What makes you think it was Saturday and not Sunday?"

Greg did not want to elaborate on his fabrication any more than necessary. "Just a hunch. I guess it could have been Sunday."

"Someone in particular you want me to look for on the list?"

"If it's not too much trouble, maybe you could just read the list for me? There could be more than one person in on the joke."

"Why not just stop down and look on the way out?" Al suggested. "Got a lot of names on the list. It was a busy weekend."

"Al, would you mind faxing a copy of the list up to me? I need to know right away. I want to send the person an e-mail in response to the joke before I leave."

With jovial protest Al agreed to fax the information up to Greg. "Just give me a few minutes," he quipped lightheartedly.

"Thanks, Al. I owe you one."

While waiting for the fax, Greg used the time to check his voice mail from the afternoon. With the corporate auditors in the room, Greg had been unable to answer the phone. Impatiently he listened to a series of unimportant messages until he came across a call from the Information Security Department. A voice resembling an off-key baritone saxophone indicated that they had been unable to find evidence of unauthorized access to his account. In addition, no records of activity on his accounts over the weekend could be found, either successful accesses or unsuccessful attempts. However, the voice indicated that the heavy use of his accounts that afternoon might have obliterated any data from the weekend because of limitations on the amount of computer memory allocated to tracking activity. The voice further instructed him to immediately call the Information Security Department again if more unauthorized activity on his account were suspected.

Disappointed, Greg listened to the rest of his messages and then checked the fax machine. Two pages of names swam before his eyes. The short night's sleep and the pressure of the audit had taken its toll, and he was tired. He stuffed the pages in his green notebook and put it in his laptop case to review at home. It had been a long and arduous day. He had not thought of Lisa since lunchtime, and he suddenly found himself picking up the phone to call her to let her know he was on his way. He had dialed the first two numbers before the reality of the situation struck him in the face. In an uncharacteristic display of anger, he threw the phone and his laptop case to the floor and stormed out of his office, leaving the door wide open and his lights on. They would wait for him impersonally all night, this office and its accoutrements, this house of worship where Greg had spent his self-proclaimed Sabbath.

Chapter Seven

Doomed to seemingly endless night, Greg wrestled with the covers in fitful bouts of restlessness. A book on short-term investments had eventually lulled him to sleep, but dreams had begun shortly afterward. In dream after dream he found himself tallying figures for fictitious accounts that he could not balance. He looked up to see Chuck Hollis towering over his desk, red pen in hand. Mist prevented Greg from a clear view of Hollis' face as he mouthed the words, "You're fired!" Or had he said, "You're dead!"

Startled, Greg shot up from his desk, sending his chair tumbling to the floor with a muffled crash. Grabbing a ledger from a nearby shelf, he pushed past Hollis and out into the dimly lit hall. Unfamiliar employees milled back and forth, paying no attention to Greg as he scrambled for the exit to the stairs.

The smell of smoke and ashes filled the stairwell as Greg found himself in his old apartment building. A dreadful foreboding churned in his stomach. Inescapably drawn toward the charred door on the floor below, Greg trod heavily on the metal stairs, his every footstep reverberating with dull metallic echoes. The door opened before him to reveal thick blackness. A faint red glow emanated from under another door several yards away. Wisps of smoke wafted out into the hall. With dry throat and mouth, Greg called out hesitantly, "Lisa, Lisa!" He pushed open the door to find his apartment in deep scarlet flames, intense in color but dull in luster. Black smoke billowed up out of sight. Nothing was recognizable in the inferno except for his roll-top desk. A box wrapped in gold foil sat unharmed on the writing mat next to an unopened letter. Compelled to open the package, he braved the flames and stood before his desk.

An explosion from the kitchen shook the ground with a deep jolt. "Lisa!" He ran out of the study, leaving the package behind, but found his movements hindered, as if he were carrying an immense weight. By the time he arrived at the kitchen, it was engulfed in flames too deep to penetrate. Fire surrounded him on all sides except back to the front door. Unable to move, he looked up to see a glass ceiling. His father and mother stood on the ceiling, his mother clutching his father helplessly in fear. Next to her Lisa appeared with his sister. Somehow the gold package had materialized in their hands. Holding onto a ribbon wrapped around the box, they lowered it to him through the ceiling. Greg began to jump furiously to reach the package. With each jump he came closer to the package until finally he grasped it. The ledger from the office fell out of his hands, and he looked down after it. Suddenly he found himself back on the ground next to the ledger. Frantically he looked up to see nothing but smoke and flames. The ceiling was hidden as he realized he was holding onto a scrap of gold paper. The package was gone.

With a start, Greg awoke and sat up in his bed. Swinging his legs to the side, he rested on the edge and waited for the pounding in his heart to settle down. He looked down to check his hands. No ledger. No gold foil. Not even any ashes or burns.

Theresa! I've got to find her letter. In all the turmoil in the aftermath of the fire, Greg had misplaced his sister's letter before ever having read it. A few days after the funeral she had finally been able to reach him on the phone to offer her condolences. He had kept the conversation short, even though he sensed that she had wanted to talk longer. They had never been close, and contact had always been short and infrequent after each had left home. The last time Greg could remember seeing her was at Christmas the first year he had brought Lisa to meet his parents. Since then Theresa had not made any trips home.

Still shaken from his series of nightmares, Greg began to search for his sister's letter. After pouring himself a glass of water to quench his parched throat, he began with the study. Drawer after drawer turned up no trace of the months-old letter. As his frustration grew, he became less careful about putting his papers back in order until the room began to take on a markedly disheveled appearance. A quick glance at the clock revealed large red digits reading 3:16. *How long have I been searching? How much longer will I have to search? I wish I had looked at the clock when I got up.*

Twenty minutes later Greg found success in a pile of papers in the corner of his living room near the new entertainment center. He hurriedly tore the envelope open as he jumped onto the couch. In the soft light of an overhead lamp he unfolded the handwritten letter.

> Dear Greg,
> It has been such a long time since I have written you a letter. I feel just awful about that, but I guess neither of us has ever been inclined to put pen to paper. I remember how Mom made us write our thank-you notes after every Christmas and birthday. I don't know which of us disliked it more. How ungrateful we were!
> I wrote to ask you if I could come out for a visit with the children. Jared is too busy with work to make a trip, but I really could use a vacation. That's also why I would like you not to tell Mom and Dad that I'm coming. I need a rest. I've been a little under the weather lately. I hope it wouldn't be too much trouble. Jack is 4 now and is very well behaved. I can't believe that Denise is already two! You haven't even met her. She is so precious!

My life is a lot different now. I've been through a lot of changes, good ones, mostly. I'd like to tell you about them, at least some of them, anyway. For one thing, I've gotten out of that Zen group but I still meditate on my own. I'm a lot more peaceful than before, especially more so than when we were growing up. I had some health problems but they are mostly over. Don't worry - it's not contagious. I had a couple of bad falls, among other things. I sustained a bad concussion. As you know, my head's always been pretty hard, but it took a pretty good blow this time.

I'm anxious to hear about what's going on with you. How are the wedding plans? I don't think we've talked since you told me about the engagement. I suppose everything must be almost in order by now. When are you sending out invitations?

So please let me know whether we can come out, and when would be good for you. You don't have to take off from work or anything. Let's just make sure that our visit includes a weekend so we can have some time to spend with you. It will be nice to see Linda again too.

Love,
Theresa

In the quiet of pre-dawn Greg sat motionless on the couch, the edges of the letter growing moist in the clenched grasp of his sweaty fingers. Light bathed him in its warmth amidst the shadows of the night. Beyond his line of vision a lamp quietly blazed in the office. As he reviewed his sister's letter, the characters blurred before his eyes, merging together and separating again in a tango between exhaustion and reverie. With two fingers he traced a path starting beneath his eyes and running down the side of his nose. *No tears, no tears,* he scolded himself. *We've been so out of touch, she didn't even get Lisa's name right.* The letter began to tremble in his hands. *I should contact her. Maybe I'll call her after work tonight.*

The subtle hum of the clock radio drifted across the apartment, interrupting the only stretch of restful sleep he had managed to get the entire night. A few blurry moments were necessary to orient himself, as he could not remember falling asleep on the couch. He rubbed his eyes and rose to his feet, a soft crunch emanating from the carpet beneath his toes. Stooping down to pick up his sister's letter, he felt a mild pain in his lower back, the result of his contorted sleeping position on the couch. Stiffly he made his way to the kitchen for an early breakfast. Eating before getting dressed was a break in his routine, further increasing his sense of insecurity. A nine o'clock meeting was scheduled to discuss the final results of the audit. He would meet alone with the auditors, who would then meet with his superiors. In the afternoon he was due in Hollis' office to follow up.

Despite rubbernecking delays due to a three-car accident in the oncoming lane, Greg arrived at work early to gather his thoughts in preparation for defending himself with the auditors. *I've done nothing wrong. No matter how many times I go over the details, I can't find any way to explain the switching of those accounts and the loss of that money. My main concern is that they may have discovered the $20,000 I switched from my own account to cover up that first loss. I still don't know how to explain that away.*

Greg walked down the hallway, trying not to recall the details of the previous night's dreams. The usual crew of earlier risers was already buzzing, some chatting by the coffee pot, some busily typing away at their workstations. A few looked up from their desks to greet Greg by name. A head of curly red hair several paces in front caught him by surprise. "Joanna?"

Turning and smiling, Joanna waved sheepishly. "Yes, I know, I'm very early today. I already stopped by your office once this morning. I thought you'd be here even earlier, with everything that's happening today. How are you doing?"

"Let's go into my office," Greg motioned to his door several yards ahead of them on the right. He had still managed to avoid mentioning the audit to anyone except Chuck Hollis, and it disturbed him that Joanna knew about it, even about the timing of the audit wrap-up session. When they entered his office he closed the door. "I guess you know, today's the big day. The auditors have summarized their findings and are ready to issue their report."

"I know," Joanna admitted with regret. "I wanted to see how you were doing. What do you think they're going to say? There's nothing to find, is there?"

Greg was unsure whether Joanna's words were accusatory or not. She neither chided him for not telling her about the audit nor explained how she had come to know about it. "Of course there's nothing to find! I just don't know what happened." Greg felt the truth yearning to break forth, but he could not muster the necessary trust to confide in his friend sitting across the desk from him. He found himself wondering how much detail had leaked out. "I've reviewed my work countless times, but I can't find any real errors."

"Then I'm sure the auditors won't either. I can't imagine they are that thorough on a routine audit like this."

Greg noted the concern behind Joanna's pleasant smile and reassuring words. *Doesn't she know this audit is anything but routine?* "Let's hope so."

"I'm sure everything will be fine. You're in my prayers," Joanna added as she rose to go. "Is there anything I can do for you?" she offered.

Don't talk about your prayers. "No thanks, Joanna. I'll let you know how it all comes out." Greg's eyes diverted to the floor where his lap top case stood next to his lower right drawer. His mind immediately abandoned Joanna and switched to the two pages from the logbook that Al had faxed him earlier in the week. As he opened his case, heat rose in his cheeks as he embarrassedly remembered throwing his phone and case to the floor in a fit of anger. He usually closed and locked his door when he left for the evening, but the door left carelessly open must have been an invitation for the janitor to tidy up. His phone had been placed back on his desk and the case had been neatly standing upright. With the stress of the audit, the incident and his sideline investigation had slipped his mind.

Greg retrieved his green notebook and flipped through its pages for the pieces of paper he had jammed inside. After a thorough search he attacked his desk drawer. A few minutes later he became convinced that they were not inside and began to scour the floor. He had just sunk to his knees to examine under the desk when a knock on the door startled him. Narrowly avoiding a collision with the underside of the desk, he sat up on his haunches and peered over at the doorway. It was Chuck Hollis.

"Uh, Chuck, good morning," Greg managed. Color rose in his cheeks for a second time.

"I wanted to see you before your meeting," chirped Hollis, choosing not to question Greg for his activities on the floor. "Is there anything I can do for you?" he offered in his usual monotone.

Yeah, how about putting 120 grand back in the Crucis account. "No, sir. I think I'm ready for whatever the auditors have to say," he lied to Hollis and himself. "I'm ready to get this over with. It has been a colossal waste of time, mine, yours and theirs."

Hollis hesitated. "It's never a complete waste of time to have the chance to thoroughly review your own accounts. And don't worry about minor mistakes. Everyone makes them. The auditors expect that." Hollis' words brought no comfort. "I'll see you at one o'clock to discuss the results. Good luck."

As Hollis left the office, it occurred to him that in previous jobs his bosses would have taken him out to lunch to discuss such weighty matters. Jason Coates, his second boss, was renowned for lunch meetings, the more serious the topic, the more expensive the lunch. Throughout his life, Greg had always found himself at the top of the ranks, both in school and at work. He had always felt privileged, as if people treated him with special attention for his talents and abilities. With the recent adverse occurrences, he was suddenly overwhelmed by a sense of mediocrity amidst his superiors and peers at this advanced level.

Trying to shake off pessimistic thoughts, Greg resumed his search for the logbook pages. A glance at the clock reminded him that time was running short before his meeting with the auditors. He made a mental note to call Al later to ask him to fax the list again. In the remaining minutes he chose to attempt relaxation by grabbing a cup of coffee and settling down to respond to a few delinquent e-mails.

Despite the gravity of the situation, Greg could not take his eyes off the smudge of jelly doughnut on the lower lip of the woman sitting across from him in the conference room. At first glance it appeared to be a grotesque extension of her lip reaching halfway down to her chin. Upon careful inspection, however, its slightly purple hue distinguished it from the cherry red lipstick she wore in contrast to her pale peach suit. The only distraction he found from studying the remains of her breakfast was the merging of bleached blond into light orange as he traced her curly hair down to her shoulders.

The silence that overwhelmed the room made Greg realize that he had been asked a question. He quickly sorted through his short-term memory to recall the sounds that had been uttered.

"I think it's a fair assessment," he responded.

The answer seemed to pleasantly surprise the auditors. As a smile flashed across the woman's face, the line of jelly wiggled back and forth. "As you know, after we issue our written report, you and your boss will have ten working days to respond. We will review any comments you may have and then release our final report. It will remain confidential. Only your supervisors will have the authority to release it."

Another auditor, a broad-shouldered, silver-haired man in a dark suit, continued, "Since we were unable to make any definitive conclusions about the Crucis account, we will leave any disciplinary action up to your supervisors. We cannot find any basis to recommend anything specific."

"Thank you for your cooperation," chimed in the third auditor, a young bespectacled man with a crew cut.

"I appreciate your efforts," Greg smiled as he shook each one's hand. He averted his eyes when shaking hands with the woman, for fear that she had noticed his uncontrollable gawking during the meeting. He turned his back and escaped to the hallway.

Once back in his office, Greg's thoughts returned to the missing list of off-hours entries. It was nearly impossible to concentrate on actual work in the limbo between audit meetings. He rang for the security department. After the first ring he quickly hung up as he realized that Al was rarely on duty during regular business hours. Uncertain about the best course of action, he decided to take a walk down to the security department to attempt to find the information himself.

On his way to the front lobby, he found it difficult to look anyone in the eye. He felt as if the events of the audit meeting had been broadcast to the whole company, and that everyone had paid more attention than he had. He hurried past imagined piercing stares and shut himself in the elevator. By the time he reached the lobby, his composure had returned as he focused on the task at hand. Making his way to the front desk, he casually looked through the logbook as the attendant busied herself on the phone. He quickly realized that the book was brand new and did not cover the past weekend.

"Can I help you?" the receptionist queried, covering the phone with her hand.

"Yes, I was just trying to look up what day I had a particular visitor. I didn't write it down on my schedule, and I thought I would look through the log books to find when it was that he was here. This book doesn't go back far enough."

Phone still in hand, the receptionist motioned toward a two-drawer file cabinet around the side of the front desk. "Try in there," she indicated before returning to her call.

Thankful for his ability to fabricate, Greg began his search in the top drawer only to find supplies for coffee and tea. The second drawer was more promising, containing four logbooks stacked on top of each other. He paged through each several times but quickly discerned that they all predated the time of interest. A time span of about two weeks was missing. Dismayed, he waited for the receptionist to notice him again. "I'll have to call you back," she said to the caller as she hung up. "Did you find it?"

"No, unfortunately the time I'm looking for seems to be missing. Do you know where else it might be?"

"I think old logbooks are kept on file in the security department. Every few months one of the guards takes them out of that file cabinet when they man the desk at night. Why don't you try asking them? Maybe they have it."

Greg thanked the woman and headed for the security department toward the back of the building. A guard sat on duty monitoring television screens set up in strategic locations on site. A few folders sat in front of him unopened. The man seemed familiar, but Greg could not recall his name.

Greg greeted the guard, "Hi, I was just wondering if Al was working today."

A grim expression crossed the man's face. "He doesn't usually work days. But anyway, I guess you didn't hear what happened."

A knot formed in his stomach as Greg indicated that he had not heard.

"Had a bad accident. Ran off the road and hit a tree after work. He'll be out for at least a month. Got broken up pretty bad."

"But he's all right? I mean, no permanent damage?" Greg's concern was real.

"The doctors don't think so. They were surprised he wasn't injured worse than he was. Got a few broken bones including some ribs. Didn't puncture the lung or anything, though. He was lucky. They say he must have fallen asleep at the wheel, but he doesn't really know what happened. He remembers being tired and pulling onto the road but that's about all."

"I'm really sorry to hear that," Greg offered. "I guess it could have been worse." With that, Greg returned to the business at hand. "Al was going to look something up for me. Would you mind helping me instead?" Greg repeated his story and convinced the guard to look for the logbook from the dates in question. The guard agreed but could not find the book from the appropriate time period.

Greg expressed his thanks and departed for a quick lunch before his afternoon meeting with Hollis.

As he walked, Greg tried to reassure himself. *At least after the meeting, I'll know what to do! This mess will finally be resolved and I can have some peace.* Greg didn't know it, but nothing could have been further from the truth.

Chapter Eight

Chuck Hollis' door loomed before Greg like a fortress gate. He could almost hear the sound of wrought iron clashing upon wrought iron as he knocked lightly on the oak door. At the muffled sound of a toneless "Come in," he felt the need to reach to his side to unsheathe a sword to defend himself.

With a knot in his stomach, Greg opened the door and passed into the darkness within. Blinking to adjust to the scant light and gain his bearings, he was greeted by the aroma of coffee and an elusive hint of a flavor he could not quite place. Behind his polished wooden desk Chuck's face was illuminated by the glow from a small green desk lamp. At Chuck's bidding, Greg took a seat across the desk. With a grim voice Chuck began to speak.

The attractive redhead was not accustomed to visiting such places. Flaunting her self-consciousness with each footstep, she fumbled her way through the dark down to the bar counter.

Examining the profile of each male face made her even more uncomfortable, lest any of them turn and meet her eye. Whether real or imagined, the spirits of intemperance and lechery seemed to shadowbox at her every move. However, she knew they could not truly harm her.

"Joanna!" Turning, her eyes found a slightly disheveled, sheepishly grinning Greg Wesko. He sat at an otherwise empty table, a few ounces of beer remaining in the bottom of his glass. "I'm so glad you were willing to come."

"You sounded so troubled, Greg. I knew I just had to come. I'm glad you caught me before I left work." Joanna had been working hard to get up to speed on a new project, so recently she had been staying late most nights of the week. At the sound of Greg's drunken voice on the phone, she had felt compelled to come to his aid without hesitation, even though it meant finding a bar in the seedier side of town and possibly missing her Bible study group later that evening. "Tell me what happened."

Greg picked up his beer to take a last swig, then thought better of it and replaced the glass on the table with an uncalculated thunk. "The audit turned out, let's say, not so good." Closing his eyes, he paused for a moment. "You know, I'm really not so drunk anymore. I've been nursing this last beer for a whole hour."

"You do sound better now than you did on the phone," Joanna conceded.

"Chuck was very gracious. He let me keep my job."

Joanna's eyes opened wide. "Keep your job? Of course he let you keep your job! What are you talking about?"

"There was a large sum of money missing from one of my accounts." Greg delivered his words slowly and methodically as he tried to keep the drunken tone off his voice. "I don't know how it happened. It has to have been some computer glitch or something. I didn't know about it until they pointed it out, after I came back from, well, my time off."

"But you didn't take that money!" Joanna exclaimed.

"No, of course I didn't. And they couldn't find any evidence that I did take it. Even so, it was a 'grave matter,' as Chuck put it, and I was released from my responsibility of handling that account in the future. As well as any other accounts with any large sums of money. It was not a formal demotion, but I'll be unofficially on probation for six months."

"Oh, Greg, can't they find out what happened to that money? They'll have to keep searching, and when they find it, your name will be cleared."

Greg picked up his glass and finished his beer with determination. "I will be monitored closely while they continue to investigate other possibilities. They've asked to see my bank records, which I will happily supply. There's nothing to find! I didn't take the money. Hollis said he had the utmost confidence in my ability and integrity. But I think he was lying through his teeth."

"Even if he wasn't totally truthful, Greg, I have confidence in you. I know how important your work is to you, and I know you would never do anything to jeopardize your reputation and your career. And you always put forth such a great effort."

"But ultimately it was my fault," Greg admitted. "I am responsible for that account, and somehow I let the money get lost. And now that my access has been restricted, there's virtually no way for me to conduct my own investigation. I'm the one who's best equipped to find out what really happened. I tried to tell Hollis that, but I just couldn't drive my point hard enough."

"So what *are* you going to do?"

Greg smiled grimly. "Come here every day?" At Joanna's troubled expression, he corrected himself. "No, I don't really mean that. But it seemed my only choice at the time. I didn't have anywhere else to turn. I couldn't stay in the office. I came right here." He looked down at his watch. "Hey, that was four hours ago. The night's still young but I really don't want to be here anymore."

"I'll take you home," Joanna offered. "I'm sure you won't be able to drive for a while." Anxious to leave, Joanna slid forward in her chair in preparation to stand up.

"Thanks, Joanna, but I'll grab a cab. You live in the opposite direction and I don't want to put you out. I've caused you enough trouble already. Anyway, it's Friday night and you probably have something planned."

Eager to get to her Bible study, but concerned for Greg's safety, Joanna turned to prayer. *Lord, give me a sense of what to do. He needs me, and I don't want him to be tempted to drive himself home later. And I don't want to be like the others in the parable of the Good Samaritan who passed the victim by in order to get to the temple. But I missed Bible study last week and I don't want them to think I'm not interested anymore.*

"Well, I do have Bible study tonight. I can wait with you until the cab comes." The words were halfway out of her mouth before she realized it was not what she had really wanted to say.

"That's OK, you don't have to wait." He looked down and continued, "Although I really wish you would. I'm not ready to be alone just yet." The thought of a stranger driving him to his lonely apartment to work off his stupor was almost unbearable. "I've had enough of my own stinking self."

A plan formulated in Joanna's mind. "Then this is what I suggest. Why don't I drive you to my apartment where you can freshen up? You smell like beer and cigarettes."

"I stepped outside for a smoke. I only smoke when I drink," he admitted.

Joanna ignored his admission. "Then if you feel up to it, you can come with me to Bible study. Otherwise I'll drive you home from there." Her heart raced as she waited for him to accept her proposal.

Although they both knew that Bible study held no appeal for Greg, his desire not to be alone was overpowering. "I don't want to be a bother," Greg let his voice trail off.

Joanna decided to introduce some candor. "Greg, you know I'd do almost anything to get you to come to a Bible study. Come on, let's go." With that, the two rose and Greg threw some bills on the table, following Joanna to the door.

As she drove out of the city, Joanna shook thoughts of the bar from her mind so that her conversation with Greg grew more pleasant with each mile. However, the odor of smoke and beer still permeated the air. Joanna prayed that the smells would not linger in her car.

"You know, I've never been here before," Greg remarked as they pulled into Joanna's garden apartment complex.

"Neither have I been to your place," retorted Joanna. A sharp pang of regret passed through her stomach as she remembered too late that in fact she had been to Greg's new apartment one time, shortly after Lisa's death. She had brought a hot meal to him, and Greg had only allowed her to stay long enough to offer a few pious condolences and chat with his parents, who had spent that afternoon with him. To Joanna's relief, it appeared that Greg had not noticed her mistake, as he made no mention of that previous visit.

In silence they entered the building and climbed the stairs to the second floor. Once inside, Joanna offered Greg a washcloth and directed him to where he could wash his face and freshen up. When he returned to the living room, she offered him a cold caffeinated soda. The two sat down on dark blue sofas placed perpendicular to each other around a long wooden coffee table.

"How are you doing?" inquired Joanna expectantly.

"You know, I was just thinking about when we used to share that tiny cubicle on the fifth floor. How did we ever survive? Or, I should say, how did you ever survive with me in that cubicle? You put up with all my foibles, and you made it so pleasant to be at work."

"Honestly, Greg, you did a lot more for me than I did for you. Watching you excel really spurred me on. It was a blessing for me to have you there."

"I guess we have a little mutual admiration society going on here," Greg chuckled. "Let's call this meeting to order. Who's going to take the minutes?"

Joanna laughed. "I guess you are feeling better. You skirted my question earlier when I asked how you were doing."

"I'm doing fine, just fine." A wide grin spread across his face. "I didn't need to get drunk to feel good. I just needed some time with you. Please remind me of that the next time I get so down."

Joanna was overwhelmed by the flattery of his complements and the prospect of him conceding to accompany her to the Bible study. "Any time, Greg. I wish you had called me before you went to the bar to drown your miseries."

"Honestly, Joanna, I wouldn't have had the nerve. I wasn't ready to talk to anyone about this. I think the liquor helped me open up. The situation was even worse than I first let you know. A smaller sum of money was missing from a different account earlier. I used some of my own money to cover it up until I could figure out what happened and recover the money. Only I never figured it out and now I've lost that money for good. I can't even get back into the account."

Joanna, although concerned and intrigued, stole a glance to see whether it was nearly time to leave for Bible study. "How much money was it, if you don't mind me asking?"

"Twenty thousand dollars. It was money I had been saving for the wedding."

Greg's candor was beginning to wear down any defenses that Joanna usually maintained. "Greg, I'm so worried about you. This is a serious situation, and one that has been going on a long time. And it has affected not only your career but even your own finances. How are you really doing? Are you falling into debt?"

"Oh no, not at all. In fact, since Lisa died, I haven't been spending much money at all. I work, I eat and I sleep, nothing more. But it's so good to talk to you now. I hadn't even told Lisa the whole truth about the missing funds. She didn't know I had used my own money to cover it up."

"I'm grateful that you told me," Joanna admitted. *But I don't want him to compare me to Lisa. That's not fair to either of us. Why is he really telling me all this? Lord, please open his heart to go with me tonight. This could be a real chance for him to hear you speak to him.*

"I guess there were a lot of things I should have told Lisa. There were a lot of things I wanted to tell her, but I never did. There were also a lot of things I wanted to do with her, things we planned, and things I had planned that she didn't know about yet. So many things."

"It was such a tragedy, Greg." Thoughts of Bible study had temporarily slipped Joanna's mind. "You meet someone, and you hope to spend your whole life with that person. You build hopes and dreams together. To be left alone holding them all by yourself must be a terrible burden." Joanna's words hung in the air palpably.

After a long silence, Greg continued, "I've missed out on a lot in my life, Joanna. There are certain things a man needs in his life. And I've been needing them a long time. Most of my life, it seems."

"Greg, I think I know what you need. I want to help you find it tonight." Emotions rose in Joanna that she had rarely let herself experience. "Are you willing to take a chance?"

Greg glided over to Joanna's couch. "I think the more appropriate question is whether you are willing to take a chance."

The meaning of his words began to penetrate her mind. She struggled to return to the subject she had wanted to broach. "Greg, are you feeling up to going out?"

"No, Joanna, I feel like staying in. How do you feel?"

The line of questioning that Greg had begun to direct at her caught her off guard. Myriad feelings ricocheted within her person. Excitement over the opportunity to witness was waning in the wake of both the indignation and the exhilaration she felt at his advances. She had always kept her attraction for him at bay due to his relationship with Lisa. Now there seemed to be little reason to hide her feelings. The sparkle of his light brown eyes, the sharp cut of his jaw, and the luster of his voice were all taking their toll on her resistance. "What do you mean?" she found herself asking.

"Let me show you," he approached with a whisper. With his right hand on her shoulder and his left on her face, he pressed his lips to hers, eliciting a response. But as his kiss grew more passionate, he felt her hands against his chest, pushing him firmly away. Joanna sprang off the couch.

Flustered, Joanna stood speechless and searched for something to say. "It's time for Bible study. I have to go." Without a moment's hesitation, she grabbed her purse and headed for the door. She did not look back.

Greg sat bewildered on the couch, slightly out of breath. His pulse pounded in his temples. The echo of the slamming door still reverberated in his ears. Glancing down at the coffee table, he spotted a black book with gold trim and a red ribbon protruding between the pages. "You forgot your Bible," he said dejectedly. Leaning forward, he picked up the book, closed his eyes and sighed with frustration.

Chapter Nine

Driving past the parade of mercury-vapor street lamps, Joanna struggled to pray. "Lord, I can't figure out what just happened. I wanted to do the right thing. But I don't think things could have turned out worse! I blew it. I really blew it." She bit her lower lip and blinked back a few nascent tears. "I don't seem to be able to hear you any more. I thought I had the perfect chance to take him to Bible study, and instead it seems I just led him on."

In the ensuing silence, Joanna began to perceive the presence of the Lord. *Daughter, I love you! And I love the way you strive to please me with all your heart. I know your heart, and it is a good heart. Do not be ashamed of your innocence, that you did not realize his intentions. You were trying to do your best. Leave the rest up to Me. Do not worry about your inadequacies, your distractions. I will make up for what is lacking on your part.*

"Lord, but so much is lacking on my part. In the bar I felt it was best to stay and help him, even if it meant missing Bible study. But then I remembered that I missed it last week too, and I didn't want the others at church to think I wasn't interested. So I didn't take time to pray about what to do. I tried to avoid helping him so I could keep up a good image with others."

Worrying about others' opinions has cost many people dearly. Concern yourself with being pleasing in the eyes of the Lord. Trust Me, and I will take care of everything else besides. I will take care of Greg too, if he will let Me.

"Dear Lord, may he let you!"

An unseen hand tugged at Greg's heart to open the book he grasped in his cold, sweaty hands. Still dwelling on his feelings for Joanna, he unthinkingly opened the book where the red ribbon marked a place which since the beginning of time had been reserved for him to read at this moment, in this very stage of his life. He began reading at the top of the page under the guidewords "Matthew 6."

Do not store up for yourselves treasures on earth, where moth and rust destroy, and where thieves break in and steal. But store up for yourselves treasures in heaven, where moth and rust do not destroy, and where thieves do not break in and steal. For where your treasure is, there your heart will be also.

The eye is the lamp of the body. If your eyes are good, your whole body will be full of light. But if your eyes are bad, your whole body will be full of darkness. If then the light within you is darkness, how great is that darkness!

No one can serve two masters. Either he will hate the one and love the other, or he will be devoted to the one and despise the other. You cannot serve both God and money.

Therefore I tell you, do not worry about your life, what you will eat or drink; or about your body, what you will wear. Is not life more important than food, and the body more important than clothes? Look at the birds of the air; they do not sow or reap or store away in barns, and yet your heavenly Father feeds them. Are you not much more valuable than they? Who of you by worrying can add a single hour to his life?

As he read, his thoughts began to wander as wordless conflicts erupted in the battlefield of his mind. He had always felt proud to live as a man serving no master but himself. But he could not escape the sense that his treasures, which lay on earth, were rusting in the one hand and feeding thieves from the other. His attention returned to the words he was reading several verses later.

For the pagans run after all these things, and your heavenly Father knows that you need them. But seek first his kingdom and his righteousness, and all these things will be given to you as well. Therefore do not worry about tomorrow, for tomorrow will worry about itself. Each day has enough trouble of its own.

At the end of Chapter 6 Greg paused, staring down as the words on the page blurred in front of him. A few minutes passed with no perceptible motion on Greg's part. His heart struggled to accept the words he had read, but pride and arrogance fought to maintain their formidable foothold. *I am my own man. Money is not my god. I am not a slave to my bank account. Maybe my career has taken over too much of my life, but that's going to have to change now anyway. You're making sure of that, God. Don't worry about me 'storing up treasure' that men can steal. That's already happened. My career is shot. My funds are less than they should be. And most importantly the love of my life is gone, forever.* Greg's thoughts ate him up inside, yet he could not find a way to avoid them. Expressing them only contributed to his misery, for he clung to their every sentiment down to the last bitter root. Even so, each resentful word compounded his burdensome feeling of guilt. Then the events of the evening resurfaced in his mind. *Joanna must think I'm a total jerk. Getting drunk, then calling her and making moves on her when she offers to help! But I felt so lonely. So all alone.*

In an attempt to alleviate some of his guilt, Greg scrounged for a pen and some paper in order to write Joanna a note. First he stumbled on the telephone book and called a cab to drive him to the bar to pick up his car. He then proceeded to write: *Joanna, Sorry for my behavior tonight. Please don't let it ruin our friendship. I called a cab. Don't worry about me. Greg.*

Tearing off the note, he placed it on the coffee table next to the open Bible.

Back at work Greg and Joanna practiced mutual avoidance. Neither had the courage to discuss Greg's advances and the serious strain they had placed on their friendship. Greg buried himself in paperwork, including a requisite formal written response to the auditors' report. In the wake of all that had happened, he found it difficult to mount a satisfactory defense. Instead, he made a weak attempt to resurrect the issue of the alleged unauthorized access to his accounts. After signing and sealing his response, he succumbed to the irresistible urge to shut his brain off and zone out on busywork.

In his distracted state, Greg's thoughts began to wander to his sister. The length of time that had elapsed since his sister's letter embarrassed him. No mention of it had been made when she called to console him for Lisa's death. The whole issue heaped more guilt upon the ever-increasing load he was accruing. In the depth of his mind accusing voices raged with their indictments. *Why didn't you open up with Lisa? You never really talked to her. You lied about your problems at work. You screwed that up too. You're a failure! Now you've turned*

Joanna away. Can't you do anything right? You couldn't even get Lisa to go away with you. If you hadn't gone by yourself, she'd still be alive. If you had stayed, it would've been you who died instead. It's your fault she's dead!

"NO!" Greg jumped to his feet as papers flew off his desk. He closed his eyes and pulled at his hair. "It should have been me who died! It should have been me! I wish it had been me!" He looked around, shocked that he had shouted audibly at work. He glanced around but could see neither any spectators nor his accusers, although their words still echoed in his mind.

Shaking with emotion, Greg slumped back into his chair. A few moments of calm breathing eased him back to reality. With weak resolve he decided to follow through with a comeback plan. He picked up the phone and called the IT department.

"IT, Vester speaking."

"Hello, this is Greg Wesko. I seem to be having a problem with my computer. Can you come and help me with it?"

"Is it a hardware problem? I can take care of anything else remotely from the network."

"Something funny is happening when I log into my accounts. Sometimes it tells me the wrong time for my last login. And other times there are unsuccessful attempts to log in."

"Any time you put the wrong password or user ID in, it will say that there was an unsuccessful attempt to log in."

"But that has only happened to me once or twice. One time it said there were seventeen unsuccessful attempts to log in."

"Well, it could happen if someone accidentally tries to access an account of yours that they do not have access to. Or if they access the same account and they failed to log in properly."

"No one else has access to these particular accounts. Is there a computer log of who tried to access which accounts?"

A short hesitation ensued, followed with a hint of annoyance. "There is a log, but only for the last eight login activities for your account. If you logged in without a problem the last eight times, there won't be any record."

"Can I see the record?"

More hesitation and annoyance. "Those records are only accessible to ISD. I would have to forward your request to them, after you fill out the appropriate web-based forms on the intranet."

"ISD?" Greg played dumb.

"The Information Security Department. They handle matters like this."

"Oh yeah, I forgot. Never mind. Thanks." Greg hung up the phone with disgust. Unsatisfied, he grabbed his phone book and searched for the IT department directory to find another IT employee. No individual names were listed, just the main department number. Turning to his computer, he called up the electronic version of the corporate directory. Each employee was listed by name, phone number, fax number and department code. He paged down in search of the last name Vester but to no avail. Frustrated, he did a directory search on the name Vester and found a listing for Campus, Sylvester. Department 445. Assuming Vester to be a nickname for Sylvester, he searched for other employees listed in Department 445. The first one he found was Langston, Jesse. Extension 618. He dialed.

A nasal but friendly voice greeted him. "Jesse Langston, IT Department. How can I help you?"

"Hi, something strange is happening with my computer and I was hoping you could help me figure it out."

"Let's see. Are you Greg Wesko?"

At first startled that his identity was known, Greg quickly realized that the IT department certainly must be outfitted with caller-ID. "That's correct. Sometimes when I try to log into my accounts, I get a message that there have been unsuccessful login attempts, or it gives me the wrong time for my last login."

"OK, are you an account manager?"

"Yes, I have over a hundred accounts that I manage. My boss and I are the only people with read/write access to most of these accounts. There are a few people who can look at the information in the accounts but cannot make any changes."

"Who is your boss? Have you given your password or your user ID to anyone?"

"Chuck Hollis. No one knows my passwords, not even Chuck," Greg replied.

"Chuck Hollis." Langston sounded as if he were taking notes. "After three unsuccessful attempts to log in, the system should lock you out until you call someone in IT to reset your access," Langston informed him.

"Sometimes it says that there have been as many as seventeen unsuccessful attempts."

"The system keeps a log of activity. The number of unsuccessful login attempts is not reset until there is a successful log in. Have you called IT to have your access reset multiple times in a row?"

"I've never called even once to have it reset."

"This sounds like a suspicious case. I suggest that you change your password on a weekly basis from now on."

Greg wondered about the discrepancies between the information from the two IT employees. "Shouldn't we bring this to the attention of ISD for an investigation?"

Hesitation on the other end was followed by a muffled sigh. "Honestly, I don't know if I can recommend that," continued Langston in a lower voice. "At least not at this time. My experience has been that ISD investigations are not worth the hassle. Sometimes co-op students from the university get a little carried away. They poke around trying to look at people's accounts to see how big some of the figures are. I bet the activity will stop in a few weeks when the co-op terms come to an end."

Greg was dismayed by the resistance. He decided to press further. "How long does the system retain its log of activity? Is there a way to check who is trying to access?"

More hesitation. "It's not easy, but it can be done. If you give me some time, I can pull the records to determine what computer was used to make the unsuccessful login attempts. Let me pursue this on the side. It will save you a lot of hassle with ISD. I can get back to you in a few days."

Not sure whether to be thankful or suspicious, Greg decided that a few days of waiting was acceptable. "Thanks, I appreciate it. In the meantime, I'll go ahead and change my password."

"Good idea, sir. Thank you, and have a good day."

"Thanks." Greg heard Langston's click as he hung up the phone. As he sat in the stillness of his sterile office, his mind teemed with suspicions. *Can this Langston be trusted? Why is his story so different from the first guy's? Who could access my account? Hollis knows my account numbers but not my password. Maybe I accidentally typed my password in the user ID field when I left my office, and someone saw it.* On the login screen, the user ID field would show up as typed, while the password field would appear as asterisks. Greg did not ascribe the attempts to college-student mischief. He was certain that something more sinister was afoot.

In a symbolic attempt to escape his situation, Greg rose from his desk and headed out into the hallway. Down the corridor he followed the aroma of oxidized coffee. Upon finding the coffee pot on and nearly empty, he issued a mild oath and picked up the pot. As he worked his way through a village of cubicles, he caught sight of Joanna heading for the break room. Upon seeing her, his heart skipped a beat and his palms instantly moistened with sweat. The break room held the only nearby sink, and he needed to rinse out the stale coffee residue in order to make a fresh pot. With the knowledge that eventually facing Joanna was inevitable, he braced himself and passed through the break room doorway.

"Howdy stranger," he offered with a tentative grin.

Already seated at one of only two tables, Joanna jerked her head up. In an agonizing moment, her expression passed through phases of surprise and regret before settling on a forced smile. "Hi Greg. Are you doing OK?"

Greg tried to ignore the sudden acidic pain throbbing in his stomach. "I'm hanging in there, Joanna. How are you?"

"OK," she managed, casting her glance down at the table as if searching for a knife to cut the expected awkward silence.

"Joanna, I'm sorry about the other night. I shouldn't have called you when I was drunk."

"You shouldn't have gotten drunk." Regretting her quick quip, she tried again, "I'm sorry, I mean..."

"No, no, you're right. I'm sorry. I was the one at fault. I know I probably said and did some stupid things." If only she knew that his mind was alive with the vivid memory of every word, every image.

"I forgive you." The unfamiliar words rang surprisingly sweet but shrill in his ears. These were words he had heard only a handful of times. People usually tried to reconcile with him using expressions like "It's OK," or "Don't worry about it," as if brushing it off. But Joanna's words brought to mind the fact that a wrong had indeed been committed, but that there was hope to move on from that point.

"Thank you," was all that Greg could translate from his heart to his tongue. Joanna nodded, rose from her seat, and slipped out with a quiet goodbye before Greg could catch sight of the moistening of her eyes. Greg remained motionless, the coffee pot now cold in his hands as he waited for his mind and heart to return from a painful place. As he began the mundane task of rinsing out the pot, he was sideswiped by a memory from several months earlier.

Seated as his desk, eyes glued to a monstrous spreadsheet, Greg gasped when a figure in his office doorway jolted him out of an intense focus. "I'm sorry, how long have you been standing there?" he asked, embarrassed at allowing himself to be startled without cause. The figure was hardly threatening.

"Just a minute or two," Joanna smiled. "I couldn't bear to interrupt. You looked so engrossed in your work, as usual."

"Have a seat," Greg offered, motioning to a maroon swivel chair. "How are you doing?"

Joanna fidgeted with her hands. "I was going to ask you something, but now I don't know what I could have been thinking."

Greg shot her a quizzical look. "When have we ever been afraid of asking each other anything?"

"It's just that you're so busy, I don't want to be a bother." She paused, but Greg's expression enticed her to continue. "I need to prepare for a meeting at nine o'clock, but my computer keeps locking up. I wanted to ask if I could use your computer for a few minutes. I need to print a couple of items."

"No problem. I can take this opportunity to meet with Sam Bingham. He works on the fourth floor, and he's been trying to get a half hour of my time for the last two weeks. I guess today is his lucky day."

Joanna thanked Greg as he grabbed a pen and pad of paper on his way out the door. Sam Bingham was notoriously garrulous. When Greg returned to his office two hours later, he found a thank-you note penned in Joanna's flowing script. There was a computer message on the screen indicating that due to inactivity at the keyboard, the system had automatically logged him out of his accounts.

Joanna had access to my accounts that day. He recalled a few other times when he had let Joanna use the privacy of his office to make personal phone calls. *In cubicles like Joanna's, every conversation was party to many ears. It's ludicrous to think that Joanna would have anything to do with the problems in my accounts. She's a good friend. She's also a religious nut, and even I know that the Bible is against cheating and stealing. It's just a terrible coincidence.* Still, the thoughts would not leave his mind.

Absentmindedly, Greg found himself walking back to his office, fresh coffee in hand, unable to recall returning to the coffee maker, brewing a fresh pot, and pouring himself a new cup. The gravity of his situation washed over him anew, and he sat down in his office chair and pondered. He struggled over the possibility of betrayal by his own friend. Too much to bear, he made a conscious decision not to entertain the idea any more for the remainder of the day. "After all, tomorrow is another day," he quoted to himself.

Overhead, wicked plots took shape, their dark forms converging towards his impending doom. *Soon, very soon, it will happen. We will drive you to the edge. We will take you down. We will make you do it to yourself.*

Greg's guardian angel shuddered to think of Greg's ill-preparedness. *Open your eyes, Greg. Open your ears, that you may hear. Open your heart. Turn and be converted. Before it is too late to be healed.*

Chapter Ten

Enveloped in a swirling torrent of crisp leaves, Greg approached the large glass doors of the East Granby mall. His cheeks still stinging from the biting frost, Greg braced himself to enter the already thickening Christmas shopping crowds, rubbing and blowing on his hands as he walked. Late November was never too early for a foretaste of brisk Connecticut winter. It was the Saturday before Thanksgiving, and every year shoppers seemed to hasten the commercial Advent with seasonal sales, holiday music, and pictures with Santa Claus. This time Greg had mistakenly thought he would beat the crowds. His Christmas list seemed to dwindle every year, but without Lisa the list was frighteningly sparse. "Mom, Dad, Joanna, Theresa and her kids," Greg murmured to himself absentmindedly. The season held no joy for him at all this year. For the first time Greg truly realized why holidays could be so depressing for some. A spark of compassion flashed in his heart, helping to dispel some of the darkness of his self-pity.

With a penchant for jewelry, Greg's mother was easy to shop for. Greg tended to alternate between necklaces and earrings. One year he had dared to buy his mother a ring. Afterwards, his father had taken Greg aside and reprimanded him for stepping on his territory. "Only husbands should give rings," he muttered in a tone that fell somewhere between humor and chastisement. This year was the year for earrings, and Greg promptly picked out a pair of gold hoop earrings adorned with tiny diamond chips, and he bought a matching pair for his sister. For his father, he found a handsome golf bag to replace the one he had lost in a golf-cart accident. Greg's father had been driving over a muddy hill when his cart tipped over and slid sideways into a water trap. He escaped unharmed but his golf bag had not fared as well. Not sure what his niece and nephew would enjoy, Greg finally selected a classic set of board games he remembered from his own childhood. Lastly, he found himself faced with what to buy for Joanna.

Greg and Joanna had started exchanging gifts the first year they met, when they shared a cubicle at work. Joanna had initiated by leaving a neatly-wrapped silver box on his desk while he was at a late afternoon meeting. When he returned from his meeting, she had conveniently vacated the building for the day so that he would not have to awkwardly explain that he had not bought anything for her. Immediately after work Greg stopped at a drug store and purchased the largest box of assorted chocolate creams he could find. As was his habit, the next day he arrived at work early, left the gift on her desk and then found excuses to be elsewhere when she arrived. She was overjoyed, and the two finished the chocolates before the end of the week. She had given him a small Christmas plaque to hang on his cubicle wall. Since then gifts had escalated in price but still remained modest.

Greg now found himself pondering not only over the selection of a gift for Joanna, but also the selection of a partner to accompany him to the corporate Holiday party. This would be the first year attending without Lisa, and Greg's mind was working overtime to find excuses to do something else. As an employee of notable standing, Greg was expected not only to show up but to make a memorable appearance. Usually he and Lisa arrived in garb that was elegant but designed to call attention. In recent years, Greg had even been invited to make the Holiday toast. In Greg's first few years with the company, when the affair was still billed as a Christmas party, an elderly low-level executive had offered grace before the meal. With his early retirement, however, the prayer had been quickly replaced with a toast.

"Can I help you with anything?" A pleasant brunette offered Greg a flirtatious smile. Even with his wind-blown hair and pensive stare, he still made an attractive appearance. "Are you looking for anything in particular?" she continued, eyes sparkling.

"No, not really." Greg shook off the fog of his brooding dilemma. "Well, actually, I don't know what to get."

"Who do you have left on your list? Your mom, your sister, maybe a special friend?" The one-sided flirtation continued.

Taking a glance at his surroundings, he found himself on the border of the women's and men's sections of the mall's larger anchor department store. "I'm looking for a co-worker. A woman. I don't know what to get her this year."

The saleswoman made mental notes and planned her moves. "So you've known her a long time. What kind of things does she like? What have you gotten her before?"

"Last year I bought her a scarf. In other years, chocolate, CDs, books. It shouldn't be hard, but I'm all out of ideas this year. I'm open to any suggestions."

The young woman advanced towards him. "It all depends on where you want this relationship to go. Do you want it to heat up, cool down, or stay the same?"

"Frankly, it's been a little too hot lately." Greg's own words made him blush. "I don't mean it the way it sounds. What I mean is that I've made some mistakes and still feel the need to make it up to her."

Grabbing him by the arm, the saleswoman pulled him over to a nearby counter. "Perfume. That's the answer. Get her something that shows that you think she is special, attractive, feminine."

"I don't know if I want to send that message," Greg hesitated. The woman's forwardness made him uneasy, and he was relieved when she released her grip on his arm.

"Isn't she special? I'm sure she is."

"She is all that and more, it's true. I just don't want her to take anything the wrong way." Even as he spoke, the memory of their one and only kiss burned in his mind.

"Take it from me, we women can take things any way we want to. If she wants you to send her a message, she'll get it. If she doesn't, she'll ignore it."

Her words did not seem to match his experience, but despite his doubts he proceeded to say, "OK. Which perfume do you suggest?" In the next few minutes he received an unsolicited lesson in the meaning of various fragrances and colors. He tuned out in order to study the pleasant features of the young woman's face, and returned from his thoughts just in time to realize that she was expecting a response. "Uh, sounds good. I'll take it," he fumbled. Within a few minutes he found himself, packages in hand, once again blasted by the wind as he wound his way through the rows of cars in the dark numbing night.

In the background, Greg's mind counted rings as he continued to study the figures on his computer screen. After the fourth ring, he picked up the phone just before his voice-mail would have activated. "Wesko," he chirped.

"Hello, Greg, this is Jesse Langston from the IT department. I'm sorry it's taken so long for me to get back to you. I have some information." Ripping his eyes off the monitor, Greg's attention was fully captured and he indicated for Langston to continue. "I've been able to locate the computers used to access your accounts. I can give you the inventory numbers of the computers, as well as the names and locations of each. However, our computer inventory information isn't always accurate. You may want to do some snooping of your own. I can't officially recommend any course of action, and the information I'm giving you is all a matter of internal record, but nothing is top secret." Langston continued to relate the details to Greg. The unsuccessful login attempts were made from two computers, one registered to Bob Gurth on the eighth floor and another to Jay Drock on the fifteenth floor. Besides Greg's own computer, successful logins had been made from the security desk computer and from a public computer on the tenth floor. "That's all I can tell you. If you find any new information, I may be able to help again." As Greg began to issue a "Thank you," he heard the phone click in his ear as Langston abruptly hung up.

A quick glance at his clock revealed the late hour. Within fifteen minutes, most of the building would be empty, and Greg found it a convenient time for some detective work. Postponing his spreadsheets until the next day, he shut down his computer and made his way up the stairs to the fifteenth floor as he decided to work from the top down. Breathless from excitement rather than exertion, he listened at the stairwell door for silence before pushing the door open. An empty sea of cubicles met his eyes as he entered the room, now dimly lit as he walked past a row of continuous glass windowpanes looking out on the moving red and white lights of the city's evening rush hour. Each cubicle's nameplate passed one by one as he methodically circuited the large, still room. Within ten minutes he had covered the entire floor without finding the name Jay Drock at any of the cubicles. The floor also contained one row of offices, but none belonged to Drock either. Frustrated, he found a corporate directory at someone's desk and flipped through the pages. Upon finding the entry for "Drock, Jason," he discovered that Drock was now located on the eleventh floor. Descending the stairs two at a time, he slowed just before pushing open the door marked "11."

Another room of quiet cubicles greeted Greg's eyes. Relieved at encountering another empty floor, he resumed his circuit of the cubicles. Soon he came upon the name "Jay Drock" emblazoned in white upon a fake wood background. He slid into the cubicle and began to investigate the computer. From the top of the hard drive he removed a framed picture of a plump couple in their late forties sipping tropical drinks at a Caribbean bar near the beach. Pulling the hard drive forward, he peered behind to confirm the identification number with the one that Langston had given him. To his dismay, it did not match.

Frustrated once again, he shoved the computer back in place and returned the vacation picture to its rightful place. "What is this going to tell me anyway?" he asked himself. "After hours, almost all the computers in the building are fair game. Anyone could use someone's computer in a cubicle." Yet despite his discouragement, he decided to proceed to the tenth floor in search of the public computer to which Langston had directed him.

Forgetting himself, Greg opened the door to the tenth floor and treaded right into an ad-hoc meeting at the cubicle nearest the stairwell. Two people threw glances his way, but the other heads remained hovered over a computer screen full of numbers. Caught off guard, Greg struggled to maintain composure and headed towards the elevator. He was within reach of the down button when a man's deep voice called him back, "Can I help you?"

Compelled to answer the request, yet desiring to retain his anonymity, Greg paused before the elevator door. "Are you looking for someone?" This second question could not be ignored. Trying not to appear suspicious, Greg thought of a quick story.

"I was hoping to find a public computer. My computer is on the fritz, and I just needed to check some information." Greg turned toward the crowd as he spoke but could not identify which man had spoken to him.

"Darren Lado," a tall man with graying temples to match his gray eyes stepped forward. The frosting of the man's hair belied his age, which was better ascertained by the lack of wrinkles on his face.

"Greg Wesko. Nice to meet you," Greg put on his best face. "Is there a computer on this floor I could use for a few minutes?"

Lado led Greg around a corner and between two rows of cubicles, indicating a public computer Greg could access. "Depending on what information you want, you can just log in as a guest." Greg indicated that this would be sufficient, thanked the man, and waited for him to leave. Once he was alone, Greg peered around the back of the hard drive and found an identification number matching the one given him by Langston.

"Finally, one positive note," he mused to himself. After a few minutes, Greg found that he could enter his own passwords and access his accounts from the public computer, just as he had suspected. Still uncertain if his findings proved anything, Greg logged out and headed for the eighth floor.

Most of the eighth floor was under the direction of his former boss, Jason Coates. Coates often worked late, and Greg wondered if they would encounter each other. On a whim, he decided to head directly for Coates' office.

"Well, if it isn't Greg Wesko!" a friendly voice greeted him as he started to knock on the open door. "This is a great surprise!"

The warmth of the greeting brought a long-absent smile to Greg's downcast face. He even felt some light return to his eyes. "Jason, it's good to see you. How's the family? It seems like it's been a long time."

"It has been a long time. Too long. Have a seat," Coates offered. His squeaky voice did not match his tall, athletic appearance. As he leaned back in his chair, he ran his hands through his curly mop of sandy brown hair and rested his head on the back of his laced fingers. It was his usual posture, welcoming others to be open and comfortable. "What's on your mind?"

Without prior planning, Greg found himself divulging some of his troubles to his former boss. After hearing of Lisa's death, Coates had previously made a few attempts to visit Greg at his office, but each time Greg was away from his desk. To Greg's surprise, his audit and unofficial probation were news to Coates.

"I can't believe that you would ever embezzle money from the company. I know you, and you are way too honest and too committed. Money doesn't disappear like that either, so something suspicious has to be going on." Coates abandoned his relaxed position and sat forward with fingers nervously tapping.

Greg relayed the information he had received from the IT department, without mentioning Jesse Langston by name. Coates was surprised to hear that some activity had occurred from Bob Gurth's computer.

"I'm not sure what to say about Bob," Coates mused, rubbing his chin. "He's been on assignment in the Far East for the last two years, based mostly in Singapore and Hong Kong. He maintains an office here for when he's stateside, which totals maybe one or two months a year. Someone could have used his computer just about any time, either with a master key while he was away, or in a spare few minutes while he was here and left his office door open. When he is here, he often works late and goes out for dinner. Anyone who knew his habits could have monitored his activity and slipped into his office when he stepped out. I doubt that he was involved in this in any way."

Greg had heard of Bob Gurth but had never met the man. Greg trusted Coates' judgment and agreed that the information told them virtually nothing. Still, Greg wondered aloud why there were both successful and unsuccessful login attempts, and why the successful logins had occurred at certain computers while the unsuccessful had occurred at others. A quiet, persistent beeping broke Greg's train of thought.

"My Blackberry," Coates exclaimed, looking down at the number on his screen. "Greg, I'm afraid you'll have to excuse me. Let's both think this over a bit more and touch base again later." The two shook hands and Greg hastened out into the hallway, again deep in thought.

A week of nights with little sleep left Greg bleary eyed and wired with caffeine. A dozen half-baked plots tortured Greg each time he lay down and closed his eyes, and in his exhaustion he could neither refute nor substantiate any of the potential sinister schemes to which he had fallen victim. On a rainy Wednesday night he found it difficult to stay awake on the way home.

His eyes traced the scattered red streaks from the traffic light along the wet road until they blended with a splash of purple neon. Looking up to discover the source of the color, he observed a small dark construction across the street blaring "Psychic Readings." Although he had always scoffed at mediums and horoscopes, he now found the prospect almost appealing. *Maybe they can tell me what happened, and how to get out of it.* Just as quickly another voice broke through, aided by the prayers of a saint. *Lies, lies! Don't let yourself be tricked.*

The turning of the light shook Greg from his thoughts and he proceeded through the intersection, passing the psychic parlor by. Unseen, however, a dark shadow seemed to leap out of the store windows and attach itself to the top of his car. Unaware, and weary of life, Greg plodded home, parked and ran through the cold punishing rain to his apartment, shadows following him in the dark night.

Once inside, Greg shook off his wet clothing and instinctively turned up the temperature on the thermostat. Futilely he ran his fingers through his hair to restore some semblance of order to the wet windblown mess. "As if there were anyone here to see me," he told himself in the hallway mirror.

A red blinking light on the phone indicated that he had missed someone's call. He set the unit to speaker phone and listened as he flipped through an assortment of bills and junk mail.

"Hi, Greg. It's Joanna. I hope everything is OK," she paused. "I'll try you at work tomorrow. Let's have lunch some time. Bye." A computerized voice indicated that the message had been left just a few minutes earlier, and there were no more messages.

"I hope everything is OK too," Greg murmured to himself. Not ready to face Joanna or decide about the company Holiday party, Greg put aside the mail and turned to the newspaper. He skimmed the front-page article about the recurring unrest in the Middle

East, brushed past the daily comics, caught the weather report, and headed for the sports section. To his surprise, the sports section seemed to be missing from its usual place between the classifieds and the home and garden section. Muttering under his breath, he returned to the front page to find the table of contents. As his eyes traveled down the column, they seemed to catch at the title marked "Horoscope." At first just a pause, then a lingering, then a full stop, his eyes braked to a halt and his mind began to race. Although he had always dismissed horoscope readers as superstitious, and although he had always prided himself on not wasting his time on such matters, he now found an irresistible urge to dabble in the unknown. *What can it hurt? It's just for fun. And just maybe you'll learn something you need to know, something to make you feel better.*

He let his fingers take him to page D-4. *What am I, a Leo? No, a Capricorn, I think.* Greg thought back to a seemingly innocent discussion from college. In a spat with a girlfriend, she had thrown in a comment such as, "It figures. You're such a Capricorn!" When pressed on the matter, she had proceeded to describe the typical qualities of a Capricorn, and Greg was surprised to find a ring of truth to her words. Indeed he did exhibit a practical, responsible attitude and desired to accomplish whatever he set his mind to in order to make his mark on the world. He loved making money and did not mind working hard to get it. He also agreed that he found faith difficult and rather relied on proof, something his former girlfriend also ascribed to his

Zodiacal birth sign. Since that conversation, he had noticed in his life an emphasis on the characteristic traits and even a subsiding of other typically non-Capricorn qualities, such as emotional attachments and joviality.

The words from Capricorn danced and laughed on the page in front of him. "Capricorn, there may be trouble in your future. Take some time to get reacquainted with yourself, and beware of a good friend who may betray you. Trust your instincts. Now is not the time to pursue any romantic interests. Spend some quiet nights at home relaxing. Read a good book."

Far from the harmless fun and comfort he had hoped to find, Greg found instead two sweaty palms, an increased heart rate and an acidic churning in his stomach. The words sounded so true, seeming to confirm all the thoughts and fears he had been harboring. He felt as if he had been careening down the road to disaster and had caught himself on a branch just before he would have plummeted over a cliff. Chaos circled overhead as myriad thoughts swirled in a funnel cloud and descended into his mind and heart. *I can't go to the party with Joanna. I can't trust her. Maybe she even had something to do with my scandal at work. She may be the one who will betray me. Or Jason Coates. I shouldn't have let him in on my predicament. What did he do for me – nothing really! And then he got that mysterious phone call and had to cut our conversation short. Maybe his office was bugged, or maybe they were calling him to get me to leave. I'm being watched. I know I am. They're out to get me. I have to rely on myself. There is no one else.*

Unwittingly, Greg had crossed a line and opened himself up to an oppressive presence. The dark shadow that had followed him home now fell upon him like a pall, latching its occult talons onto the foothold Greg had provided through the astrological reading. To anyone with the ability to see such things, it would have seemed as if an angel of light were bound about the ankles and wrists, hindered in offering any help. Or was it not Greg who was bound?

Chapter Eleven

The December nights grew longer, matching the intensifying darkness of Greg's turmoil. He was becoming acquainted with the late-night television line-up as his ceaseless worry twisted him into various stages of insomnia. Chuck Hollis had taken an extended business trip to Southeast Asia and Australia. Greg was grateful for the tentative freedom, both his late arrivals and his bloodshot eyes undetectable by his traveling boss, for the moment. Although he had always prided himself on faithfully logging long hours in front of his computer screen, he now found that sleep deprivation interfered even with this ritual. Feelings of guilt mounted but were not burdensome enough to force him to arrive on time for work. One Tuesday afternoon Greg's eyelids fell shut, his head dropping forward in an awkward position.

A knock on the door jolted him out of his snooze. Color rushed to his cheeks as his heart pounded in his ears. "Greg? Are you OK?" Joanna called from the doorway. Greg quickly calculated that with his back to her, she might not have noticed his dozing. He struggled to quickly regain his composure.

"Hi, Joanna. I didn't see you there."

"Apparently not." Joanna vacillated between amusement and concern. "I've only been standing here for twenty minutes!"

Greg managed a wry smile as he realized that indeed Joanna must have observed his accidental nap. "I didn't sleep well last night. I did get to watch a team of surgeons separate conjoined twins on a late-night TV show, however. It was a success."

"I'm glad," Joanna answered methodically. Television was not what she had come to discuss. "I haven't been sleeping well either. Maybe we can have lunch tomorrow and commiserate."

With only days left before the company Holiday party, Greg had wanted to avoid Joanna so there would be no chance to discuss the topic. Asking Joanna to accompany him seemed logical and fitting, but his inclination was to go solo. He hoped that he would simply slip into the final decision as the week raced towards its conclusion. Avoidance was still appealing. "Tomorrow is packed, Joanna." He did not know whether or not he was lying. "I don't think I could manage a long lunch."

"OK then, let's do Thursday. I'll come by around 11:30. You can pick the place." Before he could reply, Joanna added, "I've got to run. See you Thursday." With that, she exited the doorway. Dazed, he sat listening to the clicking of her heels fading down the hall.

The black and white flicker of an old B-movie cast shadows over Greg's face as he slept fitfully on the couch the following evening. After a quick dinner, Greg had retired early to his living room in an attempt to get a jump-start on his sleep. A paperback spy thriller lay open, face-down on his chest. As he fidgeted, it slid off his chest and into an empty bowl of ice cream on the floor, the spoon resting inside clattering against the side of the bowl. The noise brought him unwillingly out of sleep, and he sat up dejectedly. The clock glared 8:20 at him with its red digits. The thought of going for a drive suddenly felt appealing, so he clicked off the television and changed into warmer clothes.

The region had experienced its first dusting of snowfall the night before, and Greg decided to try to let its beauty comfort him. He turned the car's vents directly towards his chest and face, enjoying the contrast of the frosty view with the strong, steady flow of heat. For a tentative moment, he felt a long-awaited sense of happiness, although he could find no reason to celebrate except for the warmth of the burning fossil fuel filling his small, portable space.

The purple glow of a neon light caught his attention and sparked his memory. To his right he found the same psychic shop he had first noticed a few weeks earlier. A smaller sign indicated that the establishment was still open for business. Unhesitating, he turned into the parking lot.

Greg was surprised to find his legs shaking as he made his way to the entrance, a side door in the shadows at the edge of the small lot. Ascribing his shivering to the cold rather than to nerves, he took a deep breath and passed through the door. A dimly lit parlor greeted him with dark paisley sofas and matching antique chairs. Green light from the chandelier reflected back in the gilded wallpaper that flooded the room. A standing brass lamp illuminated a small indoor pond with goldfish and a smiling Buddha. Fake foliage blocked the window and filtered out all but a few wisps of purple from the neon sign. Movement caught Greg's ears, and he turned to see a figure emerge from a back room through a curtain of dark beads.

The proprietor extended a hand with fingers pointing downward bearing large bejeweled rings. She appeared to be in her late fifties, long gray hair emerging from a peach and red bandana and straggling down her shoulders. Greg attempted to return her smile, taking her hand and managing, "How do you do?"

"My name is Madam Isis. You are in need of some advice. Come, come into my parlor." Maintaining her grip on his hand, she led him through the beaded curtain. A small room with a wooden table and three chairs stood in the center. Greg noticed that statues watched from the four walls, but in the darkness he could not see their features clearly. He was comforted by the fact that he could find no crystal ball. A pile of cards lay on a small podium near one of the chairs, which Madam Isis soon occupied as she indicated a chair for Greg across the table.

"This is your first time seeking the art, isn't it?" she began in a soothing, friendly voice. "Don't be put off by all the paraphernalia. Just enjoy it. Think of it as part of the show," her frankness beguiled him and he began to relax. "Since this is your first time, I expect you are nervous."

"Somewhat, I guess," Greg replied. *Out of my mind!* "I've never given any credit to this sort of, uh, venue." *I should go now.*

"I sense your hesitation, and I understand it. I'll make a proposal to you. For tonight, I will offer you a free palm reading. Then go home. Think it over. Then come back for a full incantation."

Incantation? "OK," thought Greg, relieved. *At least my foolishness won't cost me anything. Just read my palm and let me go. Tell me I'm unlucky in love. Tell me I'm smart and talented. Whatever.* He stretched his hand open before her.

Taking his hand, she traced lines up and down his palm. Greg studied her fingers, then studied her face as her brow began to furrow. He resisted the urge to pull his hand away, although every fiber of his being screamed to do so. "What is it?" he asked with concern.

Madam Isis forced a smile and blinked at him. "You have had a lot of success in business, haven't you? You work in finance, either as an accountant or an actuary. You are among the highest, if not the highest, person in your department." She closed her eyes, then opened them and looked directly at him, although Greg felt as if she were looking through him at something against the wall behind him. "You have recently lost someone very dear, but there is someone else in your life."

Greg sensed that she was holding back. "There's more to this than what you're saying. Tell me!"

Madam Isis hesitated. "Perhaps that is enough on those topics for today. Let's look at your life line." As she re-examined his palm, her grip suddenly tightened, causing Greg to gasp.

"What is it?" he exclaimed. "You must tell me."

"I'm having trouble getting a clear reading. Perhaps you should come back."

"Tell me. I'll pay for the reading. Just tell me!" The urgency was frightening.

"No, you don't have to pay. I will tell. Your lifeline, it does not show a long life. It does not show a happy life. It does not show love. That is all for now." With that, she released his hand and rose from the table. "I cannot say more at this time. Perhaps you will come back at another time. I can help you more then. We can go through the cards, try a few other things. I think this is enough reading for now. But take this," she said, reaching into a tiny drawer on the small nearby podium. "It is an amulet. You can carry it in your pocket for good luck. Take it as a free gift. My hours and phone number are printed on a label on the bottom." She handed him a token the size of a quarter with unfamiliar designs on one side, the label on the other.

As if in a dream, Greg returned through the parlor and back to his car without feeling the earth beneath him. He seemed to move in slow motion, the world heavy and dark about him. He had retreated into a new world and needed time to adjust.

Across town Joanna fidgeted in her seat at her weekly Bible study, now held mid-week instead of on Friday nights. Although the readings were very familiar, she could not concentrate on the meaning, and so she remained unusually quiet. Only a young man sitting across the circle of chairs seemed to notice. After the closing prayer, he stood up and approached Joanna.

"Hi Joanna, how are you doing tonight?"

Joanna stood and looked up a full twelve inches into the young man's eyes. "Hi, Peter. I feel very distracted. I hardly paid any attention tonight."

Peter Monday had the classic beach boy appearance with blue eyes, medium-length blond hair, and an athletic build. His disarming smile had caught Joanna's attention at church a few months earlier, before Peter had begun attending Bible study. Several years her younger, Peter seemed to volley between gentle wisdom and youthful immaturity. Joanna was careful to exercise caution around him, lest she cave into his handsome appearance and attractive voice. Peter was less cautious about his feelings for the vibrant, feminine redhead with the equally charming smile. Joanna's innocent and classic beauty was almost too much for Peter to handle.

"Is there anything you want to talk about?" his white teeth flashed from a lightly bronzed face.

Joanna paused a second to pray. *Go ahead, it's OK.* "I can't place my finger on what's wrong.

Would you mind praying over me? Maybe we can get Shirley to help too." Joanna motioned, and an older woman with permed, dyed black hair approached. "Shirley, can you and Peter please pray over me? I feel such a loss of peace, and I don't know why."

Peter and Shirley began to invoke the name of God as they laid hands upon her shoulders. Shirley led the prayer for peace. Peter listened inattentively, struggling to subdue his disappointment that Joanna had not asked him to pray over her alone. When the "Amen" caught him off guard, he quickly summoned a heartfelt "Amen" to match.

"Feel any better?" Shirley asked. Just then, noticing the prayer was over, a woman called to Shirley across the room. Shirley took notice but kept her eyes on Joanna, awaiting the response with genuine concern.

"I think so. Thanks, Shirley. Thanks, Peter. Shirley, why don't you go see what Martha needs?" she responded, indicating the woman who had called to her.

"OK, but call me at home if you need me," Shirley offered. She leaned over and kissed Joanna on the cheek. "Thanks, Peter," she took his hand and squeezed it before hurrying off.

"You look like you still need to talk. Do you want to go somewhere for a decaf or a piece of pie?" Peter tendered hopefully, studying Joanna's rosy complexion, dotted very gently with the perfect sprinkling of light freckles.

Joanna looked up into his sparkling blue eyes. It was difficult to resist the handsome smiling face. Everything about Peter was refreshing. Yet her mind and heart kept returning to the brooding, sullen image of Greg. "I think I need to go home. Thanks anyway, Peter. Maybe next time."

"OK," Peter replied dejectedly. "Next time. Goodnight, Joanna." Joanna bid him goodnight and turned to go. Suddenly, Peter reached out and touched her arm. "Wait, Joanna," he pleaded. "Please wait. You may not need to talk tonight, but I really do. I need a friend."

The puppy-dog look on Peter's face was more than Joanna could bear. She offered up a quick pleading of her own. *He needs someone to talk to. And although I thought you wanted me to go home and pray, I think you're calling me to be an ear for Peter tonight.* "OK, Peter, let's go somewhere."

"I'll drive," Peter offered. "I know of a new little Italian restaurant that's open late. They serve a mean decaf cappuccino and cannoli until midnight."

Willing to entrust herself to the man not only with the model's appearance but also of strong faith, Joanna submitted, "Wherever you want to go."

Greg's waking nightmare continued as he drove methodically back towards his apartment. A traffic light caught him on red, and he braked to a slow halt. A few cars rolled by in front of him. Another car pulled up across the intersection. Greg glanced over at the couple. In the light from the streetlamps, Greg observed a young blond man at the wheel with a redheaded woman sitting beside him. The two seemed to make an attractive couple. As the light turned green, Greg began to accelerate through the intersection. Just as he was about to pass the other car, the realization of the passenger's identity struck him. In seemingly the same instant, Joanna took notice of Greg. They locked eyes for a millisecond, shocked expressions overtaking their faces.

Dozens of questions barraged Greg's mind, followed by spirits of betrayal, anger and shame. *What is she doing with that man?* Greg tried in vain to remind himself that he and Joanna had never dated, had not spoken of going out, and had not even professed any feelings for one another. Yet anger still pricked his mind while bitterness pressed heavy upon his heart.

Joanna felt hot color rise into her cheeks. She wondered whether she had gasped audibly. *What will Greg think about Peter driving me through town together at night? I should have gone home to pray as I had planned. I did not feel peaceful about going out with Peter tonight. Now I know that I was supposed to pray for Greg instead. What impression have I made on Greg now? But why should it bother him to see me with Peter? And why should it bother me that he saw? Maybe that is one of the things I need to pray about tonight! How am I going to get out of this now?*

Forget going to the Holiday party with Joanna now! I'm going alone! And I'm going to get good and drunk there too. Who cares! Who needs to get drunk more than I do! Self-pity cast its wicked spell over Greg's burdened mind.

Unaware of the event that had just transpired, Peter continued towards his destination with a simple smile. For Peter, the intersection was just a short delay on the way to his long-awaited first date with Joanna, unofficial or not. In fact, Peter hoped to hit every traffic light on red just to extend the evening. He had been enjoying the conversation with Joanna very much. But suddenly, something seemed to have lagged.

I've got to think of something. Joanna's mind raced to formulate excuses. Peter spoke up, "Hey, is something wrong?"

In anger, Greg's foot grew weightier upon the gas pedal. He was almost at the junction of a two-lane road, leading into the dark countryside on the left and towards his apartment on the right. The traffic light at the upcoming intersection turned amber. Angry at another influence trying to control his life, Greg accelerated. The light blared red, still a hundred feet in front of him. *Go ahead, make me stop!* He pushed the gas pedal to the floor just as a pair of headlights caught the corner of his eye.

"Nothing is wrong," Joanna hesitated, still scrambling for words. "Peter, I really hate to do this to you. I..."

"Please Joanna, don't say you have to go home!"

Without prompting, Joanna exclaimed, "Pray with me, Peter! Now!"

In a fraction of a second, Greg's foot lifted off the gas pedal and slammed down on the brake. A patch of ice caught his tires and sent him spinning toward the intersection. Passing sideways under the traffic light, Greg's car faced an oncoming, speeding car. In a moment that seemed to last an eternity, Greg felt no regret, no remorse, not even fear.

Surprised by Joanna's sudden urgency, Peter found himself braking abruptly and pulling off onto a dark residential side street. Joanna proceeded, "Dear Lord, help a lost soul! Protect him! Save him from himself! In this very moment, Lord, hear our prayer!" As Joanna continued, Peter added his voice to hers in earnest supplication for a stranger.

Greg skidded out of the intersection to the angry, prolonged blast of the oncoming car's horn. The car had passed so close that Greg could feel its headwind helping to push him to the other side. In another quarter turn, his car screeched to a halt, facing back towards the city. He had missed death by less than an inch. Yet Greg found himself only slightly shaken, almost numb to the night's events, not only the nearly fatal accident but also the sighting of Joanna and the disturbing messages from the psychic. He mechanically headed for his apartment.

Finally dressed for bed, Joanna sat cross-legged on the beige bedroom carpet. The lamp on her nightstand was turned down low, its light blanketing a small area near her and fading away into darkness in the far corners of the room. She continued to review the night's events. She and Peter had continued with their plans, and for a short while she had enabled herself to put aside her worries about Greg. In their conversation, she had found the opportunity to broach the subject of Greg, as she ascribed her outburst in the car to the sudden sense from the Lord to pray for a friend. She and Peter had then continued talking easily and freely. It had turned into a truly enjoyable evening for Joanna, a thoroughly exciting one for Peter. Only with great restraint had he resisted giving Joanna a goodnight kiss. Unexplainably, it had not seemed appropriate.

Now in the quiet solitude of her bedroom, Joanna communed with the great Counselor, laying out her own fears, her own plans, desires and worries. As she prayed, a severe and strange dread fell upon her. Although she felt completely at peace with God about her own life, her spirit remained perturbed by an inexplicable foreboding.

"It's going to be a long night, Lord, isn't it?" she prayed aloud.

Hand on her shoulder, her guardian angel prayed, "Yes, Joanna. Pray as hard as you can."

Chapter Twelve

The few hours that Joanna had slept seemed to have counted double-time. She walked confidently and energetically towards Greg's office. For the first time in months, Joanna felt she understood the plan.

Instead of waiting in the doorway for Greg to notice her, Joanna initiated with a steady "Good morning, Greg."

The night had not treated Greg as well. Although he had fallen asleep quickly, fitful bouts of semi-conscious dreaming plagued him all night long. In his exhausted stupor, he stared at her out of his sunken eyes, not knowing where to begin.

Joanna continued, "I saw you last night in town. I was coming back from church with a friend." Joanna had decided to broach the subject of their sighting one another without denial or apology. "You were going the other way."

Greg cleared his throat. "I thought I saw you too. I wasn't sure," he lied. "I didn't get a good look at the man, but I didn't think I recognized him." *Now that's the honest truth.*

"He's just a friend from my Bible study group. His name is Peter. We haven't known each other very long." Joanna fought to subdue the fond feelings engendered by the mere mention of Peter's name.

"I almost had an accident later last night."

Joanna's eyebrows rose with concern. "What happened?"

"Oh, nothing really. I misjudged a light and ran through it on red." *More lies.* "There was a car going in the other direction, and we almost collided. Just missed each other by a nose." *Ah, the truth again.* "Lucky, I guess."

"You know how I feel about luck," Joanna gave him a wry smile. "Maybe somebody is trying to tell you something."

Greg did not feel like taking the bait amicably. "And just who would that somebody be, Joanna?" Greg's words grew more acerbic. "The guy in the other car tried to tell me something with his finger and his horn. I got the message!"

Helplessly Joanna felt her confidence ebbing away. Flustered, she struggled to continue with the plan. "So are we on for lunch today? Just before noon?"

Greg did not need any time to reconsider his decision. "Today I'm all booked up, Joanna. I didn't expect to have a busy day, but you know how things change. In a New York minute."

Her plan was unraveling. "I thought we had agreed to lunch today. I was counting on you, Greg."

"Some other time, sorry." He let his ostensible indifference work its hurt on her. "I'm sure there are lots of other hungry people out there. No lack of people to eat lunch with. Me, I brought a sandwich." He patted the brown bag on his desk with a smug grin.

Joanna quickly formulated an alternate plan. "OK, tomorrow then. I'll be by at 11:45. I'm not letting you out of this. If you bring your lunch, I'll simply throw it out the window!" With a smug grin of her own, she turned and headed out the door with her red hair bobbing to the tune of her gait. *Touché!*

The busy day Greg had fabricated to avoid lunch with Joanna promised to be another study in futility. Instead of continuing to spin his wheels at his desk, Greg decided to resume his investigation into the mystery of the disappearing funds. According to Jesse Langston's information, someone had tried to log into Greg's accounts from Bob Gurth's computer but without success. Greg decided that it was time to pay Bob Gurth a visit.

The eighth floor was quiet and deserted. Muffled voices carried down the hall from a conference room through a door that was slightly ajar. Surmising that a group meeting was in progress, Greg found his way to Bob Gurth's office. As he approached the empty desk of the administrative assistant, he noticed that Gurth's office door was closed. Recalling his discussion with Jason Coates, Greg cursed his luck, assuming that Gurth was still abroad as usual. "Plan B," Greg thought to himself. "Maybe this is an even better opportunity than I thought." He reached over to try the door. The knob refused to yield. Cursing again, he quickly perused his surroundings. The administrative assistant's desk called to him, and he furtively opened the top drawer. As if his luck had changed, he immediately found a set of keys. Retrieving them, he returned to the door to try the first key. With a barely audible click, the key slid into the lock. Silently he turned the knob and opened the door.

A loud gasp emitted from the dimness of the office interior. In the scant light, Greg could make out a figure huddled over a computer at a contemporary slate-colored desk. The figure quickly rose to its feet. Greg stepped back, prepared for an attack. The figure stopped, and Greg braved an obvious query. "What are you doing?"

For a brief moment, the tall figure stood silently. Then it responded, "I'm the computer guy."

"What?" The answer caught Greg off guard.

"I'm working on the computer in here. Has some sort of hardware problem," the figure replied.

"Why are you in the dark?" Greg questioned. Some rays of light filtered in through the closed blinds, supplementing the light that Greg had introduced through the open door.

"It's an electrical hardware problem. I need to have the lights off so I can see the flow of electricity inside the computer."

Even to Greg's non-technical ears, this explanation sounded highly implausible. He reached to turn on the lights. The figure started to make a protest but quickly dropped the attempt. The overhead fluorescent lights flickered to life, revealing an agitated man dressed in jeans and a brown shirt. A wisp of blond hair protruded from underneath a hat bearing the label "Takai Computing Services." The man stroked his bushy mustache nervously and pushed up on an unfashionable pair of thick-rimmed glasses.

"Show me some ID," Greg demanded. Reluctantly, the man reached into his pocket and produced a security badge with his picture and the name Phillip Thompson. In the photo, the flash reflected off the man's enormous lenses, obscuring part of his face. Greg turned the card over and found the initials TCS and a logo matching the one on the man's hat. "I still don't understand why you had the lights out," Greg challenged.

The man looked about the room nervously and took a deep breath. "Oh man, please don't get me in trouble. I have a new baby at home, and I don't get much sleep. I just wanted to doze for a few minutes." Glancing down at his watch, the man grimaced. "I think it turned out to be a few hours."

"It's a good thing Mr. Gurth didn't return," Greg mused, managing to chuckle slightly. "I'll keep your secret safe, as long as you're not charging the company for your nap time."

"Thanks a lot, man. I really appreciate it. Everybody knows Mr. Gurth is away most of the time. Actually, I really did need to work on his computer. I can keep the lights on now."

"Good idea," Greg smirked. "And keep the door open too."

"Don't worry, I will. Hey, do you know Mr. Gurth well? If you're going to tell him, please don't mention my name," he pleaded.

"Actually, I don't know him at all. I only know him through a friend."

"Who's that?"

"Jason Coates," Greg responded mechanically, not having intended to share any information with the stranger.

"Don't know him," Thompson replied. "I promise I won't do this again."

"OK, now you try to get more sleep at night," Greg admonished the man as he turned to walk away, frustrated that Gurth's visitor was preventing him from snooping further.

"Yeah, right," Thompson laughed.

Tucked away in her cubicle, Joanna sat drumming her fingers as she stared at the computer screen. *Lord, I know that you want me to meet with Greg. I have such a sense of urgency, but still I have to wait. Even so, I know you work all things to the good for those who love you.*

The ringing of the telephone brought Joanna back to attention. The caller ID indicated that it was a transferred call.

"Providential Insurance, Joanna Pearson speaking. How may I help you?"

"Just by talking," a man's voice answered.

"Excuse me?" Joanna rolled her eyes and began to expect an irritating exchange. "This is not a 1-900 number, sir."

"Uh, Joanna," the man stumbled over his words. "It's me, Peter. Peter Monday. I'm sorry, I should have identified myself right away."

"Peter!" Joanna felt relieved and embarrassed. "I wasn't expecting your call. In fact, I didn't even know you had my number," she continued.

Protected by the phone, Peter's flustered appearance remained undetected. "I looked up the main number and asked them to connect me."

Joanna wondered if there was a serious reason for his call. "What's going on, Peter? Did something happen at the church? Is it Pastor Marley's heart?" Their pastor had recently undergone emergency bypass surgery after several angioplasties had failed to correct the recurring blockage of his arteries.

"No, nothing like that," he paused. "I was just thinking about you and our, uh, time together last night. I really enjoyed the restaurant."

"It was nice." *More than nice.*

"Maybe we can have a repeat sometime." He waited for her response.

"That would be nice, sometime." *Blast it, can't I think of any words besides 'nice'!?*

"How about right now?"

The spontaneity was overwhelmingly attractive. "Now? But it's only 10:30 in the morning!"

"Meet me at *That Pizza Place* downtown. You know where it is? I figure it's about halfway between your work and mine, maybe a ten or fifteen-minute drive for each of us."

"Yes, I went there with a friend from work a few times." It was one of Greg's favorites, owned by his old friend, Joe Tropetto.

"Don't bring her along. I'd like to have you all to myself."

Joanna felt both indignant and attracted by his forwardness. It was a side of him that she had only recently begun to see. Today was her day to beat people at their own game. "OK, I won't bring *him* along," she paused for effect. "It's too early for lunch now. I'll meet you just before noon. It doesn't get crowded until a little after twelve."

"Great, see you there."

Joe Tropetto had the classic Sicilian look that belied the Irish ancestry on his maternal side. The name of his restaurant, *That Pizza Place,* had originated in college when he and his girlfriend Marina had been unable to remember the name of the corner pizza parlor and had come to refer to it as "that pizza place." Marina, now his wife, managed the restaurant's finances while Joe directed the artistry of making pizza in the kitchen. They had worked hard to bring about an old-world, friendly ambiance to their quarter-acre of the American dream. Business had grown enough to support two waitresses and a cashier/hostess during the lunch rush. The hostess greeted a young blond man as he entered the lobby, decorated tastefully for the Christmas season. Joanna watched him as he scanned the restaurant, trying to quickly acclimate his eyes to the dim lighting from the red lamps hanging over the dining tables. His eyes passed her by, then stopped and returned to where she sat in a booth by a window obscured by red Venetian blinds. Identity registered, and an irresistible smile enhanced his face. She returned one of her own.

"Sorry I'm late," he apologized, sliding into the seat across the table from her. "I got caught up in something at work."

"What exactly is it that you do again, Peter? I'm sorry, but I can't remember," she glanced down at the table for an instant, then returned to meet his gaze, her green eyes sparkling with life.

"I don't think I ever told you. I sell advertising space in newspapers and magazines."

"How interesting! I never would have guessed it."

Peter laughed. "It's not that interesting, really. What did you imagine I did for a living?" he inquired.

Before Joanna could answer, a waitress approached to take Peter's drink order. He noticed that Joanna had already finished half her diet soda by the time he had arrived. Greg and Joanna frequented the establishment together, and the waitress had remembered to bring Joanna's standard drink without asking.

"So then, who is this man you are friends with who takes you here all the time?"

"It's not *all* the time," Joanna retorted with a playful smile. Becoming more serious, she continued, "Actually, we haven't seen much of each other recently. He's retreated into himself so much since his fiancée was killed. He's the man I prayed for last night."

Compassion softened Peter's sense of rivalry with this other man in Joanna's life whom he had never met. "Tell me the story."

The following day Joanna found herself back at *That Pizza Place*. A completely different atmosphere enveloped the two like acrid smoke. With Peter she had drunk in the old-world charm of the restaurant and the youthful spark of Peter's face, but now she tasted the bitterness of her disintegrating relationship with Greg. The wood edge of the bench seat cut into the back of her legs. Greg scowled down into his iced tea.

Joanna had arrived at Greg's desk fifteen minutes early to minimize the chance of him backing out on their lunch date again. He had protested nevertheless, only agreeing to go out if they went to *That Pizza Place*, much to Joanna's dismay. Greg had wanted an excuse to escape to the kitchen to catch up with his old friend Joe in case the conversation led down any paths he wanted to avoid. However, Joanna had cringed when she realized that she would be seen there with two different men on consecutive days. Nevertheless, she had acquiesced in order to keep their lunch date alive.

At the restaurant, Joanna offered up a silent prayer of thanksgiving when an alternate hostess seated them. After taking their drink order, she left the two to sit in icy silence for a few awkward minutes.

When the waitress brought their drinks, she commented casually to Joanna, "I'm surprised to see you back so soon." Joanna shot the waitress a knowing look, causing her to bite her lip. She took their pizza order and scurried away.

"Here recently?" Greg inquired. At last the silence was broken.

Joanna decided that revealing part of the truth was good enough. "When you canceled on me yesterday, I met a friend from church here for lunch instead."

"The same man I saw you with the night before?"

"If you must know, Greg," she sighed, "Yes. It was Peter."

"You two dating?" Greg was brief.

Joanna was immediately flustered. She did not know the truthful answer. "No, no. We're not dating. Anyway, that's not what I came to talk to you about."

"Why not? What else is going on in your life?"

"What else is going on in *your* life, Greg?" she threw back at him.

"Nothing, absolutely nothing. And certainly nothing is going on with me and you."

"What do you mean, Greg?"

Greg rubbed his forehead. "Joanna, we have to discuss what happened that night at your apartment."

"That's one of the main things I wanted to talk to you about today."

"Good," Greg leaned forward. "Because it's eating me up. I think I made my feelings very clear that night, maybe not in words, and maybe not in the most tactful way. But I think we both know what I wanted to convey."

"Yeah, your actions said it loud and clear. You wanted to get me into bed!" Joanna was surprised by the frankness of her harsh tone.

"Not necessarily, Joanna. Don't make things more than they seem."

"Not necessarily? What then did you mean there on the couch? What were your intentions?"

Greg sat back in his seat. "Honestly, I don't know. I was getting carried away in the moment. I was coming off a strong buzz. I wanted to see where things would lead. I wanted to know how you felt about me. How do you feel about me?"

Joanna struggled to control her words, but her tongue began to take on a mind of its own. "I think you are one of the most selfish, most confused, most attractive men I have ever met. I think you are consumed by your job so much that you worship it. And I can't figure out if it's the money or the power you worship, or if it's just that it has become such a part of your identity that you can't live without it. I have seen your pain, I have witnessed you spiraling downhill, but I have not been able to share it or even discuss it with you. Because you are so caught up in yourself."

Greg had turned red. "Listen here, you self-righteous, stuck-up little temptress! You have been leading me on for years, even while I was engaged to Lisa. You talk about how offended you were that I made advances on you, but now you listen up! You have pursued me like a Jezebel, like a hypocrite! You religious people are all hypocrites! When *you* want something, it's 'God's will,' but when *I* want the same sort of thing, it's evil and depraved!"

"How dare you call me a hypocrite! I'm not perfect, that's for sure, but I mean to have good intentions. I really do. You can't judge me any more than I can judge you. You asked me how I felt about you, and I told you. Maybe it's *you* who don't want to hear what I have to say." The conversation had grown loud enough to attract the attention of an adjacent table as well as Marina Tropetto, who peeked out of the office next to the kitchen. She wondered if she should ask the waitress to just box the pizza she was about to deliver.

"How can you say you don't judge me when you accuse me of being selfish and immoral?" Greg's voice grew hoarse with emotion. "You don't know what I've been through!"

"Sometimes people bring things on themselves. And whatever you've been through, God has allowed in order to make you turn to Him."

"Is that why you're joining in the plot against me at work? A little toppling of my worldly idols, and maybe I'll turn to your God? Is that how you've been thinking?" Greg's words took on a steady and vicious tone. "I'll tell you something. I tried your God. I gave Him a chance with me when I was in the desert, and the first thing He did was let Lisa die!" In a single motion, Greg stood up, threw a wad of money on the table and turned to go. He stormed out of the restaurant and passed Marina without a word. He ventured out into the cold cloudy day without taking the time to put on his winter coat.

With tears streaming down her face, Joanna knew that this was going to be the saltiest pizza of her life.

Speeding in between traffic lights, cell phone in hand, Greg called into work to inform his assistant, Gina, that he was taking the afternoon off. In such turmoil over Joanna, his feelings for her, his suspicions about her, and his guilt over Lisa, he could only think of one answer to give him some guidance out of the chaos.

Pulling into an icy parking lot, he noticed a small Christian bookstore across the road emblazoned with the sign "God Saves." Shaking his head, Greg scoffed and headed into Madam Isis' psychic parlor.

"I saw you coming," she chanted in a low, sultry voice. "Today is the day for you."

Like a trained dog, Greg mindlessly followed the medium back through the beaded curtain. The inner room was as eerie in the day as it had been at night. Silent eyes continued to glare at him from the myriad statues and idols. Student and pupil sat down.

"You are confused. You are afraid. You are hurting," uttered the sunken-faced medium, shadows deepening the circles under her eyes. "Let me show you your cards."

Taking a large deck of intricately designed cards, she laid them out before Greg on the small table between their seats. With calculated melodrama she encouraged him with a whispered invitation, "Select your destiny!"

Reaching forward, Greg's hand began to shake uncontrollably. He felt as if his arm were made of lead, yet at the same time an irresistible force drew his fingers forward. As he touched the card he was led to, it seemed to burn his fingers with an electric spark.

"Place it face down on the table." Greg did as he was commanded. "Now turn it over!"

A smiling skeleton in a black robe greeted him with a sickle dripping dark-red blood. Not wanting to know the answer, Greg asked nevertheless, "What does it mean?"

The medium stared in horror and whispered ominously, "Death!"

The phone light blinked its one eye at Greg as he entered his apartment. With great dread he turned on the speaker phone and accessed his voicemail. An unwelcome voice chirped at him he headed for the kitchen pantry.

"Greg, this is Chuck. I'm back from the Far East. I tried to track you down and eventually your girl Gina let me know that you had taken a half day vacation. I wanted to talk to you this afternoon. It's rather important. The Holiday party is tonight, and I know you must still be planning to attend. Cocktails start at seven, so why don't you come by my office around that time. I've got some business to attend to until then, so I'll be waiting." Without a final acknowledgment, the message abruptly ended.

With his life seeming to unravel around him, Greg had decided to drown his sorrows in a bottle of liquor at home. "I guess I'll have to make this a public intoxication instead," he mused aloud. He began to open the bottle for a first swig to start off the evening but then thought better of it. Treading with unsure footing, he made his way to the closet to dress himself for the party. "Might as well go out in style tonight," he thought, selecting a smart black tuxedo with a subtle black cummerbund and bow tie. His sense of dread was strong, and his only coping mechanism was to cover it with dark humor. For an added sense of security, he found the amulet the medium had given him and slipped it into his shirt pocket. Then he stood in front of the mirror to check his appearance.

"The most stylish funeral suit I've ever seen," he sneered contemptuously.

Chapter Thirteen

The clinking of glasses, the soft laughter of polite conversation, the innocuous hum of voiceless cocktail music in the background all greeted the man in black as he strolled in through the white double doors. This year there was no woman on his arm, no charming smile on his face, just the wry grin of a man in search of oblivion in a glass. He sauntered up to the bar and slapped down a hand.

"Mr. Wesko, sir, what will you have?"

An intern whom Greg recognized from the previous summer stood at attention before a vast array of bottled liquors. All seemed to call his name, and none stood out from the rest. He rubbed his chin. "Bourbon, straight up, make it a double."

Having downed the shot in a flash, Greg began to survey the growing crowd. From the large windows of the penthouse office suite, Greg could see the streams of white and red lights from the evening traffic eighteen floors below. Across the room Tony Franco met his eyes with a wink, causing Greg to wince inwardly. "Someone more unstable than I am," he convinced himself. Greg mustered a fake smile for the man and then glanced at his watch. It was five minutes after seven, and he was already late for his appointment with Chuck Hollis. He turned to head across the room back through the double doors to the elevator lobby.

A flash of red hair caught his eye as he took his first step. With just one glimpse of Joanna, Greg's heart began to pound. The strapless royal blue evening gown complimented her exquisite figure. Curiously unaware of the effect of her physical appearance, Joanna had chosen to expose most of her flawless back. "She sure doesn't look like a church girl," Greg thought to himself. Her gaze drifted randomly to where he stood motionless. Trapped in her sight, Greg took a small step backwards and grabbed the side of the bar counter. His heart ached.

Don't let her get to you. Remember what she said. Remember what she did!

"Give me a shot of whiskey. Whatever you have." Greg could not take his eyes off Joanna, even as the stunning green of her eyes intensified with sadness. He downed the shot. "Another one," he barked hoarsely. Only then did he muster the courage to turn away. Or was it cowardice?

After taking a moment to steady himself, Greg headed toward the double doors with determination. Joanna stood directly in his path. Apprehension registered in her eyes at his ominous approach. But as he started to pass her by, he paused, turned and intently spoke her name between his teeth, "Good night, Joanna." She found it impossible to respond until after he had passed into the elevator lobby.

"Goodbye, Greg."

Chuck Hollis' door was open a fraction and gave way under Greg's spastic knocking. "Come in," the impersonal voice rang harshly in his ears. Ballpoint pen in hand, Hollis remained with his head bent over a small stack of papers. A brass desk lamp with a green shade played shadow and light on Hollis' face such that dark crevices gouged out pockets beneath his eyes. "Have a seat, Greg. Have a drink," he offered.

Greg plopped into a chair. The liquor had worked quickly on his empty stomach and frazzled nerves. "You wanted to see me, sir?" He reached for a glass of what appeared to be Scotch. Hollis had a glass of his own, empty but for two half-melted ice cubes.

Hollis put down his pen and looked up. His eyes seemed to focus on a distant object directly behind Greg's head. He cleared his throat. "Greg, you have always been an outstanding employee." The foreboding in Greg's stomach acidified. "One of our most valuable people. Someone headed straight for the top. And fast."

"Sir," Greg's feeble start was dismissed with the wave of Hollis' stubby hand.

"Greg, let me say what I have to say. I will get right to the point. Another sum of money is missing from one of your accounts. Fifteen thousand dollars and change."

While Hollis paused for a breath, Greg started in. "I didn't take it!" he blurted out. "I swear to you, someone is framing me! I know it!"

Hollis continued as if Greg had not spoken. "There are computer records showing that the money was transferred to an untraceable account somewhere in Europe."

"You're not listening," Greg slurred. "It wasn't me!"

Hollis raised his voice. "No, Greg. You're not listening. We have computer records showing that the money was transferred by you. We have proof!"

"It's a hoax," Greg was frustrated almost to the point of tears. The more indignant he became, the more slurred his speech. "How can you even prove the untraceable account is mine? And how could I be so stupid as to steal from the company three separate times, especially this third alleged time, after the audit?" Greg inadvertently betrayed the first incident, which had never been discussed.

Hollis mustered as much of a sympathetic tone as he could. "Greg, I want to believe you. I really do. But you have to understand the position I am in. I have documented evidence of an unauthorized transfer of money by you. There's a history of money disappearing from your accounts. How would it look if I didn't take action?" He paused for an interminable moment, as if expecting a response to his rhetorical question. "I tried to defend you to Amos Stockley. I was partially successful. We have a compromise for you."

If Hollis had intended to offer Greg some hope, he had failed. Greg realized his glass was empty and put it down.

"Amos and I will keep this incident to ourselves. But you must comply with certain conditions. If you have taken the money, keep it as a sort of, well, let's say, 'severance package.' But you are immediately off the payroll, although not officially fired. We will circulate the story that you have quit. There will be nothing further on your record, that is, in addition to the previous audit findings. Tell people you left of your own volition. You were not fired. It was your own initiative to leave. But do not go back to your desk. Leave straight away. We will have your personal effects packed and sent to your home. Discreetly."

"Chuck, I don't know what to say," Greg moaned.

"Then say as little as possible. Why don't you take a few moments, gather your thoughts, and even return to the party if you like. Or why not go up to the roof for some air? Don't do anything rash. If you come back down, we can even make a formal announcement of your leaving. I can lead into it with an introduction."

The open air of the roof sounded appealing despite the cold December weather. "I do need some time to be alone and think," he mused. "This is a lot to comprehend."

"Don't try to comprehend, Greg. Just try to accept. You don't want things to get any worse, that is, any worse than they already are."

Greg's footsteps echoed heavily in the dirty white stairwell. He had chosen the route least likely to place him face to face with anyone else. With the planting of each foot, the sound reverberated dully in his ears as if there were a series of other footsteps following him. He paused to listen. Silence. Continuing, the effect of the liquor and the climbing of the stairs combined to send his head into a dizzying tailspin.

The roof. Get to the roof. There's freedom on the roof. Open air, no ceiling, no people, no guardrail, no witnesses.

Reaching the top, Greg pushed his way through the steel door and into the neon glow of the company sign. All else was darkness.

In the ladies' room, Joanna pretended to adjust her make-up and fix her dress in the floor-length mirror. Inwardly she prayed for Greg. Halfway across the country another member of the Church Militant fell on her knees and prayed for a lost soul. A member of the Church Triumphant incorporated a special intention in the Beatific Vision. A life was at stake. And more than that, an eternal life.

Some time later, shaken from the turmoil of the day, but hopeful from his contemplation on the roof, Greg emerged from the obscured stairwell door and re-entered the party unnoticed. The warmth of the busy room burned his cheeks. His heart felt as if a giant burden had been lifted from the inside, even as the medium's amulet had been lifted from his shirt pocket and fallen over the edge of the roof. His eyes were bloodshot from both the alcohol and a flood of tears, now wiped away. Avoiding conversation, he acted preoccupied and headed through the crowd with occasional smiles and nods. Chuck Hollis stood laughing affectedly with a gaggle of senior executives. Greg caught his attention and motioned for him to join him in a semi-private area near a pair of empty tables. A flash of mild surprise fleeted across Hollis' face.

"What is it, Greg?"

"I'm ready for you to introduce my announcement, Chuck. Pick an appropriate time, but the sooner, the better."

Hollis agreed. "Yes, but there has been a slight change in plans. We weren't sure if you were going to come back. Amos said that if you did return, he wanted to do the introduction himself. He'll start, but you'll have to finish it."

It was Greg's turn to be surprised. Amos Stockley rarely spoke publicly about anything other than the bottom line and how to improve it. "You wait by the podium. I'll find Amos. As soon as your speech is over, you'll have to leave immediately. Don't stay to talk to anyone."

Greg did not speak but headed towards the podium, which stood on a small raised platform at one end of the large, open room. The penthouse office suite had four corner offices, with one workstation tucked neatly away to the side for an administrative assistant. A large floor-to-ceiling window separated each pair of offices. Two spotlights reflected off the window behind the podium. Greg's gaze fell back to the crowd, just in time to see Joanna approaching him through the throng of jolly, drunken officemates. Amos Stockley arrived and stood at the podium. Greg slipped through the crowd again towards Joanna.

"Ladies and gentlemen, can I have your attention please!" The shrill feedback from the microphone helped to bring many eyes front and center. Greg cast Joanna a pleading look. She squeezed through a cluster of unobservant partiers and stood next to Greg. Both wanted to speak, but Amos Stockley's commanding voice silenced all residual conversation. He proceeded to welcome everyone to the Holiday party and thanked them for a year of hard work and good results.

"I need to talk to you, Joanna," whispered Greg. "Something big has happened."

"I need to talk to you too," Joanna returned, as two nearby heads swiveled around to cast them angry, silencing glares.

After ten restless minutes, Stockley wrapped up an address on the financial state of the business, unsuitably detailed for a party speech. "And now, I want to introduce one of our most valued employees. This is someone who has been a strong asset to Providential Insurance Companies for quite a few years." Greg's heart began to pound with nervous anticipation. Stockley continued, "A top performer with a promising career. A bright star in his prime, with an announcement that may come as a surprise," he paused for effect. "Greg Wesko."

An audible gasp issued from Joanna. Greg stepped with heavy feet up to the podium amidst an otherworldly silence in the room. As he looked out on the crowd, two blinding lights served up the illusion of a press conference. Suddenly Greg felt his mouth turn to cotton. He cleared his throat and tried to clear the haze from his mind.

"I have worked at Providential Insurance ever since college graduation. I know many of you personally, and I have come to enjoy some good friendships over the years," Greg said, letting his eyes come to rest upon Joanna, then upon Jason Coates. "When I came to work here, I was certain that I would retire from PI, wealthy, famous, and only forty years old." Light laughter rumbled across the sea of onlookers.

"But no one ever knows what is in store," Greg paused, choking on his words. "What God has in store. But recently, very recently, I have started to realize what is important and what is not so important. Many of you know of my personal tragedy, and what could have pushed me over the edge. In fact, you could say I almost went over the edge, even tonight." He scanned the faces in the room, now waxing somber. "And so I have decided that the time has come for a big change in my life. I've spent the last however many years worshipping my job, and I have done my best to be a faithful employee. And now I am going to embark on something new, a sabbatical, if you will. I have put in my resignation, and I will no longer be with Providential Insurance."

Greg waited for the quiet exclamations and whispers to subside before continuing. "I have been honored to work with you all. I will miss you dearly." Greg spoke slowly and sincerely. "It has truly been a pleasure. I hope to see you all again someday." The room remained in stunned silence. "Thank you, thank you all," he added. A few scattered hands began to clap, and soon the noise of applause grew to a dull roar. Amos Stockley and Greg changed places on the platform, and then Greg stepped down and headed towards the side stairwell. Stockley took over the microphone, and eyes focused on the senior executive.

"Thank you, Greg," Stockley began as the applause quickly died off. "As I said, we have certainly enjoyed working with you. You will be sorely missed, but I'm sure you will do well wherever you go," he stated with authority and confidence. Very few people noticed Greg slip out the exit to the stairwell.

Joanna watched his figure disappear through the side door. She brushed away a tear along with the urge to follow him. Just then a warm hand fell gently upon her shoulder. "There you are! I lost you somehow in the crowd."

Joanna turned to stare up into two crystal blue eyes sparkling with affection. She took his other hand and squeezed. "Peter!" she smiled. "Don't lose me again!"

A thrill of excitement tingled up and down Peter's spine. Inwardly he promised, "I won't lose you, Joanna. I won't."

Chapter Fourteen

The striking split in the mountain ahead took Greg by surprise as he traveled Interstate 68 westward on a cold, clear winter afternoon. The previous night's sprinkling of snow still dusted the landscape. His eyes remained fixed on the man-made crevice, blasted out of the rock to help motorists speed their way across the western sliver of Maryland. Old U.S. Route 40 snaked up the curves of the mountain but no longer connected to the other side. A rest area with a four-story visitor center reminded Greg that he owed his body a break.

Pulling into the parking lot, Greg was struck by the massiveness of the geological formation before him. Over 800 feet of folded layers of exposed rock towered over the divided highway curving through it below. A walkway climbed a short distance up the side of the mountain, and Greg braved the biting wind to treat himself to a closer view of the rock strata. He marveled at several frozen cascades of ice issuing from the side of the ruddy mountain. The sun was beginning to set, and Greg tried to stay warm as he enjoyed the play of orange and yellow amid growing shadows on the sun-facing portion of the gap. He drew in a deep, cold breath. The crispness of the air, the awesome mass of rock and the ability of man to subdue the earth all combined to whisper in his ear of the majesty of God in his creation of nature and mankind. For the first time in many months, Greg's ears opened slightly.

Back on the road, Greg reviewed his schedule for the remainder of the day. He had decided to travel without an exact plan, just an urge to move westward and southward rapidly. He was considering turning south on I-79 at Morgantown and traversing the heart of West Virginia. He figured that he could probably arrive in the capital city of Charleston in time for a late dinner. He hoped and almost prayed for safety in the mountainous terrain ahead. Although he had found the highways free of ice and snow in the daylight, the encroaching darkness and plummeting mercury could make for treacherous driving.

An hour after dark, Greg passed the last exit for Fairmont and continued twisting around the peaks of the Mountain State. Traffic had dwindled to the point where Greg often found his view unaided by the light of any cars in either direction. Before the solitude grew unbearable, Greg decided to turn on the radio. He found little but white noise, occasionally interrupted by the twang of a banjo or the voice of an irate preacher. Desperate after three full trips around the dial, he settled on the only music station he could find. Only a few minutes later, the station succumbed, disappearing into the growing static. The search continued. He stopped at the sound of a deep powerful voice.

"And in the Gospel of Matthew, Jesus says:

" 'O generation of vipers, how can ye, being evil, speak of good things? For out of the abundance of the heart the mouth speaketh.

" 'A good man out of the good treasure of the heart bringeth forth good things, and an evil man out of the evil treasure bringeth forth evil things.

" 'But I say unto you, that every idle word that men shall speak, they shall give account thereof in the Day of Judgment.

" 'For by thy words thou shalt be justified, and by thy words thou shalt be condemned.'

"Then certain of the scribes and of the Pharisees answered, saying, 'Master, we would see a sign from thee.'

"But he answered and said unto them, 'An evil and adulterous generation seeketh after a sign; and there shall no sign be given to it, but the sign of the prophet Jonah.'

"The Gospel of Matthew goes on to speak of the sign of Jonah, how he had to endure three days and three nights in the belly of the whale. Now compare the generation of the Scriptures with the generation of today. We are no different! We demand signs, we look at the stock market, we look at our horoscopes, we look at the weather. But do we see? No! We don't see the signs God has put right before our very eyes. They didn't see in Jesus' time either. The sick were cured, the lame walked, the dead were raised, but even John the Baptist had doubts that the Kingdom of God had really come in Jesus Christ! We have to try to believe harder than John the Baptist. But how can we do that? John believed so hard, it cost him his very life! His head on a platter!"

The radio preacher's words stung Greg in the heart. He began to ask himself what sign he had expected to receive from the medium. He had only received signs of death. But he was still alive. There had been no signs warning of Lisa's death. But now she was gone. He wondered what signs he was missing as he sped through the cold and ice and darkness.

Sudden waves of fear crashed over Greg's body as he felt the vehicle slipping out of his control. A hidden patch of ice had initiated a frightening skid towards the guardrail, with nothing but darkness on the other side. "Oh God, help me!" Greg cried out. His vision blurred. Brakes hissed. Tires squealed. He imagined himself careening over the embankment and into oblivion, with no one to witness and no one to rescue. Time seemed to move in slow motion. Metal crunched against metal. The sound continued for a virtual eternity as the car slowed mercifully to a stop.

Shaking, Greg stumbled out of the car and stood on the shoulder of the highway to observe his situation. The car had scraped along the guardrail for a few hundred feet. Greg had tensed the muscles in his legs to the brink of cramping. Hobbling over to the edge, he peered over the guardrail. The earth gradually sloped down about twenty feet to a small ledge and then disappeared into darkness below. It was difficult to estimate whether he would have survived the crash, or if he would have continued over the ledge and into the void. He inspected the vehicle. Other than a sizeable scrape running the length of the passenger side, there was no apparent damage. He judged the car to be operational.

For the second time in recent memory, Greg was thankful to be alive. He returned to the driver's seat and waited for his nerves to calm down. The tension in his legs began to subside. Starting the engine, he prayed, "Please, God, no more signs for a while."

"Hello, Theresa? Are you still there?" Greg stood with his hand covering one ear, the phone pressed tightly against his other in an attempt to hear over the highway traffic. A passing truck had obliterated the response to his introduction. He wanted to confirm that he still had a connection.

"Greg, is that really you?" His sister's voice was full of elation and surprise. "You said you were *where*?"

"Just south of Austin on I-35. I'd love to come see you."

"Yes, yes, of course!" she exclaimed. "Come and stay with us! You're just about an hour and a half away. We're out in the country on the northwest side of San Antonio."

"I'll need directions."

The winter Texas sun was a welcome change from the bitter Northeast cold. Greg turned off the heat and cracked the windows as he bore right onto Doppler Road, a lonely byway disappearing into the hill country just a few miles outside the expansive city limits of San Antonio. Low, leafless trees dotted the golden-brown terrain. In the distance an occasional tall oak tree reached toward the sky. He glanced down at the directions he had scribbled on a gas station receipt.

A dilapidated grain silo ahead on the right matched the description his sister had given him. He slowed down to make a right turn at the landmark onto a dirt road. A small road sign read "Retten Ave." It was the first unpaved road Greg had ever seen with the epitaph "Ave."

Greg's eyes followed the road ahead as it sloped down to a beautifully landscaped adobe estate in a small valley below. The grounds were divided into several segmented garden areas. An expanse of trees headed out of sight over the next hill behind the house to the east. To the right of the house another grove of trees disappeared beyond the horizon to the south. An ornate sign with silver recessed letters proclaimed, "McAllen Orchards."

The sound of Greg's tires rolling over the white stones in the parking area caught the attention of two friendly dogs. Tails wagging and barks greeting, they bounded out of a screen door on the left side of the house and circled his car. Two small children also gyrated towards him, several paces behind the dogs. Unsure how to handle either the dogs or the children, he waited in his car for a moment until a woman appeared in the doorway.

She waved and called out to him through the screen door, "Hi Greg! Come in!"

When it did not seem that his sister would come to his rescue, Greg cautiously opened the door. Immediately he was greeted with two paws on his leg and a tongue in his face. Then the second dog pushed the first out of the way and repeated the salutation. When the dogs backed away, he found himself staring down a stone walkway at two pairs of wide, silent eyes. The younger one, a girl, appeared to be on the verge of tears.

"It's OK, I'm your Uncle Greg," he proffered. No response. The excitement with which they had vaulted toward the car had led him to expect a chatty, chaotic welcome. He wondered if they had intuitively sensed his uneasiness with children. The awkwardness of the situation was heightened when Theresa prodded from the doorway, "Don't just stand there, kids! Go give your uncle a hug!"

Still standing, Greg bent over to receive his hugs. Instead, the kids quickly squeezed him around the legs and then ran back into the house. Greg looked up at his sister with a touch of bewilderment.

"You'll have to excuse the kids. They haven't seen a grown man in years," she joked from her station in the doorway. "Come in and take a load off. Jared can help you with your bags later." She opened the screen door and shooed the dogs away. Greg entered the house and received a warm hug from his sister. The he followed her into a parlor decorated in typical southwest array. She took his jacket and hung it on a wooden coat rack, empty except for a white cowboy hat and a set of antique skeleton keys. She motioned him out of the parlor and down a hallway to the right. "You can have a tour later. Let's go to the kitchen and sit down."

The hallway led past several closed doors and a few large archways revealing a poolroom and main foyer on the right and a large sitting room and formal dining room on the left. The corridor spilled out into a spacious, bright kitchen with handsome pine cabinets and a white marble floor. A matching pine table and chairs to the left appeared to be the usual eating area. As Greg accepted a seat at the table, he marveled at the massive picture windows that graced the kitchen walls on three sides. The east window looked out on a patio eating area, the south towards an orchard in the distance, while the west window on the front of the house faced back up a hill towards the road.

"So, how was your trip?" Theresa approached him with an inviting glass pitcher decorated with lemon designs. "Iced tea?" she offered, setting two matching glasses down on the table. "It's sweetened."

"Sounds great," Greg accepted. "The trip was just fine. I have some extra time so I took the opportunity to stop and see some sights along the way. Honestly, I started out with no final destination in mind. But even so I took a fairly direct route here. I passed through Louisville, Nashville, Memphis. I took my time."

"So what happened, did you lose your job?" Theresa guessed. "Is that what you mean by having 'some extra time?'"

Greg smiled. "It's a complicated story. You could say I was forced into it. But in any case, it was time for a change."

"We all need a change sometimes. I've experienced some changes myself," she hesitated as the din of approaching children grew louder. "But we can talk about that some other time. Let's try to get a better welcome out of the kids." Theresa leaned over in her chair and picked up a little freckled girl, sliding her onto her lap. "Say hello to your Uncle Greg again, Denise."

"Hello, Uncle Greg," the little girl whispered timidly.

"Hi, Denise. Do you know who I am?"

"No." Denise had never met Greg.

"You're Mommy's brother," the little brown-haired boy spoke up. "I saw an old picture of you when you were a kid. You and Mommy were standing next to Granny and Pappy. Why did you look so funny?"

Silence reigned as Greg fumbled for something to say. He remembered an awkward family portrait taken when he was in high school.

"Uncle Greg hasn't been around children much," Theresa interjected. "Why don't you show him the playroom? If you ask nicely, I bet he will read you a story. Pick one off the bookshelf." Theresa shot Greg a look that combined expressions of "I hope you don't mind," with "Being around children will be good for you."

The idea of having a story helped the children overcome their shyness. Calling "Uncle Greg, come on!" they bounced out of the kitchen and into the adjoining playroom. "Let me pick the story!" they shouted in unison.

Three books later, Theresa trod into the playroom to rescue Greg. "I've got dinner cooking on the stove. It'll be ready in another fifteen minutes or so," she informed them as she leaned against the doorframe.

"I'm home!" entered a voice through another door opposite Theresa. The children jumped up to greet a tall, sturdy man with jet-black hair and sun-darkened skin. After greeting his children, the man approached Greg and extended a hand for a hearty shake. "Hi, Greg. It's good to see you again. Been a while."

"Good to see you too, Jared," Greg returned the greeting. "I don't think I've seen you since right after Jack was born."

"I'm basically the same," his grin revealed a perfect set of white teeth. "Still busy all the time. Orchards are doing great, though. In fact," he said, turning to his family, "I have to go away on a business trip tomorrow."

"But tomorrow is Sunday!" Jack protested.

"And you already worked all day today!" Denise chimed in with her own objections.

"I have to be in El Paso for a meeting with a big potential customer on Monday morning. That's over 500 miles, so I have to leave tomorrow. I'm driving the truck out so I can bring along some plants for show-and-tell."

"Can we come?" Jack pleaded.

"Sorry, buddy, not this time. Besides, your Uncle Greg is going to be here. You don't want to miss his visit." Greg cringed, anticipating rejection from the boy. "Greg, you are staying awhile, aren't you?"

"You're welcome to stay as long as you like, Greg," Theresa offered. "Greg's out of a job," she added, turning to her husband. "Dinner's about ready." The proclamation of mealtime put a quick end to the discussion.

Bright sunlight streamed through the Venetian blinds to notify Greg that he had slept long enough. The quiet Sunday morning house was a welcome break, as Greg was not accustomed to the random noise of young children. After dinner Saturday night, he had been invited to attend church with the family the following morning. He had tentatively agreed to go if he woke up in time. He purposely slept in.

Greg threw on a summer robe and decided to explore the house, which was a maze of hallways and open arched doorways. A brick-red tile floor meandered throughout the first floor, dividing it into four uneven quadrants. Greg's guest room adjoined Denise's room and faced the playroom. From his window, Greg could see the master bedroom and its adjoining office jutting into the backyard. Deceptive in the cool winter sunlight, a blue pool sparkled invitingly some distance behind the house. Two small gardens abutted against the wrought-iron fence surrounding the concrete pool area. The entire grounds had a neatly manicured appearance, as expected of anyone in Jared's business.

Greg wandered into a carpeted sitting room across the hall from a side entrance to the guest room. Two pairs of arched doorways let a good quantity of light from the hallways into this interior room. Through two of the doors Greg could see a main foyer leading to a recessed area, which Greg surmised to be the formal entrance. Through the windows flanking the front door, a garden patio area was visible with two large wrought-iron gates.

Greg began to peruse the titles on the bookshelves in the sitting room. One stand-alone white bookshelf contained collections of uniform appearance, such as encyclopedias, bound National Geographic issues, and two sets of classical Roman and Greek literature. One wall was completely lined with darkly stained oaken bookshelves over a row of cabinets. The books were organized according to category, and Greg soon recognized his sister's taste and interests from various stages of her life. A literature section containing the complete works of the Brontë sisters. A horror section predominated by Stephen King. A cooking section focused on Chinese and Indian cuisine. Craft books on flower arrangement, sculpting, interior decorating. Half a shelf of paperback crossword puzzle books. A philosophy and Eastern meditation section containing interesting titles such as "The Voice Within Me," "Zen and the Computer," and "Aquarius Now."

Greg's attention was drawn to three identical volumes with red velvet covers and gold lettering proclaiming, "Buddha, Savior." Reaching up to feel the fabric covering, he accidentally dislodged one of the books and sent it crashing to the floor. It landed with a dull thud and a metallic ringing. Intrigued,

Greg picked up the book to investigate the unexpected noise. Opening the front cover, Greg let out a gasp as he realized the book contained a secret compartment. He paused for a moment as he contemplated whether he should snoop into his hosts' private matters. Overcome with curiosity, however, his fingers fumbled frenziedly to open the compartment. Prying away the compartment lid, he found two dazzling white gold rings, one studded with inlaid diamonds and the other with a large princess-cut solitaire. Unable to control himself, he nervously grabbed the other two Buddha books to investigate. The second revealed a wad of folded five-hundred dollar bills. Palms breaking out in sweat, he began to pry open the compartment of the third book. His heart pounded in his ears and his adrenaline pumped as he anticipated learning the identity of the contents with excitement. A rush of disappointment and disbelief overtook him as he discovered that the compartment was empty.

The sound of sudden inhalation stabbed Greg in the chest. He wheeled around just in time to be greeted with the indignant query, "What on earth are you doing?"

Chapter Fifteen

Like a criminal caught in the act, Greg felt the urge to flee. Common sense prevailing, however, he stammered to formulate an answer.

"Theresa, I was just looking at your books," he fumbled weakly, uncertain of what else to say. His mouth instantly turned dry.

"You should not have opened these up," Theresa frowned sternly like a well-practiced disciplinarian. "These are private."

"I'm sorry, Theresa," Greg apologized. "I didn't mean to stumble onto your hiding places. The books looked interesting so I picked them up. I didn't know there was anything inside, at first. You've got to believe me," he pleaded.

Theresa's scowl softened. "I do believe you, Greg," she admitted, the hint of a smile straining to emerge. "How could you have known they were secret books? I bought them a long time ago. What titles! I should have thrown them away."

"I shouldn't have pried. It was not my intention," he said as he handed over the books.

"When I saw they had a secret compartment, I should have just returned them to the shelves."

Theresa accepted the books. "Why don't we sit down," she offered with a sigh. "This is a good time for me to find a new hiding place. I can't blame you for being curious once you found them. Who could resist looking inside? I doubt that I could." She began opening the compartments without commenting on the contents. When she opened the empty book, she gasped and looked up at Greg. "Can I have it back?"

"Have what back?" Greg's stomach knotted up as he realized that the third compartment was not expected to be empty, and he was the most likely suspect. "Have what back?" he repeated.

"Um," she hesitated, "the thing that was in this third book."

"What was it?" *She doesn't want to tell me!*

"I have the money, I have the rings. The third book is empty."

"There wasn't anything in it when I opened it. It was already empty," Greg insisted.

"Then help me look on the floor!" Theresa entreated with a hint of panic. "Please," she added.

Brother and sister stooped to their knees and scoured the floor. "It would help if you let me know what it is," Greg asserted. "Describe it for me."

"You'll know it if you see it," Theresa returned.

The sound of children's feet pattered down the hallway. Before Greg could turn to look, he was ambushed with a fifty-pound weight on his back. "Gotcha, Uncle Greg!" On his hands and knees, Greg struggled to regain his breath and stabilize himself under the load. "You're a horse, and I roped you! Now giddy-up!"

Deciding to play along, Greg forced himself to trot around the room a bit with Jack. Laughing, Theresa sat on the floor and watched. Denise veered around the corner and stumbled into the room. "My turn, my turn!" pleaded the three-year-old girl.

Theresa elected to come to Greg's rescue. "Let's give Uncle Greg a break. After all, he still needs to get dressed for the day." She grabbed onto a nearby sofa and pulled herself to a standing position with some effort. "I'll get some lunch together. Greg, I'll continue this later by myself."

The plan seemed agreeable to everyone, and they quickly vacated the room. Assured that she was alone, Theresa returned to the floor and began searching for what was lost.

"Tell me again how you and Jared met." Greg and Theresa sat enjoying a pot of gourmet coffee on the patio outside the kitchen. In the afternoon sun it was warm enough to forgo jackets on the San Antonio winter's day.

Theresa put her mug down and embraced it with her hands. "I was working at the college newspaper," she began. "I was assistant editor at the time. He came into the office and wanted to place a full-page ad. It was against the rules to have a single ad that large. I don't even remember why," she smiled, reminiscing. "He was tall and sturdy, although I didn't think he was particularly handsome at first. But he was so charming, and so persistent, that I was ready to let him do almost anything he wanted."

"So he placed the ad?"

"Yes, a full page and at a discount too. He was running his own business, even then. All sorts of things, but mostly he helped students find help with tutoring, writing papers, and so on. He was a headhunter as well. He helped me find my first job out of college."

"Was that when you were a journalist for the Zen Times?"

"No, not at all," Theresa chuckled with a slight blush. "Jared never approved of any of my 'weird hobbies,' as he called them. He found a position for me as a product tester for a cosmetic company. I wrote freelance for the Zen Times on my own. I almost shudder to think about it now." Theresa seemed lost in a melancholy memory.

"I can't quite put my finger on it," Greg began, "but you seem like an entirely different person, Theresa. You were always buzzing about the latest movement you had joined to 'set yourself free.' Always adamant that everyone else should join you. Looking for peace but never finding it. You seem peaceful now. But I've never known what to expect from you, and in that way, nothing has changed!"

Theresa's eyes had lost their glaze so familiar to Greg over the years. Instead they burned with life. "I *am* a different person, Greg," she smiled gently. "I'm becoming the person I was meant to be, not the flighty, unsatisfied non-conformist I had made myself into." Pausing, she laughed lightly. "You may think that I'm only going through my latest phase, but you will find that this time there is a difference. And it's not me, it's *Him*."

"Who, Jared?" Greg surmised that Theresa had finally convinced Jared to join her in the hottest new spiritual movement.

"No, not Jared," Theresa smiled. She continued with slow, purposeful words. "It's God! Mysterious, unchanging, all-loving, unfathomable, awesome God!"

Greg paused to take in Theresa's meaning. "I have to say, those aren't words I usually associate with God." Words like distant, authoritarian and dull came to mind. Yet Theresa's excitement was contagious. He continued, "After a long absence, I started to come to God and found nothing but heartache and loneliness. I've had a rough time with God."

Compassion covered Theresa's face. "I can't begin to imagine your pain, Greg. What you have been through in the last year!" Theresa remained silent about the nights she had lost sleep crying and praying for Greg. "A tragedy, a true nightmare. I have learned two things about tragedy. First, God never leaves us alone in the storm and the cold. And second, every difficulty can be used for transformation to holiness."

Transformation to holiness did not appeal to Greg. "We've all heard the saying, 'What does not kill us will make us stronger.' But I disagree, not on principle but on experience."

"It's often difficult to see progress in our own lives. Just like looking at a speck on your nose, your eyes are too close to focus well. I have trouble seeing change in my own life, yet as an outsider you observed it right away."

"Why would God want to send someone a tragedy to help them out? Surely there must be a better way."

"God does not necessarily send the tragedy, but He does permit it. The Bible says that all things work to the good for those who love God."

"And so for those that don't love God, all things work for the bad?" Greg challenged accusingly.

"Those are your words, not mine," Theresa replied. "If a person is not in touch with God, it does make it hard for His plan to unfold in their lives. And so by their attitude and actions, a person chooses whether to allow a tragedy to be used for the good, or whether to allow the tragedy to destroy their lives, and that is where the real tragedy lies."

"Hey, I didn't ask for Lisa to die! I didn't ask for my career to go down the toilet! I was doing just fine without tragedy, and I will never see how these things have made me a better person." Greg's defiant eyes raged with indignation.

Theresa reached over to touch Greg's hand. "I'm sorry, Greg. I didn't mean to make you feel judged. I know that what happened is not your fault. I just don't want you to become a slave to what has happened in your life. I want you to be empowered to overcome. I know you can rise above and be better than you were before."

"I've tried to tell myself that, but I've had no success with picking myself up by my bootstraps."

"That's because you can't do it alone. You need God. You need faith to overcome."

Greg thought back to his time in the desert before Lisa's death. "I may have had a speck of faith at one time, but I lost it. I don't have any faith," he lamented.

"No," Theresa corrected, "You do have faith. I know you do. I can sense it. I can hear it in the way you talk. It's not that you doubt or deny God, it's that you don't seem to let Him into your life. To do what He wants to do. What you need Him to do."

Dumbstruck, Greg sat pondering the wisdom Theresa had revealed. No one had ever confronted him with this truth about himself. He did believe. Somehow, he had always believed. But he had never come to the realization that he believed. The bald truth of the matter compelled him to respond. "Theresa, you are right. I have a lot of thinking to do."

"A lot of praying to do, Greg. God has brought you here for a reason. What a wonderful opportunity you have now, Greg. Stay here as long as you need to. We have a big house. You don't have to worry about expenses if you stay here. Take time to sort out your life."

Greg had arranged for mail collection and electronic bill payment during his open-ended absence from home, and he had no other obligations to meet. "I do appreciate the offer," Greg answered slowly. "And I accept. As long as Jared doesn't mind."

"I'll worry about Jared," Theresa remarked with growing elation. "I'm so glad you are going to stay! I have so longed for us to get reacquainted. I want you to know my children too."

"I do too, Theresa, but I really don't know what to do with children. I don't have any experience with them."

"They'll break you in."

Greg crossed his arms and frowned. Even in the fading sunlight, the scrape along the passenger side of his car screamed for attention. "What happened to your car?" inquired a small little voice. Greg turned around and shot Jack a half-smile.

"I ran into a guardrail on the way here," he admitted.

"Why did you do that?"

"I didn't do it on purpose!" Greg quickly checked his tone and continued in a less defensive manner. "I skidded on a patch of ice."

"Why?"

"I didn't see it," explained Greg.

"Mommy says she doesn't buy that excuse when I say it," Jack reported. "I told her I didn't see the statue on the front patio when I ran into it with my motorcycle."

"You have a motorcycle?" Greg questioned incredulously.

"Not a real one," Jack confessed. "Anyway, why don't you get your car fixed?"

"I don't want to spend the money," Greg replied. "I don't have a job right now."

"Too bad," Jack commiserated. "Neither do I. Come to think of it, neither does Mommy, but she still pays for stuff."

"That's different. Your mommy is married to your daddy, and he has a job. A real nice job."

"I guess so. Aren't you married?"

"No."

"Why not?"

"I don't want to talk about it."

"Why not?" Jack repeated.

"Because I say so," Greg managed in his best parental tone. "Let's go inside. The car's not going to get any better just by looking at it."

"Why not?"

On the third ring, Greg spoke up. "Would you like me to answer the phone?"

Theresa looked up from her bowl of chili. "We try not to answer the phone during dinner," she informed him.

"But Daddy does!" Denise blurted out. Jack smiled slightly, his eyes flitting from mother to sister to see how the dispute would be handled.

"Sometimes Daddy has to answer the phone during dinner because of work," Theresa responded. "Since Daddy isn't here, the person will have to call back."

From across the room, an antiquated answering machine picked up and began to relay its message aloud. Theresa winced. "I forgot to turn down the volume. We might as well listen to see who it is."

At the end of the recorded greeting, a voice on the other end of the line began to speak. "Hi Theresa, it's me." Greg recognized Jared's voice. "Things are going well, but I have to stay a second week. I'll try to come home earlier if I can. Don't count on it, though. Kiss the kids for me. Love you, honey. Bye."

Protests and complaints erupted from the children. Theresa allowed them a few moments to vent their disapproval before she spoke. "I'm sorry, children. Daddy will be home as soon as he can. You know he loves you."

"Does he go away like this a lot?" Greg questioned.

"Sometimes. I'll call him later tonight or tomorrow. I've gotten used to him being away, but the kids never do."

Eerie darkness greeted Greg at every turn. Low light cast shadows all about through the thick, humid air. As a tickle in the back of his throat grew in intensity, a feeling of panic mounted in his stomach. Greg feared that his best efforts to stifle a cough would be futile. To his horror, he broke out into a coughing fit that reverberated in the cavernous room.

The tour guide paused, unable to compete with Greg's outburst. The coughing fit subsided, Greg cleared his throat, and the guide resumed his speech. "Natural Bridge Caverns is the largest in the state of Texas," he continued. "The room we are standing in now is called Pluto's Anteroom. Over one hundred feet below the surface, this was the first large room to be discovered in the caverns."

Greg kept a tight grip on Denise and Jack to keep their natural curiosity from leading them into trouble. He had offered to give Theresa a day of rest and peace by taking the children on a field trip.

At the end of the tour, Denise and Jack were bubbling over with excitement. As they ordered lunch at the snack bar, the children discussed the adventure.

"I loved the Hall of the Mountain King the best! Or maybe Purgatory Creek!" exclaimed Jack.

"The White Giants scared me," Denise admitted. "I was afraid they would come to life."

"Stones can't come to life!" Jack chortled.

Lunch in hand, Greg corralled the kids to a nearby table. He divided up the food and raised a French fry to his mouth. Jack broke in, "Aren't we going to pray?"

Embarrassed, Greg put down the half-eaten fry and folded his hands under the table so as not to be seen. "Do you want to say the prayer, Jack?"

Jack and Denise bowed their heads, closed their eyes and joined hands with each other and with Greg. In a conspicuous voice, Jack prayed, "God is great, God is good, and we thank him for this food."

Greg looked around uncomfortably. He was thankful that no one seemed to have noticed the public display of religion.

"You don't pray much, do you, Uncle Greg?" Jack challenged but without judgment.

"Don't you pray?" Denise chimed in, wide-eyed.

The second fry stuck in his throat. "Of course I do," he started. "I pray, sometimes. Everyone has a different way of praying, I guess."

"Like Daddy," remarked Jack. "He says he can't always make it to church because of work, so he prays in the car. He says you can make your work a prayer."

Greg's experience had always been making work a god rather than a prayer, so the idea was unfamiliar to him. "I guess you can," he reflected.

"Mommy says you have to pray to God every day just like you have to talk to your family every day," Jack continued. "But I guess you forget to pray sometimes, just like Daddy forgets to call home sometimes when he's away."

"Is he away a lot?" Greg asked.

"Every day!" Denise pouted.

"No, not every day," Jack corrected. "I don't know how much, a lot, I guess. We like having him at home, but it's OK that he goes away too."

"Your daddy must love you a lot," Greg offered with consolation. "He works so that he can give you lots of good things, like your house, your toys, good food. You two are really lucky."

"Yeah, we are!" exclaimed Denise.

"I guess so," Jack agreed tentatively. "If he loves us so much, then why does he go away so much?"

"Sometimes we have to go away from the people we love, even if we don't want to. But we always come back when we can, like your daddy does."

Greg's mind began to wander. *If I love Joanna, then maybe I have to be away from her for a while. If I love God, or if I ever come to love God, do I have to be away from Him too? Or have I already passed through that time of being away? Theresa will know the answer.* Greg offered up a silent prayer of thanksgiving for the opportunity to stay and learn from his sister.

Greg's guardian angel looked on, thankful for the answer to many prayers.

Chapter Sixteen

"Shut up, or I'll kill you!" The outburst penetrated Greg's door and roused him from his light morning sleep. The subsequent crash brought Greg to full attention. Springing to his feet, Greg followed a string of venomous insults across the hall into the toy room. "Take that, you beast!"

His heart still racing, Greg stared in amazement at the sight before him. Jack stood on a chair, towering over a large stuffed dragon and holding a plastic sword. Denise wore a princess hat and lay behind the dragon, ostensibly its prisoner. Jack closed the faceplate on his toy knight's helmet and jumped down on top of the animal. "That's the end of you!" he cried, jabbing the green monster with fierce thrusts of his sword.

"What are you doing?" Greg exclaimed. He did not know whether to be amused or horrified by the play display of violence.

Jack continued his fight. "I'm saving the princess from the nasty dragon! He caught her and put her in his cave. He made her lie down on the floor all morning and wouldn't let her play."

Greg shot Denise another glance. She lay quite still with ashen face, seeming to fill her role well. On closer look, she appeared to be shaking. "Are you OK?" Greg asked.

"I don't feel so good. My tummy hurts. Jack scared me."

Greg heard a few footsteps clicking down the hallway. Theresa entered the toy room. "What's going on?" she asked, adjusting her earrings. With a smart cobalt pants suit, she was already dressed for church. "How did Jack scare you?" she continued.

"I felt tired so I lay down behind the dragon. Then Jack started yelling at me and the dragon."

"I wasn't yelling at her, just the dragon!" Jack defended himself. "She was his prisoner. He wouldn't let her go."

"Did you see anything?" Theresa turned to Greg.

"I heard someone yell, 'Shut up, or I'm going to kill you.' I didn't know it was just play, so I ran in here."

"We don't allow our children to talk that way, play or not." Theresa turned to the children, "Do we, kids?"

Jack murmured a dejected, "No," but Denise remained silent. While the room waited for a response, Denise suddenly sprang from the floor and headed for the doorway on the other side of the room. Just at the entrance to the kitchen, she stopped short and projectile vomited. Greg winced at the splattering sound on the marble-tiled floor.

Theresa hurried over towards Denise to the tune of Jack's comments, "Gross! I'm out of here."

Greg stood feeling helpless and paralyzed at the other end of the room. "Do you need any help?" he offered tentatively.

"Could you grab me some paper towels, please," Theresa called from a crouched position next to Denise. "On second thought, never mind. You're not used to this, and I'm not going to put you through it. Why don't you go ahead and get dressed."

Greg's flesh wanted to jump on the invitation, but his conscience triumphed. "If I'm going to stay here for a while, I want to earn my keep. Let me get the paper towels. Do you want some wet ones?"

"That'd be great, Greg. Thanks. Just watch where you step."

"Mommy, what if I throw up at church?" Denise whimpered.

"Do you think you are going to be sick again, sweetie?" Theresa asked. Denise nodded in the affirmative.

"Hey, Theresa, I can stay home with her," suggested Greg. "If you can clean her up first," he added sheepishly.

Theresa hesitated. "OK, Greg. Thanks again. I'll change her into her pajamas and set her up with a DVD and some soda water. Hopefully she won't throw up again."

In his thoughts Greg echoed Theresa's sentiment. *Yes, hopefully she won't throw up again!* He headed for his room to get dressed and wondered at the change in himself. *Perhaps I'm beginning to see the speck on my nose after all!*

The feminine figure crouching amidst the garden plants held Greg's attention. From the easy chair in the guest room, he followed her movement up and down the rows of bushes, devoid of any fruit or flowers in the middle of winter. The vivid hues of her multi-colored sun dress were enhanced by the afternoon rays and nicely complemented the darker tone of her skin. As she turned her face toward the house, her long black hair floated just a moment behind. Her dark sparkling eyes seemed to meet Greg's gaze for an instant, although he was certain that he was imperceptible amidst the shadows inside the house.

Soon afterward, the aroma of cumin wafted into his room from the kitchen. Lured by the prospect of a late lunch, Greg arose and followed his nose down the hall. As he passed by the dining room, he met Theresa coming down the hall with a tray of taco shells. "We're going to eat in the informal dining room today," she said with short breath.

"Can I help you, Theresa? You seem short-winded. Are the tacos made out of lead today?" he joked.

"No, it's just a heavy platter," she groaned, handing the platter over to Greg. The tray was thick and plated with Mexican silver. "Ana María is back. She made tacos for us today."

Greg received the tray and set it down carefully on the green runner stretching lengthwise across the table. Matching green place mats sat in front of each of the ten chairs around the dark cherry table, polished to almost mirror-like finish. The dark paneled room with its intricate molding work around the baseboards and ceiling struck Greg as anything but informal. On the opposite side of the room, another doorway opened onto a hall leading to the formal dining room, which remained hidden behind closed doors. Greg was curious to see the décor in the formal dining room but had not yet taken the opportunity to peek inside.

Greg began to return to the kitchen to help bring the next dish out. He gasped inaudibly when he found himself eye to eye with the woman from the garden. "¡Hola!" she greeted. When he hesitated to answer, she continued, "I am Ana María Astuza. You must be Gregory. Please take the vegetables." She offered him a business-like smile and handed him a bowl of diced tomatoes and shredded lettuce. Then she hastily returned to the kitchen. Greg brought the taco fixings to the table, wondering how she had managed to prepare the meal in the short time since he had seen her in the garden.

Theresa joined him in the dining room. "So you met Ana María. She's a great help to us, tending to our gardens and taking care of some household chores. She just returned from visiting her family in Mexico. I'm so grateful for the help." She paused to set down a ceramic sombrero adorned with guacamole, sour cream and pico de gallo. "She's been away for a while, and it's been very tiring without her," she added. "We do have a big house to keep up."

"I noticed, Sis," Greg smiled. "You and Jared have done very well for yourselves."

"I suppose we have," she chuckled. "Still I find it odd that we hire someone to tend to our gardens, when Jared runs his own orchard and nursery business."

Ana María entered the room with the taco meat and the children in tow. "Lunch is served. Let us pray." The three adults and two children stood behind their chairs as Ana María made the Sign of the Cross and led the blessing of the meal, to which Jack added his standard, "God is great, God is good, and we thank him for this food." All answered, "Amen," and then sat down to eat. As Ana María passed the taco shells to Greg, their fingers briefly touched, sending an electric pulse up Greg's arm. She winked at him and he nearly fell out of his chair.

Greg sat outside on the patio enjoying the afternoon sun. To his right he could see into the kitchen through a large glass window. He had waited for Ana María to finish cleaning the dishes before he had ventured out onto the patio. He would not have been able to relax knowing that her deep dark eyes could wander across his shoulders as he sat studying the countryside.

A strong and unusual attraction had caught him unaware from his first sighting of Ana María. He judged her to be just a few years younger than himself. Although her hands were adorned with several rings, none seemed to be suitable as an engagement or wedding ring. Furthermore, the children had referred to her as "Señorita Astuza" rather than "Señora." His initial attraction to Lisa had been sudden but playful, in contrast to his attraction to Joanna, which had grown slowly with time. However, the emotions flooding him over Ana María seemed irrational yet sobering in their intensity. He felt almost morosely pulled towards her, although the only things he knew about her were that she could cook and she could pray.

The sound of a door closing softly stirred him from his pondering. Theresa approached and sat across the table from him. "Penny for your thoughts," she offered.

"I'd be willing to give *you* money if you could help me straighten out my thoughts," he challenged.

"Try me," she responded.

"Oh, I don't know," Greg trailed off, not certain what to say. The two sat in silence for a few moments. "Do you ever wish you could know more than you do?"

"Sure, Greg. That's why I get the newspaper and read my books."

"No, what I mean is, do you ever wish you could know more than you can find out from a book? Things that aren't written down or broadcast on the news."

"Well, when I pray, sometimes God shows me things I didn't know. Sometimes about myself, sometimes about Himself or even other people."

Greg gathered the strength to bring up a painful memory. "I visited a medium once. Actually, more than once. You know, with the Tarot cards and everything."

"Oh Greg, why on earth did you do that?"

"I wanted to know things. I wanted to know what would happen in the future, and what was happening around me. I especially wanted to know about Lisa and about my career. Something just came over me, and I went."

"Did you find out what you wanted to know?" Theresa asked with some trepidation.

"Not anything that I wanted to know. It was a disaster. Death and misery, that's all I found. I was looking for comfort and assurance."

"You know why, Greg? There are some things we are not meant to know. Especially about the future. We can only take one day at a time. We're not meant to handle tomorrow before its time, just today."

"You mean we can't plan for the future?" Greg objected.

"No, we should plan but we shouldn't worry. Were you motivated to know the future so you could plan, or was it out of fear?" questioned Theresa.

"I was definitely worried. I was practically paralyzed with fear. It made it difficult for me to fight back to save my job. And to save my life."

"What do you mean?"

"After consulting with the medium, instead of peace I found chaos. And in despair, I wished to escape any way I could, even through death. There was a time when I would have welcomed it."

"And now?" Theresa asked, eyes wide with concern.

"Now I want to live at least long enough to find out if my life can be salvaged. I think it can."

"Of course it can, Greg. Yes, with God's help, you will have a better life than you ever dreamed possible."

"I hope so," Greg mused wistfully. "I'm going to try to do my part."

Sunday morning burst bright and early through Greg's guest room window. During the week he had tried to break the habit of sleeping in late. Yet every night he and Theresa had sat reading books or conversing until all hours. Through their discussions, Theresa had convinced Greg to attend Mass with them. In the meantime, she prayed that no excuse would arise to hinder his attendance yet again.

Dressed in a navy blue suit and maroon striped tie, Greg joined the children in the kitchen at the breakfast table. Theresa stood sipping a glass of water near the sink. "You're going to be overdressed, but that's OK. I like it," she smiled.

"Aren't you going to eat breakfast with us?" Greg suggested.

"No, thanks. I fast before Mass. I guess you don't remember the rules."

"I don't think I ever learned the rules well enough to remember them. Once I had squirmed my way through Confirmation class, I considered myself graduated from church."

"Something will come back. Don't be nervous."

"Who's nervous?" Greg joked, shaking his glass.

A few minutes later, Theresa drove the foursome in her brown SUV away from town. "We usually go to a small Mexican church a few miles west of here. The 8 AM Mass is in Spanish and the 10 AM is in English. I thought we should go to the English Mass, since it's your first time in a while," she teased.

In the distance Greg caught sight of a darkly-clad woman walking on the side of the road. As they approached, Theresa slowed down. "It's Ana María," she announced. "Sometimes we see her walking to Mass." Theresa pulled up and rolled down the window. "Hi Ana María. Can I offer you a ride?"

Without speaking, Ana María smiled somberly at Theresa through her black veil and climbed into the back seat between the two children. Greg marveled at her apparel and wondered whether she had been widowed at an early age, or whether her outfit was a nuance of Mexican culture. Silence prevailed in the car until they arrived at a quaint adobe-style church. When Ana María stepped out of the vehicle, she whispered a "Gracias" and proceeded into the church. Greg followed Theresa inside. Denise held Theresa's hand while Jack took Greg's.

The interior of the church was somewhat dark, but when Greg's eyes adjusted after a moment, he was spellbound. The walls were decorated with frescoes of New Testament scenes, and the ceiling was painted with Old Testament figures, which Greg recognized as Noah, Abraham and Moses. In between the bas-relief frescoes, sunlight streamed through intricate stained glass windows, splashing multicolor swaths of light among the rows of pews.

Greg followed Theresa's lead by dipping his hand into the holy water font and making the Sign of the Cross. Despite the cool temperatures outside, Greg was pleased to find the water crisp and refreshing. He felt as if he were cleansing himself, even if ever so slightly. Following Theresa up the aisle, he noted that Ana María sat in the very last pew in the back of the church. She stared blankly ahead and did not seem to notice the entourage passing by. Jack tugged Greg into a pew, and he turned to see the magnificent altar in the front of the church. Although they sat in the fifth row, the first rows were almost empty so that Greg had an unobstructed view of the sanctuary.

Greg followed the Mass intermittently in the missalette. He studied the statues, the gilded tabernacle, the marble altar, and the inscriptions and paintings behind the altar. He followed the congregation's lead in sitting, standing or kneeling at the proper times. Much of the Mass felt vaguely familiar, and he could recite several of the prayers along with the parishioners. After the Scripture readings, he tried to listen to the words of explanation and encouragement from the priest, but he found his mind wandering to myriad topics.

Joining the others on his knees, Greg realized that the Eucharistic Prayer had begun. The old church was unusual in that there were no kneelers, and as he thought about the feeling of the hard stone floor against his knees, the sound of a small brass bell chime caught his attention. Looking up to the altar, Greg saw the priest holding the round Communion host in his hands. Light from an untraced source illuminated the host, causing it to gleam as if it were a heavenly body descended from the sky. Overwhelming feelings of God's presence washed over him. For several unmeasured moments, he lost himself in the wonder of God's love for him. Greg did not feel a need to respond with words, but he knew for the first time that the possibility of his returning God's love was within his reach. He resolved to find out what his own part was, and to take the first steps to do it.

In the spiritual realm, unseen by the worshipping mortals, a beam of light radiated from the Eucharist to Greg's heart, where it flooded him with grace and mercy. A crack formed in the hard concrete shell around his heart, and a glowing light could be seen coming from inside as God began to take up residence.

The first candle of holiness had been lit, but the forces of evil were gathering to try to extinguish it.

Chapter Seventeen

Greg brought the last of the lunch dishes to the kitchen sink. The family had chosen to eat outside, the spicy salsa making up for whatever heat the afternoon sun lacked. Still in his church attire, Greg excused himself to change his clothes.

Unraveling his tie, Greg heard the sound of a male voice through his bedroom door. The pitter-patter of feet accompanied by shouts of "Daddy!" followed almost immediately. Greg slowed his pace so that the children would have ample time to get reacquainted with their father, and so that Theresa could reconnect emotionally with her husband. He opened a paperback novel he had borrowed from the sitting room. The enticement of sleep caught him unaware, and soon he nodded off.

As he slept, the events of the morning Mass danced before his mind's eye. Comforting images passed before him. A statue of Mary smiled with peace and tranquility. From the large wooden crucifix, Jesus' passionate eyes seemed to say that he understood and loved Greg. As he envisioned the priest holding up the Eucharist, the words echoed: "This is my Body, given up for you." Light emanated from the host, illuminating him in a warm bath. Fire burned in his heart as if something were being scorched away. As he looked down into his chest, he was alarmed to see only a small candle surrounded by overwhelming darkness. A figure approached in a dark robe and clasped onto his arm. Greg let out a choking cry.

Sitting up in his chair, Greg became aware of a tapping on the door, barely audible over the pounding of his heart. He glanced at his watch and realized that he had dozed for over two hours. Stiffly, he trudged over to the door and called out, "Coming!"

Greg was surprised to find the intriguing young Mexican woman at his door. "Uh, hello Ana María." When she did not respond, he continued, "I'm glad you woke me up. I was dreaming, and it was just starting to turn ugly. But I hadn't intended to fall asleep in the first place."

"No need to apologize for sleeping, Greg. I sensed that you needed to wake up."

"You...sensed it?" he stammered incredulously.

"You did cry out," she added.

"Of course," he fumbled. "Well, I'm grateful to you. Anyway, I thought you had Sundays off."

"Normally I do. But Señora Theresa asked me to come baby-sit the children for the evening. She and Señor Jared wanted to go into town for a dinner date."

Greg was puzzled at the decision to hire a babysitter while they had a live-in guest. "I'm perfectly capable of watching the children," he thought aloud.

"Of course you are," Ana María's dark eyes shimmered. "But they did not want to disturb you. We did not know how long you would be asleep. They left about twenty minutes ago. I think they wanted to go to the cinema before dinner."

The appeal of dinner and a movie was suddenly so overwhelming that Greg spoke before he could think. "Perhaps sometime you can show me a good restaurant and movie theater." His face became awash with crimson.

"That has all been arranged, even tonight. I will cook you a good dinner. We can find a good movie. Señor has cable, you know."

"I know." Greg was relieved that Ana María did not seem offended by his forwardness. She flashed him an enchanting smile and excused herself to the kitchen.

The children chattered away over dinner so that Greg and Ana María were barely able to exchange more than a few sentences with each other. Greg found himself wondering what would happen after dinner. Their earlier conversation left him doubting whether they had truly set up a date for themselves, or whether the whole idea required confirmation. Suddenly Greg realized that he had been asked a question. "I'm sorry, what was that?" he returned to the three faces awaiting his response.

"What would you like to do after dinner, Señor Greg?" Ana María repeated.

Greg thought that the title "Señor Greg," although charming, hardly seemed an appropriate antecedent to a date.

"I was hoping to watch a movie," he put forth tentatively.

"Oh, let's watch Jingle Mouse!" Denise exclaimed.

"No, Jingle Mouse is for babies," Jack retorted. "Rescue Bears is much cooler! I just got the latest DVD. Let's watch that!"

Greg surveyed the room and found the idea agreeable to Denise. He was unable to read Ana María's expression, which was directed toward her plate. Feeling relieved that the decision seemed to have been made for him, he agreed, "OK, then I guess it's Risky Bears. I mean Rescue Boars." Jack and Denise chortled at his joke. "Risk Your Beers? Oh, I mean Rusty Boards!"

"No, Rescue Bears! Rescue Bears!" Denise and Jack shouted in unison, giggling.

"OK, Rescue Bears it is. Then bedtime. I can pick another movie after that." Greg shot a glance at Ana María. She smiled ambiguously and stood up to clear the table. In Theresa's absence, Greg took her place in encouraging the children to bring their own plates to the sink. He followed suit.

A few minutes later, Jack helped Greg search through the children's DVD collection for the selected movie while Ana María finished popping popcorn in the microwave. The enticing aroma preceded her as she brought out heaping bowls of the hot buttery treat into the family room. The children sat on the floor while the two adults reclined in comfort behind them.

"I'm so excited. I've never seen this movie before," Greg joked quietly to Ana María.

"I can sense that," she joked back.

"What else do you sense, Ana María?"

"You're making fun of me," she protested lightly.

"No, not at all. It's just that you seem to have this innate sense of what people are thinking or feeling."

"True," she said. "It is a gift from God. I thank the Lord for it. He helps me to see in the spiritual realm. You know what I mean?"

"Not exactly. Tell me." Greg was fascinated.

Ana María leaned in closer. "You can see a lot with the eyes of faith," she confided in hushed tones. "Alma. Corazón. Soul. Heart."

"What does God tell you about me?" he whispered.

Ana María's eyes darted around the room as if she were looking for someone. She pointed to the children and then motioned for him to step outside with him. They exited through the adjoining playroom into the corridor leading past Greg's room to the outside. A porch skirted the house in front of a bay window so that they could see the children and the movie inside.

"I feel a great sadness in you, and yet some hope. You have been through something terrible, but I do not know what."

Greg related the events of the past many months, starting with the disappearance of the money at work and Lisa's death. Although Ana María's compassionate expression and comforting words put him at ease, he chose not to disclose anything about his dabbling in the occult or his trip to the roof. He did not mention Joanna at all.

"And now I find myself here," he ended his synopsis.

"Your soul has endured great distress," Ana María commented. "You need prayer of healing."

"What?"

"You need to lift the burden of this curse against you. Someone has invoked black magic against you. You need to heal. You need the white magic to heal you so you can be whole again."

"You mean the light?" Greg asked, contemplating the image of the shining Eucharist.

"Yes, the light. We must pray. But now is not the time. Look, soon Señor and Señora will be home. We must go inside."

Suddenly breathless, Greg followed Ana María back into the house. Their absence appeared unnoticed by the children. As Greg sat down in the chair, he shivered. Whether it was due to the chill outside or to something moving inside him, he did not know.

Moments later the voices of Theresa and Jared floated in through the playroom from the kitchen. Greg rose to greet them while the others remained seated.

"Welcome back, Jared," Greg stretched out his hand. "I trust you had a good night out with my sister."

"Hope I didn't break her curfew," Jared winked as he extended his hand in return. "May I call upon her again sometime?"

"How do I know your intentions are honorable, son?" Greg joked.

"I promise I won't lay a hand on her until we're married, sir."

"Gentlemen, please!" Theresa interrupted. Blushing, she changed the subject. "How did the children do? Are they still up?"

"We're watching a movie. Come see," Greg offered. The trio exited the kitchen into the playroom and then stepped up into the family room addition. Cartoon characters continued to dance on the television screen, unaware that their audience had fallen asleep. Jared squatted down and picked up both children, one in each arm. He carried them off to their bedrooms with Theresa close behind. "Goodnight, Greg."

"Good night Theresa. Good night, Jared." He surveyed the room. Ana María was nowhere in sight.

"Gin!" Greg slammed his cards down triumphantly on the kitchen table. "Read 'em and weep!"

"You sure are on a winning streak! That's at least four in a row today," Theresa lamented lightheartedly. "I've been losing to you all week!"

The creak of the patio door caught their attention. A sweaty Jared huffed over to the sink and poured himself a glass of water. "Must be nice to be able to play games all day long," he muttered.

Taken aback by his implicit accusation, Greg did not know how to respond. Theresa spoke up. "Having a rough day, Jared?"

"Real rough. I don't want to go into it. What do you all care anyway? Go back to your game."

"No need to take out your frustrations on us, Jared," Theresa protested. "Greg is on vacation and I..." she trailed off.

Although Greg wondered how Theresa had planned to finish her sentence, he decided to speak up. "We'll gladly stop our game to help you out if we can," he offered. "Just let me know anytime you need something. I never intended to become a freeloader."

Jared's mood visibly softened. "I'm sorry. I just got so frustrated and so I took it out on the nearest people," he apologized. "At least I ran into you two first instead of the kids."

"What has gotten you so upset?" Theresa asked.

Jared frowned. "My bookkeeper was totally incompetent. I fired him when he came in on Monday. He hadn't done anything the whole time I was away on the business trip. Now I'm way behind, and I have to do it all myself."

Greg saw an opportunity to make himself useful. "Why don't you let me help you out? I'd be happy to work on your books for you. I've got the qualifications."

Waving his hands, Jared declined. "No thanks, Greg. It's better if I do it. No need to get you involved in this. After all, you are on vacation."

"Longest vacation of my life," Greg mused. "Believe it or not, I miss work. I would love to have something concrete to do."

After a moment of hesitation, Jared responded. "It's a tempting offer, but I have to decline. Thanks anyway."

"Keep it in mind. The offer still stands."

"I will." Jared poured himself another glass of water and returned to the outside.

"I'm sorry for that, Greg," Theresa apologized once Jared was out of sight. "Don't feel obligated to offer any help. Jared is a very private, very self-sufficient businessman. I was surprised when he hired an accountant. I think he only did it because I started complaining about his late hours. I usually try to hold my tongue, but he was coming to bed after I was asleep. This went on for weeks before I said anything. After that, he hired a man named Ulsta to help out. He lasted almost a year. His getting fired was news to me."

"I am serious about helping out," Greg asserted earnestly. "I don't know how long I want to stay here, or how long you want me to stay. But I could certainly justify my existence better if I were gainfully employed by the head of the household. I would welcome the opportunity."

"I'll work on Jared. Maybe he will reconsider," Theresa proposed.

"Now about you claiming to 'hold your tongue!' If this is so, then you truly have changed! I've never known you to stifle any of your opinions," he jested.

"I've learned that sometimes it is better to remain silent and appear wise than to open my mouth and show how foolish I really am. I've also learned to respect my husband's authority over his own life. I can gently prod and suggest, but I cannot make him do anything against his own will. It's futile to try, and it brings nothing but frustration."

"You have changed!" exclaimed Greg. "Now I want to ask you about something else. It may be none of my business, but I am your brother so I need to try to find out. You excused me to Jared because I was on vacation, and you started to excuse yourself but you did not give the reason. Is something wrong with your health?"

Theresa's expression betrayed the truth Greg had discovered. "I am sick, Greg," she admitted, "but the doctors are not sure what it is. I think it may be chronic fatigue syndrome. Jared doesn't believe in that."

Greg rubbed his forehead in an attempt to jog his memory. "I have heard of this disease. Apparently it's very hard to diagnose."

"True. In reality, the diagnosis is by process of elimination. I've had numerous tests. It's not cancer. It's not Lyme disease or AIDS or anything like that. It's not my heart. I've just been very tired for a few years now."

"And you bruise easily?"

Surprise ran across Theresa's face. "Yes, I do."

"I noticed a bruise on your arm and another on your face when I first got here. I was afraid that Jared was beating you."

Theresa immediately became flustered and wrung her hands. "Oh no, no. Nothing like that. What an awful thing to think! How could you say that?"

"I'm sorry, Theresa. You are my sister, and I have to watch out for you."

"I appreciate that, Greg. No, I just go so tired. I'm glad to have some extra help. Ana María used to come once a week to clean and tend the garden. But when I started feeling sick, we hired her full-time. It seems she's here more and more," Theresa sighed.

"How did you find her?"

Theresa refreshed their glasses of iced tea as she began her story. "When I was pregnant with Denise, I suffered from severe hemorrhaging. I was sent to a specialist in high-risk pregnancies."

"I didn't know about that," Greg furrowed his brow.

"Jared and I decided to keep the matter to ourselves. He didn't even want to let anyone know we were pregnant until we were fairly certain that the baby would live. I wanted to let people know, but we waited until I was about five months along."

"I do recall the announcement being late."

"Anyway, the specialist's name was Gabina Perez. Over time we became very good friends. Gabina was a very faithful woman, and she offered to pray with me in the office. We had some very good talks, and she was instrumental in deepening my conversion. She was able to answer a lot of the difficult questions I had. For those questions she couldn't answer, she encouraged me to talk to a priest. She even arranged for a meeting with her own pastor."

"What type of difficult questions?"

"For example, I had a lot of trouble understanding the role of Mary and the saints. Some people accuse Catholics of worshipping Mary and praying to idols. I knew that wasn't true, but I didn't know how to explain it."

"How do you explain it?" Greg asked.

"When Mary and John stood at the foot of the cross, Jesus looked lovingly at them and said to Mary, 'Woman, behold, your son.' Then to John he said, 'Behold, your mother.' John is often called the Beloved Disciple rather than by his name. When Jesus gave Mary to John as his mother, he gave her also to us all. We are all beloved disciples. And when we honor Mary, we honor Jesus too. For one way to honor someone is to honor his parents."

"I don't remember that from CCD," Greg admitted.

"And as for statues, we certainly don't worship them. They are not idols. They are merely tools to help us focus. Just like when we want to think about a friend or family member, we might go look at their picture on the wall or in our wallet."

"What about praying to saints? Don't we only pray to God?" Greg challenged.

"You can ask a person to pray for you, can't you?"

"Of course," Greg replied.

"Praying to a saint is really just asking a person in Heaven to pray for you or someone else.

But the person in Heaven doesn't have earthly cares to distract them anymore."

"So we can also ask them things? Call on them to appear like at a séance?" Greg questioned.

"No, not at all. We don't try to conjure up the dead. We don't ask them to tell us the future. This is forbidden. Jesus told us to focus on doing right today and trust tomorrow to him."

"I have a lot to learn," Greg mused.

"So did I. And I have a lot to learn still. Gabina has been so helpful. I wanted to do something for her in return. The opportunity came when I found out that her cousin had lost her job. The day care where she had been working closed after a dreadful fire. Thankfully no one was hurt. Jared and I had already talked about hiring someone, so I told Gabina I would offer her cousin the job."

"And the cousin was Ana María," Greg surmised.

"Yes. At first Gabina was very hesitant. I think she was afraid that I felt obligated. But I assured her that I had been considering hiring someone for quite some time. So she agreed, and the rest is history, I guess."

Sunday morning began with a knock at the door. Staggering to his feet, Greg trudged across the room. Still rubbing the sleep out of his eyes, he murmured, "Who is it?"

"It's Jake! Time to get up, Uncle Greg. You don't want to be late for church!"

"OK, thanks," Greg managed. More than anything his body wanted to return to bed, but he had set his mind to investigate the merits of attending Mass. Remembering his resolution, he mustered up the energy to shower and dress himself.

Several minutes later Greg joined Jake and Denise at the kitchen table. They had begun their second bowl of sugar cereal as Greg poured himself a glass of juice. Theresa hurried into the kitchen to check on the children.

"Won't you sit down?" Greg invited. "There's plenty of time before we have to leave."

"No, thanks. I don't eat at all before Mass. I like to feel hungry at church. It reminds me of my need for God," she explained as she hurried back down the hallway.

Inadvertently flying in the face of Theresa's words, Jared entered the kitchen a few moments later and sat down for a bowl of cereal.

Still in a sleepy fog, Greg found himself in the back seat of the family vehicle, speeding towards church. Again they passed the darkly-clad Ana María, her outfit in stark contrast to the dazzling white or bright colors she typically wore around the McAllen estate. Jared slowed down and offered the woman a ride. She nodded with a faint smile and climbed in between Jared and Theresa in the front seat. At the church, she took her usual seat in the back while the family proceeded towards the front of the church. Greg resisted an urge to sit with Ana María in the obscurity of the back.

After the Scripture readings, a swarthy priest ascended to the podium for the homily. He began with a "Buenos días," followed by a torrent of unfamiliar Spanish words. Greg shot Theresa a quizzical look. She leaned over to softly explain that the man was a priest visiting from Mexico. "I can fill you in on the meaning later," she whispered.

The prayers seemed slightly more familiar than they had the previous week. Greg looked forward to the consecration, hoping for another vision of light emanating from the Eucharist. However, when the priest held up the host, this time Greg's eyes saw only a piece of bread. But in his heart he heard the words, "It is more than it appears." Repeating the words inwardly brought great unexplainable comfort.

After Mass Greg lingered behind as the family exited the church. As Theresa engaged in a conversation with an elderly couple, Greg searched the faces of the parishioners for Ana María. The largely Mexican crowd was alive with happy smiles and quiet laughter. Although most of the dialogue was in Spanish, Greg could sense the joy and reverence of the congregation. It was entirely inviting. Across the patio outside, Greg caught a glimpse of a woman in dark garb resembling Ana María. Pushing his way through the crowd as politely as he could manage, he rushed to follow the figure as she disappeared around a corner. He ran in pursuit down a path along the side of the church. Rounding the building, the walkway spilled out into a small paved area surrounded by neatly-spaced mesquite trees. He peered down each of the rows to no avail. The figure had disappeared among the dark twisted branches of the low-growing mesquite.

Chapter Eighteen

"Does your offer still stand?"

Greg rose to greet Jared as he entered the sitting room. He put down his book and asked for clarification. "Do you mean the offer to help with your accounting?"

"Yes," the admission seemed difficult to utter. "I'm totally swamped with work. I fear I may lose some customers because I don't have enough time to devote to them. If I could solicit some help, especially with tax season coming up, it would be a real load off my mind."

"I'd be glad to help," Greg smiled. "Can we start today?"

Jared smiled tentatively. "Let me clear out an office space for you. When I hired that lazy good-for-nothing Craig Ulsta, I cleared out the front office on the north end of the house, off the side parlor. I retired to the back office down the hallway. Ulsta worked out of the front office. Although to actually say 'Ulsta worked' is somewhat of a farce."

"Can I help you with getting the office cleared out?" Greg suggested.

"Sure, let's go."

In the ensuing weeks, Greg began to feel more like a contributing member of the family rather than a guest. Although Jared offered to pay Greg, he declined any salary, citing his living expenses as adequate compensation. Not being on the payroll also gave Greg the opportunity to take off once or twice a week without guilt. Although McAllen Orchards had a large customer base, Greg could not find enough work to occupy him full-time. Jared's preference was to run a one-man show, and it was apparent that he had only accepted Greg's offer out of desperation.

Working for his brother-in-law was much less stressful than working for Chuck Hollis at Providential Insurance had been. Although both men had a hands-off management style, Greg felt that Jared valued his opinion more than Hollis ever had. As a self-made man, Jared had acquired the skill of listening to all with an open mind. In several instances, Greg found opportunities to apply his large-corporation experience to Jared's benefit. At the same time, Greg found himself learning new ways of working effectively that would not have been accepted at Providential Insurance.

Sitting at the kitchen table for an afternoon snack, Greg munched on a tray of nachos while catching up on the latest headlines. At the sound of someone entering the kitchen, Greg looked up from the newspaper to see Theresa carrying a small package. "This came for you today," she informed him.

Greg reached eagerly for a small box wrapped in brown paper. "I wasn't expecting anything," he admitted, examining the writing. "It's from my friend Joe back in Connecticut." Greg noted to himself that he had not said, "back *home* in Connecticut" and wondered if the omission was significant.

"Open it!" urged Theresa eagerly.

Greg obliged. First he pulled out a handwritten note and began to paraphrase. "It's an item I apparently left on my trip out West last year. I called the hotel a few days afterward and reported it missing. It eventually turned up, and it's taken this long for it to catch up with me. Joe apologizes for opening the package without asking first."

"What could it be?" wondered Theresa.

Greg already knew. He finished opening the package and held up the contents. A fashionable two-tone watch sparkled in the sunlight streaming in through the kitchen windows. Greg's voice crumbled as he explained, "It's the watch Lisa gave me for our last Christmas together." Theresa put a comforting hand on Greg's shoulder as he fought off tears. He clutched the watch tightly and bit his lip.

"Oh, Greg," Theresa offered, loading the words with a heavy dose of compassion.

Greg reached up and gave Theresa's hand a squeeze. "I think I need to be alone for a little while," he managed, standing up and exiting the room. Theresa remained in the kitchen and prayed for his consolation.

On a bright Saturday morning, Greg awoke with a yearning to explore. The sunlight slipping through the blinds beckoned him. He arrived at the breakfast table with a plan in mind.

"It's such a beautiful day. It would be a shame to waste it inside," he put forth.

"What are you suggesting?" Theresa shot him an inquisitive look. Denise and Jack cast eager eyes upon him.

"It would be a perfect day for you to show me around the city. I haven't been to downtown San Antonio for a long time."

Denise and Jack piped up, "Oh, please, let's go!"

Jared and Theresa exchanged glances, trying to read each other without betraying their thoughts to the children. "Can you break away for the day?" Theresa pleaded. "After all, it is the weekend."

Jared conceded, "Sure, let's all go in for the day. It will be fun. I haven't been downtown in a while myself."

Just then Ana María arrived with a large serving dish of scrambled eggs and a side dish of salsa.

"Ana María, perhaps you can come along too," Greg suggested.

Greg barely noticed Theresa's scowl out of the corner of his eye. The children immediately shouted their approval of the idea. "You're welcome to come along, Ana María," Jared offered. "We can fit everyone in the van. You can help us keep track of the children. They tend to get lost in the marketplace."

Theresa remained silent on the matter. Greg made a mental note to ask about her tacit objection at a later time.

Two hours later, Jared parked the van in a downtown lot with numbered spaces. A large yellow box contained slots corresponding to each number, and Jared handed Jack a few bills to stuff into the appropriate slot. "That will be good for the whole day," he remarked.

Jared and Theresa led the way while Ana María and Greg brought up the rear with the children in between. Greg noticed Theresa take Jared's hand as they walked. Soon they approached the familiar shape of the Alamo, seemingly out of place in the bustle of downtown San Antonio. Hollywood had conditioned most visitors to expect an encounter with a lonely old structure amid barren, dusty scrubland. Over the centuries, the open spaces had given way to encroaching skyscrapers and traffic-laden streets. Since 1724 the mission had stood in its current location a short distance from the San Antonio River. On the way inside, a guide reminded them that the Alamo was still a shrine and therefore they should conduct themselves with reverence. Theresa translated this to the children as: "Don't talk. Don't run. Stay close to us."

Inside the Alamo, Denise took Jared's hand while Jack took Theresa's. Suddenly alone, Ana María and Greg browsed among the displays of historic artifacts. Glass cases contained swords, uniforms and other items from the famous 1836 battle in the Republic of Texas' war for independence from Mexico.

"I can feel the spirits of the dead all around me," Ana María whispered, leaning toward Greg. "Almost like you can touch their souls. I wonder what they could tell us. They have seen the face of El Señor and the face of El Diablo."

Ana María's words were both captivating and eerie. "Certainly a lot of men died here," he mused uncomfortably. "Not one Texan solider escaped with his life."

"You can pray to hear them," she uttered in hushed tones. "They speak to your heart."

"I don't think I want to listen right now," Greg's flesh began to crawl. "How do you know they're all in Heaven?"

"Not all are," Ana María answered. Greg stared at her with wide eyes full of horror. "I'm sorry," she apologized. Her excited countenance visibly softened. "I don't want to make you uneasy. What I mean is that it's just like praying to the saints. Sometimes you can hear God through them."

To Greg's relief, Theresa's sudden approach offered a change in topic. "Time to head for the River Walk. Jared is ready for lunch. Are you hungry?"

"Famished," Greg exclaimed. "Let's go."

A few moments later, the group stood up as the amicable hostess called, "Jared, party of six." They meandered down a concrete aisle past quaint tables hidden under a sea of brightly colored umbrellas. As they studied their menus, small boats motored leisurely by on the San Antonio River. Over the hum of the engines, Greg caught a few words as the tour guides on the boats recounted the history of San Antonio and the River Walk.

"After lunch, let's go to El Mercado!" Jack suggested with enthusiasm. "I want to buy some armadillos for my collection."

"Armadillos?" Greg jovially raised one eyebrow.

"Jack collects little onyx figurines. Armadillos are his favorite. They are imported from Mexico. El Mercado is supposed to be the largest Mexican marketplace outside of Mexico," Theresa related as the waitress arrived with their drinks and two bowls of chips and salsa. The conversation paused as the waitress took their lunch order.

"I recall seeing an onyx statue of the Virgin Mary in your parlor," said Greg. "It was swirled with white and tan. On first glance I thought it was marble."

"That was an anniversary gift from Jared," Theresa smiled in remembrance. "He bought it for me after my conversion," she continued.

"I didn't know what to do with her," Jared explained as color rose to his cheeks. "My parents got me in the habit of going to church as a child. When I married Theresa, she was always into some new weird cultish fad. It was a little embarrassing. When I finally got her to go to Mass, I never thought she'd grow to like it more than I do. Now I feel like *she* takes *me* to church!"

"Were you baptized again?" Greg inquired of his sister just as she stuffed a salsa-laden chip into her mouth.

"No, not at all," Theresa started to chuckle. "Once baptized, always baptized. You and I were both baptized and confirmed. No need to do it again. In fact, it's not allowed."

"Not allowed?" Greg looked at Theresa quizzically.

"Baptism and Confirmation put indelible marks on your soul. They cannot be erased. When you've been away from the Church, all you have to do is go to Confession."

"Oh, come on," Greg scoffed. "What do I need to go to Confession for?" Greg realized that suddenly the conversation seemed to be aimed at him. "I can just tell God I'm sorry. I don't need to have a priest translate it. Or does God only speak Latin?"

"That's not fair," Theresa frowned.

"What's Latin?" Denise questioned.

"I'm sorry," Greg apologized to Theresa. "I just don't understand the purpose of public Confession." Turning to Denise, he added, "Latin is a dead language. That means no one speaks it anymore."

"Frankly, neither do I," Jared added through a mouthful of chips. "I mean, I don't really get Confession either. But Theresa makes me go once a year." Then he added awkwardly, "And I don't speak Latin either."

"Why did Latin die?" Denise looked concerned.

"I'll explain in a minute, honey," Theresa softly patted Denise on the head before turning to the men. Just then the waitress returned with their plates, distributing to the children first. Theresa continued, undaunted. "First of all, Confession is private, not public. The priest would never betray anything said in the Confessional." She paused as the waitress set down a plate of soft tacos in front of her. "Secondly, sin hurts your relationship with God and with the Church. Of course God can forgive you any time, but to be at unity with the Church again, you need to confess to God and to the Church."

"And God gives you grace there," Jack piped up. "I learned it at CCD," he added proudly as the waitress brought Greg a plate of enchiladas. "Grace is a gift from God. That's what they said."

A gasp heralded a sudden crash as plate and serving tray toppled out of the waitress' hands. Ana María's meal of flautas lay plastered over the back of a man sitting at an adjacent table. The mortified waitress began apologizing profusely as she rushed to clean up the man's shirt. The man seemed inexplicably unaffected by the incident and continued eating his fajitas. All nearby conversation stopped as the diners curiously gawked at the spectacle. The middle-aged manager rushed over and apologized to the victim. He exchanged words with the waitress who motioned with hand gestures that eventually pointed to Ana María. The manager approached their table and addressed Ana María.

"My sincerest apologies for your meal. We will bring you a new one as soon as possible, free of charge."

"It won't come out of her pay, will it?" Ana María inquired, indicating the waitress.

"Don't worry about that," he assured her. "We will take it off your bill."

With the commotion dispersed, conversations were resumed, but the topic of Confession was conveniently dropped. The remainder of the meal centered on their afternoon plans. Greg noticed that Ana María sat quietly, lips moving without sound until her replacement meal arrived.

At the market, Greg wandered through the stores seeking trinkets for Denise and Jack. A collection of beautiful silver jewelry brought images of Joanna to mind. She always preferred silver to gold, claiming that silver better suited her red hair, although Greg disagreed. He suddenly ached to return home to see her. Before leaving, he had made all the necessary arrangements so that bills could be paid and other business taken care of. He had hired a neighbor from his old apartment building to vacuum and dust his apartment once a month. He had promised to check in with Joe Tropetto periodically, who also was in charge of watering his plants once a week. But he had not made any plans to contact Joanna or anyone else from Providential Insurance. In effect he had disappeared off the face of the earth, practically unreachable. As his hands ran through a swath of silver necklaces, he pictured Joanna and wondered how she was faring, and whether they would ever speak again.

A familiar voice broke his rumination. "You look troubled. I have the perfect solution," Ana María smiled. "Come, I show you."

She led him to a shelf with small yellow boxes. "Worry dolls. You take one out of the box at night, tell it your worry, and leave it by your bed or under your pillow. Then in the morning, the worry is gone." She handed him a box, which he opened. Six small dolls stared up at him.

"Cute. Are they Mexican?"

"No, actually they are from Guatemala. But the magic is the same," she winked.

A mysterious sense of déjà vu caused Greg's head to spin. "I feel like I've done this before," he thought aloud. "Maybe on a previous trip to San Antonio. But I can't remember any of the details." Ana María shrugged and smiled at him. He picked out a box for himself and one for each of the children. He then followed Ana María to the counter for the purchase. Booty in hand, the two headed to rejoin the others.

Arms folded, head bent, Greg sat on the edge of his bed and listened. Through the side door of his bedroom, a pair of muffled voices exchanged hostilities. The venom of the deeper voice was apparent even after its trip down the hall past Denise's room and through Greg's door. The other voice returned in a softer but strong soprano. The volley continued for several stressful minutes. Greg rose and began to pace back and forth on the guest room carpet. A faint knock on the door startled him. Opening the door, he cautiously peered out.

"Uncle Greg, can I stay with you for a while?" Denise looked up with pleading eyes brimming with tears.

"Let's go read a book," he suggested. Taking Denise by the hand, he led the small, frightened child down the hall toward the playroom, away from the noise. Crossing through to the family room, Greg lifted Denise onto the couch. He browsed among the titles on the children's bookshelf until he found a fairy-tale about a princess and a dinosaur. Book in hand, he took a seat next to Denise. She leaned over to rest her head against his arm.

A few pages into the story, Denise's snores informed Greg that she had drifted off. He closed the book and carefully picked up the little girl to carry her back to her room. After laying her down in her bed, he gently tucked her in and softly pulled the door shut. Without a sound he returned to his room. Opening a plastic bag on his dresser, he removed three little yellow boxes. He made a mental note not to forget to distribute the gifts to the children in the morning after Mass. Retrieving a little orange doll, he whispered a prayer, "God, please give this worry to the doll. Take away the fighting and the anxiety, especially for Denise and Jack." The little doll felt hot in his sweaty fingers as he laid it next to his bed on a night table. It was not to be a restful night.

Chapter Nineteen

Drifting off to sleep, Greg wondered whether telling worries to little dolls was harmless superstition, an appropriate form of prayer, or something disturbingly wrong. His thoughts ran back to his desert experience shortly before Lisa's death.

The mid-afternoon sun penetrated the car windows with brutal fervor. Speeding down Route 93, Greg's back was drenched with sweat while his chest shivered in the full-blast air conditioning. He had taken a few minutes to stretch his legs at Hoover Dam, and he continued to review the remarkable sights in his mind as he drove. The deafening roar of the falling water and the wind tunneling through the canyon lived on in the hum of the engine. He took up a silent conversation with himself.

What an awesome sight! It speaks of the glory of God! Greg marveled at the beauty of nature and the amazing power of the concrete structure holding back the mighty river.

But God did not create the dam. Men did! Doubts threatened to steal God's thunder and tarnish His victory in Greg's mind.

Then a wiser voice spoke out: Yes, *but God created man who built it. And He gave man the ability to form and to invent. God's glory is revealed in man and nature, and the synthesis of the two.*

Greg was astonished by the grand thoughts playing out in his head. Normally occupied with the trite and worldly, he felt refreshed by the divine. The contrast between the brashness of Las Vegas and the tranquility of the Mojave Desert struck him profoundly. *But mankind, whom God created, also made Las Vegas.*

Cutting southeast through Arizona, Route 93 transitioned Greg out of the treeless Mojave Desert to the foothills of the Cerbat Pinnacles. Patches of colorful wildflowers bloomed with urgency on rapidly drying flatlands at the base of impressive ruddy rocks reaching heavenward. The strong overhead sun bleached the shadows of the surrounding cliffs. In the distance, Greg could discern a scruff of trees climbing towards the harsh summits. Liberating his characteristically serious nature, the magnificent isolation invited him to freedom. Only the oppressive heat helped Greg resist the urge to pull to the side of the road and run through the dusty valleys with wild abandon. *Soon enough.* Up ahead, flashes of light traveled in a straight line, signaling the 16-mile stretch of highway shared by Interstate 40 and US

Route 93. A sign indicated that the town of Kingman would soon offer Greg a welcome break.

A few moments later, Greg pulled into a strip mall with an iced tea and a sandwich on his mind. Finding no close parking spots, he circled the parking lot three times before finding a vacancy at the far end of the mall. Stepping out of the car, he stretched his legs with relief. He followed a covered sidewalk as it passed a variety of stores. Halfway to the café, Greg found himself meandering through the tables of a bookstore sale that had spilled out into the walkway. Deciding to search for good reading material for his trip, he browsed the varied collection of titles. First he leafed through a selection of trashy spy novels and cheap paperbacks. Nothing appealed to him. Turning, his eyes came to rest on the gold lettering of a green hardbound book. "*New American Bible.* What could be new about a Bible?" Greg asked himself. Curious, he leafed through the pages. The paragraphs had been separated into groups with descriptive titles. One reading from 1 Samuel Chapter 28, "The Witch of Endor," caught his attention. He read:

> So he disguised himself, putting on other clothes, and set out with two companions. They came to the woman by night, and Saul said to her, "Tell my fortune through a ghost; conjure up for me the one I ask you to..."
> Then the woman asked him, "Whom do you want me to conjure up?" and he answered, "Samuel."

When the woman saw Samuel, she shrieked at the top of her voice... "I see a preternatural being rising from the earth."

"What does he look like?" asked Saul.

And she replied, "It is an old man who is rising, clothed in a mantle." Saul knew it was Samuel, and so he bowed face to the ground in homage.

Samuel then said to Saul, "Why do you disturb me by conjuring me up?"

Saul replied: "I am in great straits, for the Philistines are waging war against me and God has abandoned me. Since he no longer answers me through prophets or in dreams, I have called you to tell me what I should do."

Greg looked away from the book in astonishment, asking himself, "Where are all the *thees* and *thous*, the *hasts* and *shalts*?" The text seemed utterly readable, as good as any of the novels he had seen on the bargain table. He recalled the story of Jesus and the woman at the well, which the campus minister, Travis Grenley, had related to him on the flight to Las Vegas. Convinced that the Holy Scriptures could prove both informative and entertaining, he closed the book and tucked it under his arm. Unaccustomed to things religious, Greg squirmed at the thought of parading through the book sale with a Bible. Although the appearance of the book did not betray its identity, Greg quickly sought a large coffee table book under which he could conceal his secret holy treasure. Spying a shopping basket next to the entrance, he walked in and buried the Bible in the basket under the large book. Trying to act inconspicuous, Greg pretended to interest himself in the hobbies section before braving the counter to make his purchase.

"Just these two?" the clerk asked with a smile.

"Actually, just this one," he smiled back, pointing to the smaller green book.

"Oh, just this Bible?" The clerk turned the book about, opening and closing it several times. "I don't see a price on this Bible. Do you remember how much it was?"

"No, I don't," Greg replied while trying to hide his sudden agitation.

"Hey Bob," the clerk yelled loudly. "Check a price for me. *New American Bible.* The one with the green cover. I think it's outside."

A young high-pitched voice squeaked back, "*New American Bible*? Just a minute."

Greg's face began to flush. He chided himself for feeling embarrassed at the purchase. He was certain there must be a Scripture quote chastising his reaction. Price confirmed, Greg quickly paid and started to exit. "You want a bag for that?" the cashier called out after him.

"No, thanks," Greg replied, hoping that his denial of the bag would be worth at least partial redemption for his thwarted efforts to conceal the Bible in the first place.

Rising suddenly from the flat desert, South Mountain Park was one of several collections of peaks circling the Phoenix metropolitan area. As he traveled down Seventh Avenue, the mountains seemed utterly lifeless and dry before him. Small Mexican shops lined both sides of the wide, fairly empty roadway. Turning onto Baseline Road, he noticed that the rugged mountains looming above had many secrets to reveal. Cacti scattered the landscape, and the mid-morning sun played with the shadows of the flora amid the peaks.

After entering the park, Greg navigated his jeep up the winding mountainside road with care. A few hairpin curves required extra caution, and Greg was thankful not to meet any oncoming vehicles. The wind whipped through his hair, and Greg released one hand to check the security of the coffee he had picked up earlier in the morning at his hotel on the north side of the city.

At the top of the mountain, the roadway spilled into a parking lot seemingly halfway to heaven. Disembarking, Greg downed his coffee and picked up his backpack. A short distance away, several terraces offered nearly panoramic views of the Phoenix valley. The altitude and the magnificent beauty conspired to take Greg's breath away. A guidepost pointed out the names and distances of other peaks across the valley as well as man-made Phoenix area landmarks. Far in the distance, Greg spotted Interstate 17 rising upwards and out of sight on its course northwards towards Flagstaff and the Grand Canyon.

Toting his backpack, Greg headed down a trail amidst tall Saguaro cacti. Although he had traveled through the Southwest before, he had never experienced an area so densely forested with cacti. However, even at the heaviest concentrations, the prickly plants were spaced far enough apart that the sparse and leafless branches offered Greg no shade. As he hiked up and down the hilly summits, he marveled at the ancient patience of the Saguaro. Often requiring up to fifty years to produce even one branch, most of the surrounding plants were well older than he and yet would still outlive him.

Although the air temperature was bearable, the growing intensity of the sun began to take its toll. Setting his backpack on the ground, he retrieved a bottle of water, still cold from the hotel. Emptying it in a flash, he decided to save the second bottle for the return trip. He observed the tans and peaches of the surrounding terrain, mostly hard-packed earth rather than stony clefts. Finding a solitary boulder protruding near a cliff, Greg dragged his backpack over and sat down. After a few moments of reflection, he reached into his backpack almost mechanically and pulled out his newly purchased Bible. Out of guilt he resisted the urge to confirm the lack of any spectators. The pages fell open to 1 Corinthians Chapter 6.

Do you not know that the unjust will not inherit the kingdom of God? Do not be deceived; neither fornicators nor idolaters nor adulterers nor boy prostitutes nor sodomites nor thieves nor the greedy nor drunkards nor slanderers nor robbers will inherit the kingdom of God. That is what some of you used to be; but now you have had yourselves washed, you were sanctified, you were justified in the name of the Lord Jesus Christ and in the Spirit of our God.

The words *sodomites* and *boy prostitutes* rang shrill in Greg's ears. Regardless of the politically correct agenda he had always been fed at school and work, he had always found homosexuality repulsive. To lump these items in with fornication and drunkenness did not seem appropriate and engendered an uneasiness in the pit of his stomach. He recalled his recent conversation with Lisa and her decision not to accompany him on the trip. Although he still did not agree completely with her moral stance, he now felt relieved to have avoided the issue and the temptation altogether. In any case, it was clear to him that God had other purposes for this trip. His thoughts wandered next to the *thieves* and the *greedy*. Thinking about the missing money at work, he began to question whether it was a case of clerical error, or if criminal activities were truly to blame.

Moving onto the end of the passage, Greg tried to apply the passage to himself. Indeed, some items came close to describing what he 'used to be.' Yet he could not say how far removed he had become from these things, if at all. Certainly he did not feel washed, as the passage claimed. Neither did he know what it meant to be sanctified or justified. "I don't even really know you, Jesus, or your Spirit," he whispered aloud.

You will. It was the sound of a sudden gust of hot wind blowing up from the valley and enveloping him. In an instant it had passed through him and could not be recalled. Greg longed to replay the message, to discern whether he had truly heard anything or rather simply fallen victim to his own imagination.

"Will I?" he called out tentatively, then a moment later, loudly, "Will I!"

The only response now was the echo off the neighboring peaks.

Dry, majestic summits emerged from the flat, desert scrubland as Greg sped southeast along Interstate 10 towards Tucson. Greg could not decide whether the terrain seemed fascinatingly wicked or inspiringly holy. Greg felt called to explore to find out.

A sign indicated the turn-off for Saguaro National Park. Following the directions, Greg guided his jeep into an area of native desert flora, heavily populated by southern Arizona standards. After refreshing himself at the visitor center, he headed with map in hand towards a marked trail. In the 110-degree heat, Greg prepared himself by downing a liter of water at the start of the trail. The park ranger recommended bringing copious amounts of water and not straying from the path.

Greg browsed among the brittlebush, catclaw acacia, and the flowering feather tree. Never a naturalist, Greg was surprised by the variety of plant life in the desert, most of which he could not name. A small lizard darted in front of his feet and disappeared out of sight. The heat of an approaching high noon was intense, and Greg walked slowly. Although he was sweating profusely, his shirt remained mostly dry in the extremely arid conditions. He unburdened his backpack and consumed another liter of water. The path continued up a hill to an outlook, and Greg decided to take the opportunity to rest. Dropping his backpack, he found a flat, barren area and planted himself on the coarse, sun-bleached earth.

From his vantage point, Greg could survey a wide portion of desert valley sloping gently down from his outlook and back up to an opposing set of crags. The sun's rays burned the landscape with intense heat. After several moments, the movement of distant figures caught his eye. Far below, a man ran over a hill and disappeared into the hazy distance, blurred by the heat rising from the scorched valley floor. Two people crouched over an exposed boulder. As he watched, they remained perfectly still as if focused intently on something on the rock table between them. Suddenly one of the two, a young man, stood up and staggered backwards. Turning, he proceeded hastily to exit the scene over an opposite hill. When Greg's gaze returned to the table, the other figure was nowhere in sight.

To his amazement, Greg spotted what looked like yet another person, this time at the top of a steep rocky peak directly across the valley. The figure swayed slowly back and forth, arms sometimes extending and sometimes falling back to its sides. As he watched in horror, the figure leapt from the lifeless precipice and disappeared into the desert flora. At such a great distance, no sound was heard. Greg's heart pounded in his ears as he sat in utter disbelief at what he had just seen. Grabbing his backpack, he jumped to his feet and raced towards the cliff. He tried in vain to keep his eyes on the spot where he thought the person would have landed. With no direct path, Greg soon lost the exact location as he jumped over sagebrush and skirted small clumps of prickly pear. In a five-minute time-span, which seemed an eternity, Greg arrived at the base of the cliff with his head pounding and ears ringing. He scoured the foot of the precipice below the leaping point. Not a trace of humanity could be found. Ten minutes and one liter of water later, Greg sincerely doubted the credibility of his own witness. He determined that the vision, and perhaps the other people he had seen, had simply been mirages, the product of his heat exhaustion and the rippling of the hot air. With no water remaining, Greg decided to return to the visitor center and his jeep.

Heading back across the valley, Greg slowed his pace and kept his eyes on his footing. Soon he came to an impasse, a peninsula of earthen floor surrounded by growth too thick to penetrate. He surveyed the area and found a more suitable pathway to his east. Greg was relieved to rejoin a trail, which led him up a gentle incline toward an area close to his original overlook. The way led by a stand of remarkably tall, branchless Saguaro cacti slightly off the path. Taking a moment to pause, he studied the desert sentinels. He soon noticed that the cacti bore unusual markings. Stepping over to take a closer look, Greg gasped in shock. In each cactus, someone had carved demonic faces with writing underneath. The titles jumped out at him: GREED. LUST. PRIDE. OCCULT. BLASPHEMY. THE UNNAMED IDOL. Shuddering at the sight, Greg felt an urge to bow down in fear. Resisting, he stood motionless as he tried to break himself away. The names seemed to call to him.

"God, help me!" he gasped. One step at a time, Greg methodically lifted each foot off the ground and backed away from the six idols. A phrase came to mind that he had read earlier in the day in the Gospel of Luke:

> Behold, Satan has demanded to sift all of you like wheat, but I have prayed that your own faith may not fail; and once you have turned back, you must strengthen your brothers.

"Lord, I am prepared to do whatever it takes. I will not fail," Greg pleaded with God and himself. "I will not fail."

Greg awoke with a start, still repeating his mantra, "I will not fail." He sat up in bed and listened to the pounding of his heart. As it subsided, he assured himself item by item that he was safe, back in his sister's house, back in the guest room, with the dark blue covers and the Painted-Desert patterns on the walls. The familiar clock shouted silently at him with its timely message. His experiences in the desert had returned to the forefront of his mind with such clarity that Greg felt as if he had truly just relived it all.

As he sat in the darkness, Greg suddenly knew without a doubt what he had to do. First, he crushed the little orange worry doll on the night table under his fist. Second, he knelt down on the ground by his bed and uttered a prayer.

"Lord, I did fail you. You spoke to me and I turned away when things got tough. I relied on myself and worshipped so many things besides you. Even after you warned me, I still let myself slip away. I've never been religious, and I don't know how to start. All I do know is that I want a relationship with you." Greg paused as a tear rolled unexpectedly down his cheek. "Lord, lead me step by step. Help me not to turn away again. I cannot do it on my own. I want to do only what is right from now on. I don't know how. I will try." With a new-found peace, with a plan to talk to Theresa in the morning, and with utter exhaustion, Greg collapsed into his bed to sleep the remaining few hours of the night.

Chapter Twenty

A fierce knocking at the door startled Greg out of his sleep. The early morning sun was barely strong enough to cast any light through the small partition in his curtains. The urgency of the knocking roused Greg to his feet. Throwing on a robe over his night shorts, he ran across the room and opened the door. Ana María stood in the doorway. The concerned look on her face alarmed Greg immediately.

"What's wrong?" he pleaded.

"Is your sister. She no feel good. Jared called me to come right away. He took Theresa to the hospital. He called from the car."

"What is wrong with her?"

"Yo no sé." She continued in Spanish for several more sentences before returning to English. Greg had never heard her speak in broken English or lapse into Spanish before. He attributed it to her nerves.

"Why didn't they wake me up to help?" Greg wondered aloud.

Ana María took Greg's hand. "I'm sure they no think about it until afterward. You no have phone in your room, so they no can call you after they leave, I guess."

Coincidentally, the ringing of a phone echoed softly down the hall from the kitchen. Greg could only hear it when his door was open. He raced down the hall. "Hello?" he gasped, breathing heavily.

"Greg, it's Jared. I'm at the hospital with Theresa, but don't worry, she's fine."

"Ana María just told me. What happened?"

"They don't know for sure yet, but it was probably just a hypoglycemic attack. Low blood sugar."

"She's not diabetic, is she?" Greg questioned.

"Not as far as we know. We'll have to have some tests run, but we should be home later this afternoon. Are you OK with the kids and Ana María?"

"Yes, Jared. I can send Ana María home. It's no problem handling the children."

"No, keep her there, why don't you. Let her fix a nice brunch and then prepare something we can heat up easily for dinner." Then he added, "She can stay the night if necessary. If we need extra help."

"If you think so, Jared. But if Theresa is OK then I don't see why Ana María would have to stay."

"We'll see," Jared sounded distracted. "Listen, I have to go. The doctor is here."

"OK. Tell Theresa I love her."

"Will do."

Greg returned to his room to find Ana María sitting on the edge of his bed and looking distraught.

"Was that Jared? Everything is OK?" she asked. "Come, sit and tell me." She offered him a seat next to her on the bed. Still exhausted, he sat down.

"They think she just had an episode of low blood sugar. I suppose anyone can have an occasional attack like that."

Ana María took Greg's hands and held them tight in her lap. "I worry about her. She is always so tired." Her anxiety subsided somewhat and her good English returned. "You look tired, too, Señor Greg."

"I didn't sleep very well." The events of the previous night came flooding back. His uneasiness grew as he recalled the worry dolls that Ana María had given him. Although he felt it was meant as cute and harmless gift, he nevertheless sensed that its origins were not pure.

"Would you like me to massage you back to sleep?" Ana María offered. "I'm sure the children are still in bed. I think they were up late last night." Her warm hands reached under the collar of his robe and began caressing his shoulders. So much time had passed since he had experienced the touch of a woman, and for the moment all thoughts of worry dolls and desert dreams vanished. He sat still, lost in the enjoyment of feminine fingers working the tense muscles in his neck and upper back. A rush of moist, warm air tickled his ear as it preceded a close, soft question. "How does that feel?"

"Wonderful," he admitted.

"I can sense that something is troubling you. I have been thinking about the situation with the money at your old job. I think I can help," she whispered sultrily.

"How?" Greg turned his head in an attempt to shoot her a quizzical look.

"You know I have some special gifts," she started. "I can use them on your enemies."

"Enemies?" Greg was puzzled.

"The people who stole your money. Or stole the money that you had to pay. I can fix them."

Forgetting the massage, Greg turned fully to face Ana María. "What do you mean by 'fixing' them?"

"I mean, we can pray for the magic to come and make them give the money back."

Greg stood up. "Do you mean a curse?" he exclaimed.

"I don't like to use the word 'curse.' It's just to make them feel the pain until they give the money back and do what they should. To help you out."

Greg was outraged. "Ana María, I do not believe in placing curses or casting magic spells on anyone!"

"Oh, it works! You can believe it. I have done it a few times before. And now I have a new special charm to help me." She joined him in standing as she lifted a necklace that had been hidden under her collar. It held a dendritic crystal amulet with silver markings on the ends. "It is so powerful. You remember at the River Walk, the manager who was so mean to the waitress who dropped the tray of food?" A malicious smile filled her lips as she waited for Greg to hesitantly nod his recollection. She continued with an eerily sinister tone. "I used this amulet to curse him for his cruelty. Later he fell into the river. As he was climbing out, he sprained his back." Her eyes danced with delight.

"Ana María!" Greg exclaimed. "I will not participate in any magic spells or charms or potions or anything of the sort! And I destroyed one of the worry dolls you gave me. I plan to do the same to the rest. I think they are evil!"

Hurt and anger overtook Ana María's face. "A child's toy! They were meant to help you with your worries, and the children with theirs. You destroyed something that was meant to be beautiful. How sad, Señor Greg!"

"Their cuteness is deceiving," Greg retorted.

"The worry dolls are nothing compared to the power of a true charm."

"That power does not come from God!"

"Don't limit yourself, Señor Greg. There is power in God and there is power in magic. Why not use both? Each has its own end."

Once again, Greg was deafened by his own heartbeat. "What end is that? I don't want to be part of that end. Look at you!" Greg glanced down at himself, sweat glistening on his chest half exposed under his robe. "Look at us!" he continued. "I don't want to talk to the unknown dead. I don't want to cast spells on my enemies. I don't want to place my trust in a little piece of cloth and sticks when I don't know why it's supposed to help. And I don't want to give into my desires with you. Get out, Ana María, and leave me alone! We cannot be what I had hoped we would be. What we never talked about being but were fast becoming. I'm sorry, but I must stay away from you for my own good!"

Crimson overtook Ana María's face. "You are a foolish and selfish man, Señor Greg. I only want to help. I only want to make the most of it all. But you insult me by twisting it into some kind of devil worship! I am a religious woman. You cannot judge me! But do not worry. I will go, for today. But I will be back. I have a friendship with this family, not just a job. Tell Señor Jared you asked me to go home today. He does not have to know why. I will be back on Monday as expected. If you want to avoid me, the burden is on you. I will go about my business as usual. After a while you will leave, and I will remain. I will never go away." With a chilling look, she stormed out of the room and down the hall, calling back, "And you fix your own dinner today!"

The crunching of tires on the rocky driveway was a welcome sound. Greg sprang up from the office chair and raced out to meet the car. Jared opened the passenger door and helped Theresa out. The pallor of her face struck an uneasy chord in Greg's heart.

"How is she doing?" Greg addressed the question to Jared.

"I'm still here," Theresa answered. "Don't act as if I'm not! I've got some fight in me yet."

"I never doubted it for an instant," Greg smiled. "What did the doctors say?"

"It's related to my chronic fatigue syndrome," Theresa started.

"That's not what the doctors said," Jared interrupted.

"True," Theresa attempted to regain control of the conversation. "Those weren't their actual words, but they did say that whatever caused this episode probably is also responsible for my constant tiredness."

"When will they know something more definitive?" Greg asked as he opened the door leading inside to the parlor.

"In a few more days," Jared answered.

Once inside, Jared started to lead Theresa down the shorter of two corridors. "No, I don't want to lie down," she directed. "Let's go to the kitchen." Altering their course, Jared helped Theresa towards the longer corridor, which ran the width of the house to the kitchen. Greg followed behind.

"Let's ask Ana María to get a snack together," recommended Jared. "Theresa didn't eat anything at the hospital."

"Yes, and I am hungry," admitted Theresa. "I told Jared to run down to the cafeteria to grab a bite to eat when they took me away for some tests."

Greg fumbled over his prepared explanation. "Ana María, I sent her, I told her she could go home." Jared and Theresa both looked questioningly at Greg. Compelled to continue, he elaborated, "It seemed best. It seemed that there were other things she needed, wanted to do. So I let her go home."

"What are we going to do about dinner?" Jared exclaimed with vexation. "I thought we discussed having her stay overnight to help out!"

"I'm afraid it just didn't work out," Greg explained. "She had things to do, and I knew I could take care of the children. And dinner."

"I smell something cooking. Greg is a bachelor, after all, so he must know how to cook for himself," Theresa defended Greg. "I think that sometimes we take advantage of Ana María, always calling her up. You would think she lived with us."

"The idea has been suggested before," Jared quipped, "but was always struck down."

"I'm not incapacitated, Jared. I'm perfectly capable of taking care of the whole family. I do appreciate the extra help, though." Theresa politely broke free of Jared's hold and sat down, resting her hands squarely on the surface of the kitchen table.

"Not right now, you aren't," Jared retorted. "You need to rest. Maybe there is something to this chronic fatigue syndrome after all," he conceded.

The oven timer interrupted the conversation with a series of electronic beeps. Greg rushed over to silence it. "I made a ham and cheese casserole. It needs a few minutes to cool off." Grabbing oven mitts, he continued, "I didn't know when to expect you, so I had planned to keep it warm in the oven. The children are already fed and in their pajamas. I set them up watching a movie, but they may already be asleep."

"Were they worried?" Theresa asked with concern.

"No, I didn't even tell them you were at the hospital. I just said you didn't feel well so Daddy took you to the doctor. We had a nice day playing and reading books."

Theresa looked relieved. "I'm sorry we were gone so long. I thought we would be back in the early afternoon, or at least before dinner."

"You are back before dinner," Greg smiled. "It's just a late dinner."

"And we missed Mass today," Theresa fretted. "I felt so bad this morning, and then we spent the whole day at the hospital."

"I think God understands," Jared added. Theresa nodded her agreement. Greg's face flushed as he realized that the idea of church had completely escaped his mind. "The church will still be there next Sunday," Jared added.

With that comment, Jared excused himself to freshen up. Greg informed him that dinner would be on the table in about ten minutes. Once Jared had left, Greg took the opportunity to broach the real reason behind Ana María's dismissal for the day. He recounted her advances and her offer to place a curse on his enemies. As he related the story of the irate restaurant manager, Theresa's countenance adopted deeper shades of concern.

"And she showed me an amulet she recently acquired that supposedly has special powers. It was a long crystal with silver markings on the ends."

Theresa gasped with a look of surprised horror. "Greg, describe the amulet further," she urged. "Was it about this long?" she asked, holding her fingers about an inch apart. Greg nodded. "What did the markings look like?"

"I don't know exactly. I didn't get to see it for very long."

253

"Come with me," Theresa demanded, rising suddenly and exiting the room. With sudden haste, Theresa led Greg to the library. She rifled through the titles until she found a wicked-looking tome called "Aquarius Now." Greg recognized it from his initial browsing among the unique collection of volumes.

Greg watched his sister flip through the pages with fury until she seemed to find her objective. Without a word, she flipped the book into Greg's face, where he found himself confronted with a black-and-white photograph of the amulet Ana María had shown him. "That's it!" he exclaimed.

Theresa's eyes narrowed with anger as she cast an incensed glare at an imaginary victim. "She stole it from me."

"What?" Greg gasped, upset by Ana María's additional offense and bewildered that Theresa had owned such an object.

"Remember the day you stumbled on my secret hiding place? There was one item missing, which was never found. I didn't want to tell you what it was. It was an object from my past, when I used to collect talismans, crystals and other occult items. I was embarrassed, first because I had ever collected them, and second, because I had held onto this one."

"Why did you?" Greg asked.

"Because Jared gave it to me. He never encouraged any of my strange fads except this one time. It was a birthday present. I suppose I justified keeping it by telling myself it was given as a gift with good intentions. I convinced myself it was just a piece of rock and silver. And I still suppose that it is, but there is so much meaning behind it all. So much evil."

"What is its purpose?"

"It's supposed to be an idol to the incarnation of some ancient Persian or Hindu spirit. The writing is in the Devanagari script, and I forget what it says. I don't want to remember."

"And I don't want to know," Greg heaved a sigh. "Now what?"

"I have to confront Ana María. I have to get the crystal back. And I have to destroy it."

"Do you believe it really has power?" posed Greg.

Theresa hesitated. "Greg, there are many sources of power in this world. There is the power of Good and the power of Evil. There is the power of Light and the power of Darkness. Ultimately, there are only two sources. I don't believe that a piece of rock or a form of metal has any significance of its own. But power, holy or unholy, can be attached to it either by man or by spirit. I don't claim to know how it all works, but that's the best explanation I can offer."

"Seems reasonable. I'll have to consider it," he reflected honestly. "Let me know if you need help when you talk to Ana María. What are you going to say to Jared?"

"I don't know," Theresa frowned as she returned the book to its place on the shelf. "I have to tell him. How can I trust that woman in my house, with my children anymore? I had grown suspicious of her as time went by. As I said before, I've gotten to know some of her family fairly well. They're very devout, truly lovers of God. But something always seemed different about Ana María. I discounted my suspicions because I knew so much good about Gabina, her siblings and her other cousins. But I guess even Jesus had an enemy in His own camp."

"When will you talk to Jared?"

"I don't know yet," she mused as they exited the library back towards the kitchen. "But certainly not before dinner. Let's eat. I'm famished!"

Chapter Twenty-One

Yelping, Greg fought in vain to protect himself from the onslaught of ice-cold water. As the shriek of the crowd melted away into laughter, Greg smiled and began to wring out the water from his shirt. Next to him Denise and Jack hysterically gyrated back and forth, brimming with excitement at the killer whale show at Sea World of Texas. "Again, again," they called, hoping that the giant sea mammal would douse the crowd another time.

Still tasting salt water at the end of the show, Greg suggested that the trio eat an early dinner. A nearby food stand offered a menu of children's delights: chicken fingers, hot dogs and pizza. Arms encumbered with food and drink, Greg led the children to a splash of tables out in the sun. It was still early in the season, and Greg hoped the rays would dry their wet clothing as quickly as possible. Family membership came with unlimited free visits to the marine park, and Theresa often took the children for a late afternoon outing. Greg had offered Theresa some peace and rest by taking the children out for her. So far the day had been thoroughly enjoyable, and it came with the added bonus of avoiding contact with Señorita Astuza. With prior consent from Theresa, Greg made sure to extend the trip long enough to miss after-dinner cleanup by Ana María. He had encouraged Theresa to confront her, but Theresa cited her illness as grounds for postponing her discussions with either Ana María or Jared.

"Uncle Greg, do you live with us now?" Denise asked.

Greg smiled. "It may seem that way. I've been with you for a couple months."

"But you're not going to stay forever, are you," Jack guessed dejectedly.

"I do have to get on with my life at some point," Greg mused.

"What does that mean?" Denise asked, wide-eyed.

"Well, your mommy and daddy have each other, they have their own house, and they have you two children. I have an apartment back East, and somewhere out there I hope there is a wife for me."

"And children?" smiled Denise.

Greg laughed with slight embarrassment. "Someday, I hope so. Someday."

"Why don't you have a wife?" Denise continued her innocent interrogation.

Greg paused as painful memories rushed to the surface. "I tried, I tried, but God had other plans." He choked back an unexpected tear. "I don't know why."

"But God knows?" Jack's words were both an answer and a question.

"Yes, God knows," admitted Greg. "And I suppose only He knows best."

The dinner conversation with the children burned in Greg's mind all night and into the following day. As he sat in the front office working with Jared's financial records, his thoughts drifted to his former life hundreds of miles away in Connecticut. More than distance and time seemed to separate him now, as he found himself increasingly engrossed in his pursuit of God. He felt some of the old desires and priorities slowly fading into dim memory.

However, the exercise of reviewing McAllen Orchards' finances reawakened his theories on the disposition of the missing money from his prior accounts. The overwhelming sense of having become the victim of sinister activity burdened him. A renewed confidence in his abilities led him to excavate the idea that he had been framed, rather than having made multiple grave clerical errors. He regretted his efforts to hide the money with his own, and he lamented his own resulting financial harm. He stopped short of grieving the loss of his job as he realized the great spiritual benefit he had achieved in unburdening himself from that distraction. Even so, as he knew that joblessness needed to be a temporary state, he found himself starting to long for full-time gainful employment.

The image of Joanna leapt to the forefront of his mind. A sudden desire to call her instinctively brought his hand to the phone. He punched in the first three digits of her phone number before he realized that he had not included the area code. The mistake gave him time to collect his thoughts. As he remembered the tone of their final moments together, he realized that he could not call without a plan for the conversation. Disappointed but relieved, he pressed the disconnect button. Still craving a voice from the past, he kept the phone by his ear and dialed Joe Tropetto.

"You have called *That Pizza Place*. How can I help you?"

"Hi Joe, it's Greg Wesko."

"Greg!" crackled the line. "Good to hear from you. How are you doing? Where are you, anyway?"

"Still at my sister's in San Antonio. Hey, thanks for helping out with things while I'm gone."

"Sure, no sweat. I'm just glad to know you're still alive, not lying dead in an alley somewhere!" chuckled Joe. "I haven't heard an update from you in forever."

Greg's tone conveyed his smile. "I'd better call more often, or you might start selling my stuff!"

"Well, if you ever do return, you will notice something missing. Marina's the one with the green thumb, but I'm the one who's been stopping in at your apartment. I killed your plants, Greg. Sorry. We had the funeral last week."

"Oh, they probably just died of loneliness," Greg joked. "Anyway, how is Marina?"

"She's doing well. She recently told me about the fight you had with that pretty redhead in our restaurant a while back. She had forgotten about it. I don't know what made her remember it all of a sudden."

"Does she come in anymore?"

"I think Marina said she came in with a group of people from that company you used to work for," Joe recollected. "That's probably what triggered Marina's memory about the woman. I'm not going to pry by asking what you two fought about that last time you were here together."

"And I'm not going to volunteer any information," Greg purposely avoided the bait, not desiring to reopen old wounds. "I just wanted to call to see how things were. You still have the phone number here?"

"I do. So when do you think you might come back?"

"Probably sooner rather than later."

"Real specific," cracked Joe.

"I'll call you next week. Thanks, Joe."

"No problem, man. You take care of yourself."

Wednesday morning had barely begun, but the air was thick with tension. Having awakened early, Greg prepared himself a simple breakfast with the intentions of getting an early start on the workday. Efficient and experienced, Greg had adeptly streamlined McAllen Orchards' accounting process. Maintaining the affairs required less than a full work week, leaving Greg with ample free time for other pursuits. Today's plan included wrapping up work before noon and heading into town by himself for lunch and shopping. He wanted to update his wardrobe in preparation for eventually rejoining the public arena in the workplace and the social scene. Thinking about his demise at Providential Insurance still caused Greg to wince with emotional pain. He was finally at the point where he could review the details without shuddering. In many ways he felt violated, unable and unwilling to trust the systems that had been put in place to protect him. Now removed from the immediate situation, Greg was more convinced than ever that he had been framed for embezzlement. Thoughts of Tony Franco kept popping into his head, but Greg could not imagine Franco capable and sane enough to pull off a crime. Chuck Hollis had let Greg go so easily that it seemed suspicious. However, Hollis liked to play his cards close to his chest, and so would prefer to save face rather than admit to scandal within his ranks. Greg assumed that Chuck had only permitted the audit of Greg's accounts under extreme pressure.

As he finished up his scrambled eggs, mulling over his past and his future options, an unwelcome figure entered the room from behind. Feeling a noticeable change in the atmosphere, Greg turned his head. Steely eyes locked with his. His heart skipped a beat. "Good morning," she hissed, leaving out her normal courteous addition, "Señor Greg."

"Good morning," Greg responded automatically. "I was just leaving," he added as he stood to bring his dishes to the sink.

"Leave it," she snapped. "I told you I would be here long after you leave. Soon you will be gone. As for me, nothing has changed in my position in this family. I run this house, and I will continue to run this house," she said icily, each word laden with venom. "I am in charge here!"

"Don't be so sure!" The unexpected outburst caused both Greg and Ana María to jump. Theresa had overheard the conversation as she walked down the hallway in her morning slippers. "I need to have a word with you, Miss Astuza."

Greg had never heard Theresa or Jared address her as anything but "Ana María." He was surprised to see Ana María appear slightly shaken. Apparently her self-proclaimed position of running the household was not exactly in the job description given by her employers.

"Greg is a welcome guest in this house. I expect you to treat him with respect. He is my brother," she stated very plainly but firmly. "You, on the other hand, are a paid employee. Yes, your work is valuable and you have always done a good job. I have always appreciated your hard work and your flexibility. But you have done something that has broken my trust."

"And what is that?" Ana María's somewhat contrite tone belied her seething anger.

Theresa approached Ana María until the two were separated by only one foot. "Show me your necklace!" demanded Theresa. Out of the corner of her eye, Ana María shot a hateful look at Greg. "Show me!" repeated Theresa insistently.

Ana María took a step back at Theresa's words. With great reluctance, Ana María brought her hands towards her throat. Hesitating for a moment, a look of strong defiance overtook her countenance. With purposeful movements, she dug underneath her collar and produced the amulet, which hung from a thin gold chain. Despite the expectation, Theresa and Greg both gasped at the sight. "Is this what you wanted to see?" Ana María taunted them with contempt.

"You thief!" Theresa accused her. "You stole from me in my own house! I welcomed you into my home and you betrayed my trust and confidence. What do you have to say for yourself?"

Theresa spoke with cold and calculated words. "You were wasting it," she began. "Such a precious item as this does not belong hidden among books on a shelf. Call it borrowing, call it rescuing, whatever you like. What harm did I cause anyway? Were you saving it for a rainy day, Señora? I left the money and I left the rings. I happened on your whole cache by accident in the course of my cleaning. But it really was no accident. It was my destiny. The amulet called to me to release it from its prison. How could I refuse?"

"Give it back!" commanded Theresa, stretching out her hand.

Ana María kept her tone calm and even. "No, Señora, I will not," she refused. "Take it out of my salary, if you like, but I feel I have *earned* it!" she challenged.

"I'm warning you, Ana María, give it back!" Theresa's tone rose an octave.

"Again, I say no."

"Ana María!" Greg exclaimed. "Do what Theresa says!"

Like a viper seeking a new victim, Ana María turned to face Greg. "You stay out of this! I offered you the power of the amulet, but you refused. We could have defeated your enemies together. But still you hold onto your silly notions. Weakling!" she fumed. Turning to Theresa, she added, "Now as for you..."

The sound of palm on cheek reverberated through the kitchen. Greg felt as if it were he whom Theresa had slapped. As Ana María stood silently holding her face, the world seemed to grind to a halt. Anger seethed in Ana María's eyes.

"How dare you treat me this way, after all I have done for you and your family!" The woman began to shake. "I will leave, but I will be back. You will ask me back!"

With this remark, Ana María turned to go. As she did, Theresa reached out and quickly caught hold of the necklace, which consequently tore. Ana María turned around and glared with hatred at Theresa, who stood triumphantly clutching the thin gold chain with the amulet. Without another word, Ana María fled from the kitchen and out of sight.

"Goodbye, Daddy!" Greg rounded the corned just in time to see Jared, suitcase in hand, heading down the path towards his SUV. Denise and Jack stood waving and blowing kisses in the doorway. Theresa stood by with hands on their shoulders.

"What's going on?" Greg questioned.

"Hi Greg," Theresa smiled. "Jared had an unexpected business trip to Dallas. He'll be back sometime Saturday night. He said he left a few instructions for you on the desk in the front office."

As Jared pulled away, the children called out a final farewell and then headed back towards the playroom. Theresa and Greg followed at a slower pace.

"What did he say about Ana María?" Greg asked.

Theresa's hesitation in responding clued Greg in. "He didn't say anything," she started. "Because I didn't have a chance to tell him yet."

"Didn't have a chance?" Greg repeated incredulously.

Theresa continued to blame her exhaustion and sudden illness and promised to discuss the matter with Jared when he returned on the weekend. She admitted that the situation would have to be acknowledged shortly, as Jared would require an explanation regarding Ana María's long absence.

The remainder of the work week passed quickly, and the adults decided to turn Friday evening into "movie night." Theresa and Greg took the children out for an early dinner at a local seafood restaurant just off Interstate 410. Greg ordered the special, a bucket of steamed crawfish, and Jack was delighted to help his uncle with the shellfish cracker. Country music sounded sweetly from the juke box in the hall, and Greg took the opportunity to relax with a mug of local brew. After a satisfying meal, Theresa drove them to a nearby movie theater. On the way, Greg stared out at the endless flow of traffic as the children sang songs in the back seat.

Two hours later, a half-full popcorn bag still in hand, the foursome returned to the car with sticky fingers and smiling faces. As they crossed the parking lot, Greg noted to himself that any outsider would think he was the head of a family with two children. The thought awoke in him a deep melancholy and a strong yearning.

As expected, the children fell asleep on the way home. Greg carried them to their rooms one at a time, first Jack and then Denise. As he quietly closed the door to Denise's bedroom, the creak of a floorboard caught Greg's attention. He paused and listened. The sound repeated from the direction of the library just across the hall. Quietly, Greg tiptoed to the doorway and peaked in. He decided that the carpeted room could not have been the source of the noise. Without a sound, he crossed through the library and into the adjoining hall on the opposite side. Before stepping out, he peered around the corner to scout the area. To the left the hallway led to the kitchen, dimly lit by a fluorescent lamp over the stove. Another sound caught his attention to the right where the hallway passed the poolroom and spilled into the front parlor.

Greg stealthily made his way towards the parlor. Heart pounding, he bounded in and braced himself for a confrontation. The parlor was empty. He tried the door to the office but it was still locked as he had left it earlier in the day. The door leading outside also appeared undisturbed. Through a door next to the office, another corridor led towards Jack's bedroom and the master bedroom, eventually ending at Jared's back office. As he passed between the front office and a second guestroom, Greg heard a shuffling sound emanating from the master suite. He raced quietly down the hall and stopped short at the entrance. Cupping his hand to the door, he heard what sounded like drawers opening and shutting. Surprised at the volume of the noise, he wondered whether it was simply Theresa searching for something. At this point, the occupant was not masking his or her movements very well. As he debated, he lost his footing and fell full force into the door. The latch had not caught, and Greg burst in through the door as it opened.

A small shriek flew up as the intruder whirled around. Greg shouted in astonishment, "Ana María!" As she stood there motionless, Greg's eyes quickly observed the open drawers and ransacked contents.

"I have a right to be here!" Ana María shouted. "I still work for Señor Jared," she defended herself defiantly. "I have been in this room many times to clean and to help Señora Theresa."

"I believe you were asked to leave!" Greg challenged.

"No one asked me to leave. I said I would be back, and here I am!"

"You have no right to rummage through their personal items. What are you trying to steal this time?" Greg accused her.

"I steal nothing!" she denied. "I am only looking for what is rightfully mine!"

The uproar had filtered down to the family room, and Theresa arrived to join the confrontation. "Get out of here, Ana María!" she shouted as she ran into the room.

"I came back tonight for my amulet," Ana María admitted. "It is mine. I deserve it." She paused before putting forth a shocking statement. *"Señor Jared* gave it to me!"

In horror, Greg observed Theresa's face turn ashen. After a period of stunned silence, she managed softly, "No, no, it can't be true!"

"Of course it's true," smirked Ana María. "I asked him for it, and he gave it to me. It was obvious that you didn't want it anymore."

Theresa stood frozen, dumbfounded. "When did this happen?" Greg came to her aid.

"Quite awhile ago," Ana María sneered matter-of-factly. "Señor Jared thought I deserved a bonus, and I told him what I wanted. I had found the amulet by fate, as I said. But I did not take it outright. How could I use the magic of the crystal if I had gotten it dishonestly?"

Ana María's revelations and logic left Greg and Theresa bewildered. "But you are taking it now?"

"Yes, you are right. I am *taking* it back, not *stealing* it. I haven't been able to find it so far. Now tell me where it is!" she demanded.

"I don't believe you," Theresa cried. "Your story is a lie!"

"And we will not tell you where it is. Get out of this house!" Greg chimed in.

"You are wrong on all counts. The story is true, whether you believe it or not. I want the amulet now. Give it to me, or else Señor Jared will give it to me when he returns tomorrow. And then we would have to raise this whole ugly issue with him. Wouldn't you like to avoid that?" challenged Ana María through clenched teeth.

"We'll just see about that!" Theresa shouted. "I'll show you where it is!" Greg choked on his voice of protest as Theresa stormed into the master bathroom. Flinging open the medicine cabinet over the sink, she retrieved a small box. She threw the cover onto the floor and grasped the amulet, letting everything else crash to the tiled floor. "Here is your precious crystal!" she screamed, holding it up in the air and waving it at an enraged Ana María. "You want it?"

Ana María lunged at Theresa to grab the amulet, but Theresa moved aside and dropped to her knees. Grabbing a stone soap dish, she shouted, "I should have done this years ago!" With that, she cast the amulet onto the floor, raised the stone above her head, and thrust it down towards the crystal. The ensuing clamor of the crystal shattering between the stone and the tile floor reverberated throughout the room. With fierce determination, Theresa continued to pulverize the crystal to the tune of Ana María's wailing and shrieking. When only dust was left, Theresa collapsed against the nearby wall. Sitting down to comfort his sister, Greg noticed that Ana María was gone. Jack and Denise looked on in shock and horror.

"Mommy, Mommy, what happened?" Denise managed to say as she fought back tears.

Theresa offered her arms to the children. "Oh, my sweet children! I had to destroy something that was very bad. It's all right now. Everything is going to be all right. You'll see." Theresa paused to catch her breath. She continued softly, "And Mommy's not sick anymore!"

Chapter Twenty-Two

Early Saturday morning, Theresa found Greg sitting on one of the leather couches in the library. Already dressed, he sat with his Bible open on the seat next to him. Theresa greeted him and asked how he was doing.

"I was trying to figure out what to say to you," he smiled. "I can't decide whether it's my place to give you advice. I am your brother, after all. But I'm not skilled in relationships."

"Did you find something to say from the Bible?" asked Theresa, noting the book.

"Honestly, I was looking for something to encourage you to speak with Jared about everything that happened. Especially about the amulet and about Ana María. What I found is from the first letter of John, Chapter 4." Picking up the book, he read:

> Beloved, do not trust every spirit but test the spirits to see whether they belong to God, because many false prophets have gone out into the world.

This is how you can know the Spirit of God: every spirit that acknowledges Jesus Christ come in the flesh belongs to God, and every spirit that does not acknowledge Jesus does not belong to God. This is the spirit of the antichrist that, as you heard, is to come, but in fact is already in the world. You belong to God, children, and you have conquered them, for the one who is in you is greater than the one who is in the world.

"Ana María claimed to acknowledge Jesus, but at the same time looked for power in a piece of glass, something that can be shattered. What a paradox!"

"What about you, Greg?" Theresa asked.

"I'm ready to acknowledge Jesus Christ as my God. I've tried other gods. Work and greed and my own pride require a lot of sacrifice, but they can't save my soul. I've even dabbled in the occult in order to find assurance of the future."

"What are you going to do?"

"What do you recommend?"

"Can I pray with you?" suggested Theresa. "Then let God lead from there. And when you're ready, I would encourage you to talk to a priest and go to confession."

"What is to prevent me from doing that right now?"

"Nothing," Theresa smiled. "Nothing at all. Let's pray. But before we do, just let me assure you,

I will talk to Jared tonight when he comes home, regardless of how I feel or how late it is. And incidentally, I am no longer sick. When I smashed that crystal last night, I felt the sickness leave my body."

"It's a miracle!" Greg exclaimed.

"I wouldn't necessarily call it a miracle," said Theresa. "But it certainly is a healing."

"Your letting go of that crystal inspired me to smash my own idols," Greg admitted.

"How wonderful, Greg!" She waited to see if he would elaborate, but when he remained silent, she continued, "Let us pray." Greg arose and stood next to Theresa. Turning to face him, she extended one arm to his left shoulder while raising her other hand heavenward. She closed her eyes, and Greg followed suit. Two angels hovered behind them, encircling them in a cloud of protection. As Theresa continued the prayer, Greg felt a warm burning sensation rush through him.

"Dear Heavenly Father, we come into your presence in the name of your only Son, Jesus Christ, and in the power of your almighty Spirit. Come upon my brother today and fill him with your peace and your wisdom. Break the idols that have clutched his heart, mind and soul for so long. Touch his heart to know and welcome your love. Open his mind to understand something of the mysteries of your power and mercy. Cleanse his soul as he accepts the precious salvation that you won for us on the Cross of Calvary, dear Jesus. Richly bless him, and cause your Holy Spirit to dwell with him, so that he may gaze upon your face forever. We love you and trust you to do this all in your good timing. Amen."

Lost in the moment, Greg choked out an "Amen." Several moments passed before he could manage to open his eyes. He wondered if the world would look different. The incandescent bulb of the adjacent light shone so brightly that he could not bring himself to raise his eyes, but instead kept his vision slightly pointed downward. "Thank you," he whispered.

"Thank you," Theresa softly responded.

Greg sat on the edge of the seat in the soft lighting of the church and rested his head against his folded hands on the back of the pew in front of him. The backlit marble altarpiece resembled a Gothic cathedral with spires reaching toward Heaven. "What do I say to you, Lord? I don't know where to begin."

I love you. The words seemed as clear to him as if they had been spoken aloud.

"I love you too," he responded. "I want to love you more. But I don't know how to do that."

Get rid of the things that are in the way. Again, the message rang clearly in his mind.

"Oh God, help me to break down the idols in my life. I turn away from them now."

Name them.

"Lord, I surrender all my idols over to you. First, Greed." As he spoke the words, an image flashed before his mind's eye of a pillar crashing toward the ground. It collided with the arid ground and raised up a cloud of dry earth to the sound of a hollow, resounding rumble. When the dust settled, broken pieces scattered the landscape. He named the next idol. "Lust." Another column toppled. One by one, the remaining idols crumbled in succession as he named each one. "Pride. The Occult. Blasphemy. The Unnamed Idol."

"Forgive me, Father, for I have sinned. It has been, uh, many years since my last confession." Greg trembled with nerves as he knelt behind the curtain in the dim light.

"How many, my son?" responded a kindly voice.

"I haven't been to confession since I was a kid. I've been away from the Church and from God since then."

"God always welcomes the sinner back. As a loving Father, He is overjoyed when His children return home. Tell Him what you are sorry for. He is ready to forgive."

The peace that surpasses all understanding overtook Greg as his knees pressed into the cold stone floor. "I want to renounce all my idols, that is, the things I have set up in my life to compete with God. I never thought of it in these terms, but somehow I must have known.

"First, Greed. I desired wealth. I worshipped my job. I worked to excess, putting my career above relationships, above family, above God. I felt secure when I had money. I could rely on myself rather than on God or anyone else.

"Second, Lust. I went too far with girls in high school and college. I claimed to love them when I really just wanted them. I put myself into dangerously tempting situations with the one woman who truly was the love of my life. She was purer and stronger than I wanted to be. She was killed," he choked back a tear, "but thankfully, she went to God with a clear conscience." He paused. "Some time later, I tried to express my feelings for another woman, and I ridiculed her when she refused my advances.

"Pride. I have always tried to rely on myself, even when I should have accepted help from others. I never allowed people the chance to truly help me, but instead I would choose to manipulate them and use them on my own terms. I wanted to make a name for myself. I felt it was owed to me.

"Next, the Occult. I sought counsel from fortunetellers and tarot cards. I thought that I could make God give me the answers to my questions rather than wait for Him to reveal them in His good timing.

"Blasphemy. I had a vision that this is one of my idols, and I had a difficult time knowing how it applied. But I think it means that I put myself before God. I refused to attend Mass for years, thinking that God and church were for fools and for the weak. I thought that true men stood on their own, perhaps as our own little gods unto ourselves.

"Finally, the unnamed idol. I have been away for so long, and there are so many other things I have placed before God, more than I can number or recall. I am truly sorry for all the sins I remember, and I can't imagine that there are any sins that I have forgotten that are worth holding onto. I will try my hardest to do what is good and pleasing in God's sight from now on and not offend Him anymore. I want to learn how to love Him more. But I cannot do it on my own. I need God's help."

A peaceful silence reigned for a moment as Greg's words faded into the air and presented themselves before the throne of the Almighty, who had prompted, listened to, and welcomed Greg's every word from His newly-reclaimed seat on the throne of Greg's heart.

"You have made a good confession," the priest spoke with emotion-laden words. "God has worked a miracle in your life. He has forgiven all your sins. For your penance, read the parable of the Prodigal Son in the Gospel of Luke, Chapter 15." After the absolution and dismissal, Greg rose with a bursting heart and headed up the center aisle towards the altar rail. He genuflected and remained on his knees before the tabernacle. On the rail lay a Bible. Amazed, Greg noted that it was open to the Gospel of Luke, Chapter 15.

A man had two sons, and the younger son said to his father, "Father, give me the share of your estate that should come to me." So the father divided the property between them. After a few days, the younger son collected all his belongings and set off to a distant country where he squandered his inheritance on a life of dissipation. When he had freely spent everything, a severe famine struck that country, and he found himself in dire need. So he hired himself out to one of the local citizens who sent him to his farm to tend the swine. And he longed to eat his fill of the pods on which the swine fed, but nobody gave him any. Coming to his senses he thought, "How many of my father's hired workers have more than enough food to eat, but here am I, dying from hunger. I shall get up and go to my father and I shall say to him, 'Father, I have sinned against heaven and against you. I no longer deserve to be called your son; treat me as you would treat one of your hired workers.'" So he got up and went back to his father. While he was still a long way off, his father caught sight of him, and was filled with compassion. He ran to his son, embraced him and kissed him. His son said to him, "Father, I have sinned against heaven and against you; I no longer deserve to be called your son." But his father ordered his servants, "Quickly bring the finest robe and put it on him; put a ring on his finger and sandals on his feet. Take the fattened calf and slaughter it. Then let us celebrate with a feast, because this son of mine was dead, and has come to life again; he was lost, and has been found."

The image of the father embracing his lost son was still vivid as Greg processed up the same aisle the next day. He followed Theresa, who held Denise by the hand. Jared had taken Jack out for an emergency trip to the men's room. As he took each slow step, Greg felt as if he were participating in a marriage ceremony, where the Savior waited as a bridegroom in front of the altar. The anticipation had been building in the forefront of Greg's mind all night and all morning, and in fact had been building unacknowledged in his heart for years. "Lord, I am ready," he repeated silently. "Make me ready." As Theresa moved to the side, he realized that the moment was upon him. The priest held up the Communion host but Greg could barely hear over the pounding of his heart in his ears and could barely see through the tears suddenly flooding his eyes. He uttered "Amen," aloud. As he received, he felt the floodgates of God's grace open to release their blessings upon him. The experience enveloped him such that he arrived back at his seat without remembering the return trip.

Meanwhile, in Heaven, a new saint rejoiced to see her beloved communing with the Alpha and the Omega, the First and the Last, the Beginning and the End. From her vantage point upon the lap of the Father, she shared the moment with him through the fellowship of the Spirit and the person of Christ. A sense washed over Greg, causing him to look up. For an instant he could imagine the Heavenly throne and the angels and saints gathered around. "Lisa!" he called silently, as if able to see her shining face.

Just as suddenly, the image was gone, and Greg merely gazed at one of the light fixtures suspended from the ceiling.

On the way home from Mass, Greg sat quietly, basking in a peace he had never known before. It struck him as odd that the sun did not shine any brighter, the trees still bore the same colors, the roads still twisted up and down. Outwardly, nothing seemed to have changed. But inside his own soul, Greg knew a great transformation had occurred.

Back at the house, Greg changed into more casual attire. As he headed towards the kitchen, the sound of an argument met him in the hallway. He quickly ascertained that Jared and Theresa were discussing the situation with Ana María.

"And I broke it into a thousand pieces. I had to!" he heard Theresa exclaim.

"What a stupid thing to do!" Jared lambasted her. "You overreacted to a simple misunderstanding. Now you've fired the best help we ever had, and broken one of my gifts to you besides! How ungrateful!" Greg was just about to offer them privacy by returning to his room when a slap pealed out from the kitchen, followed by a shriek.

Greg tore down the hall and burst into the kitchen to find Theresa rubbing her face and bearing a look of shocked offense. Jared raised his hand as if to slap Theresa's other cheek. In an instant Greg jumped on Jared and pulled his arm back. In the ensuing struggle, the two men thrashed themselves into counters and tables, eventually knocking over two chairs. Several sets of punches were thrown before Theresa's pleas and cries managed to break through and bring the men back to a reasonable frame of mind. Fists only partially lowered, the two remained poised against each other.

"No one slaps my sister!" Greg shouted.

"This is none of your business," seethed Jared. "You have freeloaded long enough. Now get out of here!" he commanded.

"No, no!" Theresa pleaded. "Let's all calm down."

"You go ahead and calm down," Jared hissed. "I'm going out of town on business again. I'm leaving now, and I'll be back Friday night. You had better be gone by then, Greg, or I'll call the cops to evict you. You are no longer welcome here." Jared enunciated Greg's name with enough contempt to make his skin crawl. "Have I made myself clear?"

"Jared, please!" Theresa began.

"Shut up! We'll deal with this when I return." Jared shot Theresa a hateful look and proceeded to storm out of the kitchen. As he passed Greg, he forcefully knocked into him with determination.

Theresa broke down as she stood in the kitchen. Greg rushed over to comfort her. "I fell asleep waiting for Jared last night," she sobbed. "I didn't get a chance to tell him about Ana María and the amulet until after church."

"He didn't take it well at all," Greg understated.

"You don't have to go, Greg. I'll work on Jared. Let's let all this settle down. Maybe we can get Ana María back, and..."

"No, Theresa. Don't go back on everything good that has happened in the last few days. You smashed the crystal. You don't want to bring it back, do you?"

Theresa wiped her eyes. "No, no, of course not. I just don't know how to make it right with Jared now. He doesn't understand."

"He won't understand, Theresa," Greg fumed. "You should throw him out of the house. He can't hit you!"

"Greg, no!" Theresa exclaimed. "Divorce is not an option. And believe me when I tell you that this is the first time he's ever hit me. We have to work it out. God established marriage to be a sacrament that binds for life. Our marriage is valid, so we are joined in God's eyes, and no one can undo that."

"I don't necessarily mean divorce," he said as he led her to the kitchen table. Stooping over to pick up the two chairs that had been knocked over, he continued, "Just separate until you can work out your differences. I don't see a happy marriage here, Theresa. And I don't mean just today."

Theresa sat down. "We do have a lot of work to do," she sighed. "We've grown apart. I feel like I used to be on one side of him, now I'm on the totally opposite side, and he remains in the middle. I am triangulating, I suppose."

"Theresa, you are right where you need to be. Don't change for him. He is the one who needs to change. All you have to do is stop letting him make you feel inferior."

"I don't feel inferior. I believe in being loyal to my husband. I have to give him the benefit of the doubt. I also know that I have to encourage him to fulfill his duty to protect me. From Ana María and even from himself sometimes. He governs and provides for this family well enough, but I have to make him see me as a valuable partner. Now that I feel well again, I know I can make this marriage really work. Trust me, Greg."

"I do trust you," he furrowed his brow. "But I worry about you, Theresa. And I worry about Denise and Jack as well. What kind of model do they have here?" Greg rose to put on some coffee.

"You know, I've thought about leaving Jared before. Not permanently, just for long enough to make him think. But he's away so often that I doubt he would miss us much at first."

"You and the kids are always welcome to come visit me in Connecticut," invited Greg as he scooped coffee grounds out into the filter.

"Are you really going to go back now? When you first came here, you said you were going to travel out West. I thought we were just a pit stop. But then I was hoping you were going to stay for a long time."

"Thanks, Theresa," Greg set out two mugs. "How many months have I been here? I'm surprised I didn't wear out my welcome sooner. At least I felt my stay was somewhat justified by helping Jared part-time. But I'm ready to go back. It's time to pick up my life again."

"God had a purpose in you coming out here."

"He sure did. And I'm not returning in order to get my old life back. I want to make a new start with the gifts God has already given me. Plus I want to clear my name and my conscience regarding my old job. I'm convinced that I'm the victim of a crime, and I want to find out what happened and set it right. I've been thinking about returning for a while now anyway."

"Mommy! Daddy's going away again!" interjected Denise as she and Jack ran into the kitchen. "He just kissed us good-bye. When will he be back?"

Greg could not bear to burden the children with the news of his own upcoming departure. He exited the kitchen and returned to his room to pray and ponder.

The week flew by much more rapidly than anyone had wanted. Greg and Theresa had tried to pack the remaining days with as many memories as possible. They returned to Sea World, visited the Zoo, ate dinner downtown on the River Walk twice, and toured some of the old Spanish missions. The evenings were occupied with games and singing songs to the tune of Theresa's acoustic guitar playing. Without Jared and Ana María, it seemed that a pall had been removed from the household. They would all recall it as the best week of the entire visit.

Friday morning brought the dreaded inevitable. As Greg packed his suitcases, his sister knocked on the open door.

"Can I help?" she offered.

Greg looked down at the overstuffed bags. Clothes peeked out of every opening. "I've fit almost everything," he chuckled. "I didn't pack some of my older clothes. Do you know of anyone who could use them? I bought so many new items since I've been here."

"I know a very pious Mexican family at church," Theresa smiled. "They make a trip once a month back to Mexico to bring food, clothes and other articles to the poorest of the poor. They would be glad to receive these."

"Then please, take them," Greg indicated a pile of clothes on the dresser.

"What time do you plan to leave?" she asked.

"Just after breakfast. I have over 2000 miles to drive. If I can make it to Memphis today, I should be able to make it home by Sunday night in time to check in at my friend Joe's house. He and his wife Marina have been watching after my apartment."

"Where will you stay tomorrow night?"

"Probably in Virginia, maybe Roanoke. We'll have to see how tired I get on the road."

During breakfast, conversation began to lag as the foursome sat dreading Greg's impending journey. Jack spoke up. "Uncle Greg, I really wish you could stay. I'll miss you something awful."

"I'll miss you too, all of you. I've really enjoyed staying with you this whole time. But you'll come out and see me sometime."

"Really? Will Mommy and Daddy come too?"

Theresa chimed in, "I'll certainly come. We won't wait long."

"Oh good!" the children cried in unison.

"You found God," Denise remarked.

Greg and Theresa sat for a moment, flabbergasted. "Yes, Denise, I did," Greg finally responded. "What made you say that?"

"You changed. You got better. You smiled more. God makes smiles. I think you found your smile because you found God."

Amazed by her unspoiled heart, Greg patted Denise softly on the head. "You're absolutely right. And I am going to smile a lot more when I go back home."

"God lives in Connecticut too!" Jack laughed and the others all joined in.

"Yes, he does. He always has, but I just never knew it."

Moments later, Greg started his car and rolled down the window. "One more hug!" Denise cried and ran over to embrace him through the window. This maneuver required Greg to unbuckle and lean out of the car. Jack joined Denise and embraced his uncle again. Theresa called out another farewell from her spot at the edge of the drive. The children returned to their mother and clung to her side, shivering in the uncharacteristically cold morning.

"Thanks for everything! I love you all!" he shouted as he started to back his car up in order to turn around. The three waved and called back, "I love you too!"

Tears welled up in Greg's eyes as he drove past the McAllen Orchards sign and turned left onto Doppler Road. In the distance he could barely distinguish the three figures huddling together and waving. He beeped his horn and glanced in the rearview mirror one last time.

Chapter Twenty-Three

A seasonably cold rain pelted Greg in the face as his black shoes sank into the waterlogged cemetery soil. Pulling the collar of his gray raincoat up, he huddled under the barren branches of a majestic oak tree. He adjusted his hat and shivered in the bone-chilling dampness. In the distance he observed a small crowd of people clustered around a fresh grave. From his vantage point he could barely discern a few familiar faces. Chuck Hollis, the last of his bosses at Providential Insurance, stood with shoulders hunched against the steady rain. Next to Hollis stood the executive Amos Stockley, Chuck's manager. Greg recognized a tall man towering over the crowd as Darren Lado, whom he had met when investigating suspicious computer activity at work. Two other acquaintances, Sam Bingham and Janet Semolini, also stood in attendance. On the fringe of the gathering paced the small, stout outline of Tony Franco. The grim expressions of those gathered remained unchanged as the burial ceremony ended and the group dispersed. After a few minutes, only one figure lingered behind. Greg decided it was safe to approach. With each step his shoes sank deeper into the mud.

"Quite a gloomy day," the man greeted him without removing his gaze from the grave below his feet.

"Hi Jason," Greg greeted his friend and former boss. "Thanks for meeting me." He followed Jason Coates' eyes down to a temporary plaque, an island in the midst of a rippling puddle of rain. The name *Robert Jackson Gurth III* was emblazoned in bronze letters upon a black background.

"You didn't know Bob, did you," Coates emitted hoarsely. "I worked with him for several years."

"I'm afraid not," Greg answered. Coates remained motionless. After a minute of silence, Greg suggested, "Do you want to get out of this rain?"

Coates glanced nonchalantly about and, seeming satisfied, motioned Greg toward a navy-blue sedan parked nearby. Coates unlocked the car and Greg sat next to him in the passenger seat.

"I'm sorry for all the cloak-and-dagger arrangements, Greg," began Coates, "but I'm not ready to take any chances. Not the way things have developed of late."

"What do you mean?" Greg was intensely intrigued.

"The stress level at work has been at an all-time high. I don't mean our regular deadlines or threats of a reduction in force. There is something going on that feels like a cross between a whirlwind and a silent plague." Answering Greg's puzzled expression, he continued, "Politics are running rampant, with people taking sides and dividing into war camps. But it's not the battles that are killing people; it's always something unexpected and seemingly unrelated."

"I'm still confused," Greg admitted.

"Take yourself as an example. As you told me, there were questions raised over the integrity of your accounts, but the audit could not convict you of anything. It seemed your future at the company was still stable, but then you suddenly quit without warning."

"There was another accusation made against me, the details of which were not made fully available," Greg explained. "I was asked to leave quietly on good terms rather than face possible charges. Of course I'm completely innocent of any wrongdoing. But my mental and emotional state was such that I welcomed the opportunity to escape."

"That's what I mean," Coates became agitated. "Why was there a problem with your emotional state? Normally I would have expected you to stay and fight in such a situation. It doesn't make sense to me that you were willing to leave so easily. But other things don't make sense either."

"Like what?" Greg pressed him for more information.

Coates nervously scanned the grounds through the windows. The uncharacteristic behavior worried Greg. He could not detect any trace of his usual exuberance and confidence. "Bob Gurth was supposed to leave for Singapore two Fridays ago.

As you may know, although Hartford was his home base, he traveled to Asia about eighty percent of the time." Greg recalled Coates' previous description of Gurth's travel abroad. Coates continued, "He was found dead a week later, apparently having choked on a chicken bone in his home. The mystery is this: what was he doing at home? He had told me he was leaving for Asia. But upon investigation his schedule showed he was planning to remain in town for another two weeks. And nobody reported him missing for a whole week while he lay dead at his kitchen table. Wasn't someone expecting him somewhere, either here or in Singapore?"

"He was already dead for a week when he was found?"

"Yes," Coates shuddered. "A neighbor happened to look in the kitchen window and saw him slumped over. He called the police. You see, Bob and his wife separated several years ago, and he has been living on his own since then. His lifestyle didn't support any long-term relationships anyway. It's hard to keep a marriage together when you're half a world away all the time. But they never divorced, and his wife was here today with their two grown children. They have a daughter in Sacramento and a son in Omaha."

After a moment of silence, Greg turned to Coates and earnestly began his proposal. "Jason, I need your help. That is why I called you to arrange a meeting. I've just returned to town, and one of my primary goals is to clear my name. My only questionable act was to cover missing sums of money with my own funds rather than bring the situation to the attention of Chuck Hollis. My pride was in the way. I thought I could figure the matter out in a short amount of time. I didn't suspect anything sinister until it was too late to do anything about it."

"I understand your problem," Coates sympathized. "I received a few disturbing calls at home that I haven't responded to yet. A man identifying himself as Tom Phillips wants to meet with me to discuss something that he said would 'be in my best interest not to miss.' He suggested that it's related to work. I have my own misgivings about some of the business practices at work recently. I'm afraid the company is either under federal investigation or is in trouble with organized crime, or both, and I don't know which side Phillips is on."

"What do you plan to do? Will you meet him?"

"I don't think I have a choice," Coates groaned. "I can either plan the meeting on my own terms, or I feel I will eventually meet him in a way I don't desire."

"Do you want help? I can be a distant third-party observer in the background."

Coates looked at Greg for the first time. "You came to ask me for help, and now you're offering to help me?"

"I think it will help us both," Greg smiled seriously. "If this Phillips character really has something to do with work, then I'm sure it involves me somehow too. What do you propose for a meeting?"

"Let's call on my cell phone now," Coates suggested. "He left a number for me to call. We can arrange to meet at a restaurant."

"I know a good one called *That Pizza Place* in East Hartford. I'm friends with the owners. They are very trustworthy, and I could enlist their help in arranging our seating."

"Good, I'll try." Coates' excitement began to surface at the prospect of positive action. He dialed the phone. Greg listened intently to one side of the conversation. It became readily apparent that their suggestion would not be accepted. After a few minutes Coates clicked off the phone dejectedly.

"He didn't like the plan," Coates frowned. "He picked out a bar in a seedy part of the city. He'll be waiting at a booth in the back tonight at ten o'clock. I am to look for a man in a dark blue polo shirt." Coates recited directions to the bar, and Greg took mental notes.

"I'll ask some of my friends to help out if they can. We'll stake out some of the booths in the back of the bar where he said he'd meet you. If we're lucky, he'll pick one near me or one of my friends. That way we can overhear what's going on. We'll try to arrive at 9:30 or earlier."

Plans formulated, the two men parted company. Greg stepped up onto a short grassy embankment to avoid being splashed with mud as Coates pulled away in his car. He gazed out at the sea of headstones and painfully longed to visit the grave of the one person he most desperately longed to see. But Lisa had been buried in the family plot he would never be a part of. A tear of yearning merged into the other streams running down his rain-soaked face.

Two cars pulled down a dark side street and parked in tandem along the curb. From one vehicle emerged a couple with curly black hair matching in color but not in length. They crossed the street and headed through a doorway under a neon sign announcing, "B-Street Bar" in flashing red letters. One minute later, Greg followed them into the bar and headed for the back. Five booths lined a fake brick wall. The nighttime crowd had not yet peaked, and Greg quickly spotted the couple. They had split up, with Joe Tropetto in the second booth, Marina in the third. Greg winked at Marina as he passed by to take a seat at the fourth booth. Greg hoped that the seating arrangement would allow flexibility for wherever Phillips decided to sit. If necessary, they could double-up or switch seats with each other to make sure there was an empty booth for Phillips to occupy next to Greg.

Ten minutes before ten o'clock, a tall, blond man entered the bar alone and headed immediately for the rear. In the dim lighting, a dark blue shirt was barely noticeable peeking out from under a light jacket. Greg, Joe and Marina followed his movement while trying to remain inconspicuous. As the man passed by, Greg was surprised by the youthful look of his face. Greg offered a silent prayer of thanksgiving when the man chose the seat directly behind him. A barmaid followed him and raised her eyebrow at his order for a coke. Greg sipped his draft beer slowly and declined another as she stopped by to check on him.

Shortly thereafter, the tall, athletic figure of Jason Coates pushed through the door. His sandy brown hair poked out from under a baseball cap. He surveyed the interior for a moment before walking with determination toward the booths. His eyes did not flicker in the slightest toward Greg as he passed him by.

"Phillips?" Greg heard Coates squeak hoarsely. Coates' voice had always seemed incongruous to his appearance.

"Mr. Coates," greeted the stranger quietly, "Have a seat."

"I want to know why we are here," Coates demanded softly.

"Of course," Phillips replied as he waited for Coates to sit down. "Like I started to explain before, I have reason to suspect that there are certain unethical activities occurring at your company," Phillips responded. Several sentences were exchanged in tones too hushed for Greg to hear clearly. Greg grew distressed and began to conjure up pieces of the conversation in his mind. Marina and Joe both faced him in their booths. A look of concern appeared on Joe's face as he stood up and began to approach. Suddenly Greg realized that Coates and Phillips were both standing at his table, towering over him in their above-average heights. His heart skipped a beat.

"Greg, this is Tom Phillips," Coates introduced the shorter of the two.

"May we sit down?" he offered a professional smile and handshake. Greg shot a glance at Joe, but Joe decided to maintain his secrecy and calmly sat down with Marina in the booth next to Greg.

"Tom is a private detective," Coates' words were almost drowned out by the growing din in the bar as carousers began to fill the establishment. "He wants to offer us his services."

"How so?" Greg challenged him with a quizzical look.

"I like your style," Phillips responded. "I appreciate customers who know how to play by the rules. Bringing a backup is a sharp idea. Any others here with you?"

"First of all, we're not your customers," quipped Greg.

"Hear him out," Coates interjected.

"You can ask the couple behind you to join us if you like," Phillips smirked. "You don't have anything to fear from me."

"No thanks," barked Greg. "I don't know them anyway."

"Suit yourself," continued Phillips. "I'm not the bad guy here. I've had two clients at Providential Insurance in the last year. Both wanted me to investigate some unusual unauthorized transactions they could not explain. They believed that someone was embezzling money in their name."

"Then why didn't they go to the authorities?" questioned Greg.

"No hard evidence. And they suspected that the parties involved went up the ladder pretty far. Very influential people, these crooks. There was no way to bring the crime to light without putting themselves in the hot seat. So they hired me."

"Greg, let's see if Mr. Phillips can help us out," pleaded Coates. "He said he was working for Bob Gurth before he died."

"And Jack Fishburn," Phillips added.

"Fishburn?" Coates waxed pale.

Greg recalled the name from his time at Providential Insurance. "You mean you've had two clients from PI who have ended up dead in the last year?" His hands started to shake where he hid them under the table.

"I told you, these crooks are powerful. Fishburn's heart attack seemed authentic enough. I didn't get suspicious until later, but Gurth's accidental death sealed it for me. We have embezzlement, framing and murder on our hands."

"Then why would I want to get involved?" Greg argued.

"You already are involved," countered Phillips. "And you want to settle this, otherwise you wouldn't have teamed up with Mr. Coates here tonight."

"I'm free and clear right now," Greg exclaimed.

"These people don't give up," Phillips frowned. "I was already watching you. My contacts informed me that you were poking around, asking questions, the kind of questions Mr. Fishburn and Mr. Gurth had asked. I had planned to get to you before they did. In fact," Phillips looked intently at Greg, "I let myself into your apartment one time in order to find out which side you were on."

Greg's sat wide-eyed in astonishment. A host of questions jumbled in his mind and left him tongue-tied in silence.

"I couldn't find anything suspicious in my investigation of you. And so when you left town, I decided to let you go. But now since you've come back, you're in danger."

"I don't believe it," Greg began to fret.

"The truth is true whether you believe it or not," Tom Phillips opined.

All week the conversation in the bar pervaded Greg's waking and non-waking moments. He had never felt any sense of danger at or away from his Connecticut home. Now fear compelled Greg to make a late-night trip to a hardware store so he could install an extra dead bolt on his apartment door. Tom Phillips' story left him dismayed and perplexed. The mystery seemed more sinister than he had ever imagined, and Jason Coates' agreement only intensified the gravity of the situation. They decided to hire Phillips to investigate further. A lunch meeting was set for Monday to review the status of the investigation.

In the remainder of the week, Greg sought to acclimate himself to his old surroundings. He restocked his refrigerator and canceled the forward on his mail. On Friday a large envelope arrived from Texas containing mail that had already been forwarded. Enclosed inside one small envelope he found a picture of Theresa with the children and a personal note assuring him that things were improving with Jared. When Greg placed a call to

Theresa one evening, Jack answered the phone. He was overjoyed to hear his Uncle Greg's voice and said that his parents were out on a date. Further questioning allayed Greg's fears about Ana María; Jack said they were testing a new babysitter named Talia.

Greg began to surf the Internet for any local jobs even remotely related to his areas of expertise. The job market seemed momentarily bleak, and Greg found himself applying for positions far beneath his previous salary. The idea of hiring himself out as a consultant began to sound appealing.

Sunday morning Greg found himself scrambling to find Mass times. Having forgotten to set his alarm, he slept late, a habit he had acquired during his extended stay with his sister. While getting dressed, he flipped through the phone book with one hand and arrived at the listing for Churches – Roman Catholic. He dialed the phone and rested it between his ear and shoulder as he shaved in the mirror. To his dismay, he had already missed all the Masses at the first two churches. At the third church, the answering machine picked up but did not list Mass times in the message. "Well, I tried," he thought, sitting back down on his bed, shoes already in his hands.

Keep trying.

The inner urging gently pressed him to continue, and he slipped on his shoes and laced them quickly. Checking the address of the church again, he raced out to his car and sped off. Traffic lights timed their green perfectly, and he sailed through the mostly deserted streets, hitting only one red light. As he pulled into the parking lot, a hopeful feeling flickered inside as he observed several people trickling into church. His smile fleeted away, however, as he caught sight of the billboard indicating Mass had begun ten minutes earlier.

Greg always hated arriving late, and he made plans to slip into the back pew. Once inside, however, he noted that the back half of the church was completely full. An usher met him and led him toward the front of the church. Feeling embarrassed, Greg followed the man up the side aisle to a seat in the second pew from the front. In the awkwardness of the moment, Greg forgot the customary genuflection and simply took his seat next to a cluster of elderly widows. Although nobody seemed to take notice of him, he sat in growing discomfort, unable to focus on the Scripture readings or the subsequent homily. During that time, another latecomer arrived and plunked himself down in the space next to Greg.

The sudden impatient coughing of the latecomer caught Greg by surprise, and he realized that time had arrived for Communion. The elderly ladies had already exited the pew into the main aisle, and the man stood waiting for Greg to move. He was only prevented from passing by because Greg had rested his feet on the kneeler, blocking the way. Greg quickly rose and headed for the aisle. Feeling completely unprepared, he made the short trip up to the front of church. Time seemed to stand still as the woman in front of him received. Turmoil raged inside of Greg as he waited for her to make the sign of the cross and step aside. As she began to move, Greg turned and followed her back toward their seats. When she reentered their row, Greg continued walking straight toward the back of the church as he repeatedly mouthed the words, "I'm not ready, Lord. I'm sorry. I'm just not ready today."

Chapter Twenty-Four

Greg felt as if here were in a movie as he pulled into the parking garage at Providential Insurance. His conversion experience and the passage of time had collaborated to make his old life seem like something he had read in a book, not actually experienced. The sights and sounds were all familiar, even down to the cracks on the pavement by the elevator. However, he no longer felt ownership of all the details. They belonged to someone else.

It was mid-morning, and Greg hoped he would not encounter any of his former co-workers. His plan was to make a quick strike without being noticed. As Greg walked toward the parking garage elevator, he could not help but notice a new luxury car, shiny black with temporary tags, parked at the end of a row. As he passed by, his heart skipped a beat as he noticed an occupant in the driver's seat. The dull hum of a radio vibrated the closed windows of the car. A set of shocked expressions were exchanged as Greg and Tony Franco locked eyes through the window. Greg stood motionless as the door flew open and the stout figure erupted from the vehicle.

"Greg, Greg Wesko?" stammered the surprised Tony Franco.

"Tony, what are you doing here?" Greg lamented his misfortune.

"Greg, I, I could ask you the same, the same question," Tony managed. "You can't take your old job back, you know. You've been replaced."

The news, although to be expected, took Greg aback. "Replaced? By whom?"

"Janet Semolini," Tony answered. "You remember her? I used to work for her when I first started at Providential."

"I thought you worked for Brian Hodges when you started," Greg recalled.

"Oh, oh yes. Well, I wanted to work for Janet. I used to help her out sometimes."

"Did you really? I don't remember that."

"You're right, I didn't help her out. But I wanted to. I tried. I would always make sure there was a fresh pot of coffee in the afternoon. She liked to drink coffee after lunch."

Conversation with Tony Franco was as confusing and frustrating as ever. "Nice car, Tony. You must have gotten a handsome bonus," Greg changed the subject.

"It's not mine. It belongs to my wife. I bought it for her. Then she gave it back when she moved out. She wasn't going to work today, so she said I could take it," Tony explained in rapid-fire fashion.

"I thought you said that she moved out. How could you take her car if she moved out?"

"Well, she moved back in. It happens. She's moved out several times now."

Greg searched for a way to quickly end the painful dialogue. "Hadn't you better get back to work, Tony? You won't get a hefty bonus again this year if you spend all your time listening to the radio in your car, I mean, your wife's car," Greg suggested.

"I'm on my way to the doctor," Tony offered. "I got to my car early, so I decided to sit and listen awhile."

"OK, Tony. Good to see you," Greg fibbed.

"Nice to see you, too," Tony returned. "Welcome back."

"I'm not back, Tony," Greg corrected him. "I was just in the neighborhood and decided to stop in for a minute. Providential Insurance is over for me." As the words left his mouth, Greg realized that they were far from the truth. PI was a demon that still needed to be exorcised from his life.

"Nice to see you anyway," Tony replied as he stepped back into his car.

As Greg watched him back out of his space and drive away, he realized that he had missed an opportunity. Despite all the strides he had made in his walk of faith, he had treated Tony Franco with the same subtle contempt and disrespect he had always harbored for the disturbed man. *I could have asked him how he is doing, if he is holding up OK despite the instability of his marriage. I shouldn't have brushed him off and hoped he would quickly leave. I'm sorry, Lord. Please help him. He seems headed for a psychotic break. Amen.*

A moment later, Greg passed through a revolving door into the front lobby of Providential Insurance. He entered the waiting area and approached the front desk. He was thankful to see a new receptionist whom he did not recognize. "Can I help you?" she greeted with a smile. A new shiny gold company logo flanked by the letters P and I hovered behind the woman.

"Greg!" a familiar voice called out just as Greg was about to answer. "Long time no see!"

"Al Finch!" Greg was amazed at his luck. "Just the person I wanted to see! Can we go back to your office?"

Al motioned to the receptionist that it was unnecessary for Greg to register as a visitor. Al hobbled back to the security office. He offered Greg a seat in the corner, out of view of the office window. After closing the door, he sat down in a swivel chair, his back to a panel of video monitors.

"I'm so glad you called," Al began. "I haven't felt like I could talk to no one about this. At least, not no one who wouldn't think I'd went crazy. Sometimes I don't know who to trust no more."

"Tell me," Greg prodded.

"Last year you asked me to look through the record books to see who was coming in on weekends. You said someone was playing a joke on you. Well I looked but some of the log books was missing. I went snooping around and couldn't find them nowhere. Well, I finally got to suspecting our newest security guard, Jodah Sherman, of misplacing them. When I accused him, he got all defensive on me."

"You think he took them on purpose?"

"Not at first," Al continued. "I thought he might have put them in the wrong place, or maybe he threw them out by accident, not realizing we're supposed to keep 'em. But the way he answered me, I thought he knew more than he was letting on. And it didn't seem harmless like just some prank."

"Why would he hide them?" asked Greg. "He must have wanted to erase the records of who was coming and going."

"My thoughts too," Al agreed. "I was thinking, maybe he had a friend or a girlfriend coming in on the weekends to hang out with him. But on the weekends, there ain't no receptionist, so visitors got to sign in with the security guard. If Sherman had a friend come over, he could cover it up by just having them not sign in at all."

"Sure, just like you didn't have me sign in today. Someone could have been paying Sherman to hide their own weekend activities. On the weekends, even employees have to sign in for safety reasons," Greg recalled.

"They changed that rule after you left. Actually, while I was out recovering from my accident."

"I heard about that. You hit a tree?"

"They say I fell asleep at the wheel, and that's true, I did. But I wasn't tired when I left. I think someone slipped me a mickey."

"A mickey? I thought that was something from the movies."

"Well I don't know what it is, but someone put something into my drink. I always nurse a diet soda all afternoon. I was driving, wide awake one minute, and the next thing I knew, I was coming to in the hospital. They tested me for alcohol and drugs. They said the test was clear on alcohol but they found traces of some kind of prescription drugs that ain't supposed to be available in this country or something. When I told them I wasn't taking nothing, they didn't believe me. In fact, I could have got in big trouble with the company. But they had a meeting about me and decided to let me stay on, giving me the benefit of the doubt."

"Wow, Al. I didn't know." Greg paused. "Who cut you the break?"

"I don't know, upper management I guess. My boss, Pat, is the one who told me."

"Has there been anything else weird going on?"

"No, nothing." Al sighed. "Maybe because Sherman quit about three months back."

A few moments passed before Greg broke the silence. "As I said on the phone this morning, I think I was framed for something I didn't do. And so I was wondering if you could help me out on another item or two?"

"Sure thing, Greg. What is it?" offered Al.

"First, could you get me a copy of the company phone directory? I want to call a few people."

"I can do that. Who you want to call? Maybe I can give you the low-down on some of them."

"Jesse Langston, in the IT department. Also Vester Campus."

"Don't know Langston," Al thought. "But I know Campus left the company. Didn't bother showing up for work one day. Never handed in a resignation. Haven't seen him since. Who else?"

"That's actually all for now. What do you know about any of my former bosses?"

"Well, I can't say I really ever knew who your bosses were."

"Chuck Hollis, Amos Stockley."

"Oh, the real high-ups. Same as always, I guess. Stockley never comes through here. He's got his own private keys to the building." Al handed Greg a two-inch binder. "Take my copy of the directory. I'll get another one from the storage room. Anything else you need?"

"Thanks a lot, Al. Just let me know if anything unusual happens. I've got a private detective working for me named Tom Phillips. You ever hear of him?"

Al rubbed his chin pensively. "Can't say that I have."

"In any case, he may contact you."

"No problem, Greg."

Greg departed the Providential Insurance parking garage and headed for his lunchtime appointment with Jason Coates and Tom Phillips. Again Tom Phillips rejected Greg's suggestion to meet at *That Pizza Place*. Instead, they agreed to meet in an out-of-the-way diner in New Britain, about twenty minutes from the PI office building. When

Greg arrived, Jason and Tom were already seated in a quiet back corner booth. Tom sported a Mets baseball cap, which hid most of his blond hair. As a Yankees fan, Greg found one more reason to hesitate trusting the cocky young detective.

"Now that Greg's here, start at the beginning," Jason urged Tom.

Tom leaned forward. "Over a year ago, Jack Fishburn noticed unusual activity in some foreign accounts he was responsible for. Certain European accounts that had remained largely inactive suddenly experienced some large withdrawals. He tried to follow up with the clients, but they were difficult to reach. In fact, he couldn't get any positive confirmation as to the validity of any of the transactions, although everything appeared legit on paper. When he brought it to the attention of his boss, he didn't think there was any reason for concern."

"And his boss was..." Jason prompted Tom to continue.

"Chuck Hollis."

"Wait a minute!" interjected Greg. "Chuck Hollis was my boss too. I didn't know Fishburn reported to him!"

"Most people didn't," Jason explained. "Julia Pratt and Chuck Hollis were the two managers in the Specialty Clients department. Hollis oversaw Domestic Accounts while Pratt covered Foreign Accounts. But because Pratt was a new manager, a few of the Foreign Accounts folks actually reported to Hollis with a dotted line to Pratt."

"Who were those people?" Greg asked.

"Besides Jack Fishburn, just Yoku Asahi and Eva Bernardino," Jason answered.

"Our two groups never intermixed," Greg mused. "I guess that's why I didn't know. I do recall seeing Eva in Chuck's office one time. Yoku Asahi I didn't know at all."

Tom Phillips resumed telling the story. "As I came to find out, the protocol at Providential Insurance is to bring any suspicious activity to your manager. The manager examines the information and decides whether to bring it to the next level. At Hollis' level, he has the option of bringing it to his manager, Amos Stockley, or taking direct ownership of the situation by filing a report with the Information Security Department, ISD for short."

Jason interrupted. "As you may recall, Greg, anyone can actually initiate a report with the ISD if they feel that management will not handle their situation properly. However, the ISD is notoriously incompetent. In all my years at PI, I've only known of one case that was actually solved."

"What was that about?" asked Tom.

"Someone was filing expense reports for personal items like an iPod, a DVR and so on," explained Jason. "He was fired but not prosecuted."

Tom picked up the narration again. "When Jack Fishburn reported suspicious activity to Hollis, he wasn't satisfied with the response. He never got a straight answer out of Hollis about whether he brought the matter to the attention of his boss or to ISD. So he hired me to do some investigation."

"Any paid with his own money?" Greg asked.

"The checks came from his personal account with a local bank, not from PI, so I suppose so. At first the investigation was fairly low-key. He just asked me to look into the welfare of some of his clients, mostly in Europe. Especially the clients whom he could not reach by phone but who had allegedly made some large withdrawals. It wasn't easy to do from here, but Fishburn didn't want to pay for me to fly to Europe. I did what I could, and we concocted a plan for him to do some investigation on his next business trip overseas."

"What did you find out?" Jason leaned in closer.

"Jack never got to take another business trip. When the company didn't make its quarterly goals, they placed restrictions on travel overseas. Jack had a heart attack and died before the restrictions were lifted."

"I don't recall any restrictions," Greg mused, "but then I never had any reason to go abroad on business." Greg's eyes were drawn involuntarily to Tom's Mets baseball cap. Something more than sports rivalry was chipping away at him, but he could not pin down the underlying reason.

"I don't travel out of the country either," Jason stated. "However, it does ring a bell. We certainly had a few quarters in the last two years where the company didn't make its financial goals. The idea of restrictions is plausible."

Tom stroked above his upper lip while planning out his words. "In the meantime, I poked around to see what it would take to divert funds or make fraudulent withdrawals. I got a tip from an associate about a guy in the IT department who had helped the police nab a co-worker who was stealing office supplies. He seemed like a reliable start, and he was somewhat willing to cooperate."

"Without help from ISD, I suppose," Jason mused. Tom nodded agreement.

"What was his name?" Greg asked.

When Phillips hesitated, Jason reminded him, "Remember, you are on our payroll."

"Jesse Langston. He worked with me to identify a relatively new IT employee, Sylvester Campus, as a possible suspect. He said that Campus acted suspiciously. For example, he always worked late, but never seemed to finish his assignments. He didn't seem to have respect for authority or rules. Langston said that Campus seemed like the kind of guy who wouldn't mind selling people's access passwords for a price. Jack Fishburn and I set up a sort of sting operation. I hooked Jack up with a wire and then sent him to find Campus at the end of the day, when they could be alone. He asked Campus what it would take to get a password to someone's e-mail account so he could play a joke. At first, Campus played the good boy and refused to even acknowledge Jack's offer. But when Jack offered him two hundred dollars, his ears seemed to pick up. Unfortunately, someone else came into the office just at that time. After that, Campus refused to talk to Jack anymore."

The waitress arrived to take their lunch orders, forcing the conversation to subside. The diner was filling up with customers, and the noise was a welcome mask to their discussions.

Tom continued, "I used some of my contacts to check into activities of other PI employees. Mostly we looked for people who had a sudden change in lifestyle or who seemed to be living above their means. One obvious candidate was a man named Tony Franco."

"Yeah, I know Tony," Greg frowned. "Quite an unstable guy."

"And quite a spender," Tom elaborated. "He bought an expensive sports car recently. He took a two-week trip to Europe by himself. He bought a second home in upstate New York. His wife had a few shopping sprees at the jewelry store. These are not the activities of a junior accountant."

"I don't know," Greg mused. "Before I left PI, Tony confided in me that he was experiencing marital problems. And when I ran into him when I went back to visit PI, he said his wife has since moved in and out several times. It seems he's been throwing a lot of money at her to try and regain her affections. I think he's headed for a nervous breakdown. He had been institutionalized for a short period of time during college, he once told me," Greg recollected.

"Yes, that's true. As of yet, I don't have any solid evidence on Franco, but he acts like a guilty man. I'm still working on him," Tom continued.

"I think he's just unbalanced," Greg suggested as the waitress arrived with their sandwiches. Inexplicably, the wisp of blond hair protruding from underneath Phillips' cap continued to agitate him.

"In any case, Jack Fishburn helped me get some information that uncovered some suspicious activity in Bob Gurth's area. We eventually met with him, similar to the meeting we all had last week. Gurth agreed to work with us. At first I think he just wanted to get us off his back. But when he did some investigation of his own, he found that some transfers had been made from some of his Asian accounts without the proper protocols. Just about that time, Jack had his heart attack."

"Last time you suggested that the heart attack was suspicious," Greg recalled.

"Jack wasn't a health nut, but he was in decent shape and only forty-five years old. No history of early heart disease in his family. But since the death was not ruled suspicious, they quickly concluded that an undiagnosed case of arteriosclerosis had led to his heart attack." Tom lowered his voice and leaned forward to add, "There are a dozen drugs you can slip someone to trigger a sudden heart attack. Some can be administered right through the skin. I'm convinced that Jack Fishburn was murdered."

Tom's repeated accusation sent shivers up Greg's spine. Jason whispered his agreement, "Bob Gurth's untimely death convinces me you're right."

Tom addressed Greg directly. "Jesse Langston told me that you were asking him questions. He didn't really want to be involved in the situation. I started watching you."

"Was I suspicious?" Greg raised his eyebrows and studied Tom's face intently.

"Not very. I didn't think that you were perpetrating anything. But it seemed that you were caught in the web."

"The computer guy!" Greg jumped to his feet as the words spilled out of his mouth. Pointing at Tom Phillips, he repeated, "You're the computer guy from Bob Gurth's office!" Embarrassed by his outburst, Greg quickly sat down while Tom motioned for him to calm down and speak quietly.

"Way back then, yes. So you do remember. I was wondering if you were going to figure it out," Tom smiled.

"What are you two talking about?" demanded Jason.

Tom laughed. "Quite a while ago, Greg caught me in Bob Gurth's office. He had given me a key, and I would use his office to launch investigations, under the guise of being a computer repairman for Takai Computing Services. I went by the name Phillip Thompson. I tried to access other people's accounts to see how easy it could be. Trust me, it ain't easy."

Greg continued the story of their first encounter. "So I caught him snooping in Bob's office in the dark, and he made up a phony story about having a new baby and being tired all the time. He claimed he was taking a catnap. I only recognized you because of your Mets cap. That day you were wearing a cap too, and that's what triggered the memory." To Greg's surprise, the realization helped lend validity to Tom. Greg felt trust beginning to grow.

"Let me tell you what was going on with me, and why I was doing my own snooping," Greg offered. "Money was disappearing from my accounts. The first time it was $20,000. I figured I had made a mistake, and to cover myself, I used my own money to make up the missing sum. I planned to recoup the money when I found out what had happened. But I wasn't successful. Then some unauthorized transfers were made. Chuck Hollis took notice and was forced to call for an audit. Nothing positive could be found, but I was placed unofficially on probation. Finally Chuck called me into his office one last time. He informed me that additional moneys were missing from my accounts. He claimed that he didn't want to suspect me of anything, and that if I resigned immediately then they would forgive me of any possible wrongdoing. He never divulged the details, and I was too, uh, well," he hesitated, "I was too out of my mind at the time to press him on it. So I left."

"So how did you come to contact me?" Jason asked Tom.

"Before his death, Bob told me that if anything should happen, you were a trustworthy man. When I found out that you were Greg's former boss, so much the better. And in our first chance meeting, Greg mentioned your name."

"I did?" Greg was perplexed.

"Somehow you mentioned that you didn't know Bob Gurth, but you had a mutual friend," explained Tom. "When I asked who it was, you sang like a canary. You must be terrible at keeping secrets."

"I was under a lot of stress. Usually my tongue is not so loose," Greg defended himself.

Jason turned to Greg, "Before you got here today, I told Tom that you had confided in me back then. As it turns out, Jesse Langston had given you that information at Tom's prompting. He was helping us out before we even got on board."

Tom resumed his narrative. "I checked out two men, Darren Lado and Jay Drock, whose computers had been linked to unauthorized activity. Both men checked out clean, so far," Tom informed them. "They were away on business during at least some of the suspicious activity, and they've had no change in lifestyle or gross additions to their bank accounts."

"What's the next step?" Greg asked.

"Two main things. First, I'm in the process of investigating the employees at PI more thoroughly. Second, I have a lead to follow that I'm not yet ready to reveal."

"Why not?" demanded Jason.

"I don't want to upset you in case it goes nowhere. You won't benefit by knowing what it may be." Tom settled his eyes on Greg as he spoke.

Tom's statement went unchallenged. "Then let's meet again soon," Jason suggested. "How about Friday?"

"No, I'll call you when I have something worth sharing. In the meantime, be careful. These are dangerous criminals we're dealing with. Some of them have to be people you know. They are responsible for at least two murders, maybe more," Tom said very seriously. "I'll be in touch within a week. In the meantime, stay close to people who love you and can protect you."

On the way home, Greg watched the world with a new sense of alarm. Every oncoming car seemed menacing. When he stopped at red lights in the city, every pedestrian was a potential assassin. His list of people who loved him and could protect him was very short. He felt the overwhelming urge to flee. His thoughts turned to his sister. He began to pray.

God responded. Tension slowly ebbed as Greg accepted God's outpouring of love. Although the threat to his life could hold merit, a sense began to develop that God's will would not be thwarted. He prayed aloud.

"God, I put my life into your hands. I don't know if someone will try to kill me. I don't know if it's worth pursuing this case. I could let it go, but I think you want me to work for justice. Help me. I don't know what to do."

Greg awoke to the soft creak of a floorboard. Heart pounding, he sat up in bed and stared into the darkness beyond his open bedroom door. The soft moonlight peeking through the curtains illuminated a path from his open bedroom door through the living room to the kitchen. Over the pulsing of his heartbeat in his ears, Greg strained to listen for a repeat of the noise. His eyes scanned the shadows. Wishing for a gun, Greg reached over to his nightstand to pick up his battery-operated alarm clock, the only weapon at hand. It calmly displayed

3:16 in green digits as if nothing were wrong in the world. Two endless minutes passed before another solitary creak broke the stillness. Two additional minutes passed in utter silence. Greg started to convince himself that the noise was merely the sound of the building settling. He prayed a quick prayer of forgiveness for all his sins and resolved to get out of bed. An investigation would either prove his fears were unfounded or would accelerate an unwelcome end. In any case, he knew that sleep was not an option.

Still gripping the alarm clock, Greg stepped quietly out of bed. He crossed the floor without a single creak. Bracing himself, he exited his bedroom and entered the living room. Nothing happened. Walking a few steps, he found the wall switch and bathed the apartment in blazing light. No movement. No sound. Feeling more confident, he toured the rest of the apartment. No intruders lurked about. He sat down at the kitchen table and sighed in relief.

Lisa died in the kitchen.

The thought struck him so suddenly that he almost fell out of his chair. Lisa had died in his apartment, in his kitchen. Another untimely death. The chilling thought penetrated to his innermost being. "Oh Lord, was that fire meant for me?" The sense came upon him with such vivid urgency that he could not mistake its truth. "Oh God, they wanted to kill me!" he called out. "She died instead of me! Oh why, oh why?" He fell to his knees on the hard kitchen floor and wept bitterly.

Chapter Twenty-Five

Greg's face lit up to see the caller-ID register a Texas number. He clicked the button on his phone with haste.

"Theresa!" he exclaimed. "How are you?"

"Excellent, Greg. Really excellent," Theresa responded. Greg was overjoyed to hear his sister sounding so happy. With just a minor amount of probing, Greg learned that Theresa and Jared had started marriage counseling with their priest. The results were apparent even over the phone. Theresa relayed how Jared had started spending more quality time with the family. He had also taken the initiative to reserve special time for just the two of them. With Theresa's miraculous cure, her energy returned, and they no longer felt the need for a full-time housekeeper.

"Losing Ana María has been a real blessing," Theresa continued. "At first, as you witnessed, Jared was irate. I'm sorry he directed some of it at you."

"My fight with Jared was over him slapping you, not over Ana María," Greg reminded her. "He can't ever do that to you again," Greg warned.

"He knows that. Greg, it was a one-time deal. It's no excuse, I know. But I do want to assure you that it never happened before, and it will never happen again. If only you could see how remorseful Jared is. He's also deeply upset because he thinks he ruined his relationship with you. Forever. Did he, Greg?"

Greg paused for a moment to decide what his answer should be. Even after the months he had spent at the McAllen estate, Greg still did not feel he had ever developed a solid relationship with Jared. "We'll have to see, Theresa. If you're willing to give him another chance, then I suppose I should as well. I have to say, though, I'm not feeling a great deal of love for the man right now."

"Give it time, Greg. Give it time. It's enough for me to know that you are considering it. Jared and I are married, and he's always going to be a part of my life. So at some level, you have to accept him."

"Don't worry, Sis," Greg reassured her. "I'll have to take the good with the bad."

"Anyway, Greg," Theresa continued, "The incident with Ana María really brought things to a head. I even accused Jared of having an affair with her! After all, she claimed that he let her have that horrid amulet."

"Was that true?"

"I confronted Jared about it, and he admitted letting her keep it. He knew I didn't want it anymore, so he didn't see any harm in it. But now I think he understands that it's not acceptable to take back gifts from your wife and give them to another woman!"

"I would hope so!" responded Greg. "Do you believe him that he didn't have an affair?"

"Honestly, after much consideration, I really do believe him. I've prayed a lot, and we've talked a lot. You know, after I fired Ana María, I don't think she would have had any reason to keep an affair secret. It's exactly the type of thing she would have loved to rub in my face. Her silence actually supports his case. And surprisingly, I don't think Ana María would have an affair with a married man. She seems disconnected from the truth. On the one hand, she plays the pious Catholic, adhering to the rules. I think she really believes that she is right with God. On the other hand, somehow she thinks it's acceptable to dabble in the occult, practicing witchcraft and putting curses on people. I can't understand where she's coming from. She would never miss Mass or commit adultery, but she has no issues with using magic incantations."

Greg thought about the one time Ana María had seemed to make advances on him. He decided not to make mention of it to Theresa, but inwardly he wondered what she had intended and how she might have justified it. "I hope you're right, Theresa. For your sake and the children's, I hope you are."

She is right. The ephemeral words flashed through his mind in an instant, and he longed to recall them to make sure he had heard them correctly.

Greg and Theresa's conversation lasted well over an hour, and for that time Greg felt immersed back in the comfort of his sister's company, the warm Texas sun and the cradle of his nascent faith. The time passed much too quickly.

As Sunday approached, Greg's heart grew heavier. The thought of returning to the same unwelcoming church was more than he could bear. He recalled the location of another church a few blocks away. "I don't suppose you care were I go, as long as I show up," he prayed softly.

Greg's memory had served him correctly, and he arrived at a modern looking building bearing the name Church of the New Gospel. "New is what I need," he murmured as he approached the entryway.

A man in a brown sports coat stuck out his arm in greeting. "Hello, friend! Welcome to the Church of the New Gospel. Is this your first time worshipping with us?"

The man's friendly demeanor set Greg at ease. "Yes, it is. I'm a Catholic, but I haven't been able to find a church where I feel comfortable yet," he found himself admitting. "I've only been to a Protestant church one time, for a friend's wedding."

"Good man. We aren't Protestant or Catholic. We welcome people of all faiths. You can worship any way you want here at the Church of the New Gospel. Feel at home, brother. Make yourself comfortable."

Greg found a seat towards the back of the church. Inside there were tapestries of various colors draped on whitewashed cinder-block walls. Greg couldn't find an altar, but a small table with a glass of water and a Bible sat next to a white podium on a small raised platform. The podium stood in the center of the open room, with seats arranged in concentric rings and angled toward the middle. Although less ornately decorated that most of the Catholic churches Greg had attended, the bright and informal atmosphere was warm and welcoming. Most of the congregation seemed to know each other and engaged in quiet conversation in their cushioned seats. A young couple waved in his direction from across the room. After several repeated waves, Greg realized that the greeting was meant for him, so he raised a hesitant hand in response. They countered with wide smiles.

An excited hush fell on the crowd as the organist struck a jazzily resonant chord. The whole congregation rose to their feet and began clapping in time to the music. As the crowd began to belt out the tune, someone offered Greg a songbook open to a hymn entitled, "I've Got a Friend Up There." Although unfamiliar, Greg found the upbeat spirit of the crowd contagious. Soon he was swaying back and forth to the music, humming along and repeating part of the refrain. Four verses later, the crowd sat down expectantly.

A man in a white suit entered the scene from a door opposite Greg's seat. As he passed down the aisle, he extended his hand to several members with a hearty smile. He waved to each section of the church and stepped onto the platform. "Good morning and welcome!" he shouted enthusiastically.

"What a lovely day we have been given today! Amen?"

As a unit, the bulk of the congregation responded with a definitive "Amen!" A few people responded, "Amen, Pastor Whitcomb!" Applause broke out. When it died down, Pastor Whitcomb continued.

"Do we have any visitors with us today?"

Greg's heart pounded with mortal dread that the spotlight would fall upon him. A few people stood up and introduced relatives and friends whom they had brought with them. Each group of newcomers stood up and received a hearty ovation. Finally, the pastor asked, "Anyone else? Anyone here by themselves?" After a few seconds of silence, he prompted, "Don't be shy. We're all friends here at the Church of the New Gospel."

A young brunette stood up and meekly waved. "Tell us your name, young lady," urged the pastor gently.

"Hi, I'm Sarah Huff. I just moved to town."

"Welcome, Sarah!" Pastor Whitcomb greeted her. She humbly accepted the congregation's rousing applause. "Who else?"

The urge to stand was almost irresistible, despite his penchant for anonymity. He felt that if he did not stand on his own, he would be levitated to standing nonetheless. He stood. "Hi, I'm Greg," he forced with as much confidence as he could muster. The ensuing applause embraced him. He sat down as the crowd quieted to listen to the Bible and a commentary following each passage.

A reading from the Psalms encouraged him to seek the Lord in prayer. The story of David and Goliath reminded him that the proud and arrogant soon fall. Then Pastor Whitcomb closed the Bible and held it in his hands.

"Brothers and sisters," he began, "many people want to limit our access to the power of God. They say we have to worship this way or that way. They say that we need to use this book and this book alone to know God." Whitcomb raised the Bible and shook it at the crowd. "They say without it, people go to Hell." He paused for effect. "But I say that people who think that way have already put themselves into their own private hell, the hell of their own narrow thinking. For we know that Hell is not a real place, but only a state of mind."

As the pastor continued talking, Greg looked at the faces in the crowd. He read expressions of deep concentration, pleasant acceptance, and stern agreement. But nowhere did he see the image of the confusion and questioning that he felt inside himself.

"The Bible tells us about God, but we must remember to listen to the other voices which speak of God. We can find God in each person's own version of God. God cannot be contained in one book or one person's view. He or she is in your own inner sense of right and wrong. He or she is in the voices of your children. Look even in your very own goals and desires. Follow them, for God helps those who help themselves."

The pastor's words sat uneasily in Greg's stomach. Some of his words made sense, but many of the thoughts expressed were very troubling, contrary to what Greg had come to learn over the recent months. Greg could not hear clearly enough to sort fact from fiction, but the inner working of the Holy Spirit moved him to one firm conclusion: he needed to escape. His row had completely filled up, and the shortest route out required climbing in front of a dozen people. Mustering all his courage, he offered up a silent prayer for help and rose from his seat. He did not look up to meet any potential stares, perhaps an entire room full. Instead he continued purposely and politely squirming past the pairs of legs blocking his exit. As he walked down the aisle towards the door, he did catch a few quick glances in his direction, but mostly the faces seemed transfixed on the preacher of the gospel of prosperity and self-reliance. As he approached the archway leading to the main foyer, an usher smiled at him, "Welcome, Greg. The men's room is just down the hall to the left."

"Thank you," Greg returned automatically.

As he headed towards the exit, Greg heard the harsh click of footsteps following him. Not daring to turn around, Greg quickened his pace. The pursuer matched his gait. He pushed through the doors and into the open air as a woman called, "Wait, wait!" Feeling relatively safe outside, he turned to address the voice's owner. It was Sarah Huff.

"Please wait. I need to talk to you," she pleaded in between urgent breaths.

"Why?"

"Because you gave me the courage to do what I felt I had to do. And so I need to know if you left for the same reasons I did," she pressed him earnestly.

Not knowing what words to choose, Greg prayed for quick assistance. "I couldn't accept what the pastor was saying," he started. "I don't mind finding out I'm mistaken, but the words he said were so confusing to me. Some of it sounded very good. But then what he said about the Bible, God and Hell were so opposed to what I have come to learn. I was afraid that if I listened much more, I would forget what I knew to be true. And so I had to leave."

Sarah looked at him with wide eyes. "That's why I knew I had to leave too. I just moved here from southern Virginia and I wanted to find a good church. I used to go when I was a child, but during college I drifted away, only attending church every once in a while. Since I just transferred with my job, I thought this would be a good chance to start fresh. But today I heard so many things that made me feel I had been out of the loop too long."

"My sister told me that God never changes," Greg answered. "So even if you are away for a while, He will still be the same perfect God when you return. That's how He is."

"Don't you mean 'he or she?'" Sarah returned with a facetious smile.

"Yeah, right," he chuckled. "Do you want to get some coffee?"

Chapter Twenty-Six

The sign at the entrance to the parking lot indicated that university parking permits were not required on the weekend. Greg pulled into the last vacant space.

Greg waited for Sarah Huff to exit his vehicle before activating the remote lock from his key chain. The lights winked twice at the two as they headed toward the campus chapel in the approaching dusk. Inside, two students greeted them with songbooks and missalettes. They took seats near the front of the church.

The low rumbling of chatter filled the room with a friendly ambiance. Since the university chapel was used for services of many faiths, no overtly Catholic or other denominational fixtures graced the interior. Candles were brought in and set up next to a card table covered with an altar cloth. As Mass began, students accompanied the priest with a crucifix and the lectionary in the entrance procession. At once Greg felt safely at home, yet a slight apprehension remained concerning his new non-Catholic friend Sarah. He wondered inwardly if she would find the Catholic Mass as foreign and contrary as the service they had attended at the Church of the New Gospel earlier that morning. During the entrance hymn, his thoughts briefly wandered back to their coffee date, which had evolved into lunch. Afterwards Greg had searched the phone book for a Sunday evening Mass. When Sarah expressed interest in joining him, Greg was overjoyed to extend an offer to pick her up after dinner.

Greg found the Mass familiar and soothing. At Communion time, he remained in his seat with Sarah. Although he told himself that it would make Sarah more comfortable if he stayed back with her, he knew that his feelings of guilt were truly preventing him from fully communing with Jesus. He agonized inwardly over what he felt was a betrayal by trying another church.

After Mass, Sarah remained in the pew praying. Trying to minimize his interruption, Greg softly whispered to her that he wanted to talk to the priest and would return in a few minutes.

As the priest finished chatting with two students in the doorway, he turned towards Greg. Greg noted that the man of God looked barely older than himself. "Hello, I'm Father Phillip," the man extended his hand in warm welcome. His eyes danced with life as he met Greg's gaze.

"Father, do you have time to hear my confession?"

Father Phillip led Greg to a discreet corner of the chapel. Greg began to relate his sins and struggles over the weeks since he had left Texas, finally ending by recounting the events of the morning. The priest listened intently and periodically nodded his head in understanding.

"The words of the pastor started to make me forget what it was that I believed before I entered the building. So I left," Greg explained.

"Wise choice," Father Phillip commended him. "It's OK to have your beliefs challenged, but it's vitally important to protect yourself from misinformation and hype. Hell is a real place, and people cannot wish it or preach it away. And even if people somehow thought they could find God without reading the Bible, why would they ignore the instruction book that He provided for us? And if God wanted us to call Him 'he or she,' wouldn't He have said so? Jesus didn't give us a prayer called the 'Our Father or Mother!'"

Greg chuckled in spite of himself. "You know, Father, they didn't even mention Jesus at all in that service."

"It's hard to preach Jesus and not talk about the truth. And vice versa."

Later, after Greg performed his penance, he noticed that Sarah's seat had been vacated. He found her standing outside, gazing up at the stars. In the moonlight, she struck Greg as someone who needed terribly to be kissed. "Do you want to grab a bite to eat?"

The mist from a recent early-spring rain hung damp in the mid-afternoon air. With the classified section of his newspaper, Greg prepared himself a dry seat on a green bench. The location matched the description Tom Phillips had given him over the cell phone. At Tom's prompting, Greg had ordered a new cell phone in his sister's name in order to protect the content of their conversations. Only Tom, Jason, Greg and Theresa were to have the number. However, Greg also secretly gave it to Joe and Marina Tropetto, friends whom he trusted more than any private investigator.

A man jogged by in sweats and a tee shirt. A moment later, he returned at a slower pace and stopped to take the seat next to Greg. "Seat's wet," the man muttered. Greg recognized the voice as Tom's.

"You're half bald!" Greg exclaimed quietly.

"If you look carefully, you'll see I have a skin cap on. I'm working on another case today, and I need a disguise. I entered the gym as the young, virile Tom Phillips and came out as an anonymous middle-aged health nut," Tom said without letting himself look at Greg.

"The fire in my apartment last year was no accident," Greg blurted out.

"I believe you're right," Tom frowned. "I avoided mentioning this in our last meeting because I had no proof. My suspicions started back when I was working for Bob Gurth, and I looked into the fire at that time. There was no evidence to prove that it was deliberate, but then again, there was no evidence to completely rule it out either. Officially, however, according to the police department and the insurance company, it was an accidental explosion caused by a gas leak."

"So there's no way to point a finger at anyone," Greg mused dejectedly.

"Not at this time."

"What else can we do?"

Tom sighed and leaned over on the pretense of tying his shoes. "My former employer was an expert in explosions and fires. I have to admit, I don't hold a candle to him in that department. If there were anything to uncover, he could do it. Unfortunately, we aren't on good terms."

"What happened?" asked Greg.

"I'd rather not get into it. Let's just say that I like to run an honest business, and that meant that I couldn't run with him any more. I haven't spoken to him in a few years or so."

"Could you ask him for help anyway?" Greg pleaded.

"I'll see what I can do. In the meantime, don't give your new cell phone number out to anyone else. Joe and Marina Tropetto check out OK, but next time you may not be so lucky," Tom warned as he rose to his feet.

"How did you know?"

"It's my job to know. I'll call you later." With that, Tom resumed his jog and disappeared around a corner into the woods. Greg sat for a few minutes, stunned that his little secret had been uncovered, but also grateful that his private detective was astute enough to do so.

"Hi Greg, it's Sarah," the answering machine played back fuzzily. "I found a nice church I thought we could try on Sunday. It's called St. Stephen the

Martyr." She proceeded to recite the address and Mass times. Greg was pleasantly surprised at the message. The previous Sunday night they had talked about their denominational backgrounds and church experiences, or lack thereof. Although Sarah felt no allegiance to any particular denomination, she had grown up with consistent church attendance and had maintained some level of relationship with God, even when no longer attending church regularly. She was fascinated by Greg's recent strong return to the Catholic Church after a meager start in childhood followed by years of absence.

Greg returned her phone call to make plans for Sunday morning. Before the phone call ended, a date was also set for the approaching evening.

With time on his hands, Greg had begun several small projects. In the past, between working for Providential Insurance and keeping fit at the gym, he had barely saved any time for his fiancée, let alone any projects. Judging the time required to get ready for the night's date, he figured that he could squeeze in half an hour sanding down an antique side table he had bought for Theresa's birthday. His plans were to refinish it and drive it down to San Antonio for the event, still many months away. His ulterior motive was to witness firsthand how Jared was treating Theresa and the children.

Time passed quickly, and Greg shot a look at the clock to find that he was running very late. Panicking, he threw down his materials and raced for the shower. In a flash he was ready and speeding towards Sarah's apartment. The route was familiar, following the same initial roads he had taken many times to Lisa's apartment across town. He also passed the street that led to where Joanna lived. Despite his best efforts, he could not put these two other women out of his mind. He prayed that he would not use the wrong name when speaking with Sarah.

Greg arrived at Sarah's apartment only a few minutes late. If Sarah noticed his flustered appearance, she made no outward sign. She wore jeans and a turtleneck sweater against the chilly evening. Although Greg felt overdressed for the movies in his khakis, blue shirt and tie, Sarah was thoroughly impressed.

Greg watched the film with feigned interest. He had difficulty focusing on the story as thoughts of women and dating flooded his mind. Feeling like a teenager, he wondered whether he should reach out and hold her hand. He and Lisa had reached a comfortable point where handholding was optional but frequent and always welcome. The sudden touch of the other's hand in the dark theater always sent a thrill through each of them. He had never caught a movie with Joanna, so since Lisa his hands had only experienced a brief encounter with Ana María's, quite an uncomfortable memory now. Conflicting thoughts prevented him from taking hold of Sarah's hand. However, the moment seemed to scream for it. Thinking of an excuse, he leaned over and said awkwardly, "My hands are just covered in butter from the popcorn."

"Oh, so are mine," Sarah answered as she handed him a pile of napkins. "Don't worry about it."

Missing the clue, Greg did worry about it. He wiped his hands so thoroughly that Sarah handed him another dose of napkins. Finally she leaned over and whispered, "It's OK, I don't mind."

"I'll be right back," he uttered quietly, jumping up and running out of the room. He raced to the men's room and washed his hands and face. Looking in the mirror, he noticed how signs of aging had begun to make their mark. In the ten years or so since graduation, his grand plans had taken a serious derailment. The man staring back at him looked weary, scared and unhappy.

This is not the look of a man who knows that God loves him.

The enlightenment shook him and left him wanting more.

You have to live an honest life.

Greg reflected on the message for a moment. Summoning new resolve, he fixed his hair and dried his face before heading back to the movie. When he stepped into the hallway, he spotted Sarah waiting outside the restrooms. He approached her.

"Are you OK?" he asked.

"I'm fine. I wanted to ask you if *you* are OK!" she responded with concern.

"I think so. Can we go somewhere and talk?"

A few minutes later, Greg and Sarah placed their orders and handed their menus to the waitress. The intimate atmosphere of the small café helped Greg open up.

"Sarah, there's a lot about me that you don't know."

She looked at him with inviting eyes. "And there's a lot about me that you don't know either. So let's talk," she offered.

"I want to be up front with you about my past," he started. "I've been in relationships before."

"Do tell," Sarah prodded with a smile.

Greg recounted his relationship with Lisa, from first meeting to engagement to tragic end. He paused to choke back a tear from time to time, especially as he spoke of the courage Lisa had shown in standing her moral ground. Sarah sat still, listening intently. Her expression varied, showing soft joy at some times, sympathetic understanding at others. Some of the memories seemed to pain her as well.

Greg offered a less detailed overview of Joanna and Ana María. Sarah was shocked by the devious tactics of the latter.

"And so I felt I had to be honest, right from the beginning. I don't know where our relationship is going. Truthfully, I don't know whether it's fair to pursue anything with us while I'm still straightening my life out."

Sarah took a long breath before answering. "Waiting for someone to get their life in order can be a long road, maybe a lifetime. You can't wait that long for your own sake. And I can't for mine either. But I can understand that you need a short time of adjustment. So do I. After all, I just moved to town, and I can't fall for the first guy I meet. That is, the first guy who stands up and walks out of a church with me!"

The two smiled and laughed lightly. As the waitress brought the bill, Greg decided to bring closure to the conversation on the topic. "I want to keep seeing you. Just know that I have some limitations, for now."

"I can deal with that, for now," she conceded.

Jason Coates handed a check over to Tom Phillips. "We decided to alternate making the payments," he informed the detective.

Tom looked from Jason to Greg and back before speaking. "I spoke with my old boss."

"What did he say?" asked Greg, moving to the edge of his seat.

"It's mostly what he didn't say," Tom said enigmatically. "I won't go into all the details now, but I got bad vibes from the man. His name is Ian Jacobs. I think he knows more than he's telling. The details of the fire seemed unusually familiar to him. I think someone else already hired him to investigate."

"Who?" Jason and Greg asked in unison.

"I've been racking my brains trying to figure that one out for the last two days. The best way to find out is to set up an undercover operation."

"How do we do that?" Greg quizzed him.

"I need your help. We need to send someone into Jacobs' office to do some snooping around," Tom answered.

"We're not going to do anything illegal," Jason spoke up.

"I'm not proposing any breaking and entering. Anyway, it can't be either of you. You are known to the perpetrators. We need someone outside the loop."

After a moment of thought, Greg announced, "I know just the right people."

"I knew you would," Tom smiled back.

The glass door was soaped over to minimize the view inside the small dark office. All other windows were covered with thick horizontal blinds. A single finger appeared between two blinds, making a space just wide enough for an eye to peer out. Once noticed, the finger immediately disappeared.

Joe Tropetto jumped at the sound of a buzzer as he opened the door and pushed into the darkness inside. The outside light struggled to shine in through the window, casting shadows on the floor reading, "I. Jacobs, Private Investigator" in Art Deco bold font. Joe pushed through another door and into a small waiting area. A smallish woman in her forties sat at a desk and adjusted the column of dyed strawberry blond hair resting atop her head.

"Can I help you?" she mumbled nasally through two hairpins protruding from her mouth. She removed them and stuck them in their proper places in the mountain of pink hair.

"I need a PI," Joe said in the toughest voice he could muster.

"You're in luck. We got one," she retorted. "What's it about?"

"Rather not say," Joe responded gruffly.

"Fine, I know. Marriage troubles. I'll let Ian know you're here. Just a minute and then you'll go through that door," she indicated a black wooden door as she pressed an intercom button. "Man here to see you about a woman," she barked. Joe caught some profanity thrown back her way. He heard the sound of another buzzer as the door lock released for his passage. Slinking through the doorway, he was greeted by a stale musty odor and the unwelcome click of the door locking behind him.

"In here," a gruff voice bellowed down the hallway. He traced its source to a wooden door on his left, partially cracked open. The force of his first knock opened the door fully to reveal a dark, smoky room. From an ashtray on a grimy metal desk, a trail of cigarette smoke rose up through beams of sunlight peeking in through the blinds. A man with shoe-polish black hair extended a hand through the haze. "Ian Jacobs at your service," he grunted. "Have a seat."

Without introducing himself, Joe sat in a stark metal chair with a hard green cushion on the seat and back. As he sank into the cushion, air rushed out in a quiet hiss.

"Don't be so nervous," Jacobs barked. "Tell me your name and your problem."

"Joe Tropetto," he returned. "I want you to follow my wife."

"Affair?" Jacobs smirked. "Nothing for you to be embarrassed about. Happens all the time. Don't take it personally. And hey, it may turn out that she's just selling cosmetics on the side or something. But I get paid either way, you know."

"Of course. I just want to know what she's up to."

"Let's start with a picture," Jacobs mumbled as he took a puff from his cigarette. "Then I'll need to ask you some questions."

Joe reached into his pocket to retrieve his wallet. Opening it, he removed a photo of Marina and handed it to Jacobs. While he examined it, Joe let his wallet fall to the floor. "Clumsy of me. I'm a little jittery. I never did anything like this before."

"Don't sweat it," Jacobs assured him as he turned around to rummage through a file cabinet. Joe leaned over to pick up his wallet. As he hovered over the floor, he slipped a tiny electronic device out of his billfold. Removing a small adhesive strip, he stuck the gadget to the underside of Jacobs' steel desk. He placed the removable adhesive in his wallet and returned the wallet to his pocket.

"I've got some questions to ask you. But first, why don't you go ahead and fill out this form," Jacobs said as he turned around to face Joe again.

"I'd like to keep this as confidential as possible," Joe frowned.

"Don't worry. The lady won't know I'm tailing her at all. But if you want me to work with you, you've got to work with me. I need to know her habits, her favorite stores, things like that. Does she work?"

"We run a pizza place together," Joe answered. Every time he revealed a true aspect of their personal lives, he cringed inside. Yet he agreed that tarnishing his reputation with a fabricated suspicion was less risky than trying to assume a false identity.

As the interrogation continued, Joe took the opportunity to rub his sock against the furtive bug in order to remove his fingerprints. What seemed like an eternity later, Joe thanked the man and stood to leave.

"Give your down payment to Phyllis on the way out. Three hundred dollars by check or two fifty cash."

Joe exited the office and walked back toward the door. The lock clicked to allow his passage, and he entered the small lobby. He took his wallet out and fumbled through it nervously. Phyllis smacked her gum and waited as Joe laid Greg's money down on the counter. "Do I get a receipt?" he inquired.

"Your canceled check would be a receipt. You want to do it that way instead?" she retorted, pushing the cash back towards him.

"No, thanks. He said you would give me a call to set up another appointment when he had something."

"Then you'll be hearing from me after the weekend," she smiled wryly as she took the money. "See ya."

The final chorus of "Here I Am, Lord" still seemed to echo in the rafters as Greg and Sarah exited the pew. A group of young adults chatted with Father Theodore in the back of church by the holy water font. Almost instinctively, Greg took Sarah's hand as they walked down the aisle. It was the most joy-filled Mass he had experienced since San Antonio.

"Welcome, friends," the middle-aged priest greeted them. "I'm Father Theodore Hammond. Are you visiting from out of town?"

"Oh no, Father, we live here," Greg laughed. "Not together," he added.

Father Theodore chuckled. "I don't recognize you. I must be getting old."

"Actually, we've never been here before, Father," Sarah spoke up. "Greg used to go to another church, and I just moved here. I'm not actually Catholic," she admitted.

"Then an extra big welcome to you," Father smiled. "I hope you enjoyed our celebration. What tradition is your background in?" Father Theodore's disarming eyes sparkled with life. Sarah and Greg felt completely comfortable.

"I'm familiar with a lot of different churches," Sarah answered. "The Catholic Church is new to me, though."

"You are welcome any time." Turning aside, Father Theodore called out across the entranceway, "Harry, Marnie, could you come here for a minute, please?"

Two people broke away from a foursome to heed the call. Father Theodore introduced the couples to each other. Although Harry and Marnie had only recently joined the parish, they ran a prayer and fellowship group for adults, married and single.

"We have 'Game Night' on the first Thursday of every month at 7:30 in the church hall. It should be loads of fun. There will be snacks and refreshments, and of course all sorts of games. Board games, card games, and a special video trivia quiz that Harry put together. We'd love to have you there. The more people, the better," invited Marnie.

Although the idea of socializing with strangers was not immediately appealing, Greg viewed the opportunity to spend more time with Sarah in a group environment less pressuring. Harry and Marnie's friendly demeanor was also very inviting. "It sounds like a great idea," he accepted, squeezing Sarah's hand.

Greg, Tom and Jason sat in the cafeteria of the local community college. They had chosen an inconspicuous table in the corner opposite the entrance.

"I don't see how there is any other choice," Greg asserted. "And I won't take no for an answer."

"I agree with Greg," Jason nodded firmly. "We've hit a roadblock otherwise."

"You have to admit, I am the best one for the job. I have no other commitments. I also have the anonymity that Jason does not have."

Tom Phillips grimaced and looked off to the side. "I guess it's settled then. I'll make an itinerary and get it to you tomorrow."

Having spoken, Tom rose and departed the restaurant. Greg and Jason remained seated, drinks still half full and an empty bucket of buffalo wings before them at the table. "Do you really want to go through with this?" Jason asked.

"Absolutely," Greg affirmed, trying not to reveal his anxiety over deciding what to tell Sarah. He downed his glass and flashed Jason a contrived smile.

Greg arrived at the courthouse as the doors opened. He proceeded up the stairs to the Federal Passport Agency and approached the counter. A silver-haired woman greeted him pleasantly, and Greg indicated that he wanted to apply for a passport. The clerk handed him the appropriate form, which he filled out. Then she collected the necessary identification and instructed him to obtain a 2x2-inch photo of himself. There were two photo shops within walking distance that could take the passport photo for him in the correct format. When Greg returned thirty minutes later with the picture, the clerk finished helping another man, leaving Greg as the sole customer.

"Mr. Wesko, I was waiting for you to come back," the clerk announced in a flustered voice. "I thought you said you never had a passport. When I checked our records, I found that you already have an active passport."

Stunned by the news, Greg could not hide the quizzical look on his face. He tried to recover quickly. "Well, I don't have it now. I don't know where it is and I can't find it," Greg answered truthfully. His mind churned rapidly in an attempt to figure out how he could be on record as having a passport when in fact he had never applied for one.

"You should have said something at the start. You have to redo some of your paperwork." The woman indicated some additional requirements, which Greg attended to promptly. "How soon do you need the replacement passport? Do you want to pay the fee to expedite it?"

"No, thanks," Greg declined the offer. He finished the paperwork, handed over duplicate passport photos, and thanked the clerk for her help.

Once outside, Greg whipped out his cell phone and dialed. Tom Phillips picked up immediately.

"It's done," Greg announced surreptitiously. "One snag though, Tom. They said I already applied for a passport, but I never did! I'm receiving a replacement."

Tom brushed past Greg's bewilderment. "Did you pay the fee to have it expedited?"

"No, just like you told me not to," retorted Greg.

"Good. I can actually work my magic better if it's not on the list to be expedited."

"That's what we pay you the big bucks for, Tom. I'm sure it's more than the expediting fee."

"You bet. But I can get it to you in two days," Tom grinned.

"Europe, here I come!"

Chapter Twenty-Seven

Terra firma grew more distant with every passing second as Greg watched the expanse of blue ocean spread out beneath him like a carpet. Greg knew that the short overseas night would soon be upon him. While waiting for his evening meal to arrive, Greg allowed the events of the past few days to float through his mind. He recalled Sarah's crestfallen face at the news of his sudden "business trip." Closing his eyes, he could almost feel the softness of Sarah's hand again, squeezing more tightly during the final moments of a suspense thriller they had rented on DVD the previous night. Greg's lips longed for a repeat of Sarah's sweet parting kiss, which she had given him when he stopped by her apartment on the way to the airport.

"Chicken or beef?" The flight attendant's perfunctory question ripped Greg from his reverie. He mumbled some form of reply which the flight attendant interpreted as the latter choice. Before attempting to ascertain the composition of his meal, Greg dug into his carry-on bag and retrieved the itinerary Tom Phillips had drafted for him. Greg ate absentmindedly as he reviewed the plan. With mixed emotions, Greg noted that Tom had left only a little room for sightseeing. Greg had always dreamed of going to Europe, but he never anticipated making the trip under the duress of his present circumstances. Nevertheless, he vowed to make the most of his time abroad.

Touching down in London's Heathrow Airport, Greg could scarcely contain his excitement. Impatiently he waited for the plane to taxi to the appropriate terminal. Looking out the window, Greg was surprised to find very little indication that he had left the continent of his birth. The people, words and equipment all looked familiar. He hoped that England would be an easy introduction to Europe for him.

After a painless portage through customs, Greg followed signs for the Heathrow Express, a train offering non-stop service to central London. On the way he exchanged some money and then purchased some overpriced post cards in an airport gift shop. He boarded the train with his pre-booked ticket, and less than twenty minutes later he found himself in Paddington Station. With several hours to spare before he could check in at the hotel, he decided to begin his sightseeing adventure. First he dropped off some of his luggage at a locker to lighten his load. Pulling out the subway map from his backpack, Greg found his way to the London Underground connection.

Greg chose Westminster Abbey as his first stop. The ancient building loomed magnificently before him with its spires reaching heavenward in praise. Frantically rummaging through his backpack, Greg fumbled to retrieve his camera to snap a picture of a double-decker bus passing by. The hum of the traffic and the crowd was intoxicating. A friendly-looking tourist stood nearby, and Greg asked him to take his picture with the Abbey in the background. The man suggested that Greg watch a short film giving an overview of the Abbey's history. As soon as the lights dimmed in the small theater, Greg realized that he had made a mistake. In the darkness, Greg's lack of good sleep on the plane quickly overcame his will to stay awake. A gentle prod on the shoulder interrupted his catnap at the end of the show. Somewhat refreshed, Greg proceeded into the Abbey. He marveled at the ancientness of the place, and he strove to find the oldest of the royal graves. His brochure indicated that the site had witnessed the coronation of every king since William the Conqueror. The significance of all the history was almost too much for Greg to absorb.

After exiting the Abbey, Greg walked towards Big Ben and the Houses of Parliament. On the way his stomach spoke up and urged him to find something to eat. Greg answered the call with a croissant and a cup of coffee at a small café nearby. With renewed energy, he began the trek towards Trafalgar Square, with Nelson's Column as its focal point. Greg marveled at four large bronze lions flanking its base. The column had been erected in the early nineteenth century to commemorate Admiral Nelson's victory in the Battle of Trafalgar off the coast of Spain in 1805.

Greg exited the square through Admiralty Arch and towards Buckingham Palace. The route he had chosen led him through St. James's Park. About halfway through he paused to rest and snap a few photos of some resident swans. Greg noticed an unshaven man in tattered clothes standing nearby. Greg cast a glance his way to find the man looking back at him. The left side of the man's face drooped slightly as if he had been the victim of a stroke. As suddenly as the man had appeared, he ducked behind a clump of bushes and out of sight. Greg decided to move on quickly.

Once at the British royal residence, Greg stood on his toes to steal a few pictures over the heads of the amassing crowd. He overheard chattering that an important dignitary was visiting, and onlookers strained for a glimpse of celebrity. Growing weary, Greg decided to find the closest Underground station and make his way to his next destination, the Tower of London.

After paying the entrance fee, Greg started paging through his guidebook as he walked along. Although the site had been occupied since ancient times, it gained its prominence when William the Conqueror had the Great Tower built soon after he defeated the Anglo-Saxon king Harold II. Subsequent rulers had expanded and improved upon the site over the next several centuries. He stepped off the path to touch some ruins dating back to the Roman occupation, when the city was called

Londinium Augusta. Strolling with the crowd along what was called the Wall Walk, Greg traversed the thirteenth-century battlements of the Tower's inner wall. He soaked in the British accents and wealth of history. An hour later, Greg rounded out his tour with a visit to the Jewel House to see the crown jewels. A conveyor belt crawled past a sampling of the royal collection of immeasurable monetary and historical value. Most impressive to Greg was the solid-gold St. Edward's crown from 1661, used in the coronation of Queen Elizabeth some three hundred years later. Gawking at some of the finest diamonds in the world, Greg wondered whether anyone had dared to steal any of the treasures. He later read that an Irish adventurer by the name of Thomas Blood succeeded in stealing the crown jewels in the mid-seventeenth century. The treasures were recovered almost immediately but sustained considerable damage. Rather than receiving an execution as might be expected, King Charles pardoned him and made him a friend of the court. Since that time, apparently, no further attempts had been made.

As dinnertime approached, Greg made his way back to the Underground. He returned to Paddington Station to retrieve his luggage and find something to eat before checking into his hotel for the night. Exhausted, Greg did not mind the small size of the room, and the bed felt extraordinarily welcoming. Within a few minutes he was asleep.

The next morning Greg enjoyed a continental breakfast in the basement of the hotel. Energized from a long restful night, Greg felt no traces of jet lag. He reviewed the plan in his mind, double checked the address and directions, and headed out into the bustling London streets. His hotel was just a few blocks from the Bayswater Underground Station. A few stops later, Greg disembarked at South Kensington. Once on street level, Greg followed Harrington Road, noting the numbers as he headed west. Having walked much further than he expected, he finally reached the street number he was searching for. Puzzled, he double checked the information he had written on the side of the map. The address seemed to match, but where he had expected to find an apartment building, he found an Indian restaurant instead. Too early in the morning for lunch, the door was locked. The building was connected to other buildings on both sides, and Greg had to walk quite a distance to find a passageway that would lead him to the rear alley. He headed back toward the building that housed the restaurant. Making careful judgments, Greg was certain he had picked the correct building. Hoping for an answer, he knocked on the back door. The isolation of the alley made him nervous, and he scanned both ends of the littered street for any signs of life. After another set of fruitless knocks, Greg realized that there was an apartment above the restaurant. As he ascended an old iron ladder, the stairs groaned and complained under his feet. At the top he searched for a bell next to a forbidding door, its red paint peeling off in large sections. Finding no bell, he rapped against bare wood with three authoritative knocks. No response was returned. Greg was about to knock again when he heard the release of a deadbolt. The door opened just enough to reveal a sallow face peering out from the darkness.

"Uh, hello. I'm looking for a Mr. Yates," Greg stammered clumsily. In response, an unintelligible string of words erupted from a half-toothed mouth. Greg started to repeat himself but soon realized that the attempt would be futile. He was about to leave when the door opened further. An attractive young Indian woman greeted him in the Queen's perfect English.

"Please excuse my grandfather. How may I help you?" she inquired.

Greg was relieved to overcome the language barrier. "Hello, I'm looking for Mr. Geoffrey Yates," he replied.

"I'm sorry, sir, but there is no one with that name at this residence," the young woman replied.

With further questioning, the woman insisted that she had never heard of Mr. Yates. As the conversation continued, however, Greg was made aware of his mistake.

"This is not Harrington Road. This is Harrington Gardens. They are the same road, but the name changes. Harrington Road runs further east," the young woman informed him.

Greg thanked her and returned to the front of the building. Retracing his steps, he headed back towards Harrington Road. At every intersection he checked the street signs. When the street name changed, he resumed his search for the correct address. Soon, however, Greg began to question himself. Two adjoining buildings bracketed the number he was looking for, leaving no room for the address he needed. He made inquiries at each building, but no one claimed to know a Geoffrey Yates. One storeowner let him use her phone book, and Greg found eight entries for Geoffrey or G. Yates, none of whom lived on Harrington Road. He took a pen and paper out and jotted down the addresses and phone numbers.

Greg returned to the street and spent ten minutes attempting to hail a cab. Greg showed the cab driver the list of addresses. The man guffawed when Greg said he hoped to check them all out in two or three hours. Greg lamented the time he had wasted on the Harrington Road - Harrington Gardens mistake.

"Let's do as many as we can," Greg insisted with a sigh. "Whatever order works best, ending up near Bayswater, where my hotel is."

Greg's first stop was an apartment building in a crisp, clean section of town. Several rounds of knocks revealed no answer. Scouting the area, he furtively reached into the mailbox and retrieved an envelope. The correct name, "Geoffrey Yates," spoke encouragement to him from the computer-printed address label. He took a business card from his wallet and marked on the back, "Urgent: Please call today regarding your account." Underneath he wrote his hotel number and an e-mail address Tom had set up for him. He placed the business card and the envelope in the mailbox. Greg's second stop played out the same as his first. After three strike-outs in a row, Greg realized the flaw in his plan, that most of the G. Yates were likely at work. The fourth and fifth stops turned up a *Gina* Yates and a *George* Yates, respectively. When the sixth and seventh stops also proved futile, Greg's mounting frustration neared the breaking point. "Why bother with the last stop!" Greg fumed.

"That will use up your three hours anyhow, sir," the taxi driver returned. "I'm sorry you've wasted all your time," he added in his thick Cockney accent. "Do you want to skip the last address?"

Tempted to give up, Greg nevertheless summoned the resolve to continue. "No, we might as well check it out. If we don't, I'll just keep worrying about it."

Despite his best efforts, Greg's last stop proved as futile as the others. Looking out the cab window, Greg's face flushed with anger. This time G. Yates stood for *Gregory* Yates, the name emblazoned on the doctor's office window. Greg sighed deeply in order to retain his composure before asking the taxi driver to return him to his hotel.

Greg calculated the cab fare against the money he had allotted for his time in London. His budget was far exceeded. Back at his hotel, he found a quiet dinner and explored British television while waiting for a potential response to one of his business cards. As the hour grew late, however, his mood sank further. With resignation, he prepared himself to declare his first mission a failure. Disappointed with the day's results, he offered prayers for success on the next leg of his journey.

Just before drifting off to sleep, a curious thought brought him fully awake. He wandered about the room and opened all the dresser drawers. Soon he retrieved a phone book, the object of his search. He thumbed through the pages until he found the entries for Yates. He compared them with the addresses he had visited earlier in the day. One extra name appeared in the hotel phone book. Despite the late hour, he quickly dialed the number. Several rings later an irritated voice sounded at the other end of the line.

"I'm sorry to call so late. Is Mr. Yates at home?"

"No," the young man's voice barked. "I haven't seen the bugger in over a month. Stiffed me with paying the whole rent, he did!"

"Are you his roommate?" Greg inquired.

"I was," the man replied. "And who are you?"

"His accountant," Greg replied.

"Accountant? The man could barely meet the rent! How could he have an accountant?"

Greg apologized, claiming to have called the wrong number, and quickly hung up.

Greg returned the phone book to the drawer. Right next to it lay a copy of Gideon's Bible. He picked it up and prayed for a verse. After a few pages, he came across Galatians Chapter 6. He read:

> And let us not be weary in well doing: for in due season we shall reap, if we faint not.

"Lord, I hope I'm doing well," he prayed aloud. "It doesn't seem so. When will my 'due season' come?" He paused, half expecting an audible answer. Then he continued, "Help me not to faint, Lord. Help me reap the answer I'm looking for."

Chapter Twenty-Eight

Greg took in the sights of Amsterdam's Schiphol Airport, his first taste of Continental Europe. The bustle of people rushing to and from flights clashed with human roadblocks chatting in the middle of the corridor or bulging out of myriad shops. A few glances around Schiphol Plaza, the airport's large central hub, promised Greg that his English would be sufficient to navigate the city of Amsterdam. Familiar sights included American fast food chain restaurants, but Greg chose to grab a pastry at a croissanterie. Ignoring the signs for the airport casino and sauna, Greg found his way to the railway ticket counter and purchased a pass on the train to Naarden-Bussum.

Exhausted from the events of the day, Greg dozed off against his will as soon as the train pulled out of the station. His intention had been to stay awake for the half-hour ride. Some time later he awoke with a start to find the train stopped. Flustered, he arose just as the train began to move again. With panicked voice, he caught an elderly woman's eye and asked, "Where are we?" Her smile indicated that she wanted to help but could not understand his words. He repeated the question aloud as another passenger approached. In a thick Dutch accent, a young man asked, "Where do you wish to depart?"

"Naarden-Bussum," answered Greg.

"You have luck. The last stop was Weesp. Yours is the next stop. About seven minutes."

Greg thanked the man. Although the pounding of his heart was enough to keep him awake, he remained standing just to be sure. He had no desire to get lost in an unfamiliar country. He pulled a folder out of his backpack and reviewed a map he had printed from the Internet. Within a few minutes he had committed his route to memory, although he was certain that his pronunciation of the street names was far off.

According to schedule, the train pulled into the station at precisely 11:12 AM. As Greg disembarked, he smiled at the elderly lady and the young man who had helped him. With only a little foreign travel experience now under his belt, every interaction with another human being seemed a small victory.

Before departing the station, he found a locker to store his luggage for the day. He then exited the building, passing a row of taxis and making his way down Ceintuurbaan, one of the main streets running through town. He stepped inside a small café for an early lunch. The menu was entirely in Dutch, and Greg found himself at a loss. Adding to his adventure, he scanned the list and picked at random. *Broodje paling.* When the waitress approached, he attempted a pronunciation. When she did not understand, he showed her the menu and pointed to his selection.

"Oh, *broodje paling!*" she answered. "Smoked eel on bread. Very good." She answered Greg's surprised expression with a good-natured smirk as she returned to the kitchen. When she emerged a few minutes later with the sandwich, she tried to satisfy her own curiosity.

"You are American tourist?" she guessed. "We do not get so many tourists here from America. Most do not venture outside Amsterdam."

"I'm here on business," Greg answered. "I am visiting a client."

"You have been here before?"

"No, this is my first time in Europe."

"Ah, welcome then. Perhaps you need help with directions?"

"The place is a bicycle shop on Goudenregenstraat."

The waitress winced, presumably at Greg's botching of the street name. "I know the place. It's not very far from here. The *Tweewieler.*" As she spoke, Greg produced the Internet map. She examined it and confirmed the route for Greg before leaving him to his meal. Two bites convinced him that the waitress was correct, and his culinary adventure had paid off. As he ate, he thought about the bicycle shop and marveled that it truly existed. Perhaps that adventure would pay off as well.

Some time later Greg asked for his check. "How did you like the eel?"

"Delicious," Greg answered. "I discovered something new today."

"Honestly, I was surprised that you ordered it. Mostly it is ordered by the Dutch, never by Americans. Good for you."

"Keep the change," Greg handed her a few bills.

"So why is an American businessman interested in buying a Dutch bicycle shop?"

Greg laughed. "Oh, I don't want to buy it."

"But it's for sale, so I think."

"I was not aware of that."

"Yes, ever since the owner passed away."

"Passed away?" Greg raised his eyebrows.

"Just a short while ago, maybe two or three months. Jaap van Huygen. He was, oh, what's the word? Euthanized."

"Euthanized?" Greg's eyebrows rose further.

"Assisted suicide. His doctor helped him to end his suffering. There was an article in the newspaper about it."

"The doctor was arrested?"

"Not at all. The law permits it. A person is free to choose suicide as a way out of suffering."

"Due to terminal illness?" Greg was incredulous.

"Yes, but for other reasons as well. This man was not physically sick. He claimed to have extreme emotional distress. The reason is not so important."

"That's terrible," Greg lamented.

"I don't agree with it either," the waitress remarked. "On the other hand, I cannot tell someone else how to live, or whether to live."

"I disagree. There have to be rules." Greg shook his head in disbelief. "Only God can give life, and only He should take it away."

"Maybe so. Some people feel that way. Me, I do not get involved in other people's lives. I concentrate on living my own life correctly." She flashed him a farewell smile and left to answer another customer's call. Greg gathered his jacket and briefcase and returned to the street.

Following the directions to the Tweewieler, Greg reviewed his plan. He had already accomplished his first goal, confirming that the bicycle shop did exist. He was far along the way towards his second goal, which was figuring out why Jack Fishburn and Tom Phillips had been unable to make direct contact with the business, a client of Providential Insurance. He hoped that a visit to the shop would reveal more information about the departed owner and the bicycle shop account.

A darkened store on the corner of Goudenregenstraat bore a sign reading 'TE KOOP,' which Greg surmised as meaning 'For Sale.' He peered in the window to find the store almost completely barren. Two bicycles were propped up in the storefront showcase. Otherwise the store was entirely empty except for a cash register on a counter across the lobby. Behind the counter stood a closed door, refusing to reveal any secrets of the back half of the building. Greg noted that the name and phone number in small letters on the front door matched the information Tom Phillips had provided him about the unreachable client. Greg surmised that Fishburn and Phillips' attempts to contact Jaap van Huygen would have predated his alleged suicide. Greg jotted down a note to try to confirm the timing.

Greg made a circle of the building. On one side, a door stood in the middle of an alley. Greg looked around and then cautiously entered the alleyway. Next to the door read the name 'van Huygen.' Greg rang an unassuming bell underneath the words. After a minute, Greg rang again. This time he detected movement behind a curtain covering a small glass window at eye-level on the door. Two fingers parted the curtain to allow a pair of eyes to peek through from the darkness inside. "Wat wilt u?" The man continued in Dutch until Greg put a business card up to the window. The man came into the light in order to examine the card. Greg placed him in his late thirties or early forties. The man met Greg's eyes and then disappeared behind the curtain. To Greg's relief, he distinguished the sound of a chain being released followed by the turn of a deadbolt. The door opened cautiously.

"Come in," the man said, casting glances up and down the alleyway.

Greg questioned his own sanity for following the man inside, but he reminded himself of the purpose of his trip. He stepped into a small foyer. A door presumably led to the store, while a staircase rose a few steps and then disappeared around a corner. Greg followed the man upstairs to a little apartment. He was thankful for the bright light inside.

"I was wondering who would come this time," the man said. "I trust everyone was pleased with my work?"

Greg's mind raced to calculate what the man may have meant. It appeared that he had expected someone from Providential Insurance. Tom had made business cards for Greg to distribute when necessary on his trip. They were identical to Greg's old business cards expect the name had been changed to Bill Greene.

"I have heard no complaints about your work," Greg scrambled for words. "Tell me, who was it that came last time?" Greg asked.

"The boss," he answered in unbroken English. "He brought the second installment of the insurance policy. Now I assume you have brought the final one? I hope there are no strings attached this time."

Greg thought fast. Feeling very uneasy, he decided it was safest to continue playing along. "I've come to tell you that the last installment is delayed."

The man broke into a tirade of foreign oaths that Greg was thankful not to understand. When he calmed down enough to resume English, he looked intently at Greg, fire burning in his eyes. "You tell them that enough is enough! My father told you people that he wanted out. He kept his end of the bargain, killing himself to do so. That was to be the end of it all. I was never supposed to pick up where my father left off. That was not part of the deal! I expect my money, and I do not expect anything else requested of me! You know what powerful information my father left me with. Don't make me use it."

"Information?" Greg realized he had stepped into a mine field.

"Do not play stupid with me. I am no fool! If necessary I will risk foregoing my last installment by contacting the authorities."

"What else shall I relay?" Greg probed for more information.

"Nothing except this. Tell them that I will not step out of the way as easily as my father did. I want to live!"

Greg sat in an Internet café in central Amsterdam, a few blocks from the Rijksmuseum where he had spent the morning amidst the works of Rembrandt, Van Dyck, and a host of other Dutch masters. He refused to let the air of history and culture fade away as he waited for his web e-mail account to check for new messages. In the cyber world, twenty seconds seemed like an eternity. Greg's heart skipped a beat when a message finally appeared. It simply presented a time and a chat room address. It had a single letter, Z, as the signature, as he had Tom had agreed. Glancing at his watch, Greg determined that he had ample time for lunch and a guided tour of the city by canal boat. He surmised that meanwhile his friends in America were probably just rising for the day. He spent a few minutes jotting off a postcard to Sarah before embarking on the next leg of his sightseeing excursion.

Three hours later, Greg clicked his way to the designated chat room for an Internet rendezvous with Tom Phillips. When he entered the site, he found Tom's message waiting for him.

You there? Z
Just got here Y
The info you sent about our bike friend last night was useful
How so?
The Providential account is still in his name. Somehow the dead man is still withdrawing money.
So Providential still doesn't know he's dead?
Right. Can't tell you any more now.
What do I do?
Go to destination 3.
When?
ASAP
OK
E-mail from the hotel again
Will do
You OK?
Yes
Sure?
Yes thanks
TTYL

Chapter Twenty-Nine

The next day Greg found himself wending his way slowly through the lunchtime crowds in the busy streets of Konstanz. He chided his stomach for its poor timing. One hard roll with Nutella had not lasted long enough. He spotted a nearby restaurant with a take-out window on the side of the main entrance. Taking his place at the back of a long line, he struggled to decipher the menu. Two years of high school German had all but abandoned him. Silently his mouth practiced the words "Schinkentoast." A man of Middle-Eastern descent took his order with a smile and returned a seemingly perfect string of German. Greg smiled politely. A minute later Greg was munching on a toasted ham sandwich as he navigated the small German town on the Swiss side of the Rhein.

Sandwich finished, Greg found himself lost in the zigzag of centuries-old streets. The border of Switzerland was almost upon him, leading to the Swiss city of Kreuzlingen. Greg blamed his lunch-on-the-go for his directional errors. Unable to find a garbage can, he stuffed the greasy sandwich wrapper in his back pocket and retrieved a map. After a few minutes of study, he found Rosgartenstrasse and headed north. Over the other buildings he could see the spire of the city's cathedral. The site had harbored a cathedral since the seventh century or earlier, and the spire was a nineteenth-century addition. Before reaching the church, he turned on Salmannsweilergasse and began searching for his query. Reaching a string of shops, he perused the storefront signs until he found "Georgs Buchhandlung." He stepped inside the quiet bookstore. Narrow rows overflowing with used books encroached on him from every side. A young woman sat at the cash register a short distance from the front door. Greg approached her and showed her his Providential Insurance business card. "May I see the owner, please?"

Nodding, the woman motioned for Greg to follow her towards the back of the store. She led him through the maze of books to an old wooden door cut out of the back wall. She knocked and shouted a string of unintelligible words through the closed door. A muffled response, equally unintelligible, issued from the other side. Greg picked out a few words from the cashier's reply, including "Providential Insurance." He tried his best to distinguish additional words. His heart skipped a beat when he thought he heard the words "Gregory Wesko." He assured himself that his ears were mistaken, but he searched for a quick escape route nonetheless. Suddenly something slipped out of the young woman's hand. Greg reached over to pick it up for her. As he did, he noticed that it was his business card. He glanced at the name under the company logo. To his dismay, it read "Gregory Wesko" instead of his alias, "Bill Greene." His mind raced furiously. He held onto the business card and quickly grabbed his wallet. Thumbing through it, he retrieved the small stack of business cards that Tom had prepared for him. They all bore the name of his alias. He stuffed the fallen business card back inside his wallet but in a different compartment. Greg figured that Tom must have accidentally returned his original business card that had been used as a model for the alias cards.

The door opened slowly and the cashier indicated that Greg should enter. Greg offered up a prayer and obeyed. The door closed behind him, and Greg felt trapped inside the small, dark office. Despite the pervasive clutter and paucity of light, the room held a cozy charm. Paraphernalia erupted from every shelf and desktop surface amidst stacks of ancient books. An old but sturdy wooden chair awaited him at the foot of a definitively messy desk. An elderly, hunchbacked man smoked a pipe from behind a stack of papers and envelopes. "Seat yourself, please," he beckoned. Again Greg obeyed. As he sat, he handed the man a falsified business card.

"I thought my girl said your name was Herr Wesko," the man frowned as he read the card. "Herr Greene, how do you do?"

"How do you do," Greg replied, shaking the extended hand. "I have come to discuss the bookstore's account."

"Of course," the man replied without introducing himself.

"I'm sorry if my arrival was unannounced. I was unsure of my plans," Greg apologized.

"Of course," the man repeated.

"I have brought the records and would like to go over them with you."

"Of course." Greg began to wonder if the man was actually able to understand him.

"Sir, are you Herr Georg Schrift, the owner?"

"Yes, of course!" the man intoned, pointing to a nameplate almost completely hidden behind an unruly stack of papers. "You are Herr Greene of Providential Insurance Company, are you not?"

Greg winced at the man's harsh tone and nodded in the affirmative. From his briefcase, Greg produced a file bearing the name of the bookstore. He blinked his eyes several times at the acrid smoke from the man's pipe. He withdrew a statement that Jason Coates had prepared for him before the trip. He placed it sideways on the only open spot on the desk for them both to look at. He thumbed through the pages and reviewed the activity for the past year. Several large deposits and withdrawals had occurred. Schrift declined to comment, merely nodding and puffing smoke. Greg found himself grasping at straws to elicit any response or obtain any clues. He reminded himself that he had accomplished the first goal of his task, which was to establish that the client truly existed.

To Greg's surprise, the man reached over and closed the file. "What do you want, really?" he asked with his thick German accent.

Greg paused to think for a moment. "To find out if you have any information for us," he replied.

"Herr Greene," Schrift mumbled through his pipe, "I have an errand for you."

"Yes?" Greg waited with bated breath.

"Take this camera to Mainau. In exchange you will receive your, eh, information."

Stunned, Greg asked, "How will I make this exchange?"

"Go tomorrow morning, early. Sit in the garden. The camera is obvious. You will be found," he answered. Reaching out of sight, the man rifled through his desk drawers. A moment later he produced a conspicuous yellow camera with a telephoto lens. "Do not develop the pictures," he warned sternly. "Do not remove the film at all."

"Yes, sir," Greg responded. He tried to remember the last time he had used a camera with actual film.

"I think we are done, are we not? Good day."

"Thank you, Herr Schrift. Good day."

Greg disembarked from the small ferry boat which had carried him across the Bodensee, also known as Lake Constance, to the tiny island of Mainau. The Swedish Royal family still owned a small palace on the island, a vestige of ancient political history. The remainder of the island was open to the public, and tourists delighted in the beautifully constructed gardens. Greg marveled at a variety of floral sculptures. The yellow camera hung prominently from his neck as he toured the extensive grounds. On the one hand he hoped to be noticed soon, but on the other he also feared it. After a two-hour stroll, Greg took a seat on a low concrete ledge encircling a small pool. Two wrought-iron swans performed a courtship dance in the middle of the water. Greg studied the surrounding garden and the lush hilly mainland across the lake. Suddenly he noticed a figure standing beside him. He immediately rose.

"Setzen Sie sich," a tall, lanky man commanded in a whisper. Greg resumed his seat and the man joined him. His tanned face was difficult to read behind a pair of sunglasses, but Greg placed him in his early forties.

"Setzen Sie das Photoapparat auf den Boden." Greg's mind struggled to recall the meaning of the words. Even to Greg's untrained ear, the man's accent seemed something other than German. The man repeated his request with more urgency. Greg placed the camera on the ground. "Es hat Film?" the man questioned. Greg nodded. The man waited a moment and then reached down to retrieve the camera. Holding it up, he peered into a narrow window in the back of the camera to affirm that it contained film. The man arose and walked briskly away. Greg stood up to protest his departure, but as he did, a small envelope fell off the ledge into the pool. Quickly he reached in to rescue it. He headed in the direction of the ferry dock as he dried the envelope on the side of his pants. His curiosity triumphed over patience, and he opened the envelope and peered inside. The sight of the contents stopped him dead in his tracks. Inside was a thick stack of five-hundred-euro notes.

I developed the pictures. Y

Just like I told you to. You put the blank film in?

No, not blank. Took pictures around town. Then opened the back of the camera and exposed the film.

So tell me

Young children and babies. One child per picture.

Doing what?

Sitting, standing, sleeping

Where?

Don't know. Inside rooms. Some furniture, no decorations.

And what info did you get?

50,000 euros

Nice tip!

I'm worried. Do I keep it?

Have to. May be traceable. Can't turn it over to anyone.

Serial numbers aren't in order.

Then probably not traceable. Just hide it in your bag.

I'm going to mail it to you.

No!!! You may need it anyway.

Now what?

Destination #4.

That gives me an idea

What?

Later

What?

You there?

Answer me!
Answer me!

Chapter Thirty

Through a small opening in the wooden walls, Greg peered down at the River Rhein flowing beneath him. It was early morning, and Greg's excitement had cut his night short. His excitement helped overcome the residual exhaustion from the previous day's complicated journey. By way of several trains and one bus he had trekked to his current destination, the town of Vaduz in the principality of Liechtenstein. The small country was sandwiched in between the picturesque mountains of Austria and Switzerland, with various ties to both countries over the centuries. In modern times, money laundering prospered under the country's lax banking regulations, although external pressures increasingly threatened such profitable illicit practices.

While waiting for the world to wake up and join him, he passed the time touring the tiny capital city. The wooden covered bridge afforded him entry back to Switzerland, and Greg fulfilled a juvenile desire by crossing the bridge several times. *Now I can say I've been to Switzerland ten times!* Greg chuckled to himself as he returned to Liechtenstein for his final visit.

As Greg's morning tour continued, his stomach began to call attention to itself. He found a pastry shop and purchased a fresh flaky treat. Walking as he ate, he marveled at the hills overlooking the city. One hill boasted the royal castle, occupied since the twelfth century. Greg's guidebook said that tours of the castle were prohibited to the general public. Although he was disappointed at the missed opportunity, he reminded himself that his time in Vaduz was very limited. He checked his watch and realized that the time had gotten away from him. He made a quick end of his breakfast and hurried off to his destination.

Greg brushed some crumbs off his clothes and entered the lobby of a large bank on the corner of a busy intersection. He took his place at the end of a short line. As he waited his turn, his nerves suddenly began to act up. The envelope in his briefcase seemed to scream as loud as Edgar Allen Poe's *Tell-Tale Heart*. When he finally approached the counter, he swallowed hard. "I'd like to open an account," he managed in his most confident voice. The teller asked him several questions with a heavy accent, and Greg produced his identification. She handed him some bilingual forms and indicated for him to take a seat in a row of empty chairs across the room. Greg followed her instructions, and soon a pleasant mustachioed gentleman appeared and led him to a glass-enclosed office.

"Mr. Wesko, welcome," he greeted in nearly perfect English. "So you would like to open another account?"

Another? Greg found himself scrambling to recover from a surprise yet again. "First, I'd like to review my current account."

"Certainly. Let me retrieve the records." The man typed furiously on his computer keyboard. The monitor was obstructed from Greg's view, but after a few moments, then man turned it so that Greg could see the screen.

Pointing to a line near the bottom, the man remarked, "You have nearly seventy thousand euros in your first account. Let me check on the second." After another rash of wild typing, the man continued. "Your second account has," the man trailed off. "See here." Greg followed the man's fingers. The seven-digit figure swam before his eyes. A double shock ratcheted his mind when he noticed the joint name on the account, *Emil Crucis.* Greg winced inwardly as memories of the audit at Providential Insurance flooded back.

"What type of account would you like to open this time?" asked the man, seemingly unaware of Greg's astonishment.

Greg was unable to think clearly. He felt the urge to flee. "I think I changed my mind," he announced slowly.

"Very well. Would you like to use your safe-deposit box before you leave?"

"Most definitely," Greg responded.

The man led him to a vault and retrieved a sign-in card from a locked drawer. Greg examined the signatures and dates. The signature was similar to Greg's, but not as close as Greg would have hoped. "I forgot to mention, the main reason I came in today was because I lost my safe-deposit box key. I thought I might open a second box, but I decided that I'd rather stay with the one I have. I've searched everywhere for the key, and I don't think I will ever find it."

A look of dismay wrinkled the man's moustache. "There is a very heavy penalty for key replacement," he frowned.

"I realize that," Greg replied. "But I do need to get in as soon as possible."

"Of course. We will have to get our locksmith. This will take some time." The man proceeded to instruct him on filling out an affidavit for the lost key. It took an hour to fill out the paperwork and verify Greg's identity, and two additional hours were necessary to take care of the lock. Greg waited in agony, expecting the authorities to arrive at any moment to apprehend him. Finally a new key was issued, and Greg signed for the hefty key-replacement fine, an insignificant dent in the multi-millions in his new-found account.

An attendant carried Greg's box and escorted him to a private booth. Heart pounding, Greg locked the door and opened the box in privacy. Inside Greg found dozens of pictures very similar to the ones he had developed from the yellow camera at a one-hour photo shop. Nameless young faces stared back at him, a few hopeful, many scared, and all with a good measure of melancholy. The background of all the pictures was fairly stark, with little to help identify location. After a while, Greg began to recognize a few items of furniture repeated in several pictures.

Two envelopes lay under the pictures. One envelope was blank, while another had the letters NH. Upon examination, each revealed a payload similar to the one Greg had received for the camera. Two passport-sized pictures lay in the bottom of the box, each of a different man. The first was a plain-looking, fair-skinned man in his early forties. The second man had dark, wispy hair and a droopy face. Greg studied them carefully and then stuffed them into his wallet. The only other item in the box was a short note written in a language unfamiliar to Greg. He copied it as best as he could onto the back of a receipt in his wallet. The letter was simply signed, "David."

Greg wrestled with himself over the appropriate next steps. His original intention, unexpressed to Tom, had been to open an account with the money he had received in Germany. Greg had chosen the bank in Vaduz because Tom and Jason's research had linked it to Providential Insurance. However, the newly-discovered safe-deposit box already in his own name seemed a safer place. He did not want to travel with money of suspicious origins. Even so, the additional find and Tom's advice both tempted him to hold onto the money. Greg closed his eyes and prayed for wisdom. A few minutes later, Greg placed the envelope he had received in the box and closed it up. When he exited the bank shortly thereafter, he hastened down the busy city streets, unable to bring himself to look back.

I left the money – Y
Where?
A box I already had here but didn't know about
What?
I'm suddenly a millionaire
!!!???
Don't worry, I didn't keep it
You've got a double?
Seems so. Identity theft in a good way, I think.
Hah
Will fax you some pictures, two men and some of children.
I'll search the criminal records
Will fax a letter I found too. Needs translation.
I'll do my best
Onto the next destination?
You got it

Chapter Thirty-One

Passing through one of two Gothic towers, the Charles Bridge led over the Vltava River in the Stare Mésto, or Old Town, of historical Prague. In the distance loomed the majestic Pražský Hrad, translated as "Prague Castle" in Greg's guidebook. First begun in the ninth century, numerous renovations and additions had transformed it into a large collection of government and historical buildings. St. Vitus Cathedral, a relatively recent addition, was one of the most noticeable features of the complex.

Greg navigated through the throngs of tourists traversing the bridge in haphazard fashion. Street musicians and artists set up camp between Baroque statues, added some four hundred years after construction of the bridge. The old-world charm of the city could not be diminished by the crowds and bustle. Greg was enthralled. Despite the gravity of his mission, he had decided to make time for some more sightseeing. At the far end of the bridge, he paused to admire a collection of crystal spread out on a purple blanket. A few yards away, a quartet of musicians in traditional Bohemian garb entertained a small gathering. While enjoying a few folk songs, Greg pulled out a map and studied his route. The bridge led him to the Malá Strana, known as the Lesser Town, where his ultimate destination lay.

Meandering through ancient streets with unpronounceable names, he stopped every so often to browse the wares of local street carts. He picked up a few postcards and a small pendant of the tenth-century king St. Wenceslas, martyred by his brother, Boleslas.

Resuming his trek, Greg passed the Japanese and Danish embassies. He checked his map and reassured himself that he had not wandered off course. As he continued, he observed a young couple stagger out of an ornately decorated restaurant some distance ahead of him. The echo of their laughter faded as they headed in the opposite direction. Greg crossed the street to look inside the restaurant. The glass chandeliers and large framed pictures on the wall reminded him more of an art museum than a restaurant.

Gazing away for a moment, Greg realized that the restaurant was situated on the corner of Pelclova, the street he was looking for. He backtracked a few steps and turned down the short side street. An old red door bore the numbers of his destination. Finding no buzzer or knocker, he tried the doorknob. It opened to reveal a narrow staircase leading up into darkness. Issuing a prayer for protection, he ventured up the stairs. At the first landing stood a small door. Greg paused to decide whether the door was worthy of a knock. Deeming it inconsequential, Greg continued up to the end of the stairs. A more substantial door held greater promise. Greg swallowed hard and knocked.

Soft footsteps answered, followed by a long pause. Greg surmised that he was being observed through the peephole. He looked down nervously. A stream of incomprehensible speech penetrated the wooden door. Greg called back, "Providential Insurance, Bill Greene." Some shuffling and muffled conversation ensued behind the door. The sound of a deadbolt unlocking and the slow creak of the door alerted Greg that he was bidden to enter.

Inside he was greeted by an empty, dimly-lit foyer. The wooden floor groaned under his feet. In the faint light he could discern that the walls had been painted white at some time in the distant past. Narrow corridors led to the left and right, but a short, thin man with graying hair led him into a large room directly across from the door. Greg followed cautiously, casting a glance back towards the door. To his dismay, he noted that the deadbolt had been reset.

"Have a seat. We have been expecting you," the man informed him with a thick Slavic accent. He smiled and departed back into the foyer through the open doorway, the only entrance to the room. Greg watched him disappear down one of the corridors. Rather than sit in one of the rickety wooden chairs, Greg paced quietly about the room. One wall was lined with windows overlooking an unfamiliar, deserted street. One storey below, a small balcony protruded from the building. A set of plastic patio furniture struck Greg as very un-European. A bee flew in through one of the unscreened windows.

The sound of movement made Greg jump. He whirled around to face two tall men in the doorway. Greg's stomach began to burn with the acid of panic. After an endless moment, one of the men approached. Greg's mouth went dry as he recognized him as the man with the droopy face from the pictures in the safe-deposit box in Vaduz. Extending his hand, he greeted Greg without introducing himself. "Welcome, Mr. Greene."

"Thank you. You may call me Bill," Greg offered with cotton-mouthed hoarseness.

"Very well," he responded with a distinct British accent. "Won't you have a seat?"

Greg obeyed, taking a chair facing the doorway. The other man sat next to a small desk between Greg and the exit. Greg felt as if he had been put in the hot seat. He struggled for words. "I've come from Providential Insurance," he began.

"Enough with the formalities," the droopy-faced man said. "We want to know why you are really here."

"To review the account of Mr. Rezek," Greg replied. "A review is overdue."

"On the contrary, it appears you have wasted your time," the nameless man continued. "You are just a few hours too late."

"How so?" questioned Greg, barely able to contain his apprehension. His eyes moved to the silent man and then back to the first man.

"Your colleague arrived earlier today. Are you not traveling together?"

"My colleague?"

"Mr. Gregory Wesko."

Greg felt his body start to shake. "Dear Lord," he prayed silently, "Rescue me from the snares of the enemy. I place my trust in you." A peace surpassing all understanding flowed over Greg like an anointing. He stood up as another figure entered the room from behind.

"Here is Mr. Wesko now," the first man commented.

A man in a suit jacket entered along with the gray-haired man who had led Greg into the apartment. Still recovering from the sound of his own name, Greg gasped as the other man's face emerged into the light. It was the face of the other of the two men in the pictures Greg had found in the safe-deposit box. The man locked eyes with Greg. In horror, Greg watched the man's expression develop from curiosity into evil malice.

"Restrain him!" the ersatz Greg Wesko commanded.

Leaping to his feet, Greg raced for one of the open windows. Taking a quick look over the edge, he cried, "God deliver me!" With more faith than he knew he had, he jumped out the window. The plastic table on the balcony below gave way beneath his feet, breaking in two. He crashed into one of the patio chairs, a cushion on the seat softening his landing. Without looking up, Greg regained his feet and ran towards a low railing at the edge of the balcony. He climbed over and grabbed onto it to lower himself down to the ground. Just before Greg let go, the silent man came crashing down onto the remnants of the broken table. His fall was not as fortunate, and he knocked himself unconscious against the hard balcony floor.

On the ground, Greg raced back towards Pelclova Street. As he rounded the corner, Greg caught sight of the gray-haired man. Emerging from the red door, the gray-haired man quickly spotted Greg and shouted something in Czech. Greg sped down Pelclova in the opposite direction. Soon Greg realized that he was fast approaching a tributary of the Vltava River. A park lay to his left. He sprinted across it towards a small bridge leading over the tributary. He followed the street to its end at the Vltava. To his dismay, there was no interconnected bridge over the main river. He risked a moment to survey the area. No pursuers were currently in sight, but he caught the sound of nearby shouting. Greg spotted a small crowd of tourists admiring the Lichtenstejnský Palace. As he tried to blend in, he heard the sounds of hurried footsteps behind him. Not daring to turn around, Greg huddled close to the tourists. They snapped pictures and chattered happily in an unfamiliar language. Greg's heart skipped a beat as he caught sight of the droopy-faced man and the imposter across the street. Suddenly Greg noticed the crowd moving on. He followed them only to find that they were boarding a small tour bus. Alarmed, Greg attempted to walk away quietly. His nonchalance was futile. The other Greg Wesko began walking purposefully in his direction with great haste. The man kept one hand inside his jacket as if to grasp a weapon. Abandoning all semblance of obscurity, Greg took flight. Both Greg Weskos sped north towards the familiar Charles Bridge. Hoping to lose himself in the tumult, Greg pressed his way through the crowds. Despite his best efforts, he could not shake his doppelgänger, although none of the other people from the apartment were in sight. By the end of the bridge, Greg had only gained a few extra yards as he turned left onto another main street. Greg shouted apologies as he careened into startled tourists milling about.

As Greg crossed a busy avenue, he caught sight of a bridge leading back over the Vltava to his left. For a brief moment, he considered running to the bridge or even diving into the river. However, common sense prevailed, and Greg was glad that his thoughts had not slowed down his pace.

Continuing forward, he passed a square named Jana Palacha and soon entered the old Jewish Quarter of Prague. A short distance away Greg noted a great crowd of darkly-clad tourists, mostly children. It struck Greg as a good place to get lost. He quickly crossed the street. As he approached, he noted that although the adults milled slowly about, the children were not moving. Further inspection caused him to freeze in his tracks. The small figures he had seen were not children at all, but an incredibly tightly-packed collection of headstones. Regaining his composure, he continued on towards the cemetery. As he neared an entrance, he joined a small cluster of people passing slowly though. He cast a series of furtive glances about but could not find any pursuers. A slight sense of relief helped to loosen the knots in his stomach, while at the same time sweat continued to darken his shirt.

Playing the tourist, Greg joined the somber procession through the sea of graves. Centuries-old headstones were piled five deep or even more. Greg wished he could decipher the Hebrew in order to learn the names and ages. In a secluded part of the cemetery, he crouched down to study the unfamiliar characters. He was about to stand back up when he realized that the cemetery grounds had almost completely emptied out. Afraid to call attention to himself by standing, he prolonged his study to wait for another group to pass which he could join. Two full minutes ticked slowly by. A few soft voices broke across the solemnity of the yard. Greg's legs began to ache from his crouched position. He gingerly leaned upon a headstone for support, wondering about the Jewish believer whose name was inscribed upon it. Inexplicably, verses from the book of Daniel whispered in his heart, words that the Jewish believer might have uttered in a foreign tongue centuries earlier.

Those who trust in you cannot be put to shame.

And now we follow you with our whole heart, we fear you and we pray to you.

Do not let us be put to shame, but deal with us in your kindness and great mercy.

Deliver us by your wonders, and bring glory to your name, O Lord:
Let all those be routed who inflict evils on your servants; Let them be shamed and powerless, and their strength broken;
Let them know that you alone are the Lord God, glorious over the whole world.

Greg felt as if God were lifting his head, and he raised himself back up onto his feet. He inconspicuously headed for the exit. Trying to muster an air of confidence, he headed back in the direction of the Charles Bridge, Karlův Most in Czech. Spotting a sign for the metro across the street, he joined a crowd descending deep into the earth. The strong breeze indicated that a train was approaching fast. He was thankful that he had purchased an extra ticket earlier in the day so that he did not have to waste any time and possibly miss the train. He boarded and searched for information to determine if he was heading in the direction of his hotel.

Just as the train prepared to depart, a large crowd appeared and swarmed toward the tracks. As people pushed aboard, Greg found himself forced next to the window. Looking out, he gasped in horror. The alternate Greg Wesko was at the back of the throng. Greg started to turn in order to hide his face, but it was too late. Recognition broke across the man's countenance in sordid surprise. As the doors started to close, Greg stood frozen in panic.

He prayed that the man would not make it aboard due to the size of the crowd trying to cram onto the train. Suddenly the man bolted, heading towards a back car of the train where the crowds were thinner. The train shook and then started up. Greg strained to see whether the man had boarded. His view was partially blocked. He thought he saw the man make it onto the train but he could not be certain.

Nerves overcoming courtesy, Greg pushed his way through the metro riders towards the front of the train. He passed from one car into the next. In a minute he had reached the end of the second car only to find that there was no passage to the next. He stared wide-eyed at the passengers in the unattainable car as if he were sealed in a sinking submarine watching the only survivors being rescued.

Over the dull din of conversation and rocking rails, Greg heard a recorded voice announce the next stop, "Mústek." He remembered this busy exchange. Greg nervously watched the back of the car as a minute slowly expired. He made his way to a door in order to be the first to depart. To his relief, the subway came to a halt and the doors opened without any trace of his pursuer.

As soon as the doors opened, Greg leapt from the train and sprinted across the platform. He focused on the way out, not daring to look behind. He soon entangled himself in a great multitude of commuters. He spotted another train that appeared ready to depart. He jumped aboard just as the doors closed. Once on board, he looked back onto the platform. Disbelief and panic racked his body as he witnessed his nemesis pry open the doors toward the rear of the train. Greg headed back toward the door in a vain attempt to escape. Too late for Greg to exit, the train left the station.

Greg could see that passage was not permitted between his car and his enemy's. Once again he made his way as close to the front of the train as he could. He waited nervously by the door until he heard the name of the next station, "Národní Třída." When the doors opened, he forced himself out first despite angry protests from fellow passengers. Soon he found the metro exit and ascended to the street.

A main thoroughfare led back toward the wide river, spanned by a sparsely populated bridge. As he jogged across, he spotted a series of other parallel bridges upstream and downstream. He spun himself around quickly to survey the scene behind him. In the distance he spotted a runner, but the figure was too small to positively identify. After nearly a kilometer, Greg could no longer keep his same pace. To his relief, he noticed a taxi waiting further up the road. Renewing his sprint, he headed for the vehicle. Just then a tourist appeared and stepped into the cab. Greg's heart sank and his pace slowed once again. Glancing back, Greg noticed that the runner did not slack.

Up ahead lay a large park across the street. Spotting an emptying tour bus, Greg quickly formulated a plan. As gracefully as possible, Greg joined the group of Italian tourists at a point where the bus blocked his view of the man in his pursuit. Spouting Italian, the tour guide led the group along a path winding through the park. Soon they reached a cable car. The tour guide started handing out tickets. Unsure how far he could carry his charade, Greg broke out of the line and approached the ticket counter. Along with the ticket he purchased a black baseball cap sporting the name "Mt. Petrin, Prague" in English. "Not much of a disguise, but it will have to do," he mumbled to himself.

Having rejoined the tour group, Greg rode the cable car up the mountain. Greg's heart skipped a beat for one of many times that day. Following shortly behind the cable car, the other Greg Wesko trudged up the steep incline about thirty yards away. Obviously exhausted, the man could not keep up with the car. Part way up, the cable car came to halt. The Italian tour group departed to enjoy refreshments and a spectacular view of the city below. Hoping he could continue to rest while outpacing his rival, Greg remained on board. Greg began to doubt the wisdom of his choice as he spotted the man quickly making up the distance. A few more tourists filled seats around him. Greg breathed a sigh of relief a moment later as they continued their ascent.

Once on top, Greg made his way toward a replica of the Eiffel Tower. Although only a quarter of the size of the original, the observation tower was impressive enough. A multilingual sign indicated that it was closed for renovation. Certain that he had put a considerable distance between himself and the other Wesko, Greg devised a plan. Although closed, Greg noted that he could still slip into the tower and hide. He carefully surveyed the area. Only a few people were present, and all eyes were fixed on a street performer. The other Wesko was nowhere in sight. Furtively Greg entered the tower. He maintained an even but slow pace in order to avoid attracting attention to himself.

After one hundred steps Greg lost count. He seemed to be about a third of the way to the top. Lightheaded, Greg stopped to rest on the stairs. When his heavy breathing subsided a few moments later, the sound of activity below reached his ears. Greg strained to hear what was happening. He quietly made his way to a vantage point from where he could see the tower entrance. Two teenaged boys were engaged in a shoving match. A few friends stood by. As Greg watched the friends attempt to break up the brewing fight, he noticed a figure slip into the tower below just as he had. Greg's nerves tingled with panic. He felt completely trapped. Heading back down would certainly bring him into the path of the other Wesko. The only other option was to ascend the tower in the hopes that God would provide some type of escape route.

Greg ascended the stairs as quickly and quietly as his fatigued body would allow him. Finally he reached the highest observation deck. He peered out below and caught sight of a police officer attempting to intervene in the fight. Greg yelled out in the loudest voice he could muster. No one seemed to notice him below, but he was sure he had given himself away to his pursuer. He took a deep breath and tried again. This time the police officer looked up and caught sight of Greg. From his great height, Greg could not ascertain the man's expression or words. Greg took off his black cap and waved it through the air frantically. The police officer headed for the tower while the boys scattered in several directions. Greg was relieved to see the officer enter the tower. Greg hoped that he could fend off the other Wesko until help arrived. Getting caught for trespassing was the least of his worries.

Greg searched for a place to hide, but nothing availed itself. As he walked nervously about, dread suddenly overtook him. He whirled around to face his enemy standing at the entrance to the observation deck.

"What do you want?" Greg managed in a hoarse whisper. The man did not answer. "I don't mean you any harm!"

In response the man pulled out a knife. It was obvious that the man did mean Greg harm. Greg's mind raced for words or actions to prolong his chances for survival.

"Who are you?" Greg demanded. "Why are you impersonating me?"

The man lunged at Greg. Greg dodged the knife to the left and then to the right. Two more quick swipes followed, but Greg reacted quickly enough. Hatred gleamed in the man's eyes as he planned his next move. Knife poised, he leapt at Greg. Greg managed to grab the man's right arm and prevent the knife from stabbing him. The force of the man's lunge sent them crashing towards the railing. The two men were locked together, and Greg summoned all his strength to keep the knife away. The railing dug into Greg's back. In a losing battle, Greg saw the shaking blade inching toward his chest.

Instinctively, Greg shot his leg out and kneed the imposter in the stomach. The blow caused the man to double back, letting go of Greg.

Greg jumped up onto a nearby bench in the hopes of gaining a height advantage. The man lunged at Greg again. Greg jumped up and shot out his legs, aiming his feet toward his adversary. The man sprang into the air to avoid Greg's kick. He crashed full force into Greg's chest. Greg fell backwards against the bench, but the man ricocheted towards the top of the rail. In a freak turn of events, the other Greg Wesko hit the edge of the rail just below his center of gravity. Unable to stop himself, he careened over the edge and into the air below. A haunting scream of terror grew fainter and then suddenly stopped with a sickening crash. Thinking quickly, Greg took off his cap and threw it over the ledge. Then he withdrew from sight.

Chapter Thirty-Two

A telephoto lens focused on a tall, sturdy, black-haired woman as she exited a building. The viewfinder followed her as she approached her forest-green sedan sporting a "God Bless America" bumper sticker. As she paused to retrieve a set of keys from her purse, the crosshairs came to rest on her head, tilted slightly downward. As she looked up again, a quick click rang out as an unseen man in a dark blue pick-up truck shot her picture.

Moments later, the green sedan pulled into traffic on one of the city's main thoroughfares. Undetected, the pick-up followed at a safe distance. Driving with a firm purpose, the woman wove through traffic to get ahead at every opportunity. The driver of the blue pick-up truck swore as he struggled to keep pace without calling attention to himself.

After several minutes, the woman made a right turn up an entrance ramp onto the interstate. Two cars had wedged themselves between the woman and her pursuer. Barely able to keep her in sight, he followed impatiently as the brown vehicle directly in front of him hesitated against the incumbent interstate traffic. With the woman now out of sight, he blasted the car with his horn and revved his engine to pass on the right. The driver of the brown car accelerated along with the pick-up, which prevented him from getting in front. Swearing violently, the driver of the pick-up slowed down and resumed his position behind the brown vehicle. Now fully on the highway, he took the first opportunity to pass the car on the left. As he did so, he pointed his finger at the driver and pulled a phantom trigger. Having blown away this opponent in his mind, he sought to regain his pursuit.

Speeding down the highway, the man soon caught a flash of green in the distance. Having confirmed its identity, he positioned himself two cars behind the woman as she sped towards a destination he was anxious to discover.

Taking the exit for Granby, the woman slowed down and looked in her rearview mirror. The blue pick-up truck soon appeared. The sight struck a chord of familiarity with her. Signaling for a left turn, she passed up a break in the traffic and waited for the pick-up to come closer into view. To her surprise, the pick-up signaled right and pulled out onto the road without stopping. Still wondering, she proceeded with her left turn and began driving at a considerably slower speed.

Meanwhile, her pursuer pulled onto a side street and quickly turned around. Maintaining a greater distance than he was comfortable with, he fought to keep her in his view. After several minutes, she made a right turn into a residential neighborhood. Crawling past the rows of small Cape Cods dressed in light pastels, she allowed memories to flood her mind from distant years. Finally she parked her car in the street in front of a baby blue version of the cookie-cutter houses.

A few moments later, the blue pick-up turned down the same street. As the driver searched for the shade of forest-green, he caught sight of the woman waiting at the door of the light blue house. Pulling over to the side of the road, he whipped out his camera and shot a series of photographs as the door opened. Out stepped a portly man whom the woman embraced and kissed before the two disappeared inside.

On his iPhone, the man ran the address of the house to find the identity of the owner, Mr. Nick Milano. A few more clicks revealed the man's age, occupation, credit and legal history. Nothing unusual surfaced for this unmarried grocery store manager with a high school diploma from Granby High School. He put his PDA aside and thought to himself that this would require greater investigation to establish a link.

About an hour later, the woman emerged from the house and headed for her car. Nick Milano stood in his front door and waved as the man scrambled to catch a few pictures. The woman blew a kiss as she drove off.

Tom and Jason sat next to each other on an aging couch, the only real seat in the hourly-rate motel. Greg positioned himself on the edge of the sagging bed. The sight of Tom and Jason fighting to avoid sliding toward each other on the couch amused Greg.

"So did you learn anything from the pictures? What about the note?"

Tom attempted to sit forward on the couch. "The quality of the fax was too poor. I'll need the originals," he admitted.

"Here they are," Greg opened a manila envelope and spilled the contents onto the bed. He picked up one of two passport-size pictures. "This man claims to be Greg Wesko."

Tom and Jason both shot him a look of surprise.

"I was introduced to him in Prague. When I went to the address of the client on the list, I was invited inside. I think my cover as Bill Greene of Providential Insurance had already been blown. They questioned my real motives and informed me that my colleague, Greg Wesko, had arrived before me. When we were introduced, I think he recognized me. That's when I jumped out the window."

"What?" Tom and Jason remarked in unison.

Greg proceeded to relate the events of Prague. Jason and Tom listened with fascination, especially when Greg described the chase through the city streets. "I can't even say exactly how it happened. We were fighting, but it was definitely an accident. I was hoping the police officer would arrive in time to rescue me. He didn't know that there were two of us in the tower. He had only seen me shouting and waving my baseball cap from the top of the tower. I suppose he came in to arrest me. When the false Greg Wesko fell over the edge, I threw my baseball cap after him. I wanted the police officer to keep thinking that there was only one man in the tower, the man with the baseball cap who had fallen to his death. The next day I tried to find the story in the English version of the newspaper, but I was unsuccessful. I don't know whether they ruled his death an accident or suicide. And I also don't know whether he was carrying anything identifying him as Greg Wesko."

"I'll do some digging," Tom volunteered. "Let me see what else you have." After a few moments of study, Tom packed all the items back into the manila envelope. "I'll see about translating the letter too. It's signed 'DH,' which I assume are initials. And I'll check out the receipt that it's written on."

"There's no mystery to the receipt," Greg admitted sheepishly. "At the bank, I copied the note onto a receipt I had in my wallet. The original I left in the safe-deposit box in Vaduz, Liechtenstein. For some reason I didn't think it was a good idea to take it."

"Yet you took the pictures of the two men," Tom challenged him.

"I'm not a very good artist."

Sitting across from Sarah in a diner booth, Greg concluded his sanitized version of the trip to Europe. "Originally I intended to go from Prague down to Barcelona to finish up my business. But something came up and I decided against it. It was too complicated to change my plane reservations, so

I decided to kill a few days in Munich on the way back to London."

Sarah's eyes overflowed with interest and wonder. "I'm so jealous!" she exclaimed with a smile. "What a blessing to have such choices! 'Oh, where shall I go today? London? Milan? Perhaps I'll settle for Paris!'" she teased him.

"Honestly, I've never traveled like this before. This is a first for me. And I didn't get to do as much sightseeing as I would have liked," he admitted. "I was traveling on business, you know."

"And please explain to me again, what is this 'freelance banking' that you do? It sounds so unusual, almost criminal! Nobody I know has ever heard of it before."

Greg cringed inwardly. He hated keeping secrets from Sarah. He had avoided lying to her but had also avoided telling her the whole truth. "I know it sounds strange," he began. "Basically I check up on other people's clients for them." Greg caught Sarah's skeptical frown. "I'm partnering with a particular agency and a representative of a major insurance company." More puzzlement. "I'm not a collection agent or repo man or anything like that. It's difficult to explain. In any case, my part is over for a while. I need to find something else now. I've got an interview with a temp agency next Monday to hold me over."

"I'll pray for you," Sarah smiled. "Meanwhile I'll wait to see where the next postcard comes from. I've only received your card from Amsterdam so far."

"Probably Germany," Greg surmised. "Or Vaduz."

"Vaduz? I don't even know where that is. It doesn't really matter; I'd love to visit any of those places," Sarah sighed dreamily.

"Yes, under different circumstances," agreed Greg. He smiled and reached across the table to take Sarah's hand.

"Tony Franco." Tom Phillips threw a picture down on the folding table in the small meeting room he had reserved in the local public library. "I know the name rings a bell."

Greg stared at the picture he had taken from the safe-deposit box in Vaduz. "So we have two imposters: Tony Franco and Greg Wesko, both of Providential Insurance, perhaps?"

"That's how it seems," Tom confirmed. "Listen to this. I found the police report for the death of Greg Wesko in Prague. His identification listed him as an employee of Providential Insurance working out of an office in Barcelona. Now Jason Coates investigated the company records, and Providential has no office in Barcelona."

Greg studied the picture carefully. "Tony Franco works in Connecticut. How do you know this man also goes by Tony Franco?"

"I searched for other police reports involving Providential Insurance employees in Europe. This picture matched a man who washed up on a beach in southern Spain just a few weeks ago. Accidental drowning."

Greg shuddered. "My imposter's death was an accident, but doesn't it seem suspicious that this other imposter also died? What are the chances that it was really an accident for the fake Franco?"

"Hey, I'm paid to be suspicious. In my mind, there's no chance at all."

"What about the note?" Greg asked.

"It's written in Czech. I've got a guy working on it now. I thought he would be finished in time for this meeting, but no such luck."

"I'm worried about Tony Franco, the real one," Greg fretted. "They were using my name, tampering with my accounts, and trying to kill me. Tony Franco may be unstable, but he's no criminal. What are they doing to him?"

"Hopefully nothing. I started investigating this angle with Jason already. Tony doesn't manage any money, so he's safe there. You were only in danger because they found out that you discovered the missing funds. I think they copied your identities so they could maneuver through Providential more easily."

"How so?"

"Accessing files electronically, meeting with clients, and so on. And anyone investigating could confirm that a Tony Franco and a Greg Wesko did indeed work for Providential."

"But if someone called the main office to locate them, they would have been directed to the real Tony or me, and the gig would have been up."

"I haven't quite figured that one out yet. But then again, IT probably had your phones monitored. Did you ever receive international calls?"

"Not that I remember," Greg racked his brains.

"Perhaps international calls were blocked or re-directed," guessed Tom.

"Let's check it out," suggested Greg. "Do you have your cell phone?"

Tom nodded and retrieved a small silver unit from his pocket. "Yes, but it won't register as an overseas call," Tom reminded him.

"So much for bright ideas," Greg hit his head in self-mockery.

"That's OK. I'll check out your theory. I've got a contact in England. I'll ask him to try to reach Tony Franco in the US and Greg Wesko in Spain. Although now that both imposters are dead, their cohorts may have taken steps to cover their tracks. In any case, it's worth a try."

"Sounds like a plan. I'll wait for your next call."

Greg's heart leapt into his throat as he caught sight of the attractive redhead waiting for him at a table for two. She appeared even more stunning than he had remembered. Her soft complexion still glowed despite a faint trace of anxiety in her expression.

"Hi Joanna," he called wistfully.

Joanna looked up and gave him a careful smile. "It's good to see you, Greg." She offered him her hand delicately and he gave it a gentle squeeze as he sat down. "It's a little strange to meet you under these circumstances," she added.

"I know," he admitted. "I can't share all the details right now, but I'm involved in an investigation regarding my former job. I shouldn't call or visit the company right now. I asked a friend to drop off the note to Al the security guard with instructions to deliver it to you."

"All this cloak-and-dagger is a little frightening, Greg. Why is it safe to meet me here in public if you can't show up at work?"

"Frankly, I am taking a chance. But meeting an old friend in a neutral setting is less risky than calling someone while they are behind enemy lines," Greg explained. "And I worry that my home phone is tapped." Greg didn't mention his cell phone. Tom had forbidden him to use it to call anyone else who may be able to trace his call.

"I know we didn't part on the best of terms," Joanna chose not to meet Greg's eyes, "but I am willing to help you if I can."

"Thanks, Joanna. I appreciate the offer. But I didn't ask you here today to involve you in this problem. I wanted to talk to you about our relationship."

"I'm seeing someone," Joanna blurted out. He face blushed almost to the color of her hair. "I'm sorry, I didn't intend to let it out quite that way. But now that it's said, I'm glad. I found a wonderful man in my church, and we've been dating for quite some time now. Ever since you left, basically." Her eyes rose to meet his. He wore a pained expression.

"I'm glad for you, Joanna," he said calmly. "I have to admit, I have mixed emotions about it. I'm confused. I came here not quite knowing what I wanted, for you or for me. It would be selfish of me to hope that you had been waiting for me all this time, especially because I don't know how I really feel about you, about us. There have been so many changes in my life since we last spoke."

"What changes?" Joanna prodded him.

"I found the Lord," Greg explained calmly and earnestly. "I really found Him. He finally got through this thick head of mine. I know that He loves me, and I know that I love Him. I still haven't figured out what I'm supposed to do with all this, but God will help me. Already He's made me a new man. He showed me all the things I was worshipping instead of Him, like my work and even my own self. He allowed me to go to the depths, and now He has lifted my head and saved my life from the pit."

Joanna raised her hands to her mouth as Greg spoke. A tear rolled down her cheek, soon echoed by a tear running down Greg's face. "I'm so happy for you, Greg. I've been praying for this for years."

"You have? I guess I knew you were," he smiled.

"And now I'm the one who doesn't know what I want," Joanna admitted. Greg's puzzled expression urged her to elaborate. "After Lisa's death, when we were getting closer, the only thing that held me back from you was your lack of faith. I couldn't 'yoke myself with a non-believer,' as some might say. I knew your identity was wrapped up in your work and your abilities."

"What are you saying?"

"I'm talking about what I wanted then, what I hoped could have been. But since you left, Greg, I've fallen in love with this other man. His name is

Peter Monday." Joanna paused to take a deep breath. "I think he's going to ask me to marry him!"

"And you want to marry him?" Greg asked expectantly.

Joanna closed her eyes for a moment. "Oh yes, I do. I really do," she confessed. "I'm sorry, but I do."

"Then don't let me change anything," Greg bit his lip. "Let's go back to being friends, like we were for so many years. Can we go back to being friends?"

"I don't honestly know, Greg," admitted Joanna. "We'll need to give it some time. In any case, my offer to help with your investigation still stands."

"Thank you, Joanna."

Late Monday morning an optimistic Greg emerged from a downtown office building and headed out into the unseasonably warm sunshine. His interview with Kemp's Temps had gone well, and the hiring manager had told him to expect a temporary job assignment within a week. Although his prospective wages fell far short of his previous salary, they compared well to no income at all. Already weakened by the $20,000 he had withdrawn to cover the missing funds at work, his savings were now almost completely depleted. He was grateful to have Jason Coates to help shoulder the cost of hiring Tom Phillips. At times, doubts chastised him for not taking any of the fortune he had found in the bank in Vaduz. Yet a moment of centering prayer always restored the peace he felt over his decision.

The lunchtime traffic on the drive home seemed unusually heavy. A few minutes from his apartment, a white commercial van suddenly pulled out in front of him from a side street. Greg slammed on his brakes to avoid ramming the back of the vehicle. He resisted the urge to unleash a string of swear words, but instead he allowed himself just a moderate honk of his horn. The van was large enough to obscure Greg's view of the road ahead, including an upcoming traffic light. When the van screeched to a halt at a red light, Greg found himself slamming on his brakes for the second time in as many minutes. This time a mild oath escaped from Greg's lips before he could rein it back in. He let up a quick prayer of apology.

As he sat waiting for the light to change, he attempted to calm himself down with a few deep breaths. Anger quickly subsiding, he suddenly noticed something all too familiar in his peripheral vision. Turning, he faced a purple neon sign proclaiming "Psychic Readings." This time the glow of the sign was obscured by the bright sunlight. He thought about Madam Isis inside, waiting to hasten another lost soul along the road to perdition. "Not me," Greg exclaimed aloud. "Not ever again!"

By the time Greg arrived at home, a message was blinking on his answering machine. Greg undid his tie as the message played aloud. To his delight, he was invited to start work as soon as possible assisting an accountant in a privately owned import/export company headquartered in Hartford. After a quick confirmation call to the hiring manager, he redid his tie and headed for a long overdue afternoon of gainful employment. Waves of gratitude washed over him as he approached his car in the parking lot. He began to pray quietly.

"Why have you done all this for me?" he whispered with faltering voice. "Why have you given me such rich blessings? Dear Lord, why!" Raising his head, he continued, "And you hear my prayers!"

Yes, Greg, I'm right here!

"I believe it, Lord! You have always been with me, even when I messed up my own life. You picked up the pieces and put them back together for me. I know you love me, and I want to follow you all the days of my life!"

At that moment, Greg's eyes of faith opened even more so he could see, Greg's ears opened even more so he could hear, his heart opened even more so he could understand, so he could turn, be converted just a little bit more, and be healed.

An angel, Greg's lifelong companion, threw his head back and shouted for joy.

Chapter Thirty-Three

Ian Jacobs slapped a set of black and white pictures down on his desk. Joe Tropetto picked them up with a shaky hand. "These people look familiar?" he chirped.

With all the skill he could muster, Joe feigned outrage and broke into a tirade. "How could this be true! I can't believe she's seeing him! She's been lying to me all these years!"

"It's her old boyfriend, right?" Jacobs sat back and rested his head on his laced hands, a self-satisfied smile on his pockmarked face.

"His name is Nick Milano. They dated in high school. She said they broke up. I believed her. But now I wonder if they've been secretly seeing each other all along. Marina and I have been married for over six years. Six years!"

"That's a long time to keep an affair hidden," Jacobs admitted. "But I've seen it done before. I don't have proof to show how long they've been together. Phone records don't show any calls made from home or business. Maybe she calls from other locations."

"We've got a pay phone just outside the restaurant," Joe offered in an attempt to substantiate Jacobs' conclusions.

"Hmm, I didn't catch that," Jacobs scribbled something on his desk pad. "Now that you know, what do you want to do? I could get more incriminating pictures if you want 'em," he offered, grinning.

Joe writhed inwardly to deal with such a loathsome character. "What do other people do?"

Jacobs laughed. "All sorts of things. You can do anything you want to. Some people get a divorce. Some get even. The guy can get his tires slashed or even his kneecaps broken."

"Seriously?" Joe's eyes opened wide.

"Sure. Worse than that too."

"What if I wanted to make it look like an accident?" Joe questioned with a serious tone.

"We're talking hypothetical here, right? Breaking bones don't look like no accident."

"No, it doesn't. What about a fire?" Joe suggested with premeditation.

"I've seen the 'other guy' get his house burned down before."

"What about the wife, and burning her down in the house with him?"

Jacobs wrinkled up his face and regarded Joe through squinting eyes. After a moment, he leaned forward and motioned for Joe to come closer. In hushed tones he whispered very earnestly. "Murder is a big deal. You don't want to kill them over this." A moment of silence passed in which Joe locked eyes intently with Jacobs. Joe fought to hide the torture he was feeling. He wondered if Jacobs could see his eyes becoming moist. "But it can be done," Jacobs admitted in hushed tone.

"I'm not saying I do or I don't," Joe matched his whisper. "But what about a gas explosion? Could it be set up to look like an accident? Say she goes over there, and while they're both in the house, the oven explodes?"

"Sure, it could be done. But you don't want to do that. And get this straight," Jacobs spoke very purposefully, "I'm not going to discuss the matter with you anymore. Take your pictures and go. Pay on the way out."

Jason closed the door to the small conference room. "OK, let's have it," he demanded impatiently.

Tom opened up a file folder. "I had the letter translated. It's a rough translation, so bear with me. The translator said that the Czech was very bad. It was not written by a native speaker.

Friend, your original is gone. You need to change name. Let TF handle until you make new identity. Then you handle again. DH

"Sounds ominous," Jason frowned.

"It was found in the fake Wesko's safe-deposit box, right? So I figure that the original is you, Greg. Somehow you are gone."

"Just gone from the company, I hope," Greg postulated.

"Yes, let's hope so. DH tells him to change his identity, and in the meantime TF is to handle his business."

"TF has to be Tony Franco," Jason interjected.

"Bingo. My guess is that the phony Wesko didn't want to share his business, so he killed the phony Franco and threw him into the sea."

"Or maybe the phony Wesko had something to hide from the phony Franco. But now we'll never know, since both imposters are dead, and dead men don't tell tales," Greg pointed out.

"What will happen to all that money?" Jason wondered aloud. "Who will get into that safe-deposit box?"

"The authorities, I hope," answered Tom. "At some point we'll solve this case, and then the contents can be turned over to the appropriate people."

"I'd sure like to have my twenty grand back," Greg mused. "That turned out to be the worst investment of my life," he lamented.

The Thursday morning sun broke through the small window next to Greg's provisional desk. Even though his position was temporary, Greg devoted himself diligently to going beyond the requirements of the job. The manager had warned him from the start that there was no chance of the position evolving into a permanent assignment. Nevertheless, Greg found satisfaction in giving his top performance. At the same time, he was careful not to allow the job to become an idol in his life. He reminded himself that his true value lay in being a son of God, not in his occupation.

Greg closed the file he had been working on and placed it on a stack in his outbox. Retrieving another from his inbox, he remarked aloud, "Last one!" He opened the file to find a single piece of paper, a menu from a restaurant across the street. Chuckling to himself, he closed the file and put it to the side. Tucked away amidst filing cabinets in a back room, Greg remained out of the way and mostly forgotten. With all his work complete, a nap seemed appealing and almost justified. Nevertheless, Greg grabbed his files and headed for an office down the hall.

"Julia?" he asked, knocking lightly against an open oak door.

"Greg, come in." A smartly dressed woman in her early forties peered up over the top of thin-rimmed glasses. She continued typing on her keyboard as she spoke. "What can I do for you?"

"I seem to have finished all the work you gave me," Greg responded. "I also took the liberty of reorganizing some of the file drawers in the back office. What else can I do?"

The accountant stopped typing. "You could make a histogram of the import revenue by country and category."

"I still don't have a computer," Greg reminded her. "Too bad it's against company rules to use my own laptop," he lamented, fishing expectantly for permission.

Julia shook her head. "No, no. I can't change the rules." After a few moments of thought, she turned away from her computer to face Greg. Removing her glasses, she placed them on her desk and folded her hands. "Greg, I'm afraid I don't have any more work for you to do right now. Usually the temp agency sends me someone right out of school, not someone with your credentials. You've completed a month of work in less than two weeks."

"Experience helps," remarked Greg.

"Why don't you take it easy for a few hours, take a long lunch or surf the web," Julia stopped herself as she recalled the absence of computer and even company phone. "Maybe take a walk downtown. Meanwhile I'll review what you've done. Come back this afternoon so you can answer any questions I might have."

"And then?"

"Unfortunately, I won't have anything else to keep you busy. Your assignment will be over for now. I'm sorry. But I'll certainly want you back at the end of next quarter. If you're available."

"We'll have to see, Julia. I hope to land a permanent job soon." Dejected, Greg wished that his temporary boss had helped him to see the abrupt end coming.

"You will," Julia smiled. "Don't worry about it."

"Three no trump!"

"Double!"

Greg and Sarah passed two couples playing bridge at a card table as they headed towards familiar faces. Halfway across the church hall, Harry and Marnie Hausmann stood among a group full of smiles and laughs. The newcomers approached meekly and waited to be recognized.

"Greg, Sarah, welcome to Game Night!" Harry cut short an entertaining story to greet them. "Let me introduce you around," he said after a warm and strong handshake. Introductions began, and Greg surmised that everyone was within ten years of his age on either side. Except for Harry and Marnie, the group was entirely comprised of singles.

The crowd dispersed, and Greg found himself in a conversation with Harry and a reticent man named Christopher. Harry had a talent for expressing genuine interest in other people's lives without giving an impression of being nosy or pushy. Within a short time, Harry managed to elicit a score of information about Christopher's occupation, hobbies, school history, and faith perspective. Harry's friendly demeanor stimulated a desire in Greg to share his faith and career struggles. However, the gravity of his ordeal required a more private, more trusting moment for delving into his personal life. Instead he simply admitted that he was seeking employment and generically described the work he had just completed as a temp.

A short brunette called for a game of charades. A small group of people began assembling for the game, and Sarah urged Greg to join them. He politely raised one hand and gently shook his head. But when Harry prompted him, he reluctantly conceded to participate. When Greg's turn came, he received a card reading, "Love Potion Number Nine."

"You've got to be kidding!" Greg exclaimed, laughing in spite of himself. "I can't do this!"

"Ah, come on, give it your best shot!" Harry encouraged him.

Several hand motions and incorrect guesses later, Sarah called out the right answer. Greg sat back down next to her as he received a round of applause. "I never would have done this a year ago," he admitted to her. She reached over and squeezed his hand. It was a simple gesture, but it sent tingles up Greg's arm. "I'm having a wonderful time," he added.

The buzzing of Greg's cell phone was barely detectable over the growing din. He reached into the pocket of his light jacket to retrieve it. As he answered, his heart began to pound.

"Greg, it's Tom. I've got urgent news," the voice crackled with earnestness.

"Hold on. Let me move outside," Greg told him. Apologizing to Sarah, he made his way to an exit that spilled out into an empty alleyway.

"Joe planted the bug as we discussed. I'm sure that Jacobs was involved in the fire in your apartment. I don't think he just investigated it. I think he planned it. And he was just on the phone with someone discussing you. The topic wasn't clear, but they know you are back poking around, and they want it to stop. You need to get out of town immediately."

"Right now?" Greg gasped incredulously.

"Go and pack a bag or two if you need to. But then get to a safe place. Call me from there."

"This is scary," Greg stammered.

"Yes, it is."

"I'm sorry, Sarah. Something urgent has come up and I have to leave town for a few days," apologized Greg, trying to control the shakiness of his voice.

"Is everything all right?"

"I hope so," he admitted, not knowing what to say. He had taken Sarah's hand to lead her off to the side for some privacy. As her hand remained in his, he wondered if she noticed his sudden perspiration.

"Can I help? Maybe water your plants while you're gone?" offered Sarah.

"No!" he shouted abruptly, looking intently into her eyes. "I mean, no thanks. Hopefully I won't be gone that long."

"Where are you going?"

Unable and unwilling to fabricate a lie, Greg remained vague. "I'm helping out with that project again, and it's reached a critical stage. My partners asked me to go out of town while they take care of things here."

"I thought you said your temporary assignment ended today?"

"It did. This is the project that took me to Europe. Sarah, I want to explain more, but I can't right now. I've got to leave immediately. In fact, I should have already left, but I didn't know it was so urgent."

Sarah tried unsuccessfully to mask the disappointment sweeping across her face. Looking down, she sighed, "OK, then let's go."

"Oh Sarah, no, please. Why don't you stay and enjoy the rest of the night? I feel bad enough about leaving you so suddenly like this. I'd feel better knowing that you're with other people, not all alone. Let's ask Marnie if she can give you a ride home later," Greg suggested.

"I would like to stay," Sarah admitted tentatively, "since I can't go with you now, Greg."

"I really wish you could, Sarah. I'm so sorry," he apologized again. Greg and Sarah approached Marnie, and Greg briefly explained the situation. Marnie graciously offered to drive Sarah home at the end of the night. Sarah forced a smile as she walked with Greg toward the door. He desperately wanted to add a kiss to her smile, but with the crowd, the moment seemed to call for just a squeeze of the hand. Pained, Greg walked away into the unknown.

Chapter Thirty-Four

New leaves bathed the surroundings in a light green hue as Greg sputtered up the mountain road in his car. Through occasional breaks in the trees, Greg caught glimpses of the valley below growing more distant beneath him. Soon he reached the summit and turned onto a familiar street.

Lisa's parents lived in the Watchung Mountains of New Jersey, less than an hour's drive from New York City without traffic. Since the events surrounding Lisa's death, Greg had spoken with them on a few occasions but never at length. He hoped that they would not mind his surprise visit. Greg had called them earlier in the morning from a rest area where he had spent the night in his car. Their cheerful voices had assured him that this would be a welcome, albeit sudden visit.

Pulling into the steep gravel driveway, Greg remembered how he had always dreaded making the trip in the snow and ice. He was thankful for the beautiful early spring day. He rapped on the door of their modest cottage with a large brass knocker.

"Gregory, it's so good to see you!" Lisa's mother embraced him warmly. Her father extended a hearty handshake and slapped him on the shoulder.

At their invitation, he followed them into the kitchen and accepted a cup of hot coffee. Her mother remembered that he liked one cream and no sugar.

"Thanks, Janice." Upon their engagement, Greg had been invited to call them Mom and Dad, but he continued to use their first names. As he sat now in their kitchen after such an elapsed time, he realized that he should have accepted their offer. He had felt closer to them than to his own parents.

"How are things at work, Greg?" her father inquired.

"Great! I'm currently unemployed," he smiled.

"Me too," he returned the smile.

"Sure, Sam. But at your age it's called retirement!"

Janice listed the items on the menu she had planned for dinner. They spent the afternoon engaged in light-hearted conversation. Greg thoroughly enjoyed himself, but after dinner he decided the time had come to broach a heavier topic.

"Janice, Sam," he began unceremoniously, "I believe I'm involved in a conspiracy."

Two puzzled faces remained silent.

Greg proceeded to explain the missing money at work, his forced resignation, and his current investigation. Captivated, Lisa's parents listened intently.

"My private detective called me last night on my confidential cell phone. He told me my life could be in danger and that I should leave town."

"Oh my goodness!" Janice exclaimed.

"Returning to my apartment was nerve-wracking," Greg recounted. "I was afraid someone or something might be waiting for me."

"Like what?" Sam inquired.

Greg paused to muster his courage before proceeding. "Like a bomb or explosion. I didn't want that to happen - again."

Greg let silence prevail to allow the implication of his words to sink in. Janice caught on first.

"You don't mean..." she trailed off.

"Lisa? Oh no!" Sam cried.

Greg nodded grievously. "I suspect so. The explosion was meant to look like an accident." The words were almost too heavy to utter. "It was intended for me, but Lisa got there first. I'm so sorry."

Still sitting in their chairs around the kitchen table, Lisa's parents hugged each other and wept intensely. After a while, Greg approached them, and they included him in their embrace.

Greg kicked his bag into a corner in Lisa's childhood bedroom. Her parents had offered to let him stay for a while. Sitting down on the bed, he dialed Tom Phillips on the cell phone but received no answer.

A collection of photo albums lined a bookshelf across the room. Retrieving one, he returned to the bed and leafed through the pages. Anonymous young faces laughed and smiled at him along with a teenaged Lisa. He had not known her at that age. Although they had shared details of their adolescence with each other, Greg had not taken the opportunity to make the stories his own. Now the memories were lost for a lifetime, and he knew he could never get them back. Trying hard not to let go of what was never his, he wept on the edge of the bed.

Greg awakened to the sound of his cell phone. Taking a moment to get his bearings, he scrambled to find it in the early morning light. He managed to mumble a greeting.

"Greg, don't tell me where you are. I don't know whether this phone is secure anymore. Meet me at the first place we met, Monday night at nine. OK?"

"OK, Tom." Greg planned to continue the conversation, but the click in his ear cut him off.

Sunday after church, Greg invited Lisa's parents out for lunch. The restaurant, a local favorite, sprawled at the base of a cliff and looked out at an abandoned quarry. When they arrived, the hostess handed them a beeper and informed them that there was a twenty-minute wait.

Bright sunlight took the chill off the mountain air, and they decided to wait outside where it was quieter. Sam turned to Greg and spoke earnestly. "I'm so glad you came to church with us this morning. There was a time that I didn't think I would ever see the day."

"Oh Sam!" Janice chided playfully. "We knew God would answer our prayers. We prayed for Lisa to come back to the Church for years. And she did."

"And with a vengeance!" added Sam.

"So I heard," Greg remarked with a grin. "She never spoke much about it. But some time after her death, my neighbor told me Lisa was going to church every day."

"Lisa told us that too. That last weekend she was here," recalled Sam with bittersweet emotion. "We knew she had gotten right with God earlier that year. Eventually she started attending daily Mass. She was afraid of scaring you off, so she kept it from you."

"Why would it scare me off?" asked Greg.

"Think about it," Sam advised him. "How would you have taken it back then?"

Greg frowned and then broke into a smile. "You're right. I'm a different man now. It would have weirded me out then. Too much religion can spoil a good relationship, or so I thought. But I was wrong."

"Gregory!" Janice cried out suddenly. "We thank God for you and for your faith. I just had to let you know. We are so proud of you! Your conversion is another answer to our prayers. After Lisa died, I admit I almost lost hope for you. But I prayed. I hoped that others were praying for you too, but I prayed as if I were the only one."

"There were others," Greg smiled. "My sister. She found God too, and she prayed for me. She was instrumental in helping me find my faith again. But

Lisa helped too. I tried to pressure Lisa into going away with me, but she refused. Going into the desert alone wasn't my first choice, but it gave me time to think. I experienced God, and I think He gave me a warning about where my life was heading. But my worldliness clouded my understanding, so I didn't fully comprehend. So when Lisa died, I hardened my heart for a long time. God had to bring me to the depths to get me to pay attention again. I'm glad He did."

"Sometimes that's what it takes," Sam agreed.

"We never found out what triggered a spiritual awakening in Lisa," Janice sighed. "But I guess we'll know on the other side of this life. Sometimes I just wish we didn't have to wait."

"There are lots of things I wish we didn't have to wait to find out," Greg reflected as the beeper in his hand lit up. "I guess it's time for lunch. Let's go inside," he invited.

The portion sizes at the restaurant surpassed anything one person could reasonably handle. Greg agreed with Lisa's parents that an evening meal would not be necessary. Well after dark, however, appetites awoke, and the threesome found themselves gathering in the kitchen. Lisa's mother began to prepare a platter of crackers and cheese for a communal bedtime snack. As they chatted, a faded memory surfaced in Greg's mind, a memory that still needed resolution.

"Perhaps you can help me with something," he began earnestly. "My neighbor saw Lisa the day of the terrible tragedy. She said Lisa was carrying a package wrapped in gold paper. It wasn't near my birthday or any holiday, so I wasn't expecting a present. At the scene of the fire, I found a trace of the gold paper, but I never found out what was inside the package. Do either of you have any idea?"

Sam shook his head. "I can't say I recall anything in particular," he admitted.

Janice set the tray down on the kitchen table. "Now that I think about it, she did come to me for some wrapping paper," she recollected. "I didn't ask her why. I figured it wasn't any of my business. If Lisa wanted me to know, she would have told me."

"Did you ever have any gold wrapping paper?" Even as Greg asked, Sam was on his feet heading for a closet in the hallway. A moment later he returned with a roll of gold wrapping paper.

"I'm sure that's it!" Greg exclaimed. "I only saw a piece of it after it was destroyed. If only I knew what was inside the package!" he lamented.

"I guess whatever it was, it wasn't meant to be," Sam commented.

Preparing for bed, Greg took the opportunity to search Lisa's room for clues to the identity of the mystery gift. He rummaged carefully through the drawers of Lisa's desk in search of a receipt. After a thorough investigation, Greg admitted defeat. He decided it was better not to pursue what he could not hold onto. Sitting in Lisa's desk chair, he picked up a white Bible, the only book missing from the shelf on the wall. A red ribbon marked the place where Lisa had read her last Scripture. Greg opened and read 2 Corinthians starting with Chapter 3, verse 10.

> According to the grace of God given to me, like a wise master builder I laid a foundation, and another is building upon it. But each one must be careful how he builds upon it, for no one can lay a foundation other than the one that is there, namely, Jesus Christ. If anyone builds on this foundation with gold, silver, precious stones, wood, hay, or straw, the work of each will come to light, for the Day will disclose it. It will be revealed with fire, and the fire itself will test the quality of each one's work. If the work stands that someone built upon the foundation, that person will receive a wage. But if someone's work is burned up, that one will suffer loss; the person will be saved, but only as through fire. Do you not know that you are the temple of God, and that the Spirit of God dwells in you? If anyone destroys God's temple, God will destroy that person; for the temple of God, which you are, is holy.

Greg pondered the passage, which at first seemed somewhat harsh. But as he meditated, hope began to well up inside him. *Surely Lisa helped build upon my foundation in Christ, as latent as it was at the time.* As he continued to pray, conflicting emotions of anger and compassion quietly erupted in his heart. *Lisa was a temple of the Holy Spirit. Someone destroyed her body with fire, although not her soul. How will God deal with the person responsible for her death?* Greg shuddered to think of it. Standing, he walked over to the nightstand where he had left his wallet. In a forgotten corner of his billfold, sandwiched in between two expired credit cards, Greg retrieved the scrap of gold paper he had inserted there many months earlier. He laid it in the Bible and closed the pages.

Monday morning Greg threw his bag into the trunk and turned back towards Lisa's parents where they stood in the driveway. Throwing her arms around him, Janice gave him a quick kiss and a motherly hug. Then holding him at arm's length, she looked intently into his eyes.

"Gregory, the time has come for you to move on with your life. What you had with Lisa was very special. It's true. But these last few days you've briefly mentioned another woman or two, and I can tell you feel guilty about it. Please don't. You have to know that you can and will love again."

"I want to," he confessed sheepishly.

"You should want to," Janice continued. "And when you do, don't compare it to what you had with Lisa. Learn from your relationship with her, but don't worry about whether the next one is better or worse in any areas."

"I've changed so much since then," Greg admitted. "Like I said before, we never got to share our faith, because I didn't have one."

"It was just dormant, Gregory. Lisa found her faith again at the right time. You were just a little farther behind. She knows now."

"Yes, now that she's dead instead of me."

"Don't blame yourself," Sam spoke up. "We don't."

"No, certainly not," Janice chimed in. "Maybe she was a martyr of sorts. She died so that you would live, and she died a righteous woman. If she had to die, I can't think of any better reasons. God knew what was going to happen."

"And He let it," Greg mourned.

"Yes, and we have to accept that. We don't understand, but we accept it," Sam stated, his voice growing hoarse with emotion.

"And we are not bitter," Janice added.

"It's hard not to be," admitted Greg. "But I try."

"Now go on, get on with your life," Sam urged, his voice returning. "Get the bad guys and get the girl," he winked. "Whoever she turns out to be."

"And we'll pray for you," Janice smiled.

Greg slipped into the driver's seat and waved as he drove slowly down the mountain. He could feel the guilt and shame of the past years evaporating in the warming air. As he rolled down the windows, he prayed to God for help.

"Dear Lord, help me get on with my life. Help me get the bad guys. And help me get the girl," he paused. "Whoever she turns out to be."

Chapter Thirty-Five

On Greg's second visit, the B-Street Bar seemed less seedy than it had on his first meeting with Tom Phillips. Over time, Greg's trust in Tom had grown, yet he still lacked some confidence in Tom's critical thinking abilities.

"Joe and Marina won't be joining us tonight," Tom began without a greeting. "They have to keep a low profile because of the investigation. Jacobs uncovered that Nick Milano and Marina were high school sweethearts, and he thinks they're still involved. Joe ostensibly has his proof, and the case is over. We don't feel safe sending him back to Jacobs, and the device we planted is still working. Jason plans to have lunch at their restaurant a few times a week so we can keep in touch."

"Even that is risky. I know you're good friends, but don't call them anymore, for now," Jason warned Greg. "We're afraid that they may have already linked you together, since you went to school with Joe."

Tom resumed the narrative. "Marina recently left for Italy to visit some relatives to continue the charade. She and Joe arranged to have a shouting match at the restaurant over the weekend to add some credibility. Based on my experience with Jacobs, he may have placed a tap on the restaurant phone or placed a bug somewhere on the premises. Since Joe and Marina aren't used to fighting, I actually wrote a script for them. They stayed in the kitchen so the customers couldn't hear them clearly. We want to protect their reputation with their clientele as much as possible, of course. But we especially wanted a reason to send Marina away for her own safety in case they find out Joe planted the bug in Jacobs' office," explained Tom.

"Poor Joe and Marina," commented Greg. "I never knew what loyal friends they were to me. I hope they aren't in danger. I want to pay for Marina's trip. Jason, would you tell that to Joe for me?"

"I'd be glad to. I don't whether they'll accept it," Jason stated. "I'm sure she didn't mind the opportunity to take some time off, despite the circumstances."

The waitress returned with their first round of drinks, draft beer for Jason and Greg and tonic water with lime for Tom.

"Something strange happened while you were away," Tom remarked after taking a sip of his drink. "I kept tabs on your apartment, Greg, and so did someone else."

"Who?" Greg's eyes opened wide.

"Tony Franco."

"Oh no," Greg moaned. "I don't want to hear that!"

"He acted very strange, as if he suspected that someone was following him. He waited in his car for several minutes and then trotted up the stairs to the second floor. First he looked into your neighbor's window. Your neighbor was home, and I guess Franco eventually figured out he was snooping in the wrong place. I don't think your neighbor saw him, or he might have called the police. Franco used a flashlight to peer in through your windows. He also tried the front door to see if you had left it unlocked. Then he knocked on the door several times. He waited for a minute and then jimmied the lock open and went inside."

"What?" Greg gasped. "I had no idea he could do that. Or would do that!"

"He did. He was only inside for about five minutes. When he came out, he ran for his car and sped off. I half expected the place to explode, but nothing happened. After a few minutes I used the key you gave me and checked the place out carefully. There was no sign that Franco stole anything or rigged anything up."

"Why was he there?" Jason wondered.

"I don't know the man personally, but we do know he's not the most stable guy," Tom explained. "I checked that out and confirmed that he was institutionalized on two occasions. Not the best choice for a partner in crime. I also found that he recently cashed in his 401k retirement account. That could be a sign he's getting ready to leave town. On the other hand, it could explain how he's paying for his change in lifestyle if he's actually not part of the embezzlement. Still, I have to question whether he may be an unrelated but real danger. So far we've assumed that the missing money and the fire in your old apartment are related. What if they're not?"

"What an incredibly unfortunate coincidence that would be! That'd be too hard to believe!" Jason exclaimed.

"You mean a homicidal maniac on one side, and a den of thieves on the other? All at the same company? Impossible!" Greg declared emphatically.

"I agree," Tom remarked. "We just have to keep all options on the table at this point."

"I suppose so," murmured Greg. "Tony called me and left messages several times while I was in Texas, and once since I came back. And remember, I ran into him in the parking garage at Providential Insurance when I went to pay a visit to Al Finch. He acted even stranger than ever, if that's possible, but not sinister. This whole Franco thing just puzzles me."

"He's still on the list of suspects, and I'm keeping a close eye on him," Tom promised. "But now let's get to the big news, the reason I called you back," Tom said ominously. "You remember the name Sylvester Campus, right?"

"It's a hard name to forget. He's the guy from the IT department who acted suspiciously and then disappeared," recalled Greg.

"Exacto. Turns out, when the snows melted in the White Mountains of New Hampshire this spring, they revealed something. They had been hiding the body of Sylvester Campus. His car was found half buried in the muddy bank of a mountain river. Apparently he drove over the edge of a cliff on a slippery road. The authorities estimate he's been dead since December."

"This is terrible! What he was doing in New Hampshire?" mused Greg, praying for insight.

"Foul play?" asked Jason.

"The death is ruled an accident, officially. I had one of my contacts check out the auto, but it was so badly damaged that it would be hard to find any evidence of tampering. Someone could have poked a hole in the brake line. Or he could have been suffocated, set up behind the wheel of his car and pushed over the edge. All his injuries are consistent with tumbling down a mountain, but perhaps he was first knocked out or even killed with a blunt object. But he definitely died in the crash or just beforehand," Tom related.

"Any leads on the culprit?" inquired Greg.

"There is an amazing coincidence. Amos Stockley owns a cabin in the White Mountains within five miles of the crash site."

"Amos Stockley?" Greg cried in amazement. "I knew this scandal went way up the ladder! He was our Vice President."

"Still is," interjected Jason. "Rumor has it that he's in line to fill the CEO's shoes when he retires next year. I knew he had a mountain cabin somewhere. He lends it out to the executive staff all the time. So it doesn't necessarily incriminate him."

"We know there are multiple people involved. It'll be hard to point the finger just yet," said Tom.

"Unless we can elicit a confession from someone," Greg suggested. He paused to organize the thoughts that were flowing into his mind. "Listen to this..."

Greg sat in his apartment living room, trying in vain to focus on reading the newspaper. At long last, the phone rang as expected.

"Greg, it's Tom. I confirmed that Amos Stockley owns a cabin up near where Sylvester Campus was killed in the car crash. Or should I say, murdered!"

"We have to get inside that cabin to see if we can find out whom he met with," Greg responded.

"We can try breaking in," suggested Tom.

"No, I have a better idea. My friend Joanna from work knows Stockley. They served on the company's diversity committee together. I can get her to ask Stockley to use the cabin sometime soon for a weekend getaway."

Tom paused as if he had forgotten the lines to a script. "Good idea. I'll come to the cabin too. You let me in and together we'll look for clues."

"OK. I'll talk to Joanna tonight and get back to you."

Mustering all her courage, Joanna strode down the hall towards Amos Stockley's office. As she passed through the corridor, she glanced out the ceiling-height glass windows. From this vantage point she could see the entire eastern half of the city. Somewhere out there Greg waited for her to execute the next leg of the plan. She prayed for strength.

"Can I help you?" the motherly administrative assistant asked.

"I'm here to see Amos Stockley. Can you please tell him that Joanna Pearson is here?"

"Is he expecting you, dear?"

"He'll want to see me. Anyway, I won't take but a minute."

The kindly woman conceded, "I'll see if he's busy." After a short, muffled conversation on the phone, she indicated for Joanna to proceed around the corner into Stockley's office.

"Hi, Joanna," he greeted her warmly. "What a nice surprise! Is there something I can do for you?" offered the tall silver-haired executive.

Joanna resisted the urge to clear her throat. "It's nice to see you again, Amos. How have you been?" she inquired, offering the obligatory niceties.

"Busy as usual. Doing well is a double-edged sword, you know. The better you do, the more is expected."

"I know you always rise to meet the challenge," Joanna forced a smile.

"So what's up, Joanna?" he asked, cutting to the chase but still remaining amicable.

"I have a favor to ask you," she hesitated.

"Please, tell me what you need."

"Well," she began, "I understand you have a cabin in New Hampshire. I really wanted to get away this weekend. It's so hard to make last-minute reservations anywhere good, so I was wondering if your cabin was available for rent this weekend. I've heard such nice things about it."

"Oh, it's very romantic, in a rustic sort of way. That's my way of saying it needs a little fixing up. But don't hurt my feelings by offering to pay for it. I'm not planning to use it this weekend anyway. Ski season is over, but the leaves aren't quite out on the trees yet either, at least not at the cabin's elevation. I usually don't go up at this time of year. You're welcome to it," he offered.

"Thank you very much, Amos!" replied Joanna. "I'm so excited!"

"My pleasure. I've only got one available guest key for the front door," he trailed off.

"One will be fine," Joanna caught Stockley's subtle insinuation. "But do you mind if I bring a friend? Is there a second bedroom or a sleeper sofa?"

"There are four guest bedrooms upstairs. I prefer if you use one of the first two on the left as soon as you go up the stairs. Feel free to use both, if you do need two bedrooms."

"We will. I don't want you to get the wrong idea," Joanna blushed.

"It's none of my business," Stockley replied.

"Well, it is your cabin," she emphasized. "I really appreciate it, Amos."

Stockley rose from his chair and opened a faux liquor cabinet in the back of his office. He removed a key from a half-empty set of hooks and handed it to Joanna. "All the doors and windows are alarmed. The code to deactivate it is written on the key. It's your choice whether you activate it at night or if you go out, but please activate it again at the end of the weekend."

"I will. Thanks again, Amos," Joanna accepted the key and rose to depart.

"Have a memorable time," Amos smiled affably.

"We're all set for this weekend," Joanna's voice crackled over the phone.

"Great," responded Greg. "Do you think Stockley suspected anything?"

"He got it out of me that I'm bringing a friend. Although I didn't say it was you, I think he knows that I'm bringing a man. That's not the type of impression I wanted to give him."

"Two men," Greg corrected her. "If Stockley is an embezzler and a murderer, then I don't think you have to worry about your reputation with him."

"Even so," Joanna declared demurely.

A sharp click was heard as Tom Phillips picked up the phone. "Hello?"

"Hi Tom, it's Greg. We're leaving after Joanna gets off from work on Friday. We hope to be up to the cabin by ten o'clock." Greg proceeded to give directions, giving Tom enough time to jot them down.

"Thanks, Greg. I'll see you Saturday morning, then."

"See you, Tom."

The seated man drummed his fingers nervously on the table as the standing man finished replaying the audio. "That's all there is," he slurred gruffly.

"This is a serious problem," the seated man answered. "I don't know what to do."

"Leave that to me," the standing man grinned, his shiny white teeth reflecting the dim yellow lighting of the small, stuffy room. "I've got the perfect solution."

Chapter Thirty-Six

Greg stood in the front doorway of his second-story garden apartment watching for Joanna's car in the approaching nightfall. From his vantage point, he could observe the side street traffic and the entrance to the apartment complex. His large packed bag stood clearly visible behind him. Soon a familiar vehicle pulled into the parking lot, and out stepped a woman sporting a pink baseball cap. The entrance to the stairwell took her from his sight, and he waited impatiently as footsteps sounded softly up the stairs. Greg picked up his bag and began to head out the door as the woman emerged onto the second floor walkway serving his apartment and a few neighbors. Suddenly sweat broke out across Greg's brow.

Sarah Huff's startled expression matched Greg's as the two stared at each other.

"What's going on, Greg? I thought you left last week!" A twinge of hurt crept into Sarah's tone.

"Sarah, what are you doing here?" was all that Greg could muster.

"Are you just returning? You told me yesterday on the phone that you weren't coming back for another few days. Did your work end early?"

Realizing that Joanna's arrival was imminent, Greg fought frantically to find appropriate words. He regretted his decision to waste time waiting for Joanna. "No, my work isn't finished," he fumbled, "but I had to return to pick up a colleague. We're both working on the same project. We have to go out of town again."

"How long?" she questioned.

Not answering her question, Greg repeated his. "What are you doing here? Didn't you expect me to be gone?"

It was Sarah's turn to hesitate. "I was hoping you would be back," she lied. Unable to meet Greg's eyes, she choked on her words. "No, honestly, I was checking up on you. I tried really hard to believe you, but your story didn't quite add up in my mind. I just wanted to find out whether you were here, and to make sure you weren't seeing someone else."

A noise from behind caught Sarah's attention, and she whirled around to meet Joanna as she set foot on the second-floor walkway.

"I'm so sorry," Joanna apologized as they sped up Interstate 91 towards Massachusetts. "My timing was awful."

"So was hers," Greg muttered. "Let's not talk about it."

"Just one more question," Joanna pleaded earnestly. "Are you in love with her?"

A moment of tortuous silence elapsed before Greg answered. "I think so."

"Don't worry then. It will all work out," Joanna encouraged him.

"We'll see."

The four-hour drive remained uneventful, with one stop for refreshment at a fast food restaurant near Brattleboro, Vermont, before cutting over into New Hampshire. Stockley's printed directions were flawless, and the couple pulled onto the final winding mountain road at precisely ten o'clock. Crawling slowly uphill on the dark gravel drive, the outside lights of the cabin were soon visible through the evergreens. Greg noted aloud that it would be a beautiful view in the morning.

A large illuminated deck on the side of the cabin sheltered a parking area large enough for three cars. The approach of the car activated a motion-sensitive light underneath the deck as they pulled in. Before exiting the vehicle, Joanna and Greg scanned the area for any figures lurking in the shadows. Joanna stepped cautiously toward the alarm panel next to the side door while Greg retrieved their luggage from the trunk. Entering the code written in marker on the key, she disarmed the alarm and unlocked the door. She waited for Greg to set the luggage down near the entrance. Greg motioned for her to step aside. Slowly he opened the door and stepped into the dim interior. A moment later he returned for the luggage and informed Joanna that it seemed safe to enter.

Inside the cabin, Greg and Joanna were greeted by cool, stagnant air. Greg quickly found the thermostat and turned up the heat to take the chill off the alpine night. The door opened directly into an expansive lounge area with a giant LCD television and two smaller plasma televisions. Several couches and chairs were grouped in each of three viewing areas. In the far corner, a fully stocked bar was available for the use of the guests. Across the room a table and chairs were arranged for family-style eating. A small kitchen was accessible nearby through a swinging double-door. To their right, the front door led out to a stone walkway, while to the left lay a game room, half bath and office. The property sloped such that these three side rooms had been carved out of the earth, with the kitchen and lounge having the only windows on the first floor.

Joanna turned on a set of overhead lights to reveal the twenty-foot lounge ceiling complete with skylights. A set of wooden stairs led up to a walkway overlooking the lounge. The walkway ran along two bedrooms and a bathroom and then turned a corner to access bedrooms three and four, which lay directly over the eating area and kitchen.

Toting their luggage, Greg climbed the stairs to inspect the bedrooms while Joanna unpacked some groceries in the kitchen. A few minutes later, Greg returned from the upstairs and declared loudly, "I'm all unpacked. I took the first bedroom and left the second for you. It was prettier." He then threw himself onto the sofa in front of the LCD TV. He found a basketball game and turned up the volume.

Joanna emerged from the kitchen. "Thanks, Greg," she shouted back. Approaching the couch, she whispered, "Do you think Tom will be here soon?"

"Do you want to watch something else?" Greg hollered over the game. Then softly he answered, "We have to turn down the lights first, remember?"

Greg and Joanna engaged in periodic small talk over the din of the television. After what seemed like a reasonable time, they dimmed the lights, and Joanna announced that she was going to bed. Greg broadcast that he wanted to take a short walk around the property, and Joanna cautioned him against bears as a goodnight warning. He lingered in the low lighting. After a few minutes, a single knock was heard as expected. Greg traced the sound to the front door. Double-checking that the alarm was off, Greg put on a heavy jacket and opened the front door. Stepping outside, he stooped as if to tie his shoe and picked up a rock with a small note tied to it. Heading out into the night, he turned his back towards the house and nonchalantly read the note. It indicated for Greg to proceed towards a path entering the woods from the driveway. Following the instructions, he made his way to the trail and crossed into the darkness.

"Greg, over here!" a voice whispered.

"Tom, is that you?" he called back in matching hush.

Tom Phillips emerged from the woods and walked along side Greg. "Greg, we have a real problem here!" he barked sternly.

"What is it? Did someone show up already? I checked out the house and it was empty."

Tom ignored Greg's speculation. "I thought we agreed that you would come alone! Why did you bring Joanna along? We only wanted to give the *impression* that Joanna was going to the cabin."

Greg was taken aback by the anger in Tom's words. "Joanna and I argued about it Friday morning after you had already left. She wouldn't take no for an answer, Tom. Anyway, Joanna is the one who made the arrangements with Stockley. If the criminals listened in as we planned, then they're expecting Joanna to be here. And how were we going to fool them into thinking Joanna was here unless she actually came along? We're assuming that the place is under surveillance."

"But it's very dangerous! She's risking her life."

"I told her that, but she insisted."

"You've got to get her to go back," Tom fumed.

"She's a grown woman, capable of making her own decisions."

"This was a bad idea! We should try something else."

Now Greg's temper began to flare. "Look, Tom. We agreed that we have to act quickly. Otherwise you shouldn't have called me back from hiding. I'm risking my life for this too, and I'm also in jeopardy of losing the woman I love!" Greg proceeded to briefly explain the awkward encounter at his apartment.

"I'm sorry it worked out that way," Tom began to calm down. "You're right. We do need to act. I just don't like surprises like this. I'll have to alter the plans a little."

"How?"

"I'll have to think about that. But first, let me tell you what's happened so far. I showed up earlier this afternoon in a uniform from the local utilities company. I scouted the area thoroughly enough that I think I know where all the outside surveillance cameras are."

"So there *are* cameras," Greg marveled.

"Yes. It's virtually impossible to bring me inside undetected. On the phone, I said I'd show up Saturday morning. I don't think I'll be able to get a jump-start on searching the inside tonight after all. I was hoping to have that extra time in case we are successful in flushing our suspect out of the woodwork tomorrow."

"So what can we do in the meantime?" asked Greg.

"You and Joanna get out of the house tomorrow morning by 9 AM. Stay out for at least three hours while I conduct my investigation. I'll leave you a note under your pillow after that."

Saturday morning Greg woke up to the comforting aroma of bacon and eggs. Greg dressed and headed downstairs where a cup of coffee awaited him by one of the sofas. A few minutes later, Joanna called Greg over to the table. As they sat down, Greg quietly informed Joanna that they would need to leave the cabin by 9 AM. He responded to Joanna's tacit question with a raised eyebrow and a frown. Silence reigned over the remainder of breakfast.

Once in the car, freer dialogue resumed. Greg reviewed his conversation with Tom from the previous night. For the most part, the plan remained the same. Greg and Joanna were to visit the crash site where Sylvester Campus had plummeted to his death. Although Tom had already visited the location, he wanted extra eyes to observe the alleged crime scene. Meanwhile, Tom planned to search the house for evidence of former guests, especially anything proving that Sylvester Campus had been at the cabin. Top prize would be any archived surveillance videos showing guests entering or leaving the property. Among his tasks, he was to break into the office and plant his own recording devices. Afterwards, Tom would leave further instructions for Greg and Joanna under Greg's pillow. Tom would drive off, hide his car, and double-back to the cabin to set up his own surveillance.

Joanna and Greg followed a winding gravel road until they found a small area to pull off, just as Tom had indicated in his directions. Exiting the vehicle, the two headed carefully downhill on foot, noting the lack of guardrails. Five minutes later, the road twisted in a hairpin curve. A disturbance in the gravel near the side of the road caught Greg's attention. The suggestion of tire marks exited the gravel, made indentations in the narrow muddy shoulder, and then disappeared over the cliff. The victim's last hope would have been to become snagged on one of the few evergreens protruding from the rocky slope. Greg and Joanna shuddered as they imagined the scene.

Nearby Greg could envision a circuitous path descending to the base of the cliff. He offered Joanna his hand to help her down the mountain, but she declined, opting to remain at the top.

Greg carefully made his way down the slope and encountered a mountain stream. An abrupt excavation in the embankment indicated the former resting place of Sylvester Campus' ill-fated vehicle. Greg traced the fading tracks of the tow truck that had retrieved the car and hauled it off. They disappeared around a bend, indicating that there was some other route to reach the riverbank. He took out his camera and snapped a few pictures according to Tom's request. Then he spent a few minutes taking in the sights, gratitude welling up inside him. To die a violent death in such a peaceful setting seemed entirely unfitting. Greg hoped that Campus had taken the opportunity to repent on the way down. He wondered what secrets Campus had taken with him, and he resisted the urge to speculate on Campus' eternal dwelling place. Instead he thanked God in prayer for the gift of life and for saving him from death an unknown number of times.

"Your note didn't say much," Greg chided Tom.

"What if someone else found it?" Tom retorted.

"Then you may have been meeting with a murderer out here in the woods rather than with me!" Greg pointed out.

"I would have seen them coming," Tom replied. "I watched you enter and leave the house on my little monitor here," Tom smiled, lifting up his jacket to reveal a portable four-inch screen strapped to his side. "The sound isn't very good. So I listened in on your conversation with Joanna on my other wire." Tom tapped his ear, and Greg noticed a small tan device wedged into Tom's auditory canal. "The remote recorder is in my car," he added.

"So, what did you find when you were in the cabin?" Greg asked.

"Not too much," Tom admitted. "The surveillance system is old, and the videos have limited memory and record over themselves every 48 hours or so. There's no guest logbook of any kind. I lifted some fingerprints that we can have analyzed later. I found several credit card receipts with Stockley's name on them, but none are dated in the timeframe of Campus' death. However, I did find a ticket from a local movie theater that falls within a week of the alleged murder. We'll check it for prints. Any out-of-towner would be stupid to make a public appearance before committing a murder. So maybe it will turn out to belong to Campus himself. The problem is, Campus is dead, and without a criminal record, his prints won't be on file. I may have to acquire some item of his for comparison. Perhaps Jason or even Jesse Langston from the IT department can help with that."

The sound of tires crunching gravel stopped the conversation dead short. Tom and Greg hurried to the edge of the woods to observe a silver sedan pulling up near the front door. The mid-afternoon sun cast a glare that precluded a clear view inside the car. Tom whipped out his monitor. He rapidly scrolled through the channels to select the camera with the best vantage point.

"I really didn't think anyone would come," Greg commented in a hushed voice.

"Honestly, neither did I," admitted Tom. "But this was our plan. Except for Joanna."

The car door opened, and the driver stepped out. "Chuck Hollis!" Greg gasped in a hoarse whisper. "My former boss. I should have known it!" The shadowy image on the tiny monitor seemed to indicate that Hollis had come by himself.

"He could be here by coincidence," Tom pointed out. "But I doubt it. I've got to protect Joanna. I'm going in, but you've got to let me do it alone."

"No!" Greg exclaimed. "You have to wait until we've recorded enough incriminating evidence. Then you can come in and capture him. And save us, if necessary."

"It's too dangerous."

"It's no more dangerous than before. What's with the cold feet, Tom?" Greg confronted him accusingly.

"Like I told you before, I didn't want to involve Joanna."

Tom stepped forward as if he were going to make a run for the cabin. Greg shoved him back and sprinted out into the open. "Chuck!" he called. "Hey Chuck!"

On the video screen, Tom could just barely discern the look of astonishment overtaking Hollis' face. "Greg Wesko?" the man countered. "What on earth are you doing here?"

Greg approached Hollis cautiously and ignored the question for the moment. "How are you doing, Chuck? I didn't expect to see you here!"

"I could say the same about you," rejoined Hollis.

"I guess so," replied Greg, forcing a smile and resisting the urge to look back at Tom's hiding place in the woods. "You may remember Joanna Pearson. Amos Stockley is letting us use the cabin for the weekend."

Chuck managed a laugh. "I always wondered whether you two had a thing going on." When Greg failed to produce a reply, he continued, "Let's go inside. Can you help me with my bags?"

Although Greg wanted to step inside to warn Joanna, he could not easily ignore Hollis' request. "Sure, Chuck."

Hollis opened the trunk and handed him a black overnight bag and a case of cheap beer. As Hollis reached back into the trunk to retrieve a sturdy briefcase, movement at one of the front windows caught Greg's attention. He whipped his head around to catch Joanna's expression of shock and horror peeking through the dark curtains. He returned a look indicating that he was at a loss for what to do next. The curtains quickly closed.

Hollis opened the front door with his key and entered shouting, "Hello?"

Joanna raised her eyes from her position on the couch. Greg noticed that the magazine in her hands was upside-down. She set it aside and stood up. "Hello, Chuck," she greeted tentatively.

"You remember Joanna Pearson," Greg managed confidently.

"Of course," Chuck replied. "I guess Amos must have forgotten that I was planning to use the cabin this weekend too. He didn't mention that there would be other guests. But there are three extra bedrooms, so we should be comfortable enough."

"Greg and I are in separate rooms, so you can choose from the other two," explained Joanna. "I'm so sorry about the mix-up. I just asked Amos about the cabin a few days ago. He said he had only one key, and he gave it to me." Joanna left her question unspoken.

"He keeps one extra key in his office for guests to borrow. I have my own key," Chuck volunteered. "I'm up here fairly often."

"Alone?" Greg recalled Chuck having been married.

"Now that I'm divorced, I usually do come alone," Chuck admitted. "I actually haven't been here much in the last six months."

"I'm sorry to hear about your divorce," Greg empathized.

"Don't be sorry. I'm certainly not!" chortled Chuck. "Anyway, I'll take the third bedroom as I usually do, if it's free."

"It is," Greg confirmed, handing Chuck the overnight bag. "Do you want me to put the beer in the fridge for you?" Greg offered.

"Please do, and feel free to have a few," Chuck replied. "I insist. I changed my mind and probably won't drink any of them at all," he added as he turned toward the stairs. "It's not my usual brew."

Joanna and Greg followed him with their eyes as he trudged upstairs. After hearing the bedroom door click shut, Greg explained how he and Tom had witnessed Hollis' arrival. He mentioned their argument over continuing with the plan.

"If we were trying to lure the culprit here, we just may have been successful!" Joanna remarked quietly. "Let's get whatever information we can out of him."

"Yes. If Chuck really is behind the embezzlement, we still have to prove it," Greg whispered.

"We'll ask our questions just like we planned to do if anyone showed up," Joanna reminded him. "Do you really think Chuck could be capable of murder?"

"Chuck's always been very committed to the company. But on the other hand, for him it's all about money. Stealing could be a lucrative supplement to his regular salary," Greg reasoned. "I suppose he and Sylvester Campus could have pulled it off together. Then he could have killed him and taken all the profit himself. Or maybe he partnered with someone else, like Amos Stockley. Maybe Stockley sent him here to take care of us. Maybe push *us* over a cliff."

"Let's not jump to conclusions. It could be an honest mistake on Amos' part," Joanna cautioned.

"Or maybe Hollis isn't involved at all. Perhaps Stockley lied to you about the cabin being free this weekend. With other guests here, we'd have less time for snooping around," calculated Greg.

"I wonder if I could have misunderstood Amos," Joanna began to doubt herself. "After all, with four bedrooms there is more than enough room in the cabin, whether we took one or two rooms."

"We'll have to prod Chuck a bit and see what we can learn," asserted Greg.

While Joanna remained in the lounge, Greg stepped quietly up the stairs and into Joanna's room. Cupping a glass to the wall between her room and Hollis', he listened for any sound of conversation. The layout of the land was such that the first two bedrooms were on the same level as the upper part of the sloped property, while the last two bedrooms enjoyed a two-story drop to the ground. Therefore, a person could stand right outside Greg's room and peer in, while Hollis' offered more privacy. Greg could detect a muffled conversation through the wall. He quickly slipped out of the room and to the balcony overlooking the lounge. He waved his arms to attract Joanna's attention where she sat nervously on the edge of a love seat. Catching her eye, he motioned for her to pick up the phone on the table across from her. She clicked the phone on to listen and then promptly clicked it off as she shot Greg a puzzled look. Greg tiptoed back to Joanna's room and listened against the wall again. Silence.

Back in the lounge, Greg sat down and explained what had happened. "Either he was on his cell phone, or he heard you pick up the phone and quickly ended his conversation," he whispered.

"I would guess he was on his own phone, if he can get any reception here. The land line was absolutely quiet. The other party would still have been on the line even if Chuck had hung up quickly."

"Wasn't there a dial tone?" questioned Greg.

A look of concern crossing her face, Joanna admitted, "No, it was perfectly silent."

Greg clicked the phone on and confirmed a dead line. Suddenly they noticed Chuck proceeding along the banister above them. He still wore his jacket and appeared ready for a walk outside. His eyes flitted to a coffee table where the case of beer still awaited refrigeration.

"You'll find that the phone doesn't work," he spoke down to them. "I guess Amos forgot to pay the bill." Joanna and Greg did not find the joke funny.

"We didn't bring our phones with us," Greg lied. "Amos didn't warn us. Since you spend so much time up here, you probably came prepared," Greg surmised.

"I can't get any signal here," claimed Hollis as he made his way slowly toward the stairs to make his descent. His methodical approach made Greg and Joanna very uneasy. "I'm afraid you're without connection to the outside world."

"Like Sylvester Campus?" Greg shot out. Joanna and Hollis both flinched.

"Like whom?" Hollis returned.

"Sylvester Campus," Greg repeated. "His friends called him Vester. He worked at Providential in the IT department. I'm sure you know him."

"IT people don't interest me," Chuck laced the air with venom. "They exist merely to serve."

"So you say. Did Campus serve you well?"

Chuck smiled as he completed the stairs and walked into the lounge area. "I suppose so. My computer works just fine."

"Sylvester Campus is dead," Greg hit over the net.

"Pity. Sorry to hear that," Hollis returned the volley.

"His body was found near here," lobbed Greg.

"You don't say," replied Hollis.

"I do say. Do you know anything about it?"

Hollis stopped and smiled nervously. Reaching inside his jacket, he produced a pistol and aimed it at Greg and Joanna.

Chapter Thirty-Seven

Greg and Joanna gasped in unison as Chuck Hollis waved his pistol in their general direction. "Sure, maybe I know something about Sylvester Campus. Now tell me, what do you know?" A malicious smirk contorted Hollis' face.

Stunned, Greg and Joanna sat silently, wishing they were close enough to hold onto each other for support. After a moment, Greg spoke up. "Let's not get carried away, Chuck," he stammered. "We don't know anything positive at all."

"What are you going to do with us?" Joanna demanded. "You can't kill us. We've got backup!"

"Yes, I know." Chuck smiled slimily. Just then two men burst in through the side door. A man with shoe-polish black hair supported a second man bound with ropes. He had a pillowcase tied over his head and appeared barely able to stand. The first man wielded a revolver and shoved the other man into a chair across from Greg.

"Here's your backup," the man snarled wickedly. "He won't be much help to you now!"

Recognizing his voice from the bug Joe had planted, Greg exclaimed, "Ian Jacobs!"

"In the flesh! You've been working with my former associate here."

Joanna shrieked as Jacobs whipped out a knife and stooped over the figure in the chair. He severed the rope holding the pillowcase in place and ripped it off.

"Peter!" exclaimed Joanna.

Eyes wide open, Greg stared at the man. A large bleeding wound darkened the blond hair on the side of his head, indicating the cause of his being overpowered by Jacobs. The man's eyes showed faint signs of life as his gaze fell upon Joanna, then upon Greg. A wad of cloth protruded from the man's mouth, preventing him from speaking. Despite his injured and pallid appearance, Greg recognized the man as Tom Phillips.

"Tom?" Then Greg turned to address Joanna. "Peter?"

"Peter Monday is the friend I told you about," Joanna explained. "He must have followed me here. Like the story you gave to Sarah, my story must have seemed suspicious to Peter."

"What?" Greg gasped incredulously.

Joanna turned to the injured man. "Oh, Peter, I'm so sorry I got you into this mess. But you've got to believe there's nothing going on between Greg and me!"

"I'm sure he knows," smirked Jacobs as he shoved the man into a wooden chair. "You haven't deceived him. He has deceived you. Your precious Peter Monday is also known as Tom Phillips, private detective!" Jacobs produced a two-way radio and some thick rope from his winter coat. He set the radio down and began to bind the man to the chair with the rope. "Care to explain yourself?" Jacobs reached into Peter's mouth and removed a wad of cloth that had been helping to keep Peter silent. Peter coughed and spit blood.

"You dirty scoundrel!" he accused, still gulping in fresh air.

"All this time, you've been lying to me?" Joanna exclaimed incredulously.

"Not lying, Joanna," Peter protested in a raspy whisper.

"This is good!" chuckled Hollis, still pointing the gun toward Greg and Joanna.

"Did you date me just to get close to the case?" Joanna asked, temporarily forgetting the pistol aimed at her.

"No, Joanna, not at all. You don't remember, but I met you briefly when I was working undercover as a contractor in your building. You had me from the first time I ever laid eyes on you. I found out who you were and what church you belonged to, and I followed you there. I am a detective, after all."

"Who are you really?" Greg interjected.

"Peter Monday is his real name," Jacobs answered.

"I used my real name when I worked for Jacobs. But as you see, Jacobs runs a criminal business. When I left his agency, I decided to use the name Tom Phillips to disassociate myself from him."

"You always were such a boy scout!" sneered Jacobs.

"I didn't want to tell you until after this case was over," Peter explained between coughs. "I was afraid it would put you in danger and also jeopardize our relationship. I didn't want to scare you off. I'm so crazy about you! You can't imagine how it tortured me to let you participate in this at all. I thought asking Stockley to use the cabin was enough. I had no intention of getting you involved like this. But now the worst of what I tried to avoid has come true!" Peter lamented.

"Peter, you haven't lost me," Joanna sat forward but Chuck waved her back with his gun.

"Enough with the soap opera," barked Jacobs. "Hold 'em," he ordered Hollis as he ran back out the door.

Greg turned to address Hollis. "So Campus helped you gain access to my accounts, and you logged in as me and transferred money to your own private accounts."

"Some were mine, some were my partners' accounts. There were lots of people to pay," Hollis chuckled arrogantly. "And lots of accounts to choose from."

"What kind of mess did you get yourself into, Chuck?" Greg chastised him.

"Let's just say I got myself a very profitable side business," he smirked. Jacobs returned with another coil of rope and proceeded to bind Greg and Joanna's arms and feet.

"And when people like Jack Fishburn and Bob Gurth started asking questions, you used Jacobs here to silence them," accused Peter.

"There are just so many voices to silence," sighed Hollis. "Even today's little mishap won't take care of it all. But Joseph and Marina Tropetto's recent marital problems have been quite public, so it won't be surprising when he snaps. When she returns from Italy he'll shoot her and then take his own life. So tragic!"

"How could you say that?" Joanna reprimanded him. "And what are you going to do with us?" Joanna demanded.

"Jacobs here is an expert in explosives," Hollis answered. "He can create an explosion that will seem like another regrettable accident."

"The fire investigator will find the remains of these ropes," Peter challenged. "They'll know it was foul play."

"So clever, Monday!" grinned Jacobs. "We should've kept working together, me and you," he mocked. "You have a lot left to learn. These ropes are made of a special material that's just perfect for this application. There won't be a trace of them left. The ashes will mingle with your own and those of your clothes. No one will be able to tell that you were tied up. And an empty case of beer may help explain why the accident happened, or at least why you couldn't get yourselves out of harm's way."

"Dear Lord, please help us!" Joanna cried out.

"Good show, Chuck!" called a voice from the walkway upstairs. All heads shot up to see a distinguished silver-haired man looking down on them. He held a small silver revolver. "You've incriminated yourself quite well!"

"Amos Stockley!" Joanna called out. "Thank God you've come to save us!"

"Save?" Stockley scoffed. "You wanted my cabin to lure the scam artists. Now here we are. What were *you* planning to do with *us*?"

Greg was the first to recover from Amos Stockley's admission of guilt. "We just wanted to get some information," he replied. "We were hoping to find some clues, not expecting to elicit an entire confession."

"And you weren't planning to get caught, were you, Monday!" snickered Jacobs.

"I'm not a patient man," Stockley admitted. "And neither is my friend Chuck. We don't have time for childish games. You wanted to find something to link us to the money and the deaths. I want to make it all worth your while, so sit back for a minute and let me explain. Throw in any details I may have left out, Chuck," Stockley invited. Hollis had grown visibly pale.

"How does one become a criminal?" Amos began as he walked down the stairs towards the lounge. "Sometimes it takes another criminal to get him started. Chuck had a client named David Hurley. As a travel agent, he only had modest funds. But at a certain point, he started bringing large sums of money to the table, incongruous to his meager salary. Chuck thought it was suspicious and brought it to my attention, didn't you, Chuck?"

Hollis took the cue to continue, although his reluctance was readily apparent. "It started as a joke. I told Amos, 'He must have a good scam going. Too bad we can't get in on the action.' After a while the joke turned serious."

Stockley resumed control of the reins. "What Chuck means is that we hired Mr. Jacobs to investigate our client, Mr. Hurley. He uncovered enough evidence to show that Hurley was involved in an international smuggling ring, mostly drugs and stolen items. His occupation helped provide cover, since he was accustomed to scheduling and moving people and their things from one place to another. We conceived an idea to blackmail Hurley. But rather than just collecting money, we decided to invest by getting into business with him. Becoming partners also made it less attractive for Hurley to try to have us killed, if he were so inclined."

"DH!" Greg exclaimed quietly. "We found a note signed DH. That must be David Hurley!"

"Are the pieces fitting together for you, Greg?" mocked Stockley. "Let me enlighten you further. Soon business began to grow faster than we could launder our profits. We looked for alternate sources. We started with Jack Fishburn, who had accounts in some of the European countries we were doing business with. Eventually we expanded into Asia, Bob Gurth's area. It's so much easier to handle money on a local basis, so we started manipulating his accounts.

"The heat at home was getting intense. Some of our inside agents tipped us off that Jack had hired Phillips to help him investigate."

"Sylvester Campus and Jodah Sherman," Peter interjected.

"Perhaps, among others," Stockley grinned. "Poor Fishburn. He discovered he was being framed, but he couldn't prove anything. The pressure got to him, and he had a heart attack. Of course, it didn't help that we switched his heart medication for a placebo. Then later, one of our clients who ran a phony adoption agency in Singapore informed us that Bob had been asking questions. That's when we had to arrange for his death as well.

"It's unfortunate that these necessary evils exist in the business world. But Chuck and I have done quite well for ourselves. I'm very proud of what we've accomplished. Ordering the death of Jack Fishburn was difficult because it was the first one. Bob Gurth was also hard because he and I had a long history together. Sylvester Campus, on the other hand, was not difficult for me, because I didn't order it. That was your initiative, Chuck, wasn't it?"

With all the color drained from his face, the once arrogant Chuck Hollis now appeared on the verge of passing out. "He was no longer useful to us," he stammered. "No reason to continue paying him."

"Ah, but more than that," Stockley corrected him, "He knew something that I didn't know. You and I had targeted two of Greg's accounts, but you and Campus added one more of his accounts for yourselves without my knowledge. Very clever, Chuck. What were you planning on the side?" he demanded.

Chuck's voice went hoarse. "I thought the French Riviera might be a nice place for an early retirement," he confessed.

"And a few extra dollars would help you to do that, and escape from the web of crime," Stockley added for him.

"We had planned to continue embezzling beyond the original $20,000, but we had to call it quits because Greg noticed the money was gone. We knew he was onto something because he used his own money to cover the missing funds," explained Chuck. "When he did that, I knew he wouldn't give up until he found the truth. So I paid Jacobs to set up an accident in his apartment."

"Murderer!" shouted Greg. "You killed my Lisa!"

Hollis seemed as contrite as someone of his caliber could manage to be. "That was unfortunate. When Jacobs rigged the oven to explode in your apartment, he never figured on your fiancée pulling the trigger."

"A little child was killed next door too!" Greg seethed.

"Hey, it made the accident all the more believable," shrugged Jacobs callously. "Hollis, he had to pay me extra to keep it a secret from Stockley. But I didn't have anything to do with Campus' death," Jacobs revealed. "Hollis later told me he did that himself. A little hole in the brake line and a slippery mountain road is all it took. Good work, Hollis! I didn't think you had the guts to do something like that yourself. Get your own hands dirty, I mean!"

"Chuck, dear Chuck," Stockley reproached Hollis. "What a beautiful partnership we had established. A legitimate source of income from our day jobs, plus a very handsome side business, raking in several times our honest salaries. I admire your enterprise, Chuck, trying to break out on your own. But I should have been a part of that decision. Unfortunately, my friend, I just can't trust you anymore." He nodded to Jacobs, who then knocked the gun out of Hollis' hand and threw him to the ground. Jacobs bound Chuck's hands and feet amidst his protests. Stockley walked over and retrieved Hollis' gun from the floor.

"You can't do this to me, Amos! We're partners!" he screamed at Stockley. "We are in this together!" Hollis enunciated every word with fervent desperation.

"As you said yourself, Chuck, one less person on the payroll means more for everyone else," Stockley replied matter-of-factly. "It's a shame that some of your assets are hidden away. I'll have to accept some losses now in order to achieve a greater long-term gain."

Ian Jacobs inspected the ropes of his four captives to assure that they were properly secured. Each person had been bound in such a way that movement was impossible. All four chairs were tied to a large coffee table to prevent tipping over or sliding to a different location. Jacobs then disappeared into the kitchen.

"I forgive you for this, and may God forgive you as well," Greg uttered with quiet strength.

"So do I," Joanna joined him.

"Not me," Peter Monday ranted. "I hope you burn in Hell for all eternity. And I hope it's soon!"

"My, my! What dear expressions of emotion!" Stockley exclaimed derisively. "I appreciate the sentiment, Greg and Joanna, but I think Peter has more truthfully spoken his feelings."

"I don't *feel* like forgiving you," Greg countered, "but I know it's the right thing to do. And if I'm going to die now, I want to be right with God. I've changed a lot in the last year. Maybe God was preparing me for an early end. If you kill me now, at least I know I'll be reuniting with an old friend, but most importantly, with Jesus."

"Touching," Stockley quipped sardonically. "Say hello for me."

"How can you mock God like that?" Joanna indicted him. "Even now, He still loves you and desires for you to give your heart to Him. He died on the Cross so that you could spend eternity in Heaven instead of in Hell, where we all really deserved to go because of our sin."

"If I believed in God, I guess I would worry about that when the time came," retorted Stockley. "But lucky for me, I don't believe! Aside from this unfortunate situation we find ourselves in, I really am a nice person. I care about my family's welfare. I keep to the speed limit. I vote. I even doubled my annual contributions last year in the company charitable donation program. I don't swear in front of children and I don't drink and drive."

"None of that will get you into Heaven," Joanna admonished him.

"That's not my goal," he grinned.

Jacobs returned from the kitchen and issued his report. "It's all set up. Once we activate the trigger, we have ten minutes to get away. The initial explosion may not kill everyone, but the fire afterwards will. We're quite far from a fire station here. The whole house will be ashes by the time anyone arrives. It may even set off a small forest fire. That'd be great. We can really complicate things that way!"

"I do hate to lose the cabin, though," Stockley commented with brutal selfishness. "At least my insurance is paid up. Show me how to set it off," he commanded Jacobs.

"No, you should put distance between this place and yourself," suggested Jacobs. "You need to establish location somewhere else. Go on home and I'll set it off later."

"I've already told people that I'm coming up for the weekend. My administrative assistant knows that Joanna and a friend were going to be here. I told her I wanted to check up to see how things were going. Of course I didn't tell anyone I knew Chuck was coming. I only knew that because you informed me, Ian."

"Glad to be of service," Ian Jacobs snickered.

"You betrayed me!" Hollis shouted bitterly at Jacobs. "This was supposed to be our secret. The tap on Wesko's phone was just between you and me!"

"Business is business. Your boss pays better," replied Jacobs with an indifferent shrug.

"You had this planned all along!" Chuck directed his accusation at Stockley. "When Jacobs convinced me to come up to the cabin to check on Wesko, he was acting on your orders, wasn't he?"

Stockley sighed derisively. "You're so naïve, Chuck. And therefore, you're even more of a liability than I originally thought." Turning to Jacobs, he insisted, "Show me the trigger, Ian. I want to 'get my hands dirty,' as you said."

Jacobs and Stockley disappeared into the kitchen. Chuck started to whimper. "Greg, Joanna, Peter, I'm so sorry. I don't want to die!"

"Tell that to Jack and Bob," Peter muttered. "And your friend Sylvester Campus."

"I wish I could take it back. Take it all back!" Chuck sobbed.

"Fat lot of good it does them now," Peter quipped.

"It can't bring them back," admitted Joanna, "but it can help bring you back from the dead, Chuck!"

"What do you mean?" he cried.

"The Bible tells us that if you believe in your heart and confess with your lips that Jesus is Lord, you will have forgiveness of sins and life from the dead, the salvation of your soul," explained Joanna.

"I am sorry for what I've done," confessed Chuck.

"You're sorry you got caught!" Peter scoffed.

"Peter, you have to forgive them," admonished Joanna. "Don't take this to the grave with you. I know you are a man of faith, at least the past several months if not before. Forgive them, so that God can forgive you!"

Peter hesitated slightly and then managed to say, "I do forgive them, Joanna. And I love you. I want you to believe that."

"I do, Peter," Joanna whispered hoarsely through a stream of tears. "Whatever the other circumstances, I know you have revealed your true self to me."

Greg addressed his former boss. "Chuck, do you believe in God and that Jesus is His only Son?"

Chuck shook with tears. Long-ignored memories from his childhood came flooding back. "Yes," he replied tentatively.

"Do you believe that He died for your sins?"

"I think so, yes."

"Do you believe in the Holy Spirit, the Lord, the Giver of Life?"

"I want to, yes."

"Are you sorry for your sins?"

"Yes, oh yes!"

"Will you turn from evil and instead do good?"

"I will."

"Good. Then accept God's forgiveness."

"I do," Chuck collapsed into a pile of tears.

Peter sat pensively still.

Stockley and Jacobs reemerged from the kitchen. "I've pulled the timer on the trigger myself," Stockley announced proudly. "And now that you've helped me, friend," he turned towards Jacobs, "you are no longer of use to me." The words were still dripping off Stockley's tongue as he pulled out Chuck's pistol are fired a shot directly into Jacobs' chest. Jacobs reeled backwards and collapsed to the floor in front of the kitchen without even uttering a final gasp. The captives shuddered in horror and disbelief at the body on the floor.

Chapter Thirty-Eight

Peter was the first to recover from the naked shock of the unexpected murder they had just witnessed. "You are truly wicked!" he lambasted Amos. "And foolish as well. How are you going to hide the bullet? The fire won't cover that up."

"I used Chuck's gun," he explained.

"Too much coincidence," Peter countered. "Greg and his fiancée both killed in separate fires. A shooting and an explosion at the same time. Who will believe that?"

"It's really very simple," Amos snapped. "In any case, they won't be able to link anything to me. I'll move the body to the kitchen. The explosion should take care of it all. But even if they find the bullet, the gun is registered to Chuck, who I'm sure will take the blame. After all, he won't be alive to defend his good name! I can see the newspaper story already. Chuck Hollis, having been accused of embezzlement, led his accusers to his boss' mountain cabin. There he murdered his accomplice, Ian Jacobs, in cold blood. He disposed of the other witnesses in a fire rigged to look like an accident, but unfortunately he died in his own trap."

"Amos, I forgive you," Chuck blurted out.

"Now look who's waxing religious! How quaint. Save it for the angels!"

Stockley put Chuck's pistol down on a nearby table. He leaned over the head of Ian Jacobs and positioned himself to drag the body into the kitchen. Greg was the only one who was situated to clearly see what was about to happen. As Stockley reached down and grasped Jacobs' shoulders, Jacobs' hands shot up and clutched Stockley's throat.

"You can't get rid of me that easily," he growled sinisterly. "You'll have to improve your aim!"

Gasps arose from the prisoners as they listened to the ensuing brawl. Jacobs was by far the stronger fighter, but his gunshot wound had weakened his abilities. Still he managed to flip Stockley over and onto the floor. Stockley rolled out of the way as Jacobs drew his knife and lunged at him. With a well-placed kick, Stockley struck the blade and sent it flying out of Jacobs' hands.

Meanwhile Peter instructed his three fellow captives to try to move as a unit toward the front door. Summoning all their strength, the four struggled against the ropes and the weight of the furniture to which they were bound. After several tries, Chuck exclaimed with frustration, "It's no use! We've barely moved an inch!"

Now on their feet, Stockley and Jacobs exchanged punches. A sharp left hook caught Stockley on the right cheek and sent him staggering backwards. Ducking, he avoided a second jab and planted his fist firmly into Jacobs' chest. A subsequent knee in the stomach further injured the failing Jacobs, who reeled away from his opponent. Stockley reached into his jacket in search of his silver revolver. He retrieved it and prepared to fire just as Jacobs leapt and planted both feet firmly into Stockley's abdomen. The force diverted the shot towards the ceiling and caused Stockley to lose his grip on the revolver. The weapon flew through the air and landed near Peter's feet.

"I can almost reach the gun!" Peter exclaimed. "Try to move toward the front door again! If I could only get my hands untied!" With great effort the unit strained to inch themselves and their burden in the direction of the exit.

Stockley swung wildly at Jacobs' face, just nicking his chin. In a countermove, Jacobs jumped on Stockley, and the two men fell to the ground a few feet in front of Peter. Stockley grabbed for the revolver, but his spastic motions only caused the weapon to skid across the floor under a couch. The two men scrambled to their feet and resumed their wrestling match. In a series of moves they fell through the swinging double-doors into the kitchen and out of sight.

As the clamor continued, Joanna gasped as she gazed upwards. At the top of the stairs, a man and a woman raced quietly down the stairs towards the four fettered captives. "God sent us angels!" she cried.

"Joe!" Greg exclaimed in hushed tones, "Oh how good it is to see you!"

"Untie us, quickly!" Joanna urged him. "We've only got a few minutes left before this whole place explodes!"

Joe hurried to loosen the bonds of Joanna and Peter. The woman ran over to Greg.

"Sarah?" Greg gasped incredulously. "What are you doing here? How did you get here? Oh, I don't care how! I'm just so glad to see you! I'm not dead, am I?"

"No, you're not!" she assured him with a worried smile.

"Don't untie *him*," Peter ordered, pointing to Chuck.

"Let him loose but don't untie his hands," Greg rejoined. "He's a repentant man, but let's not lead him into a near occasion of sin."

Joe explained, "The police should be here very soon. Sarah and I were approaching the cabin when we heard a gunshot. We immediately called the authorities on my Blackberry. I had no signal on my regular phone." Joe loosened the last rope. More crashes emanated from the kitchen. "Let's run!" he insisted. "My car is parked a short way down the drive."

Joe threw open the front door, and five figures followed closely behind. Each passing second heightened their growing feeling of security. A short distance from the cabin, Chuck tripped over a tree root and planted his face into the ground. Hearing the thud, Greg looked behind to see Chuck lying prostrate in the gravel. As he hesitated for a moment, a thought flashed across his mind.

If you have truly forgiven him, you will help him.

Immediately responding, Greg raced back toward his fallen enemy and helped him to his feet. The two men then strained to regain lost ground. A few seconds later, they spotted Joe's automobile parked further down the gravel drive. Just in time, Greg turned around as a violent flash of light and fire erupted through the glass kitchen window. A split second later, the entire first floor of the house exploded in a chaotic cloud of hellfire. A ball of flame glowing red and black rose slowly up into the sky as the onlookers dropped to the shaking earth.

It was so good to be alive.

Chapter Thirty-Nine

Heavy rain pelted the windowpane in big, thick drops. Joe had developed vision problems at an early age, so Greg was doubly glad that he had volunteered to drive Joe to the airport to meet Marina. Her flight from Italy was due to arrive at Boston's Logan Airport just before lunchtime. Greg expected the bad weather to add at least thirty minutes to the two-hour drive, giving them ample time to talk.

"I'm still recovering from the shock of everything that happened yesterday. I've never been so close to death," Greg admitted, having momentarily forgotten his walk on the edge of the roof of the Providential Insurance building. "After the police took my statement downtown, I was told that you and Sarah had already left. I only had a moment to speak with her when we first arrived at the police station. So Joe, please start at the beginning. Why was Sarah with you when you showed up at the cabin? And why did she return to Connecticut with you instead of waiting for me?"

Joe stared out into the thick, wet gray and recounted his story.

It was an hour to closing on a Friday night when a distraught young woman sat down in the back of *That Pizza Place*. She declined to order any food but just quietly nursed a soda. After all the other customers had left, the proprietor approached and repeated his question.

"Is there anything I can do for you?" he offered.

"Are you the owner?" she asked.

"Yes, I am. Joe Tropetto," he offered, extending his hand. She returned a compulsory shake.

"I'm Sarah. I understand we have a mutual friend, Greg Wesko," she stated bluntly.

Joe sat down across from her in the booth. *A mutual friend? After all that we've been through together, I'm sure I know all of Greg's true friends. Who is this woman?* "What do you want?" he asked, suspicion twisting his stomach into knots.

"Greg told me a strange story, very hard to accept. I figure a man will invent anything when he's caught cheating."

"Come again?" Joe repeated quizzically.

"We never agreed to exclusive dating, but I assumed as much. I may have been wrong." Joe studied Sarah's face with intrigue while she looked down into her drink. "I'm sorry if I'm not making any sense, but neither did Greg's explanation."

"What did he say?"

Afraid that Joe would see her misty eyes, Sarah continued to avoid looking directly at him. "At first he claimed to be working on a project which took him out of town for some research. When I found him at his apartment, suitcase in hand and leaving with another woman, things took a strange turn. He said that he was working to uncover an embezzlement scandal at his former company, and that he and the woman were traveling to a cabin in New Hampshire for the weekend to lure the criminals. His private detective was also going along separately."

Joe's eyes grew wide at the fairly accurate description given by the pretty stranger seated before him. She continued, "He claimed that his home phone was bugged, so they had scripted phone conversations to be overheard on purpose. The private detective was going to poke around on Saturday morning, which would be tomorrow. They assumed that their activities at the cabin would be monitored by listening devices or hidden camera. So whether he finds any useful information or not, the private detective plans to announce that he hasn't found anything."

The woman's account included details that only an insider could have known. Joe began to believe the woman had come with honest intentions. "So why come to me? Explain how I fit into this equation," he challenged.

The woman emitted a wry chuckle. "I didn't consider the possibility that you might think I was working on the other side! This lends some credibility to Greg's story. He told me to come talk to you if he didn't return. I guess he meant if he gets killed." She paused to shudder. "He said that you had worked with them to get information from a crooked private eye. Something about your wife's alleged infidelity. He said that you later staged a public fight, and she flew to Italy as a pretense."

"What did he say my wife's name is?" quizzed Joe.

"I'm sorry, I don't think he said. If this is some kind of test, I fail."

"Actually, I believe you. But first, tell me my role."

"You are supposed to stay here because someone may be watching you. But if you don't hear anything from the private detective by tomorrow evening, you will call the police and drive up to the cabin yourself. You were not discussed on the phone, so the criminals will not be expecting you."

Sarah's attitude and answers satisfied Joe. As she finally raised her head, her eyes brimmed with honesty and sadness, yet retained a glimmer of hope. He noticed a golden cross dangling around her neck. "Are you a Christian?"

"Yes, in fact, Greg and I met at church," she recounted. "We were both trying out a new one. The service wasn't biblically sound, and we had to leave. He took me to Mass later that night. I've been a Christian all my life, and that night I learned that Catholics are Christians too."

Joe smiled. "Yes, we are. You know, Greg and I haven't been directly in touch for a while. With the investigation, it's too risky for us to be associated together. I didn't know he was seeing anybody."

"We're not officially dating," Sarah admitted. "But I came here to see if I could verify his story. For my sake, I want it to be true. For his, I hope it's a lie. What a terrible mess to be involved in!" she lamented.

"I can see that you're telling the truth," Joe admitted. "There's only one detail that doesn't fit. Greg was supposed to go to the cabin without Joanna, the woman you mentioned. We all thought it would be safer that way."

"Everyone except Joanna," Sarah mused. "She was all packed and ready to go."

"I bet she insisted on going anyway. Tom, our detective, sure is going to be mad," Joe chuckled. "In any case, there's no romance between Joanna and Greg," he assured her.

Sarah smiled understandingly but remained silent.

"We suspect that a murder was committed in or near the cabin. It belongs to someone at the company, and Joanna asked to use it for the weekend. There are two main goals. First, we need an opportunity to search the cabin for clues about former guests. The cabin may be monitored, so even if we find anything, we must lead the criminals to believe that we haven't. The second goal is a long shot, which is to lure the criminals out into the open. The detective plans to keep full surveillance on the cabin. He will be visible by day but hide in the woods at night to keep watch."

"And you are the emergency backup?" Sarah guessed.

"Right again. I have to be very careful not to arouse any suspicions because I may be shadowed. I stayed here to run the restaurant tonight as I ordinarily do. But tomorrow I need to be available just in case. Since Marina is out of town, I arranged for another relative to manage tomorrow. I'll wait for a call on my Blackberry."

"I want you to take me to the cabin," Sarah proposed.

"That's not part of the plan."

"I know. But I wasn't supposed to know the plan either. Now that I do, I have to help," she insisted. "You have no choice."

"I can see that," he capitulated.

The storm had intensified the normally heavy traffic leading through the city of Boston to the airport. Marina's plane was already on the ground as Greg and Joe raced inside the terminal. "Sarah and I didn't talk much on the way up to the cabin. She slept half the time," Joe explained. "I think she was exhausted from stress. She didn't say much at all about you or your relationship. I really wanted to pry, but I restrained myself. We made small talk, and that was about it. I suggested dropping her off in town while I went up the mountain to the cabin, but she wouldn't have it. We were going to hide in the woods together and wait for Tom. Then we heard the gunshot. You know what happened after that."

"I can't get it out of my head," Greg admitted. "The details replay over and over."

"There's one thing you don't know, however," Joe frowned. "Sarah didn't ride back with me. I saw her at the police station, but I don't know when she left or how."

"Tell me you're not serious! This is not good. Oh, I hope she forgives me," Greg moaned as they joined other people waiting for international passengers to pass through customs. A large crowd had gathered at the closest point allowed by security.

"Come on, Greg!" chided Joe. "She traveled five hours with a stranger and risked life and limb for you. What else does she have to do?"

"I just want to talk with her. Why did she leave without saying anything to me? And why didn't she ride back to Connecticut with you, or with me?"

"Joanna rode back with me," Joe informed him.

"That is even stranger still!" Greg exclaimed. "I thought she rode back with Tom, I mean, Peter."

Joe shook his head. Then a big smile overtook his face. "Marina!" As Marina emerged from the crowd, Joe threw his arms around her in an embrace that would erase any doubts about the strength of their love and their marriage. Greg blushed slightly as they caught up on lost kissing time.

When the kissing came to an end, Marina turned to Greg and gave him a big hug. "How are you holding up, Greg?" she asked with concern.

"I'm good. More than good, thanks to you and Joe. How blessed I am to have friends as wonderful as you! You put your reputation and even your very lives on the line for me. I just can't show my gratitude enough. Thank you so much! Both of you," Greg choked up with emotion.

"You're more than welcome," Marina squeezed his hand.

"That's what friends do for each other," Joe smiled warmly.

Peter Monday sipped his soda and studied the menu absentmindedly as he waited in a booth at *That Pizza Place.* He broke his attention as Greg sat down across from him.

"Some weekend we had, huh?" Peter exclaimed.

"In your line of work, I suppose that's par for the course," Greg surmised.

"It does come with the territory. But you still never get used to the idea of dying. I have to say, I was very impressed with how you and Joanna handled it. I've never seen anything like that."

"As a Christian, you're supposed to spend your whole life getting ready to meet God. I got into the game only recently. But late start or not, I guess that most people don't feel ready when the time comes. But I knew that if I expect to be forgiven, I had better forgive too."

"I was hoping he'd go to Hell," Peter admitted.

"Haven't we all done something worthy of going to Hell, Peter? I don't mean we committed murder or stole from the poor. But think about this. God is all-powerful, all-loving and all-knowing. He created us out of love. He has given us everything good that we have ever had. When we break one of His commandments, don't we deserve to be cast out of His presence, like Adam and Eve were thrown out of the Garden? Hell is the utter absence of God. Jesus Christ died so that we don't have to be condemned. He took the punishment for us. He was abandoned on the Cross and cried out, 'My God, my God, why have you forsaken me?' He died a criminal's death, as we deserved to. But since He had no sin, death could not hold Him, and He rose again on the third day. And so He opened the gates of Heaven to all of us."

"I've heard this all my life, at Sunday school and at church. But it never seemed so real until now. What should I do?"

"Believe in Him."

"Like you asked Chuck Hollis to believe when we were tied up in the cabin?"

"Yes."

Peter shifted in his seat. "Hollis cooperated with the police. But from what I saw, I can't say he was a changed man. Believing in God seemed good at the time when he thought he was about to die, but I think he may have outlived his faith."

"Some people believe when it's convenient. Then they fall back into relying on themselves. There are many possible reasons. Sometimes the pressure goes away. Other times, they don't like what God asks of them. If Chuck is truly penitent, he should be completely honest with the police and show remorse for what he's done," Greg explained.

"On the surface it seems that way, but I don't think he feels that way on the inside."

"We can judge his actions in a court of law," Greg remarked, "but only God can judge his heart.

We can dish out earthly punishment. God will decide on the eternal."

"I do believe," Peter confessed readily. "I just have to live it better."

"Why not come to church with Sarah and me this Sunday?" He uttered Sarah's name automatically before considering the uncertainty their future together. "Or at least with me," he corrected himself.

"Thanks for the invitation, but I always go with Joanna." Peter shifted in his chair again. "I have something to tell you that you probably don't know," he began mysteriously. In Greg's silent bewilderment, Peter continued. "Sarah Huff rode back with me from Connecticut."

"What? Why?" Greg pressed him.

"She wanted more information about you," he answered. "And she was looking for advice. But mostly she wanted to know whether you were in love with Joanna Pearson."

In anguish, Greg's hands shot to the back of his head and he began to pull his hair absentmindedly. "What did you say?"

"Do you know what the answer should have been?" Peter questioned.

"Yes, now I do," he stated with growing confidence.

"I told her that you and I never discussed it, and so that means that if you ever were in love with Joanna, it doesn't mean anything now. Was I right?" Peter waited expectantly.

"Yes, absolutely," Greg agreed firmly.

"Good! Because I also told her that Joanna and I are in love. Sarah said she was going to need some time to sort out her feelings about everything that has happened. She didn't know when she would be ready to talk to you. She also asked me to wait until today to tell you any of this."

"I don't understand," Greg furrowed his brow. The two men sat in silence for a moment.

"I'm sorry that I deceived you about my relationship with Joanna. It became increasingly difficult to keep it a secret," Peter confessed.

"I forgive you. More importantly, has Joanna forgiven you?" Greg asked with concern.

"It will take some time to restore her trust in me," Peter admitted. "But I'm going to hang in as long as it takes. I never expected to involve her in this. As long as I was on the case, I felt it would jeopardize her safety to tell her about my occupation."

"Certainly you knew she would be upset whenever she eventually found out," Greg mused.

"Of course. But I wasn't ready to deal with that yet. I didn't know that my dreams would come true and that she would fall in love with me."

Across the restaurant, Jason Coates walked in to the cheers of Joe and Marina. "Nice to see you at dinnertime for a change," Joe winked.

"I hope this doesn't mean we won't be seeing you for lunch anymore," added Marina.

"Now that I've found the best pizza in New England, how could I stay away?" he laughed.

Joe chuckled as he led Jason to the booth already occupied by Greg and Peter. Jason greeted them heartily and then took a seat next to his former co-worker.

"So, fill us in!" Jason changed the subject to more weighty matters. "What did you find out from the authorities today, Tom?"

"Peter," Greg corrected him.

"Sorry. This is all new to me."

"It's OK. Tom Phillips is still my professional name. As my friends, however, you can call me Peter," he invited. "Chuck Hollis confessed in great detail over the weekend. Two Providential Insurance employees did not report to work today, Darren Lado in Accounting and Joan Forbis in Information Security. They were detained against their will. The search is still on for Jodah Sherman, who had quit a while ago. All the other immediate members of the conspiracy are dead, at least the ones in the US."

Jason listed the names of the deceased: "Sylvester Campus, Ira Jacobs and Amos Stockley."

"I read that people who worship false gods are eventually consumed by them," Greg shared. "These unfortunate villains were burned up in the sacrificial fires of their own idols."

"Nice metaphor," Jason commented.

Peter resumed his narrative. "David Hurley, the client who partnered with Stockley and Hollis, has been out of the country for some time. The international authorities have been alerted and are on the lookout for him. Hurley's two main partners in Europe are dead, as we already know. These are the two who impersonated Greg Wesko and Tony Franco."

"Speaking of Franco," Greg interjected, "Did you ever find out why he broke into my apartment?"

"As it turns out, I did interview Franco after we returned from the cabin. He readily admitted to the deed. He started receiving a number of strange calls, which I presume were intended for the fake Franco in Europe. Perhaps they somehow stumbled onto the real Tony Franco when they were unable to reach the imposter after he died. At any rate, one time a very strange incident occurred. Franco answered the phone in his usual manner."

"Saying, 'This is Franco, Tony Franco, of Providential Insurance,' I imagine," Greg interposed.

"Something like that," continued Peter. "The caller was shocked. He indicated that he thought Tony Franco had died. When Franco questioned further, the caller said that Greg Wesko had told him the news."

"I bet that threw him for a loop," Greg surmised.

"The man also said that he had not been able to reach Greg Wesko for a long time and was worried about him. So Tony made up his mind to check your apartment to see if you were OK," Peter explained.

"So he was just concerned for my welfare?" Greg surmised.

"Yes, he was. I also learned that the reason he cashed in his 401k was to cover all the expensive ways he tried to win back his wife. That explains his lavish change in lifestyle. Apparently there wasn't anything sinister about Tony Franco after all. I'll do my best to shield him from the police. I'm sure the spotlight wouldn't be good for his mental health anyway."

"I agree. What about our own involvement with the authorities? Where do we go from here?" Jason asked.

"Besides the characters we've already discussed, Hollis also named some accomplices in the Far East. Between the information we uncovered and Hollis' own confession, they can put a number of criminals behind bars for life. At some point we'll be called to testify. But otherwise we can return to our normal lives."

"Whatever that is," Greg mused. "What do you think will happen to Chuck?"

"Let's see. Four counts of murder, several counts of attempted murder, embezzlement, drug trafficking and other crimes... I don't think he'll ever be a free man on this side of eternity," Peter predicted. "He admitted planning to kill Joe and Marina as well. As it turns out, Jacobs uncovered the bug Joe placed under his office desk. There were no fingerprints on the device itself, but Jacobs found the backing for the adhesive strip that Joe had removed from it. Apparently when Joe took his wallet out to pay, the backing he had hidden in his pocket fell to the floor. Jacobs matched the fingerprints on it to the fingerprints he lifted from Joe's application. It was his standard practice to get prints on every client. He always did that when we were partners."

"Amazing!" commented Greg. "He would have committed two more murders. It slipped my mind, but I think he mentioned something about that at the cabin."

"Yes, I have it on the audio. Hollis told us that Jacobs was going to arrange for an apparent murder-suicide, a crime of passion. But with Jacobs dead and Hollis in prison, Joe and Marina are safe. We're all safe now," Peter reassured them.

"We'll have to re-instate you at Providential Insurance, Greg," Jason promised. "I'll do all I can to clear your name. It won't be difficult. You've done even more for the company in the last short while than when you were an employee."

"Thanks, Jason," Greg expressed his appreciation. "Honestly, I don't know if I want my old job back. I've made so many changes in my life since then."

"Who said it had to be your old job? We'll find something suitable. Try it on for size. If you don't like it, you can always leave after a while. You need some normalcy again while you sort out what you really want to do with your life," suggested Jason. "Have you ever considered a career in fighting industrial espionage?"

"Very funny," countered Greg. "But I do appreciate the opportunity to come back. Let's discuss it later in the week. I still need some time to recover from everything that's happened. I want to take some time to pray about what to do next. I'll start with today and take it one day at a time."

Joe and Marina returned with a tray sporting a large pizza pie and a pitcher of soda. "Your first pizza is on the house tonight," Joe offered. "But you've got to eat all the anchovies."

"I think I'd rather pay," groaned Greg in jest.

With rapid pulse and sweaty hands, Greg waited for his call to be answered.

"Hello?" intoned a tentative voice.

"Sarah! You finally answered. Please don't hang up! It's Greg."

After a few seconds of silence, Sarah responded, "Why would I hang up?"

"Aren't you mad at me?"

"Your story checked out. I saw it all in person, remember?"

"I know, Sarah. And I can't thank you enough. I'm sorry I had to keep so many things secret. I wish I could have let you in on the whole truth from the beginning. I wanted to protect you. How could I get you so involved when I didn't know what the future was going to hold for us?"

"Do you know now?"

"I think so. Here we go..."

Chapter Forty

The church brimmed with people. Amid the buzz of excited onlookers, Marina's distinctively joyous laugh could be heard accompanied by a hearty guffaw from Joe. A nervous Tony Franco entered and attempted a reverent gesture before joining Jason Coates and family in a pew toward the back of the church. Greg noticed with a smile that Tony was accompanied by his wife.

From his vantage point, Greg surveyed the rest of the audience. His sister beamed from the third row. Jared sat with his arm lovingly around her. Unaware of Greg's watchful eye, Jared leaned over and gave her a gentle kiss, which she contentedly accepted. Jack and Denise flanked their parents and tried their best to keep still. The only presence he truly missed was that of Lisa's parents. He knew that Lisa looked on from above.

As the signal music played, the entire congregation turned to face the back of the church. From the vestibule, the bridesmaids emerged out of the darkness and into the sanctuary. To the tune of

Purcell's "Trumpet Voluntary," they processed up the aisle one-by-one with bouquets of white roses against emerald green dresses. As they approached the altar, they filed into positions on the opposite side of the groomsmen.

Greg's heart skipped a beat as the music changed. Unconsciously he joined the organ in an internal humming of the words, "Here Comes the Bride." The church erupted in a blaze of camera flashes. In a dazzlingly beautiful, flowing white gown, Joanna Pearson emerged from the vestibule on the arm of her father. Her face radiated joy and thanksgiving. Greg had never seen her look more beautiful. His gaze wandered to the fourth row where his parents sat calmly. Seated next to them, Sarah smiled through a gentle stream of tears. He flashed her a hearty grin as if to say, "You're next." Then he turned towards the groom. Peter Monday appeared ready to burst with pride and overflowing joy.

At the reception, bride and groom were fully occupied attending to newlywed duties. They visited tables amidst the scheduled dances: bride and groom, bride and her father, groom and his mother. Joanna and Peter arrived at Greg's table just after he and Sarah had excused themselves to dance.

"Joanna, what a wonderful wedding!" Theresa exclaimed. "I just can't get over your dress. It's so beautiful!"

"Thank you, Theresa," responded Joanna.

"And thank you so much for inviting us," Theresa continued. "It's so thoughtful of you to include us in your special day."

"It was our pleasure. You know, we let each of the bridesmaids and groomsmen bring up to a whole table of guests. When Greg told us that your trip to this area coincided with our wedding, it made perfect sense for you all to come."

"Jared has started taking the whole family on business trips whenever possible. This past week we were in New York for a convention. It was just a short drive up here for the wedding. And it was well worth the trip!"

The newlyweds continued to visit with Greg's parents and Theresa's family until they were called for the cutting of the cake. Peter lovingly fed the cake to his new bride, careful not to disturb her makeup with a stray streak of icing. Joanna, likewise, brought the cake very gently up towards Peter's mouth. At the last moment, she shoved the cake in with full force, making sure to smear a healthy dollop of butter cream across his face. "That was for Tom Phillips," she whispered mischievously in his ear. "And this is for Peter Monday," she added softly under the shelter of laughter and applause as she covered his cake-laden lips with her own. When the smiling couple turned to face the crowd, a new round of applause broke forth. Joanna and Peter beamed through the frosting.

Afterwards, Greg finally caught up with the new bride.

"Joanna, I'm just speechless. You are so beautiful, and I'm exceedingly happy for you and

Peter," he enthused. "Thank you so much for asking Peter to let me be a groomsman."

Joanna truly glowed. "Oh Greg, it was his pleasure. I didn't even have to ask. He had the idea himself. I'm so delighted to have you in the wedding party. I couldn't imagine it without you. You've been such a special friend, and we've shared so much together. A lot of it has been tragedy, unfortunately, but recently things have turned to so much joy."

"I owe a lot to you, including my salvation. My soul and my life."

"Don't give me the credit," Joanna smiled. "God has done a whole lot for you and for me, countless blessings. This is the happiest day of my life!" Casting a glance over to the table where Theresa and Sarah sat talking, she inquired, "And is your happiest day on the horizon?"

Before Greg could answer, Peter approached to break Joanna away for the bouquet toss. Greg watched the couple bound over to a platform where Joanna prepared to toss her floral treasure to a rapidly amassing throng of single women. Greg searched the crowd for Sarah as Joanna lifted the bouquet up into the air. With drum roll accompaniment, Joanna tossed the flowers into the crowd on the count of three. A few howls rose up as petals showered down. Greg strained to see the happy recipient of good fortune. With the tattered bouquet, a woman rushed elatedly toward her unsuspecting boyfriend and planted her lips on his. Sarah was nowhere in sight.

Greg approached his sister who indicated that Sarah had exited into the corridor just before the bouquet toss. Greg hurried out into the hallway, empty except for a few people returning from the restrooms. Greg waited impatiently for Sarah to emerge. When his mother approached ten minutes later, he asked her to check for Sarah inside. She returned with a negative report.

Heading outside, Greg walked around the back of the white marble reception hall. A path led down to a whitewashed gazebo by a moonlit lake. A fountain shot an illuminated column of water ten feet into the night sky. A solitary figure sat huddled in the darkness inside the gazebo.

"Sarah, why are you crying?" he asked.

"I always cry at weddings," she answered.

"Not like this, I imagine."

Wiping her eyes, she sat up as Greg took a seat next to her. "Joanna and Peter are so happy together. Their wedding day is so beautiful."

"It is," Greg agreed. This did not strike him as a reason to run off and cry. "Why did you miss the bouquet toss?"

"I didn't want to catch it," she admitted.

Sarah's response caught him off guard. "Don't you want to ever get married?" he questioned, puzzled.

She cast him a brief glance of surprise. "Oh yes, I really do. But I was afraid I wouldn't catch it and then I would feel discouraged. You know I don't put faith in superstition, as if catching the bouquet really means I would be the next to marry. But I was also afraid I *would* catch it, and then there would be pressure."

"Pressure?"

"You know, pressure on you, Greg."

"Pressure to do what?"

Sarah refused to answer. Instead, she wiped away a new stream of tears. Greg rose from his seat and stood in front of Sarah. Dropping to one knee, he took her tear-soaked hands in his.

"Sarah, don't worry about any pressure. What I do I will do of my own volition. I've given this a lot of thought and a lot of prayer. In the past few years, I have loved and lost more than once, to varying degrees. God didn't intend for me to marry any of those women, that is, any woman other than you." Reaching into his pocket, he produced a small jewelry box. He placed it in her grasp and took hold of her clasped hands and the box. "Sarah, I recently found God, and I know that he is not going to go away and leave me alone. More recently, I found you too." Sarah began to shake with new tears, but the tears had turned from sorrow into joy. "I don't intend to let you leave me alone either. I ask you on bended knee, Sarah Huff, will you marry me?"

Looking through her own tears into Greg's moistening eyes, she exclaimed, "Yes, oh yes!" Greg opened the box to reveal a beautiful gold ring bearing a solitaire flanked by rows of smaller diamonds. He slipped it onto her finger easily. Since the beginning of time this moment had been ordained in every detail. Images from Greg's past floated through his mind, but this time in a new light. Old friends and loved ones seemed to cheer him on. Happy memories became fulfilled in his present, holy joy. Trials had only made him stronger, breaking him free from sinful ways and teaching him endurance and character. This is the proven character of which St. Paul speaks in his letter to the Romans. This character produces hope, the kind of hope that *does not disappoint, because the love of God has been poured out into our hearts through the holy Spirit that has been given to us.* Two angels hovering over the gazebo rejoiced and gave glory to God.

> But seek ye first the kingdom of God, and his righteousness; and all these things shall be added unto you. Mt. 6:33

THE END

Made in the USA
Charleston, SC
24 January 2013